LIAR'S CANDLE

This Large Print Book carries the
Seal of Approval of N.A.V.H.

LIAR'S CANDLE

AUGUST THOMAS

THORNDIKE PRESS
A part of Gale, a Cengage Company

GALE
A Cengage Company

Farmington Hills, Mich • San Francisco • New York • Waterville, Maine
Meriden, Conn • Mason, Ohio • Chicago

LIBRARY OF CONGRESS CIP DATA ON FILE.
CATALOGUING IN PUBLICATION FOR THIS BOOK
IS AVAILABLE FROM THE LIBRARY OF CONGRESS

ISBN-13: 978-1-4328-5318-1 (hardcover)

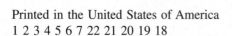

Printed in the United States of America
1 2 3 4 5 6 7 22 21 20 19 18

For my mother, Rosanne Daryl Thomas,
with all my love

A liar's candle burns only until dark.

— TURKISH PROVERB

1
THE GIRL IN
THE WHITE DRESS

Ankara, Turkey
14:45 Local Time

In Ulus State Hospital in central Ankara, in private room 309, a young American woman lies unconscious. A laminated pain scale is taped to the antacid-pink wall behind her — from smiley-face *iyiyim* to gargoyle-grimace *çok kötü* — but she's too far under to feel anything right now. There are no windows to let in the early-afternoon light.

Her chart says that she has suffered a head injury through blunt force, that her name is Penny, that she's twenty-one years old. Vulnerable as she looks right now, she could be a teenager. Her cheeks are freckled from six weeks in the Turkish sun, laced with red scrapes from shattered glass. The thick white gauze around her dark hair looks like a tasteless bridesmaid's headband, except for the blood seeping through. Somehow, the flimsy bracelet on her left wrist, a tiny blue evil eye bead on a thin red cord, survived the blast.

Outside the door, two Diplomatic Security special agents stand watch in black plainclothes. The Department of State isn't taking any risks, not after last night.

This middle-aged, practical-faced woman sitting in the chair beside the bed could be Penny's mother, but she's not. A mother wouldn't put on a crisp black pantsuit with an American flag pin to identify her daughter in the intensive care ward. As a matter of fact, Brenda has two children of her own, shiny school photos in her wallet. The hospital isn't air-conditioned. Her pantsuit is making her sweat.

Does Brenda feel a maternal twinge, looking at her intern now? Is she remembering the last six weeks, Penny's pink-scrubbed face and secondhand blazers, her straight-A student eagerness to please? The kid had been more useful than most summer interns, almost fluent in Turkish and a born translator. Anthropology major — too sensitive, too soft. Wore braids once to work and looked like she was going to cry when Brenda told her to dress like a fucking adult.

But Brenda isn't thinking any of this. She's typing a cable into her BlackBerry.

ANKARA 925311
PELECCHIA #0092531167
50X1-HUM
051145Z JUL
FM AMEMBASSY ANKARA
TO SECSTATE WASHDC IMMEDIATE
TOP SECRET ANKARA
SUBJECT: (TS) HOSPITAL VISIT TO AM-
CIT PENNY KESSLER
Classified By: Pol-Mil Counselor Brenda
Pelecchia, Reasons 1.4 (b,c,d,g)

1. (TS) Penny Kessler (USDOS intern, POL Section, Embassy Ankara) remains in serious but stable
   condition at the Ulus Devlet Has-
   tanesi (Rüzgarlı Caddesi, Gayret
   Sokağı No. 6, Ulus, Ankara). She
   has been assessed with a head injury
   and is currently under sedation.
2. (TS) Security camera evidence
   confirms that Kessler was standing
   in immediate proximity to suspect
   Davut Mehmetoğlu, and Intelligence Officer Zachary Robson in
   the Embassy garden, 20 seconds
   preceding the explosion.
3. (TS) Until Kessler regains consciousness, it is not possible to
   interrogate   her   regarding

Mehmetoğlu and possible accomplices.

4. (TS) At this time, Kessler is likewise unable to provide any statement regarding possible whereabouts of Zachary Robson.

Brenda pauses. *Interrogate* sounds bad. She substitutes *debrief,* hits ENCRYPT, then SEND.

The doorknob turns, and a wiry man steps inside, vibrating with energy, his suit still crumpled from the eleven-hour flight. He has that ropy look, Brenda thinks, that lifelong desk potatoes get when they develop a sudden middle-aged mania for biking — as if Lycra and clip-in shoes can somehow help them outspeed time. His assistant — taller, much younger, clearly ex-military — trails behind, holding a briefcase.

The wiry man sticks out his hand. "Brenda Pelecchia? I'm Frank Lerman."

She knows exactly who he is. Everyone at State does. She can picture Secretary Winthrop at his Independence Day barbecue — Bermuda shorts and that plastic hair of his. His aides interrupt to tell him about the bomb in Ankara. Winthrop's first words: "Send Frank." Brenda imagines him adding, "I won't have another Benghazi on my hands." By which Winthrop would have meant the PR side, because 256 people are already dead, 312 injured (including Penny), and there's nothing even Frank Lerman can do about that.

"I thought you'd be with the Ambassador's widow," Brenda begins.

Frank Lerman isn't listening; he's examining the sleeping girl. "That's her, all right," he confirms to his assistant. Then, to Brenda, "Coma?"

"Just sedated." Brenda conceals her surprise with difficulty. "You know Penny?"

Frank grins. "Everyone knows Penny. Haven't you seen the papers?"

Brenda stiffens. "I've been at the hospital since the explosion."

Frank turns to his assistant. "Briefcase." The tall young man hands it to him. Frank pulls out a thick stack of colorful newspapers. "I had him buy one of each."

"You read Turkish?"

"I don't have to. Look."

The headlines vary from that of the sympathetic *Hürriyet* — APOCALYPSE AT THE U.S. EMBASSY — to that of the ruling-party mouthpiece *Sabah* — REVENGE ON IMPERIALIST AMERICA? Frank's got the international version of the *Wall Street Journal* as well. Every single one has the same photo.

A young woman in a white party dress, stained with blood from her head, dragging a huge American flag out of the wreckage of the Embassy Fourth of July party. It's the kind of photo that wins awards and shows up on the cover of *Time* magazine — as this one will next week, and again on the tenth, fiftieth anniversaries of this tragedy. It's exquisite propaganda — almost too perfect to be true. Six seconds after the lens shuttered, Penny collapsed.

"Oh my God."

"I've got thirty journalists downstairs waiting to talk to her," says Frank.

"Obviously, that isn't possible."

"We need something to throw at them, before someone does the math on Zachary Robson. Brave tragic heroine. America will survive, blah blah. We have to wake her up."

For the first time, Brenda feels almost protective of Penny — possessive, at least. Penny is hers. "Mr. Lerman . . ."

Frank has already pressed the red panic button, to summon the nurse. On Frank's orders (reluctantly translated by Brenda), the doctor is sent for. A minute later, a thin, well-kept man in his late forties walks in, bleary-eyed at the end of his fifteen-hour shift.

The doctor moves at once to Penny's side,

dark eyes flicking to the monitor, the IV drip, Penny's bandages. Is she . . . ?

The girl is stable, the nurse quickly explains in Turkish, but these people . . .

Frank sticks out his hand, but Brenda is quicker. She's not about to let Frank Lerman take control. *"Ben* Brenda Pelecchia, *doktor bey.* Pleased to meet you. *Çok memnun oldum."*

The doctor smiles slightly at her accent. "Ali Denizci. The pleasure is mine. I'm sorry, but we still have over a hundred patients in intensive care. If this isn't an emergency —"

"Frank Lerman. Your English is great." That ingratiating smile of his works on almost everyone.

Dr. Denizci is no exception; he smiles back. "Should be. Johns Hopkins, class of '98."

"No way. My brother was class of '79. Way before your time." Frank sidles closer. "Look, Doctor. My colleague says the girl's sedated . . ."

"Yes. After a head injury like this . . ."

"Can you wake her up?"

The doctor's smile vanishes. "Wake her up?"

"It's very important." Frank pulls out his clunky, official-issue BlackBerry, identical

15

to Brenda's, and grumbles as he waits for it to load. "At McKinsey even twenty-four-year-old pipsqueak analysts get top-of-the-line smartphones. That's State for you." He looks anxious. "Penny's father needs to speak with her. As soon as possible."

"She may not be coherent, Mr. Lerman. Some memory loss is highly likely, at least in the short term. And she'll be in a lot of pain."

"Please. Just for a little while. If he could even hear her voice . . ."

Family counts for a lot in Turkey. The doctor softens. "If we stop sedation now, she should wake naturally in about twenty-five minutes."

"Any way to speed it up? It's very urgent, Dr. Denizci."

"Urgent?" The doctor frowns. "I could give her methylphenidate."

Brenda interrupts. "Methyl . . . ?"

"Ritalin, basically. She'd wake in a few minutes. But we don't typically . . ."

"Her father." Frank looks away, fiddling nervously with his phone. "He . . ."

Dr. Denizci takes the bait. "He's an important man?"

Frank exhales. "To put it mildly."

"Who can't wait half an hour?"

"He'll be very grateful, Dr. Denizci. And

so will I."

"And so will her Uncle Sam?" The doctor's expression is sarcastic. "I've seen the news, Mr. Lerman. I'll wake her up. But don't tell me stupid lies."

With quick instructions to the nurse, the doctor excuses himself.

"Penny's dad is a sculptor in Saugatuck, Michigan," says Brenda pleasantly, as the nurse turns off the drip of anesthetic into the girl's arm. "She showed me his website. Giant crushed soda cans. Elephants."

Frank doesn't react, at least not visibly.

They both watch Penny. Thin brown eyelashes don't flutter yet. Her brows are level, her mouth slightly, childishly open in the innocence of sleep. Her slow, shallow breathing hasn't changed.

"You can't let her talk to journalists," says Brenda. Rage and exhaustion have made her mouth dry.

Frank keeps watching Penny, as the clear methylphenidate sluices into her arm. "Did you know Zachary Robson?"

"There are only fourteen people in my Section, Mr. Lerman. Plus Penny. I know them all." Brenda lowers her voice, so it won't crack. "Knew them all."

"Did he ever mention Mehmetoğlu as a possible source?"

"I'm hardly the person to ask."

Frank's voice sounds accusing; his sweaty, shaved (clandestinely balding) head reflects the white-bluish glow of the fluorescent bars above. "Zachary Robson was your liaison."

"My liaison with them." Brenda keeps her eyes fixed on the girl, her voice too low for the nurse to overhear. "So if you want to know about Zach's other duties, I suggest you contact Christina Ekdahl at CIA."

"She said Zachary Robson never mentioned contacting Mehmetoğlu."

"Never mentioned it to me, either."

"Someone put Mehmetoğlu on the guest list, Ms. Pelecchia."

"Lots of questions, Mr. Lerman." Brenda raises a carefully plucked eyebrow. She'll be bidding for deputy chief of mission at her next post, and this high up in the Foreign Service, the aesthetics matter. "Aren't you here to handle press?"

"It helps if I know what really happened."

Brenda's lips tighten. Back in her thirties, she trained herself not to purse her lips; she didn't want her mother's wrinkles. But it's a better career move than telling Frank to take a long walk off a short pier.

He nods at the bed. "Did she work directly with Robson?"

"Once or twice, I think. She does open

18

source gists and translations for the whole Section."

"You think maybe he recruited her to CIA?"

Brenda snorts. "Penny?" She shakes her head, remembering that god-awful SAVE THE RING-TAILED LEMURS T-shirt Penny wore last casual Friday. "No way."

There's a quiet groan, not self-aware, the noise of a weak and helpless creature.

Brenda and Frank each move slightly closer to the bed. The nurse is holding Penny's wrist. The monitor shows a quickening heart rate.

"Is she waking up?" Brenda summons her best FSI Turkish. *"Uyanıyor mu?"*

The nurse smiles, nods.

Nausea. Dizzy so dizzy so dizzy. Eyes hurt to open — only one can. Woolly light. White-blue woolly blur. Pain. Not sharp, but sick. Sick heat in her head. Sheets hot too hot. Giddy, as if the pain were in another dimension, getting closer. Tubes in her nose. Then they're gone. Her head aches all the way around.

Memories that might be dreams that might be real might be making her want to throw up. A needle in her arm, paper-taped, tugging when she tries to cradle her head. It

19

stings. Her ears hurt hollow from the blast.

Under the fireworks. A young man in a suit — wavy dark hair, smiling brown eyes that always find her. He has a name. Zach. Zach's talking to someone else now, but he's smiling at Penny. She's listening, listening so hard, letting the patterns of their Turkish slide and lock into place. The man talking to Zach, the important one, holding a glass of cloudy iced apricot juice. Penny likes apricot juice. Better than sour cherry, which is too sweet and looks like fake Halloween blood.

So thirsty . . .

Carefully, the nurse lets her sip the plastic cup of water. Penny chokes a little, but gets it down. Brenda and Frank and Frank's assistant watch in silence as the nurse goes through the drill, testing Penny's reflexes. They come to the verbal stage.

The nurse asks, in that lilting nursery-school voice Turks use with foreigners, especially young women, "What is your name, *canım?*"

Throbbing head, but the voice is kind. The name comes out of the darkness. "Penny."

"Do you know where you are?"

"Ankara'dayım."

"What day is it?"

Penny answers in English this time, halting but certain. "The fourth of July."

"It's the fifth now," says the balding man.

Penny looks up from the needle in her arm. A round dark bruise has already formed beneath the itchy tape. Her eyes focus on the balding man in the suit, and she frowns hard. She wades through the grogginess. "You . . . aren't him?"

"Penny. Penny, sweetie, do you know who I am?" Brenda is more shaken than she knows.

Penny clocks Brenda's blazer, then her own hospital gown. Her cheeks are getting hot. "Brenda." She shrinks into her pillows; pain triples in her head; her heart pounds. A surge of anxiety. Work. Why isn't she at work? "Brenda. The party. I should . . ."

The nurse hushes her, but Penny won't be soothed. Her voice is getting faster, clearer. "I was going to get lemonade. Near the grandstand. Then . . ." She's still too foggy to panic, but that won't last much longer.

"There was an explosion," says the balding man, with the rubber gravitas of a soap-opera doctor. "You're going to be just fine. My name is Frank Lerman. I'm from Main State. I need to ask you a few questions, Penny, and then you're going to talk to some nice folks."

Penny is staring at the newspapers in his hand. The *Wall Street Journal* is on top, her own photo hogging half the space above the fold. "Is that . . . ?" Her voice trails off as she registers the headline.

EXPLOSION AT THE U.S. EMBASSY IN ANKARA, 256 DEAD

"A bomb?" A sick pounding fills her neck, her chest. Weak but determined, she reaches for the papers.

"We think —" Brenda begins.

Frank shakes his balding head. "Not right now."

"Please." Fear and adrenaline are making Penny sweat under her bandages. "What happened?"

Brenda sounds irritated. "It's not exactly a secret, Mr. Lerman."

"We need her memories, Ms. Pelecchia. And we have to be sure they're her own." He looks over his shoulder at the young man still holding the briefcase. "Hey, what's-your-name —"

"Connor, sir." The young man's voice carries a faint Georgia drawl.

"Whatever. Take these." Frank shoves the papers into his assistant's arms. Connor closes them back into the briefcase with an efficient click. Frank switches his kindly voice back on. "Now, Penny. What's the last thing you remember, before the explosion?"

Penny blinks hard, and her bruised eye throbs. "Two hundred and fifty-six people." Her throat feels like it's closing.

"A tragedy." Frank sounds like he's trying to sound patient. "Don't think about that right now. We just need you to try to remember. Everything you can. You were in the Embassy garden, right?"

Penny closes her eyes.

Red swirling patterns throb like fireworks behind her stinging eyelids.

The memory pulls her back.

Fireworks.

Round fizzing, flowering starbursts of blue and red sparkled high over the U.S. Embassy's garden walls.

"I typed up the expense report for those," said Ayla Parlak, the Public Diplomacy Section's summer intern. Her parents are Turkish, but Ayla's a Newarker to the bone, a senior at the Georgetown School of Foreign Service. "Twenty-two thousand dollars. Twenty-two thousand dollars! For fireworks. Our tax dollars at work."

Penny hefted the huge American flag over her shoulder. "I think my tax dollars would just about cover a box of sparklers."

"Okay, our parents' tax dollars at work.

Come on, Betsy Ross. I want some Ben & Jerry's before they run out."

The two girls wove through the crowd toward the purple ice cream truck. The six-foot American flag propped over Penny's shoulder flapped behind her like a cape. People in unseasonably warm suits and work-appropriate summer shifts clustered around the floodlit white tables, trying not to drip mustard on their patriotic ties, or let their white pumps sink too deep into the lawn. The grass felt weirdly greasy underfoot — nothing was ever quite clean outdoors in central Ankara.

"What shoes are you packing for the NATO Summit?" Penny asked. "I thought maybe just comfortable sandals — I mean, they'll just have us running errands all over Istanbul, won't they?"

"Sandals? Penny. Secretary Winthrop's going to be there!"

"I'm sure that between finalizing the peace deal, keeping President Palamut from arresting more journalists, and stopping the Russians from sabotaging the whole she-bang, the Secretary of State will definitely be giving a lot of thought to the interns' shoes."

"It's not just shoes, Penny. It's the message you're sending. Like Madeleine Albright's pins."

Penny grinned. "You could just paint HIRE ME! on your toenails."

"Do you think it would work better in red or silver?"

Overhead, the last golden sparkles fizzled into gunpowdery darkness. The Embassy garden buzzed with applause and the odd inebriated whoop. Penny could smell hot dogs and hamburgers sizzling on the grills — eight hundred frozen patties and franks had been shipped in from Iowa. As if they didn't have cows in Turkey. The brass band on the grandstand, flown in specially from Louisiana, swayed in the spotlight, their saxes gleaming as they segued into a jazz version of "My Country, 'Tis of Thee." Relations with Turkey had been so tense lately, State had gone all out on the party: in the lexicon of American diplomacy, jazz was the cheapest goodwill out there, after free Coke.

As Penny waited with Ayla in the line for the ice cream truck, coworkers kept coming up to congratulate her — none too sincerely — on winning the gigantic American flag, first prize in Independence Day bingo.

"Hang that out your window, and you can start your very own Embassy."

"So let me guess. You're . . . Canadian?"

"Have fun taking that home on the metro," drawled Brenda Pelecchia, as she strolled past, ketchup-oozing hot dog in hand.

"Ha-ha," Penny replied.

"Swirlie," wailed a small boy's voice from in front of the ice-cream truck.

"The soft-serve machine is out of order, buddy," wheedled the Embassy's Press Attaché. "Daddy can get you a scoop of chocolate and a scoop of vanilla. Is that good?" A three-year-old in a bow tie prostrated himself on the grass. "Chase, Daddy needs you to use your words."

Tiny fists pounded the earth. "Swirl-ieeeeeeeee!"

The red-faced Press Attaché grabbed his son and headed for an empty patch of grass.

The young Turkish woman in the ice cream truck smiled at Penny and Ayla as she scooped their cones. "Rough crowd." She handed them their ice cream. "Good luck out there."

Penny grinned and retreated under a tree with her flag, Ayla, and a dripping scoop of Phish Food.

"Zach totally let you win," said Ayla, through a pink mouthful of Cherry Garcia. "Next time, they should pick a more impartial judge."

"Hey, I won fair and square. I got Thomas Jefferson horizontally."

"You and Sally Hemings."

"Ayla!"

Penny could see Zach across the Embassy garden, standing near the Ambassador's grandstand, deep in conversation with a heavily bearded Turkish man. Zach snagged a hamburger off a passing tray and said something that made the tired-eyed waitress laugh. Zach could always make people laugh. He caught Penny's eye and raised the hamburger in her direction, as if making a champagne toast.

He wasn't even all that good-looking, Penny told herself. Okay, a bit like a young JFK in that suit, if JFK had dark stubble and had lived in Baku and Johannesburg.

She returned his toast and pretended to sip the cone of Phish Food, pinkie raised.

There was something about him. Confident. Complicated. Clear-eyed. Zach made a few people bristle — especially the Embassy's more hidebound higher-ups. But in the end, his wry, adaptable charm won almost everyone over. The fruit sellers near the Embassy joshed and saved the juiciest nectarines under the cart for him. Turkish officials asked if they could meet with Zach instead of his red-faced supervisor Martin

MacGowan, whose postdivorce health-food kick — he brusquely refused all tea, coffee, and sugar — had already offended half the Turkish Foreign Ministry. When Zach walked Penny home after a picnic last Sunday, even her landlady Fatma — tough as old leather — pinched his cheeks and made him stay for three whole plates of crunchy, wincingly sour green plums. Which Zach — bless him — had manfully pretended to enjoy.

People muttered that he must have serious connections to breeze so casually through the bureaucracy, as if the rules didn't apply to him. Penny wasn't so sure. Zach had an uncanny gift for listening through the noise and hearing what really mattered. A man like that can pull strings for himself. Zach was going places, and he knew it. With him, Penny felt as if she were part of some stylish drama with high stakes and sweeping cinematography: good versus evil set to a swelling score.

Penny's huge flag billowed with snappy nylon enthusiasm. She clamped it down, trying to roll it up; it flapped rudely in her face.

"Hey, Penny!" called Matt, the ex-Princeton ultimate Frisbee captain who manned the Counterterrorism desk. He raised an open can of Bud Light in each hand. "Fly it proud!"

Penny obliged with a big wave.

"That's more like it. U-S-A!" chanted Matt, pumping the beers until they sloshed onto the grass. "U-S-A!"

Penny caught sight of the guest of honor, President Palamut's thirtysomething daughter, Melek, eyeing Matt with obvious revulsion. Melek Palamut was her father's angel, unmarried as yet because, she often told the press, no man could live up to President Palamut. This evening she was resplendently self-satisfied in a tight Hermès head scarf and ankle-length gray Armani raincoat — the uniform of Turkey's elite conservative wives and daughters. It was the most expensively, aggressively unflattering outfit Penny had ever seen, offset by the world-class scowl Melek had directed at Matt's brace of Bud Lights.

Penny saw Matt grimace; he wasn't that drunk. "Shit," he muttered. "Brenda's going to kill me."

Melek stalked away, flanked by her six dark-suited bodyguards. She looked like she was headed for the exit.

"Excuse me." An unfamiliar Turkish woman touched Penny's arm. "Aren't you the girl who won the bingo?"

Penny plucked at the flag. "How did you guess?"

The woman laughed; she had kind brown eyes, a majestically curved nose, and deep worry lines in her tanned face. The pale violet scarf draped around her neck matched her purple tunic. Too stylish to be in government. Fulbright Commission, maybe? Probably a journalist, Penny thought, or somebody from a local NGO?

The woman looked from Penny to Ayla. "You seem very young to be diplomats."

"We're only interns," said Penny.

"Interns do important work, too," said the Turkish woman, smiling.

"Not this intern, I promise you." Penny grinned.

"Speak for yourself," said Ayla, straightening the American flag pin on her dress. "I make some very important photocopies."

"Everything must have a beginning," said the Turkish woman. "Here." She unfastened a string bracelet on her wrist, a thin red cord strung with a single dark blue glass bead, decorated to look like a tiny eye. "You know about the beads we wear? To ward off the *nazar* — the evil eye?"

"Oh," Penny began, "I couldn't possibly —"

"Please, *canım*! It cost one lira." The

woman clipped it onto Penny's wrist and waved away her thanks. "*Güle güle kullan!* May it bring you luck." The woman turned to Ayla. "And for you, *canım,* let's see . . . ah . . ."

Ayla held up her hand, to show off a ring with an identical evil eye bead, the same kind every tourist shop and street peddler in Turkey seems to sell. "I've got two Turkish grandmas and five Turkish aunties. Trust me, I'm covered."

"Good." The woman in purple looked relieved. "Excuse me, please. Happy Independence Day!"

"What a sweetheart," said Penny.

"Well," teased Ayla, "now that you're officially lucky, are you going to quit making eyes at your beau and ask him to dance?"

Penny laughed. "My *beau?*"

"Isn't he?" Ayla leaned forward, grinning. "You've been out together every day for two weeks."

Penny exhaled slowly. "I've never met a man like him, Ay. He has the most incredible stories — adventures he's had in the craziest places. Yesterday we talked so late the metro stopped running, and he drove me all the way home."

"Why am I not surprised the International

Man of Mystery likes talking about himself?"

"He's not like that when you get to know him. Really. He's so sweet. You should hear the way he talks about his little girl."

"Whooaa. He has a kid? Where's the mom?"

"Promise you won't tell anybody? Zach's really private about it."

Ayla nodded.

Penny lowered her voice. "After college, before he got his FSOT results, Zach was doing Teach for America in Texas. He was seeing this girl and she got pregnant. But they lived in the middle of nowhere, and her health insurance sucked. She had pre-eclampsia, and the clinic didn't catch it. She died two days after Mia was born."

"Oh my God." Ayla presses her hand to her mouth.

"Mia's back in the U.S. with Zach's sister and her husband. She's moving over here in August for kindergarten. Zach's so happy. He asked me to help pick out some toys for her room."

"He's already got you playing house?" Ayla teased.

"Stop!" Penny laughed. "I'm going to go talk to him. You coming?"

"*I'm* going to go dance with that cute

Marine." Ayla pulled out a compact to check her sparkly eye shadow and dabbed discontentedly at a tiny zit.

"Stop it. You look gorgeous."

Ayla smiled. "Good luck, Pen."

Penny crossed the garden to where Zach and the bearded man were chatting.

"Nice flag," said Zach.

"Oh, this old thing?" She draped it around her shoulders like a mink stole. "Is this Mr. Mehmetoğlu?"

The bearded man shot Zach a questioning look. He had the tawny, sun-blasted coloring of southeastern Turkey, and the extraordinarily intense blue eyes that sometimes go with Kurdish blood.

"This is Penny," said Zach, reassuring. "She's our intern."

"I'm so glad you could make it." Penny switched to Turkish to put Mehmetoğlu at ease. "Your name got left off the invite list, and Zach had me fix it."

Mehmetoğlu's cell phone buzzed; a text.

Zach and Penny watched in slow, polite silence as Mehmetoğlu slowly checked it, read it, nodded, and stuffed the phone back into his pocket.

Penny's smile was starting to go stale. "If this is a bad time, maybe I should . . ."

"Stay. Please." Zach put an arm around

her shoulder. "And since I've got a captive audience . . ." He pulled out his phone. "Mia's Daisy troupe marched in the Independence Day parade." He scrolled through pictures of a beaming little girl with round, brown freckly cheeks and a halo of tight black curls.

Penny leaned into his shoulder. "Oh, look at her on the float! Did she end up singing?"

"She was really shy. But I took your advice. I skyped her before the parade and told her to imagine everybody in their underpants. My sister said Mia sang so loud she almost broke the mike."

"Aw." Penny looked up. "Do you have kids, Mr. Mehmetoğlu?"

"One son." Mehmetoğlu smiled ruefully. "Teenager. He tells me I am stupid like a rock. Then he asks me for a motorcycle."

Zach grinned. "Wrong order of operations."

Talk turned to the traffic in Ankara. The weather lately. The recent renovations at the Museum of Anatolian Civilizations. How nice the fireworks had been.

Though Zach maintained an expression of polite interest, Penny could tell his mind was elsewhere. He turned his wrist to check his watch and dumped half his drink on the

34

lawn. "Whoops." He chuckled. "There goes the worst Bellini this side of my mom's book club."

Penny spotted a waitress handing out drinks near the ice cream truck. Martin MacGowan seemed to be scolding her about something; his face was turning crimson.

"I'm going to get a lemonade," said Penny. "You want one?"

"Stick around." Zach's hand slipped around her waist — the first time he'd ever done that. "There's something I want to tell you."

A blast of light and heat and noise.

Penny's head slammed against the wooden corner of the Ambassador's grandstand.

And then —

2
THIRTEEN DIMENSIONS

In the Ulus Devlet hospital, Penny's eyes snap open.

"Zach!" She's breathing much too fast. "Where's Zach?"

"Shh, *canım.*" The nurse puts a cool, reassuring hand on Penny's shoulder and glowers at Frank.

"Zachary Robson?" Frank Lerman's expression sharpens. His small, quick hazel eyes fix on Penny's face. Penny knows that expression. It's the look the greedier *simitçi*s and scarf sellers always give her upon the unpleasant discovery that the sweet young foreigner can haggle tough. But why should this guy care if she knows Zach?

"Yes. Zach." Penny's voice falters, and she looks to Brenda. "Oh my God. Is he . . . ?"

"We don't know, Penny. They're looking for him." Brenda's voice is level, but it sounds like she is keeping something back.

Penny's nausea has returned. She balls her

hands into fists. Her blurry gaze fixes on the peeling pink paint, the dented white door. Her mind is a vertiginous gallery of faces: ordinary, grumpy, overworked, snickering over the Foreign Service Problems blog. Matt twisting Oreos in a long meeting. Nur giving her a ride to the Embassy gym. Ayla . . .

She's got to know. "Where's Ayla? Ayla Parlak?"

"Parlak . . ." Brenda checks the spreadsheet on her BlackBerry, a highlighted minefield of murderous reds and critical-injury yellows, with a scanty scattering of unhospitalized greens. "Public Diplomacy intern?"

Penny nods.

"I'm sorry." Brenda shakes her head. "She's passed."

Penny gags. A sharp breath. "What about Matt? Sandra. Özlem. Are they . . . ?"

Brenda's face is answer enough.

Penny closes her eyes and lets her shoulders rock. She clings to the familiar sound of Brenda's calm voice — unusually deep, cracking a little now.

"Manuel, Nur, and Katie are in intensive care. Josh and Ayşegül are fine. Some cuts. Greg wasn't at the party. His son's soccer game. The others from POL . . ." Penny hears Brenda swallow. "They're dead."

Tears are stinging in the shatter cuts down Penny's face.

For a moment, Brenda looks like she was about to comfort her, but instead she folds her hands in her lap.

The nurse fusses, smoothing Penny's brow, murmuring comforts.

Frank waits a respectable fifteen seconds. Then, impatiently: "Penny, do you know the name Davut Mehmetoğlu?"

Frank has found Brenda's last nerve and stepped on it. "Mr. Lerman, if you had even a shred of simple, human —"

"Mehmetoğlu?" Penny stares wet eyed at Frank.

"Ring any bells?"

Penny is shaking her head.

"He's the only one whose name wasn't on the guest list I approved last week," says Brenda. "We think he might be the terrorist who planted the bomb. He was standing near you right before it exploded."

"Nice," snarls Frank.

"Oh my God." Penny takes a deep, choking breath.

Brenda glares at Frank as if to say, *I told you so.*

But Penny hasn't finished. She's still shaking her head. "Zach asked me to add him to the final guest list yesterday."

"*Zach Robson* told you to do it?" demands Frank.

"Mr. Lerman, stop shouting at her!"

"Zach said it was fine, Mehmetoğlu's name just got left out." Penny feels the cold sweat down her neck. "I'm so sorry. I'm so, so sorry." She tries to bury her face in her hands; the IV snags her arm. Dizzy. Head spinning, breath coming short. "Oh, God."

"Sorry?" Frank seizes on the word. Steps closer to the bed. "You're sorry?"

The nurse glares and demands in Turkish if he would treat his own daughter like this. Frank doesn't understand a word, but the tone makes it pretty clear.

Frank fixes on the nurse. "Get her out of here. Now."

Brenda crosses her arms. "Mr. Lerman, Penny needs —"

"Penny needs to talk." There is a bottled intensity in Frank's face now.

"With all due respect, Mr. Lerman, aren't you here to handle PR?"

"With all due respect, Ms. Pelecchia, I answer to the Secretary of State. Not you."

Penny startles them both. Hoarsely, in polite schoolgirl Turkish, she asks the nurse for a few minutes of privacy.

The nurse casts Frank a look of deep

mistrust. Is Penny sure?

She is.

The button is right here. . . .

Penny nods. *"Teşekkür ederim."*

When the door is closed, Penny looks Frank Lerman square in the face. She draws a deep, unsteady breath. "At orientation. I remember. They said — be careful. They said you never know who's . . ."

"Listening." Frank Lerman is not smiling. "Good advice."

Penny speaks slowly. It feels like inching along a rope, hand over hand. It takes more strength than she really has. "It happens to me. All the time. People . . . don't realize. That I speak Turkish. I overhear — all kinds of stuff."

Frank's fingers drum on the wall. "Let's stick to the point, Penny. What did Zach Robson and Mehmetoğlu talk about?"

"Nothing." Penny shakes her head; it throbs. "Kids. Traffic. Fireworks."

"That's it?" Frank sounds unconvinced.

"It was — normal."

"What exactly did they say, Penny?" cuts in Brenda. Her voice is gentle, but her stare is laser strength. "It's extremely important that you tell us everything you remember."

Tears smart in Penny's eyes. "That's it. And the museum — the Anatolian Civilizations Museum —"

"An attack?" demands Frank. His finger is already on his phone.

"The renovations," says Penny hoarsely. "And Mehmetoğlu got a text — but I don't know who from, or what it said."

"Do you think they might have been speaking in code?" Brenda asks Frank.

"Code?" Penny's jaw drops.

Frank frowns. "It's possible. . . ."

"No," protests Penny. "It wasn't like that at all."

Frank's jowls pouch out in consternation. "Do you honestly expect the United States government to believe a known terrorist came to the Embassy to chitchat about the weather on the day it *happened* to be bombed?"

Penny winces.

"Mehmetoğlu is *not* a known terrorist," protests Brenda. "He was a member of parliament for the leftist Kurdish party for eight years —"

"Until he was removed on terrorism charges." Frank has the smug certainty of a man whose entire knowledge of the matter derives from a single briefing last night on the plane to Ankara.

"Him and how many other Kurdish politicians? I'm not saying Mehmetoğlu's clean

— he's been associated with Kurdish separatist forces, especially after he got out of prison — but we have no direct proof —"

"He's on the TIDE watchlist, Ms. Pelecchia. That's good enough for me."

"What I don't understand," Brenda continues, "is why the hell Zach Robson agreed to this." Her lips are only a thin line now. "Why was he meeting with Mehmetoğlu in the first place?"

"Let's not point fingers here, okay?" says Frank.

Penny closes her eyes.

Zach.

She'd been touched when he asked for her help, even with something as little as this. She'd tried so hard to impress Brenda, to prove her worth, and nothing. But Zach pulled her aside and told her she had potential. He was the first diplomat at the Embassy who didn't look right through her. She leans against the thin pillows of her hospital bed and tries to picture him by the grandstand. Hand on her waist, joking about his spilled Bellini, so proud of little Mia. He couldn't have looked less like a man expecting a bomb.

"Penny," Brenda is saying. "Did Zach tell you anything about the meeting with Mehmetoğlu? Why meet at the Fourth of

July party, for God's sake?"

"Zach said . . . he was an important contact." Penny strains to remember; the words don't come easily. "He said it was okay, Mehmetoğlu was cleared, but there was . . . some bureaucratic problem. I think . . . his boss. MacGowan. It was urgent, but MacGowan was sitting on the paperwork."

"That figures." Brenda turns to Frank. "Zach and MacGowan had some bad blood."

"Zach didn't tell you anything else?" growls Frank.

"No."

Frank and Brenda are watching her.

Penny can tell they don't believe her. "He didn't."

"He sure told you a lot for an intern who doesn't even have Top Secret clearance." Brenda's expression is not kindly.

"He said my translations were good," says Penny almost apologetically. "He wanted to mentor me."

"I don't remember hearing anything about this," says Brenda coldly. "I am your supervisor, Penny."

"I'm sorry." Penny is blushing. "Zach said it was routine. I didn't think it was that big a deal."

"Well, Penny, my intern working for the CIA is my idea of a big deal."

"The CIA?" Penny looks from Brenda to Frank. "But Zach was in the Political Section. I mean, he's with the State Department. Right?"

There is a ringing silence.

Frank turns to Brenda. "Is she for real?"

"Don't blame me. I didn't hire her."

"But he was in our Section!" protests Penny. "He had a cubicle and everything — I translated the *Cumhuriyet* op-eds for him —"

"Sometimes, Penny," says Frank, with mocking slowness, "spies don't want everybody to know they're spies. So they use a little thing called diplomatic cover."

"I'm not stupid," whispers Penny.

"Honey," Frank says, smirking, "he's an 'information officer' working in the POL Section. What did you think that meant?"

Penny feels as if she's about to be sick. Suddenly so much about Zach makes sense. Did everyone know except for her? She tries to catch Brenda's eye, searching for some glimmer of support — or at least sympathy — but her supervisor won't look her in the face. Penny studies the ceiling. She won't cry in front of them.

"Sir?" The tall young man — Connor —

who's been leaning against the sink in the corner of the hospital room, holds out his BlackBerry to Frank. "Sir, Main State wants to know when Miss Kessler will be ready to meet the press. They're getting impatient. Top level."

"Jesus. Hello?" Frank grabs the Black-Berry and slams into the hallway.

Brenda looks to Connor. "Seriously?"

"Ms. Pelecchia, in this time of tragedy, the United States must show the world —"

"Save it." Tight lines radiate from Brenda's mouth. "We can't shove a suit behind a podium in DC? What the hell is Penny supposed to say?"

"Penny's a symbol, Ms. Pelecchia."

"Of what?" Brenda almost spits.

Connor shakes his head. "We have to do something."

"I won't have this." Without a glance back at Penny, Brenda's heels clack out.

Penny pulls her knees up to her chest. Through the nausea, she can smell sharp lemon disinfectant — same one Fatma, her stout, opinionated landlady uses.

"Hey." Connor walks over to her bed. "You — want some more water?"

Penny tries to speak, but her throat is too tight. She manages to nod.

He hands her the crinkly plastic cup. She

drains it and croaks, "Thank you."

"You've been a trouper." Something about his low, slow voice is comforting.

Penny scrunches her eyes against the throbbing pain in her head.

"Hurt a lot?"

He's not just being kind, Penny realizes through the red billowing in her skull. He's assessing her. Forcing her eyes open, she stares back at him. He's surreally untouched — a visitor from a world that didn't just blow up. Sturdy jaw, thin sandy hair like a baby's, spotless black suit, charcoal tie. Nose like a little boy's, small for his long face. American flag pin. Always the pin. They hand them out at the Embassy like candy, and for some reason, she kept collecting them. She must have seventeen in her top desk drawer.

Her desk. Was it even there anymore?

"Penny?" Connor's watchful eyes haven't left her face. "You okay?"

Penny turns away, toward the safe blank wall. Her lips are almost too dry to talk. "Look, no offense . . ."

"I get it, Penny. I wouldn't feel like talking, either." He glances toward the door, to make sure Frank is out of sight. "You want to see those papers?"

Penny nods.

He clicks open the briefcase.

Paper crinkles as Penny turns clumsily, faster and faster, from photo to photo, an endless, slightly crumpled gallery of her own bloodied face. She leans forward, bent over the blanket of colorful broadsheets. She wishes Connor would leave her alone.

"There was no sign of Zach or Mehmetoğlu after the explosion," Connor says. He sits in the chair beside her bed, right ankle propped restlessly on his left knee. In his hand, like an ungainly laptop case, is a black polyester lock bag — classified material. "Even if they died, that far from the blast their bodies would be easy to ID. They vanished. We have reason to believe the terrorists may have kidnapped them."

"Kidnapped?"

"The explosion knocked out all CCTV in the Embassy garden, but two minutes after the blast, security footage a block away caught two unconscious men being loaded into an unmarked van."

"Two men." Penny blinks. "And you think . . ."

Connor nods. "State always screws things up, so my boss wants to handle this in-house. It seems Zach broke protocol to involve you. So now we need to know exactly what you know, to maximize the chance of finding him while he's still alive."

"What?" Penny whispers.

Connor isn't listening. "Obviously, you don't have the clearance, but I have special dispensation to read you in." He emphasizes the word *I*, reveling in authority to which he is obviously unaccustomed.

"Clearance?" Penny echoes stupidly. "But I already have . . ."

"The Secret clearance State gave you? This is all Top Secret/SCI." He sounds, Penny thinks woozily, like her older-boy cousins when they were kids, trying to play grown-up. Connor opens the black lock bag and pulls out a clipboard of forms. He flips a couple of pages, suddenly awkward. "So — Zach reported that you two have been in an, uh, physically intimate relationship for the past two weeks." Connor darts an earnest glance at her over the clipboard. "Do you, uh, confirm that?"

"What?" Penny stares at him in horrified embarrassment. "Physically — no. No."

"Okay." Connor looks skeptical. "We can put that on pause. What I really need you to tell me about is the mission."

"Mission?" Penny covers her eyes with her hands. "Look, I have no idea what you're talking about."

"You know." Connor sounds impatient. "The mission Zach's had you working on. The reason he needed you to set up a meeting with Mehmetoğlu."

"What?"

Footsteps and voices outside the door. Far too noisy to be doctors.

"Don't mention this to Frank and Brenda." Connor rises to his feet. "But you know that, don't you?"

"This is ridiculous, Mr. Lerman!" Brenda's voice filters through the closed door. "She's barely conscious."

"Keep it quiet, everybody." That's Frank.

The doorknob turns, and Frank and Brenda squeeze in. Penny glimpses the jostling crowd of journalists behind them; the Diplomatic Security agents push them back. A searing flash goes off before the door can shut. Penny pulls the blanket up, all the way to her chin. Newspapers rustle untidily to the floor.

"Jesus Reagan Christ." Frank Lerman's bald patch is oily with sweat. "Conrad —"

"Connor, sir."

"You think I give a crap?" Frank glowers. "Just keep them under control. Nobody comes in until I say. Got it?"

"Sir." Connor turns to Penny. "See you after your press conference. Say cheese."

"Wait." Penny's heart is thudding so hard it feels like her whole body must be shaking with it. "Connor, wait!"

The door shuts. He's gone.

"Say cheese," mutters Brenda. Her face is blotchy; her Hillary haircut is frizzing out in the humidity. "Of all the inappropriate —"

"If you keep getting hysterical, Ms. Pelecchia, I'm going to have to ask you to leave."

"Hysterical?"

Frank sidesteps Brenda and sits heavily on the end of the hospital bed. "How's that noggin, Penny?" Now he sounds like a shopping-mall Santa Claus.

Penny pulls her feet away and stares at him in woozy mistrust. "Can I have an aspirin, please?" She licks her sandpaper lips. "And some water?"

From somewhere outside comes the faint singsong of sirens, getting closer.

"Of course, Penny." Brenda glares at Frank. "This is a hospital." She reaches for the red button to summon the nurse.

"Uh-uh." Frank covers it with his pink, hairy hand. "First things first."

"My dad." Penny turns to Brenda. "Did you call my dad?"

"We have to notify the families of the deceased first," Frank begins.

"I called the number listed on your

emergency-contact form," Brenda cuts in. "Your father's, um, studio? The message said he was in the Grand Canyon for his, his . . ."

"Found-art inspiration trip." Penny's bruised shoulders slump in the papery-green hospital gown. "I forgot."

"There was no email listed, or a cell —"

"He doesn't have one."

"Ladies?" Frank raises his eyebrows. "Back to business. Now, Penny. A few ground rules for the press conference."

Penny crosses her arms tight over her hospital gown. "I'm not dressed."

Frank ignores her. "This isn't an ordinary press conference. You're the victim here, which makes it a lot simpler. Honestly, Penny, I wish it were always this easy." He laughs.

"Easy." Penny glances down at the grave-yard headlines scattered around the floor.

"It goes without saying that you aren't an official spokesperson for the Department of State," Frank is saying. "I'll remind them of that before we get rolling. But I need you to be very careful about what you say. I'm going to walk you through it word by word, okay? I'm confident you can do this, Penny. You know why? Do you remember the Thirteen Dimensions that make a good

Foreign Service officer? Composure is number one. So you're gonna do just fine."

"I'm not a Foreign Service officer."

"Of course not, Penny, but —"

"I'm an intern." Penny's trying not to cry. "You guys don't even pay me. Did you know that, Mr. Lerman? I had to get a scholarship to cover my airfare. My rent is coming out of my student loan. My dad told me I was crazy to come."

Frank leans over and hisses, "You were supposed to translate newspapers. You got the goddamn Embassy blown up. Because of your mistake, because you put Mehmetoğlu on that list, a hundred and eighty-nine Americans are dead. So you be grateful if we don't charge you with treason. And we may yet." He leans back and switches his nice voice on again. "So let's stay on track, huh?"

Penny looks to Brenda; Brenda won't meet her eyes.

"Right." Frank cracks his knuckles; he's back on his home turf. "First of all, no political remarks. Nothing about the terrorists. Nothing about the Secretary of State. You call it an 'explosion,' not a bomb. We're not confirming anything till the forensics come through. The message is, you're fine, and America will be fine. You got up and kept walking. So will America. The Department of State is taking great care of you, and you couldn't be more grateful. You can cry if it comes naturally — that would be a good clip. You're grieving for the loss of your brave colleagues —"

"You don't have to tell me that," says Penny quietly.

"It goes without saying that you can't mention Zachary Robson." No response. "Penny?"

Penny looks him in the eye. She speaks slowly, through the grogginess. "Mr. Lerman, why do you want me to do this?"

She can see him trying to choose an answer. Finally, he offers something that might actually be true. "We need a distraction. The NATO Summit in Istanbul starts tomorrow night. An attack like this makes America look weak. Folks will want to blame my boss. We can't let that happen. There's a vacuum of information right now. You fill it."

Penny swallows. The narrow pink walls of the hospital room are starting to feel like a cage.

"You don't have to worry about the journalists. These are the tame kind. You ready?" Frank goes to the door and nudges it open a crack. "Let 'em in."

Brenda takes one last stab. "Mr. Lerman, so help me —"

But Connor has already opened the door.

3

INVITATION

Noise crashes in. Penny flinches.

"Keep it down!" barks Brenda. She steps to Penny's side with a guard-dog expression. "They can't make you say anything," she mutters.

Six journalists and six cameramen are admitted, and the door is closed again on the rest of the gaggle.

A cluster of microphones is held to Penny's face, like a bouquet. The cameramen make the best of the horrible fluorescent light.

Penny huddles against her pillows.

"Poor kid," mutters one journalist. He's wearing a flak jacket with the name tag NICK ABENSOUR — BBC pinned to it.

The woman from Fox complains, "This is ridiculous. Can't we just mike her up?"

Nick Abensour leans forward, eyes fixed on Frank. "Mr. Lerman, what will this attack mean for Secretary Winthrop's peace deal? Is this weekend's NATO Summit still on track?" Abensour speaks with a slight Parisian accent.

Frank snaps, "I'm not the one giving the interview, Mr. —"

"Abensour."

A battered memory surfaces in Penny's mind. On the BBC website she used to read Nick Abensour's Turkey column, a humane, principled voice in a cacophony of ignorant screaming.

So much screaming.

A swishy blonde leans forward. "Penny, almost two hundred of your colleagues were just murdered. How do you feel?"

Penny swallows hard. "How do you think I feel?"

"Penny, last year, Congress slashed the security budget for our embassies." A pug-faced guy shoves a microphone toward her. "Do they have American blood on their hands?"

"Seriously?" Frank explodes. "Read the press release, people. She's the *summer intern*!" He pushes the mikes aside. "We've got a roster —"

There's a sudden surge in shouting outside, mostly in Turkish. Frank's BlackBerry shrills to life. "What? . . . Who? . . . The whole *motorcade*? Jesus." He turns to

Brenda, wild-eyed. "He's not supposed to be here."

"Who?" Brenda is clearly unnerved by his reaction.

The woman from CNN focuses on Frank. "Who?"

"Oh, that is not okay. At *my* press conference?" Frank is turning purple. "Turn off the cameras! Press, out! Now!"

Two black-suited, silver-earpieced Turkish men push through the door, check the room. Outside, their colleagues herd more journalists out of the way. *"Yol verin, lütfen! Yol verin!"*

A strange hush falls.

A solidly built Turkish man swaggers in. Graying hair parted on the side. Pouty lips, handlebar mustache. Dry dark eyes. Big gleaming smile, like the Cheshire cat gnawed a box of tooth-whitening strips. He smells faintly of yogurt and soap. Penny wonders if this is a hallucination. She knows that face. Everyone in Turkey knows that face.

Bilal Bolu. The freshly minted Prime Minister of Turkey — Binky, as he is derisively known throughout POL Section. The flabby former minister of youth and sports, Binky spent twelve years presenting middle-school folk-dancing prizes, beaming behind

President Palamut on state occasions, and making as many waves as a rubber duck on a concrete slab. Everyone — including Binky — had expected him to continue serenely inaugurating volleyball courts until a plush retirement intervened. But three months ago, Binky's luck changed — because three months ago President Palamut's previous Prime Minister inopportunely sprouted a spine, daring to express pro-Western opinions mildly at odds with the President's doctrine, and even making use of prime-ministerial privilege in an attempt to deal directly with the United States.

Sniffing disobedience, President Palamut not only ousted the semi-vertebrate Prime Minister — he branded him a traitor and forced him into underemployment as mayor of a backwater town in shelling distance of the Syrian border. That left a Prime Minister–shaped vacancy for a *truly* loyal man. And who could be more loyal than his grateful protégé, the profoundly unthreatening Binky?

Prime Minister Bolu strides with newfound confidence to Penny's side.

The reporters look skittish, as well they should; Turkey jails more journalists than China or Iran.

Penny's stomach lurches. Democracy-minded Turks call Binky "Satan's Pet Hamster." She does not want her photo taken with this man.

Frank springs to life. "Sir, this is such an honor —"

The Prime Minister's security guards shut him up.

The Prime Minister puts a huge paternal hand on Penny's shoulder. Cameras are rolling. Binky's accent is surprisingly heavy; he didn't need much English on the netball championship circuit. The sour-yogurt smell is worse: *ayran,* the salty yogurt drink he and his boss guzzle on every public occasion.

Penny's head is still pounding. *Aspirin.*

Binky is saying, ". . . nothing can break the special ties between our two great countries. Turkey is strong. Turkey will annihilate these terrorists. Our minarets are bayonets!" A small cheer from the guards. It's one of President Palamut's catchphrases. "Our friend America is hurt and weak, like this young woman."

Penny tries to sit up properly. "I'm not —"

"And we will help them back onto their feet!" Binky smiles at Penny, as if about to reveal a great treat. "This young woman will stay in President Palamut's new palace. She will have the President's private doctor!" Binky grins to the cameras.

Penny stares at him in horror. "Th-thank you, but I absolutely can't . . ."

Frank makes shut-up motions at her with his hand.

"I insist!" Binky gives a small, fatherly smile; his kids are about Penny's age. Then his puffy lips purse in the stern expression Penny recognizes from his newspaper photos — people call it his pasha scowl. "I *insist.*"

Penny turns beseechingly to Frank and Brenda. Both are spluttering full blast. "Mr. Prime Minister — too generous — cannot possibly impose . . ."

The cameras are still rolling. Binky smiles at the Americans, daring them to try to take back the moment he has so thoroughly seized.

Frank and Brenda exchange helpless glances. Penny can almost see their thoughts. Turkey is still one of America's key strategic allies in the region. Insulting President Palamut's favorite protégé in front of the global press is way above their pay grade. Still, Brenda takes a stab. "Prime Minister Bolu, you are too generous, but the facilities at the hospital are surely much better equipped . . ."

"Better equipped than the Presidential Palace?" Binky's expression is derisive. "I think not." He turns to his guards. "Get an ambulance."

Once Binky is gone, it takes less than twenty seconds for his guards to expel the protesting journalists, cameras and all. Four new Turkish security guards in identical suits and earpieces materialize, followed by Connor.

Frank is snarling into his BlackBerry, *"Of course I know it isn't protocol!"*

Too much noise and too much light and too much heat, and still no aspirin. Penny scrapes together all the strength she has and whispers, "Brenda?"

Her supervisor bends close to listen, eyes intent. "Yes, Penny?"

"Why does Palamut want me there?" Fear twists in Penny's stomach. "It doesn't make sense."

Brenda presses her lips together. "No."

"Well, what was I *supposed* to do?" Frank spits into his BlackBerry. "Have our Diplomatic Security guys fight his bodyguards? Call in a Black Hawk from Incirlik? You tell Secretary Winthrop —"

Brenda leans closer. "Penny, is there anything you haven't told us? *Anything* about Zach or Mehmetoğlu?" She studies Penny's battered face. "You know you can trust me."

Penny agonizes. Connor said not to tell. But what does she know about Connor, anyway? She glances over to see if he's listening. His pale eyes stare back at her with earnest intensity. Almost imperceptibly, he shakes his head. Penny looks at her lap. Zach didn't tell Brenda, either. And Connor wants to help save Zach. Penny takes a deep breath and mumbles, "I . . . don't think so. No."

"Okay." Brenda doesn't sound convinced.

Another guard enters, pushing a wheelchair.

Penny asks Brenda, "Can you come with me?"

Frank shoves the BlackBerry into his trouser pocket. "*I'm* coming with you, Penny."

Connor is about to speak, but one of Binky's security guards cuts in, "She goes alone."

"She needs a nurse," protests Brenda.

"Come on now, fellas." says Frank, oozing oleaginous charm. "President Palamut and Prime Minister Bolu have been extremely generous. But Penny will be fine right here." The guard is stony-faced, but Frank keeps right on pitching. "She can get in the ambulance for the cameras, drive around for half an hour, and come back in discreetly. When she's a little stronger, we'd all be honored to join the President and Prime Minister Bolu at the palace for a press conference —"

"The girl goes now," says the security guard, and turns to the nurses. *"Haydi, gidelim!"*

Many rubber-gloved hands reach for Penny.

"I'm fine!" She flinches away. She slowly swings her legs over the edge of the hospital bed, one hand clamped over the IV drip to keep it in place. With Brenda's help, she balances unsteadily, barefoot on the warm floor. Her legs are laced with tiny cuts; both knees skinned like a small child's, sticky and orange with iodine.

She can feel their stares glued on her, in the papery hospital gown. Humiliating.

A guard gestures to the wheelchair.

Penny balks. "I can walk." She can't stomach the thought of feeling any more helpless than she does already.

They won't allow it. Penny is too dizzy to put up much of a fight. She sinks into the heat-sticky plastic of the wheelchair. Head spinning, spinning. Nurses produce a clipboard of paperwork for Penny to sign; the guards wave them away. Rules don't exist for President Palamut and his underlings. Not in his own capital.

"I need my clothes," says Penny. "My purse. My phone . . ."

"I'll come this afternoon," says Brenda. Her reassurance doesn't sound convincing. "I'll bring your stuff. Don't worry —"

"We need a moment with Penny alone," says Frank.

Nobody's listening.

Connor drops down in front of the wheelchair and unscrews his Nalgene bottle. "Hey, Penny. You want that aspirin?"

Penny gratefully gulps down three of the white pills. She swipes the plasticky water from her mouth. "Thank you." She looks up at Connor's kindly, boyish face. He can't be all that much older than she is, maybe twenty-six. Up close, the smell of his sunscreen is overpowering: eau de chemical banana.

"Don't worry," says Connor in a low voice. "I'll contact you at the palace. We'll get you out of there. Try to relax. You're gonna be just fine. Don't try anything on your own, though, okay?"

"I don't even know what you want me to do." Penny is getting desperate. "Zach only asked me to put Mehmetoğlu on the guest list. That's *it.* I don't know anything —"

"I'll explain tomorrow." His voice is reassuring. "Trust me. We'll fix this. You just get some rest."

"Deal with this." Frank jams the Black-Berry into Connor's hand. "Goons at NCTC want us to do their fucking jobs —" Frank's eyes latch on Penny. Sweat from his jowls bleeds into his sharp collar. "Penny. You don't say anything to anyone, okay? We'll get you out of there ASAP. Till then, zip it. Got the picture?"

"I am not letting you take her away," says Brenda. "Mr. Lerman, can't you get Secretary Winthrop on the phone? This is an emergency!"

Penny grits her teeth as the guard grabs her IV drip and slams her wheelchair through the door.

4
SIRENS

As the ambulance pulls out of the hospital parking lot, Penny rests her head back on the thin foam pillow of the gurney. She closes her eyes so she doesn't have to see Binky's four sweaty guards scowling at her. She wishes Brenda were here. Or at least a nurse. The IV needle is still in her arm, sore as a bee sting. Every pulse of the siren makes her head pound. If only Connor's aspirin would kick in already. But all she feels is strangely sleepy, and more nauseous by the second.

She's always been prone to car sickness. She remembers that awful snowy drive from Petoskey to Saugatuck, the day after Grandma's funeral. Everything she owned was zipped in suitcases in the back of Dad's Volvo: all the books Grandpa gave her; the wooden globe Grandma helped her paint.

Grandma and Grandpa's sunny house in Petoskey was the only real home Penny had ever known. After the divorce, Mom had parked two-year-old Penny at her grandparents' house, with all the other detritus of her old life. Mom was supposed to stay in California for a month "to get her land legs back." Then, when she met Bruce, she was supposed to bring Penny to live with them in Silicon Valley "as soon as we're back from the honeymoon." Then, "as soon as the twins get past the newborn stage." But "soon" was never now.

Grandma retired early from the elementary school to stay home with Penny. Dad dropped by once or twice a year. But he was just a visitor. Home was Petoskey, with Grandpa, who read to her every night in the bow window after he got back from his law practice, and Grandma, who braided Penny's hair every morning before school.

The summer before Penny started high school, Grandpa died. Two years later, Grandma was gone as well. And there Penny was, stuck in Dad's Volvo as it veered and stuttered on the February ice. Dad had to pull over at every rest stop from Boyne Falls to Zeeland so she could puke under the pines.

"It's all good, Penny," she could remember him repeating, from a splash-safe distance. "It's all natural."

The ambulance driver leans on his horn and swerves onto Fatih Sultan Mehmet Boulevard.

The vertigo, the heat, the oily, bloody stench — it's all too much. Penny sits up, ashen faced. Barely in time, one of the guards thrusts a waxy brown sick bag into her hands.

Penny retches. The three white pills come up first — they've barely even started to dissolve. So much for Connor's aspirin. When there's nothing left for her to throw up, she tries to swallow down the sour acid taste in her mouth.

She asks an unsmiling guard, "Water?"

He tsks and raises his eyebrows, the brusque Turkish gesture for "no."

He's holding a water bottle.

5
FOXFIRE

Langley, Virginia
07:53 Local Time

Blu-tacked to the door of Christina Ekdahl's office at CIA's Mission Center for Stabilization Operations is a battered red-and-black movie poster from 1990, the same year she joined the Agency. At first glance, it looks like a normal poster for *The Hunt for Red October,* with the dark silhouette of the submarine. But where the normal tagline should be, it says FIND THE SOVIET HOAGIE. It's an old Agency joke. They say that if you think it's funny, you've been here way too long. It makes Christina smile every single time. Not much else can.

A few years ago, the Director created CIA's eleven new Mission Centers, designed to integrate operations and analysis — or, as unenthused Agency lifers put it, stir scorpions into the Jell-O salad. Everyone expected Christina to pluck the plum command: the Mission Center for Counterterrorism. Instead, she gunned to lead Stabilization Operations. "STAB OPS," she likes to tell her officers, "means killing problems at the root."

Christina leans back in her office chair. She's tall and large boned — Minnesota Swedish — with strong Viking features softened by thin wire glasses. Her suburban-housewife highlights are chopped short, pageboy style. Back when she joined, she gave the ex-Marines in her trainee group at the Farm a run for their money, even with the parachute jumps. Right now, though, she's at ease, plastic spoon in her fat-free Greek yogurt, messaging one-handed on Sametime with one of those same ex-Marines — now her subordinate — who's currently on rotation to the National Counterterrorism Center. NCTC was founded after 9/11 to force CIA, FBI, DIA, and the rest of the alphabet soup to actually share intel fast enough to prevent another major attack. So far, as far as Christina is concerned, its most notable success has been defeating the nerds on the NSA soccer team at the last interagency picnic. CIA gets the real work done. NCTC is where Christina sends her officers on rotation if they do something stupid but not bad enough to get them fired, like pissing off a valuable source, or — in Dan Bishop's case — asking for paternity leave in the middle of the Assad biological-weapons crisis. It was his third wife, for Christ's sake! Dan's a good officer — not resentful of Christina's success, like so many of the forty-something macho wannabes who congregate in the middle management of the Clandestine Service. That said, he's a Division I whiner.

Christina shakes her head. After her son was born, she'd flown back to Dhaka before her episiotomy stitches were even out. It wasn't as if she'd had a choice. Twined around her desk lamp is a bendy action figure of Elastigirl from *The Incredibles.* The movie came out right before her best friend, Isabel, got posted to Afghanistan. At her going-away party, Isabel handed out identical action figures to all the other CIA moms. Elastigirl is the unofficial mascot of working mothers in the intelligence community. Succeeding as a female CIA officer doesn't mean being a babe or a bitch or a crazy hot mess, like in the movies. It means being stretched in every direction at once, and never snapping.

Being in the office before 7:00 a.m. is Christina's normal. The company of so many of her panicking subordinates is the unusual part. It happened after 9/11, after Benghazi. Most everyone else slows back down, eventually. But never Christina.

Dan Bishop-TT: Palamut's palace? The hell, Christina? I'd almost finished my report. Now it's fucked.
Christina Ekdahl: Don't get your panties in a twist. And don't call Lerman again.
Dan Bishop-TT: If you'd told me your officer was in deep cover, I wouldn't have called him. Ahem.
Christina Ekdahl: Can you hear my tiny violin?
Christina Ekdahl: Hang on. Phone.

She picks up. "Connor. Fill me in."

"Hi. Can't stay on long — our car's here in five. Basically, I can't tell. The girl says she doesn't know anything —"

"Well, she would, wouldn't she?"

"*And* she tried to pretend she wasn't involved with Zach, which was weird —"

"Probably the concussion talking. You can dig deeper tomorrow. What the hell happened with the Prime Minister?"

"Couldn't stop it. Frank Lerman tried to make it look like we were on board with it. Not sure the press are buying, though."

"Did you secure the information?" Connor can't see it, but Christina is biting her nails.

The young man's proud voice fills her ear. "I gave her *three.* That buys us what, twelve hours?" It's a good thing Connor can't see the relief on Christina's face. *"Three?"* she says roughly. "Careful there, kid. We don't want her to Marilyn Monroe on us."

"Brenda Pelecchia could be a problem. Can I put her in the picture?"

"Are you kidding me, Connor? Why don't we just send out a press release?"

"Then can you at least get her out of here?"

"Come on, Connor. I'm not your baby-sitter. Just use your common sense." Christina glances out the window. A flock of pigeons has landed on the hulking, graffitied fragment of the Berlin Wall set into the lawn. "By the way, you wearing eagle cuff links?"

"Yeah . . . ?" Connor sounds weirded out, which amuses her. It's his first overseas assignment. With operations this explosive, Christina prefers to use disposables. Worse comes to worst, it costs less than half a million to train a new Connor.

"I could see your sleeve in the CNN shot. Be more careful." She hangs up. Two seconds later, she's pounding down the hall, in the direction of the parking lot.

Her executive assistant pounces, five-foot-nothing of twenty-seven-year-old enthusiasm with an unflattering ponytail, the ink still wet on her master's degree. Bad luck for her, she can't keep up with Christina in heels. "Um, Ms. Ekdahl, there's a report from the Aleppo team about the hostage situation. They need to know if —"

"Not now, Taylor. I've got a breakfast meeting."

"Sorry." The girl jabs frantically at her tablet. "Um, I didn't see —"

"Last-minute thing. Off-site. I'll be back by eight thirty."

"Definitely. Great. Um, the Aleppo team said they really needed your . . ." Taylor trails off. The elevator has already shut behind Christina's back.

Anyone with as many medals as Christina has earned herself a decent parking spot. Within five minutes she's past security, heading away from the Agency onto the highway.

Time for some strip-mall roulette.

For a once-in-a-career source like FOX-FIRE, the read-in list is minuscule: the President, Secretary of Defense, CIA Director, and Christina herself. With the risk this high, even her own team can't know.

Foxfire — the eerie, glowing bioluminescence of fungus in rotting logs. Light from stinking decay.

Christina digs the specially modified burner phone out of her purse and pulls in at a large pet store, the kind where morons with time for that kind of thing linger for half an hour, cooing at the kittens. She shrugs off the blazer, slides on drugstore glasses and a Pink Ribbon sweatband.

Two minutes later, Christina is standing by the gerbil cage, dialing the FOXFIRE protocol.

Christina has developed thousands of foreign agents: thugs and traitors, statesmen and strippers. But FOXFIRE is unique.

"*Alhamdulillah,* Christina!" a woman's voice comes through the phone, her Turkish accent hardly even distinguishable. "I've been hoping for your call. This tragedy is unspeakable. A crime against humanity. My father has offered the United States his unreserved support —"

"It's you I'm calling, Melek."

Last year, even Christina was surprised when the President of Turkey's daughter contacted the CIA, offering to sell secrets behind her father's back if the Americans promised to help keep him in office. Melek has titanium nerves and a first-rate mind, badly underused. She's valuable. That sure as shit doesn't make her trustworthy.

"You know how much I value our partnership," Melek says. "If there's anything at all that I can do . . ."

"Are you aware of what just happened at the hospital?"

"With the flag girl? A hospitable gesture —"

"Your father just had his Prime Minister remove a U.S. citizen from our custody to your home, where we can't protect her."

"That jumped-up gym coach." Melek sounds scornful. "Bolu used to be loyal. But now? Ever since my father made him prime minister, he only cares about his own image."

"You're saying kidnapping Penny Kessler was Bolu's idea?"

"*Inviting.* Bolu's putting on a family-man act for the media. Trying to steal attention. He's selfish and he's a fool. But he's not dangerous."

"Why Penny Kessler, Melek? Why *only* Penny Kessler?"

"It's her picture on the front page, isn't it? It's not as if the girl is truly important." The not-quite question hangs there.

"She's a know-nothing intern, Melek, but she's a U.S. citizen. I don't care whether it was Bolu or your father behind this. And I don't care what you have to do. But this is a PR disaster. I need Penny Kessler back to that hospital — untouched — before the nine a.m. news."

"That isn't possible!"

"Then I suggest you make it possible."

6
WELCOME

Ankara, Turkey
15:35 Local Time

The ambulance pulls up to a monumental stone-and-iron gate emblazoned with President Palamut's starry crimson seal. Four Anatolian Shepherd dogs sniff the vehicle, each one 150 pounds of muscle, straining against their thin black tethers. The gates slide open with a low electronic hum. As the ambulance passes through, blue LED lights flicker along the ground — motion sensors, to make sure only one vehicle can pass.

Thirty-foot pines flank the road. Just in front of the Presidential Palace, hundreds of red and white rosebushes have been planted to form the crescent and star of a giant Turkish flag. Two dozen gardeners ensure there will never be so much as a brown leaf. Until a few years ago, all this was public parkland. But where else in Ankara — a

sprawling city of nearly 5 million souls —
was there space for Palamut to build his
1,150-room new palace?

Penny feels the change in vibrations as the
ambulance rolls onto smooth marble paving
stones. The guards heave open the ambulance doors.

Penny catches her breath.

The Presidential Palace is an enormous
white mansion, its neo-Ottoman façade
striped in glass and pale Turkish marble.
Blinding sunlight reflects off the marble
drive, an endless shimmering field of white.
Soldiers with rifles patrol every gate, and
every door. This is more generalissimo chic
than pleasure palace.

A clutch of construction workers in orange
vests hammer away at a fountain on the
wide third-floor front balcony. Workmen
funnel chipped marble and fiberglass down
an enormous yellow plastic tube, fat as a
playground slide, into a dirty red dump
truck below. Somebody plays a drum solo
on the jackhammer, to the accompanying
hum of industrial drills and the occasional
tinkle of glass.

Penny's head throbs. Construction workers? Isn't the palace supposed to be finished?

The guards hoist Penny's gurney and IV
drip down from the ambulance and roll her

toward the main entrance of the palace. Soldiers swing open the towering mahogany doors.

It's happening. They're really taking her inside.

She sits up to get a better look. She'd helped translate the flood of press coverage when President Palamut officially opened his new palace — it was one of her first assignments as an intern in POL. Palamut's PR people put out a press release hyping the palace in Ottomanesque Turkish as "a magnificent monument to the strength of our glorious leader, President Palamut. Never has one mighty edifice so boldly, so proudly captured the national will of the mighty Turkish people!" The reaction of the political opposition was predictably outraged; Erol Albayrak, the weedy opposition leader, milked a dozen angry speeches out of it. The few besieged bastions of Turkey's free (or at least not-yet-imprisoned) press bemoaned the palace. "Palamut's six-hundred-million-dollar penis substitute," one newsanchor dubbed it on CNN Türk. He'd used a slang word for penis that also meant "cucumber"; Penny had needed to double-check her online dictionary. An hour later, the CNN anchor was in jail on charges of "terrorist propaganda." That hadn't stopped #CucumberPalace from trending.

"You lie down," says the leader of the guards, in his harshly accented English.

"I sit up," she retorts. Adrenaline is making her rebellious.

She cranes her neck to take in the vastness of the room and feels a pang of disappointment. It's not that she was expecting Versailles, but this is just . . . *corporate.* With its angular, shiny dark surfaces, carefully staged flowers, and bland executive furniture, the cavernous, three-story atrium resembles nothing so much as the lobby of an upscale Marriott hotel.

The only thing missing, thinks Penny, are free mints and a check-in desk. The thought emboldens her. She's been rigid with apprehension all the way from the hospital, clenched from jaw to fists. But how scared can you be of a giant Marriott?

She swings her sore legs over the side of the gurney.

"What are you doing?" snaps the leader of the guards. He has the black curls and pale skin characteristic of the Black Sea coast — Argonaut country. Angry pink splotches stain his cheeks. "Get back up."

"I'm going to walk," says Penny. The glassy black marble floor is so cold, it stings her feet. But she's damned if she'll lie back down. They've got to know she's got some strength left. *She's* got to know it.

"Penny!"

From the door concealed behind a towering geometric tapestry emerges a plump Turkish man in a shiny pin-striped suit. He doesn't appear to register that Penny is liberally speckled with dried blood and iodine, still hooked up to an IV drip, and wearing a knee-length hospital gown. From his manner, he might as well be greeting a trade delegation. To her surprise, he shakes her hand. Usually, Palamut's inner circle are too religious for even fleeting physical contact with an unknown female, let alone a half-clothed foreigner. He must be part of the PR team. His hand feels as if he's marinated it in moisturizer. From sheer force of habit, Penny matches his limp grasp. The American-style steam-pump handshake is considered rude in Turkey, especially from a young woman.

The shiny man fixes her in the eye. "I am President Palamut's Chief of Staff. You may call me Ünal." His English is almost flawless. His voice drops low as he adds, "I am so deeply sorry about the attack. My most profound condolences."

Penny feels a lump rise in her throat. "It's . . ." She swallows. "It's . . ."

82

"I understand." Ünal nods. There's something almost comically supercilious about him, like the theater professor she saw play Poirot in the University of Michigan's winter production of *Murder on the Orient Express.*

"President Palamut has sworn that he will hunt down the terrorists responsible," Ünal is saying. "Already, MİT, our intelligence agency, has some excellent leads. You need not fear. We will find the terrorists. They will pay."

Penny stares at him. If Palamut's thugs can track down the terrorists, she'd forgive them an awful lot. What's that saying — the enemy of my enemy?

She asks quickly, "Who do they think it was?"

Ünal holds her gaze with his watery basset-hound eyes. "You know how things are with Syria. Now the terrorists have infiltrated Turkey, too. They know if the deal goes through at the NATO Summit this weekend, we will finally be able to crush them. They are desperate. Especially these new maniacs, these" — he almost spits the name — "Hashashin terrorists. Again and again we have warned your government. Even Daesh — you know, ISIS? Even they fear the Hashashin. And now . . ."

"You think the Hashashin bombed the Embassy?"

He sighs theatrically. "We suspect the Hashashin and the Kurds have collaborated in this terrible attack."

Palamut would blame the Kurds for snow in winter, but this seems far-fetched even for him. "The Kurds *and* the Hashashin?" Penny croaks. "But don't the Hashashin keep bombing Kurdish villages?"

Ünal waves her words away. "A terrorist is a terrorist, and an enemy of the state is an enemy of the state. The bombing of your Embassy was an act of war, Penny." Creases appear between his brows. *"War."*

Penny's knees feel as if they're going to buckle.

The strain must show on her face because Ünal quickly adds, "But I am most inconsiderate! Look at you. You must rest. I will show you to your room."

Flanked by the silent guards, Penny struggles to keep pace with Ünal down the dark gray marble hall, past shiny-looking new oil paintings of Ottoman sultans in various heroic poses. Mustafa Kemal Atatürk, founder of the secular Republic of Turkey, whose blue-eyed, ferocious-eyebrowed image used to adorn every public office, store, and living room in the country, is conspicuously absent.

Penny works up her nerve. "It was extremely kind of the Prime Minister and President Palamut to . . . um . . . invite me here. But really, sir —"

"Please, call me Ünal."

"Ünal *Bey*," she says, using the honorific, "so many people are dead. So many people are hurt. Much worse than me. I don't need special treatment. I don't deserve it." He doesn't reply as they step into the gilded, mirrored elevator, which is so vast that six guards, the scowling nurse, the gurney, Penny, and Ünal all fit in with room to spare. "I don't mean to sound ungrateful," Penny continues in a rush, "but — why *me*?"

"Because we cannot be equally kind to everyone, should we extend our humble hospitality to no one, Penny *Hanım*?" He returns the honorific playfully, smiling. "Do you give nothing to the beggar in the street because you do not have enough to give to everyone?"

"No, but . . ."

The elevator doors open on another long hallway. This one is wallpapered pearlescent white, hung with ancient-looking drawings of birds and flowers, made of contorted Arabic calligraphy. Penny had heard rumors that Palamut plundered the treasures of Topkapı Palace to furnish his own. She dismissed them as ridiculous exaggeration. It looks like she was wrong.

"You are very young, and alone, and far from home," Ünal continues. "Melek *Hanım* has a kind heart. It is only natural that she wanted to help you."

Penny is startled. "Melek *Hanım*? The President's daughter?"

"But of course. These are her quarters. Who do you think invited you?"

"But how did she even know that I . . ." Penny trails off. "Of course. The photo."

"She personally persuaded the President." Ünal gestures to the guards to halt and leans forward, swiping the keycard on his lanyard against the flat black sensor set into the door. With a gentle beep of acquiescence, the lock releases.

It *is* a goddamn Marriott, thinks Penny.

Ünal pushes the door open. It takes Penny about three seconds to realize just how wrong she was.

She's been in a few Turkish houses before — her landlady Fatma's downstairs flat for glasses of scorching tea, the apartments of a couple of the Embassy's local staff members for potluck suppers. They run, in her limited experience, to OCD cleanliness and austere

IKEA furniture, with the odd bit of kitsch to liven up mostly bare walls. There's usually nothing visibly Turkish or Middle Eastern about them. Certainly, there are few family heirlooms, little trace of a history before the foundation of the secular Turkish Republic in 1923.

Well, thinks Penny, Melek Palamut definitely didn't get the "modern austerity" memo.

The huge room is awash in whites, yellows, and golds — a stage set of feminine opulence, straight from the oligarch's handbook. Gauzy bronze drapes hang down around the head of the four-poster. The six gold velvet armchairs are overstuffed to the point of obesity, bulging as if they've never been sat on. Maybe they haven't. A crystal chandelier, drooping from the ceiling like a stalactite, refracts light from the window in tiny starbursts across the thick Hereke carpet, its millions of silken threads knotted into a pastel tree-of-life motif. It's too much — like a meal cooked entirely of butter and cream.

"Buyrun," says Ünal, gesturing her forward. He smirks at her obvious shock. "After you."

Penny steps through the door, and one of the guards rolls the little IV drip in after her. A moment of dizziness makes her wobble. Her foot catches on the corner of a carpet, and she hits the ground, sending the IV drip crashing down next to her. The scabs on her knees jar open. Oh, God, she can't bleed on President Palamut's carpet! Blushing, Penny scrambles to her feet — to find the two nearest guards have drawn their guns.

They're both pointing straight at her head.

7
THE GOLDEN ROOM

Penny stands there, her mouth stupidly open.

The moment seems to last a week. Details stab into her consciousness: the matte-black muzzles of the guns level with her eyes; the grim, set faces of the guards; Ünal's narrowed eyes and merciless mouth; the bowl of shiny grapes on the rococo dresser — plastic, no flies.

For a second, she's too shocked even to feel afraid. Then, just as the terror starts to hammer in her heart, it's over.

Ünal is patting her shoulder. He is laughing. It doesn't seem possible. "Penny! You gave us quite a scare. Here, have a seat."

She lets him maneuver her into one of the golden armchairs as if she were a doll. Her head is pounding worse than ever. She finds her voice and hears herself croak, "*I* gave *you* a scare?"

"You're our guest, Penny." Ünal waggles a

pudgy finger at her. "We can't be too careful."

"Careful?" The sheer illogic of it gives Penny a kind of mad, furious courage. "They were about to shoot me!"

"Shoot you?" Ünal is standing over her with an expression of quizzical concern. "What do you mean?"

His reaction scares Penny every bit as much as the guns. The words dry up in her throat. "I . . . don't know."

"Of course." Ünal shakes his head with a smile. "I am forgetting — you've had a terrible injury to your head. Probably you are not thinking so clearly right now. Are you feeling dizzy?"

"A little." Penny cradles her head in both her hands. She feels as if the whole room is spinning like a merry-go-round.

"Oh, Penny." Ünal gives her an indulgent look. "We're all here to protect you. Melek *Hanım*'s orders! Now, you just rest here a moment."

"Miss Penny?" A stocky man with a salt-and-pepper beard blocks the doorway. He's wearing a white lab coat.

"Good, good." Ünal ushers him in. "Penny, this is the President's own doctor. He's going to take a quick look at you."

Penny crosses her arms tightly across her

chest. "With the guards here?"

Ünal hesitates a moment. "Of course not." *Out!* he orders the men in Turkish. The door clicks shut behind them. Penny sags a little with relief. At least the guns are gone.

Ünal, however, doesn't seem to be leaving.

"And you?" prompts Penny.

"I stay."

"I'm only going to check your pulse and temperature," says Dr. Salt-and-Pepper. His hands are quick and professional. "No fever. That's good. Let me check those bandages." He slowly peels the tape away from her forehead. She feels a sharp sting as he dabs away the sweat and dried blood and freshens the antibiotic ointment. "Excellent! Already scabbing over. You've been a very lucky girl. Now, say *ah*. . . ." To Penny's confusion, he shines a flashlight inside her mouth and checks her teeth, running a rubber-gloved finger over the surface of each molar. "That looks fine." He turns to Ünal and adds in Turkish, "No hardware."

Penny blinks. She must have misunderstood. Hardware? Were they expecting braces?

"Çok iyi," Ünal says approvingly. "How's the girl?"

"Not bad," replies the doctor in Turkish.

91

"But she's very weak."

"Has she been drugged?" demands Ünal. He obviously doesn't realize Penny can understand. She keeps her face carefully blank.

"No. It's just a saline drip. You want me to?"

"Not yet. We need her sharp."

"You're shivering, Miss Penny," says Dr. Salt-and-Pepper suddenly, in English.

The hairs on Penny's arms are standing straight on end. Her heart is hammering so loudly, she's amazed they can't hear it. "I'm — cold," she stammers. "Could I maybe have a jacket, or a sweater or something?"

"Of course!" Ünal strides over to the wardrobe and opens a mirrored door. Inside hangs a deep crimson bathrobe with President Palamut's emblem, the arch of golden stars, embroidered on the back. He drapes it rather clumsily around Penny's shoulders.

"How are you feeling now, Penny?" asks Dr. Salt-and-Pepper. They're both staring intently at her, with unnaturally fixed smiles.

Penny's head is throbbing, but she'd feel safer swallowing bleach than any pills these two might give her. "I'm just so sleepy," she lies. The quaver in her voice is mostly real. "If I could just lie down for a few minutes — *alone* . . ."

"Of course." Ünal's eyes crinkle in a fatherly smile. "There is a phone by the bed." He points to an elaborate ivory-colored instrument that looks like a prop from the Doris Day musicals Penny used to watch with her grandma. "Dial six if you need anything. It will be good for you to rest. Melek *Hanım* is in a meeting right now, but she'll be up to welcome you very soon."

"Wow," says Penny weakly. "That's" — she flounders — "really nice of her."

"Let's help you up, Miss Penny," says Dr. Salt-and-Pepper. "*Haydi, dikkat* — careful . . ." He pushes back the comforter and sits Penny down on the edge of the bed. The bedspread is Bursa silk.

Ünal rolls the saline drip up next to her. To Penny's barely suppressed rage, he ostentatiously tucks her in, as if she were a tiny child. "Sweet dreams, Penny!"

Penny's mouth is bone dry. "Thank you," she murmurs, closing her eyes tight, hoping the men will leave her alone. "You're all *so* kind." With great effort, she makes her breathing slow and shallow, as if she were falling asleep. She can almost feel them staring.

Finally, she hears them pad across the carpet. There's a pause — they must have turned to check that she's really out for the count — and then an electronic click as the door shuts behind them.

Penny forces herself to lie still. One one thousand, two one thousand . . .

After two agonizingly slow minutes, she feels safe enough to open her eyes. She pushes herself upright and looks around. No sign of either of them. Penny slides her feet down onto the silk carpet and takes a determined step toward the door.

The IV snags painfully in her arm.

"Goddammit!" Penny shoves up her sleeve, rips off the tape, and yanks out the needle. It hurts, and she's made the puncture bleed, but she doesn't care. Anything's better than being chained to that thing another moment. She pulls her arms through the crimson robe and ties it snugly. She staggers over to the wardrobe and tugs open the doors. Empty. She checks what turns out to be a sleekly overdesigned white marble bathroom with what looks like a garnet and a turquoise on the gold taps. Empty. The closet doesn't even have clothes hangers in it. When she shakes the curtains, they billow limply. She squats and checks under the bed — only a patch of freshly vacuumed carpet. She really is alone.

She sits down cross-legged in the middle of the carpet and draws a steadying breath.

Not yet. Ünal told the doctor not to drug her *yet.*

Her hands are shaking. Why were they looking for hardware in her mouth? The moment she made an unexpected move, those soldiers were ready to shoot her. Who do they think she is?

She looks at the Doris Day phone. Who's she going to call, anyway? All her contacts are on her cell, and most of the people she knows in Ankara are dead.

Don't think about that. Don't think.

Besides, she's seen enough spy movies to be sure they've bugged the phone. She suddenly remembers Brenda. Her number's somewhere in Penny's email. All she needs is a computer. She walks to the door and tries to turn the handle.

Locked from the outside.

It's official.

She's a prisoner.

No panicking, Penny tells herself. It's not like they're going to hurt her. They can't. This is Turkey, not North Korea. She's a U.S. citizen. She's with the State Department, for God's sake! They're not going to let one of their own interns get hurt.

She remembers.

Fireworks.

The wet red grass.

Tripping over what turned out to be a child's severed foot, with a tiny white party shoe.

Her hand, clamped so hard around the flag she just couldn't let go, even as she ran. Even as she screamed.

A snatch of melody flares through her mind: the song the band was playing earlier that night.

And the rockets' red glare, the bombs
    bursting in air
Gave proof through the night that our flag
    was still there . . .

Sobs convulse Penny's shoulders. She can't stop, and she doesn't want to. When she finally catches her breath, her eyelashes have clumped into jagged triangles, and her nose is snotty. The pink tissues by the bed stink so strongly of synthetic roses, Penny retches.

"You've got to be kidding me." She walks into the bathroom and splashes her face, feeling a dozen tiny stings. She glances in the mirror. She *looks* like she's been in an explosion. The cuts aren't as bad as they could be — though that jagged one above her eyebrow should leave an interesting scar. She pulls her hair back into a braid and ties it with a raffia cord from the fancy bottle of rose-scented hand lotion.

Right. Clean face, tidy hair. Now she's got *everything* under control. There's just the small matter of escaping to somewhere where nobody's going to drug or shoot her.

She tries the doorknob once more, just in case. It emits an angry-sounding beep. She snatches her hand away. The air vent in the bathroom isn't wide enough for a chipmunk to crawl through. The window! It stretches from floor to ceiling, a solid glass wall, with a waist-high wrought-iron railing outside, which gives the illusion of a balcony. Penny checks the window's edges; there's no way to open it.

She thumps herself ungracefully back down onto the carpet. An elaborate silver ewer is on the coffee table, ringed by tiny golden *zem-zem* glasses, no bigger than a doll's teacup. She pours herself a thimbleful of water.

So this is what she'd always dreamed of? All those years of reading Grandpa's *National Geographic*s in the bow window, yearning to see the world; staying up every night for five months, studying to ace the tests that got her into U of M with almost a full ride; slogging through three years of Turkish classes and two summers of intensive language training; saving what she'd earned all year from work-study at the dining hall, waitressing at the coffee shop, and her weekend job at the bookstore, reusing her tea bags and living on salted store-brand pasta, a thousand tiny economies and deprivations, just to afford this internship.

Suddenly she remembers the tall CIA guy, Connor — the Southern one with the kind voice. He said the terrorists had kidnapped Zach. If it really *is* the Hashashin, Zach's got hours, days at best. Everyone knows about the Hashashin — they castrated that poor hiker and gouged out his eyes, for all the internet to see. God knows what they'll do to an American spy.

Penny's hands curl into fists. Connor said the Agency needed her. Maybe, just maybe, she could help them find Zach in time. But not if she's trapped in here.

There is a sharp electronic beep from the door.

Penny lunges for the bed.

8
DELIVERED

The door swings open. Penny tries her best to look drowsy.

It's Ünal again, looking smarmier and shinier than ever. "Please, Penny. Don't get up. I have the honor to present Melek *Hanım,* daughter of our great President."

Melek Palamut makes her entrance, a princess in all but name. She's dressed in shades of muted white, the color of mourning in Islam, from her elegant head scarf to figure-skimming trench coat, down to her white leather boots. She's a young-looking thirty-two, slightly made and chastely graceful, with powerful, arched brows and strikingly intelligent eyes, so dark the irises look nearly black. She looks straight into Penny's eyes — a searching, almost soulful stare.

Melek Palamut walks to the bed and cradles Penny's hands in her cool, manicured fingers. "My dear. You are alive, *al-hamdulillah.*" Her voice is cultured and sweet, gentle as a kindergarten teacher's. Of course her English is flawless; she's a Barnard grad. "All night, I have sat awake, praying for the souls of the victims."

Penny is suddenly ashamed of her fears. Melek Palamut wouldn't hurt a fly. "You've been very kind to me."

"I wish only that I could do more."

"You can."

Melek looks at her with surprise. "Yes?"

"You can send me back to the hospital. My colleagues need my help. Let me go back to them."

"And what will you do, poor little girl?"

Penny is stung. "I'm twenty-one, Melek *Hanım.* I graduate from college next year."

The sides of Melek's pale-lipsticked mouth quiver in what threatens to become a smile. "Of course. I forgot. You are a diplomat. Very grown-up. But you are hurt, and you need rest. And what place is safer than here, where I can watch over you?"

"You must have me confused with someone else." Penny can hear how desperate she sounds. She doesn't even care. "I'm just an intern. I'm not important."

"Oh, but you are." Melek's eyes are intensely bright. She turns to Ünal. *"Çekilebilirsiniz."* It's a royal command: *You may withdraw.*

100

Ünal's eyes dart suspiciously to Penny. "But Melek *Hanım* —"

"Now."

The door clicks closed behind Ünal.

Melek turns back to Penny. "You see, Penny, we have a friend in common."

"We do?"

"Zachary Robson."

"Zach?" Penny leans back on the poufy pillows. "You know *Zach*?"

"He is . . ." Melek blinks hard and presses a hand to her heart. "Very important to me."

Penny can't believe her ears. This can't be right. "You and Zach are . . ." She can't quite bring herself to say it. She looks up at the President's beautiful daughter with a heart-pounding mixture of astonishment, curiosity, and a sharp twist of jealousy. "You're . . . together?"

"Don't be ridiculous!" Melek jerks away. In her flash of anger, her resemblance to her father is suddenly clear. Two dark splotches of red are visible through her thick foundation. She shakes her head, and the silken fringe on her head scarf sways. "You wouldn't understand."

"I'm sorry," says Penny quickly. "I didn't mean to insult you."

Melek smiles tightly. "Be more mindful."

Penny doesn't dare do more than nod. "I

feel a little sick. Could we get some fresh air?"

"Too much fresh air can make you ill, you know."

"Just a little? Please?"

Melek walks over to the window. Sliding her manicured finger into a groove in the frame that Penny hadn't noticed, Melek pulls it open a few inches. A gust of hot and dusty air blows into the room.

Penny takes a deep breath. "Thank you."

The President's daughter sits down on the end of the bed. "I need your help, Penny."

"You do?" says Penny carefully.

"I need you to tell me everything."

Penny stalls for time. "Everything?"

Melek gives an older-sisterly smile. "I'm sure dear Zachary told you to be discreet. You've done very well. But you're safe now. You can tell me."

"Melek *Hanım,* I'm sorry, but I really don't know what you're talking about."

Melek's mouth purses. "That's enough, Penny. I'm Zachary's friend. You need to tell me. Otherwise, we may not be able to save him."

Penny feels a knot of dread beginning to form in her gut. "Tell you what?"

"Penny, please don't test my patience."

"I don't mean to," says Penny carefully.

One wrong step, and she senses Melek's gentle calm will shatter like spun sugar. "Believe me, if I knew what you wanted to know, I'd tell you."

"Penny, let me put all my cards on the table." Melek leans closer, so close Penny can smell her perfume — rose again, one note and candy sweet. "I know you spoke to Zachary and Mehmetoğlu, just before the bomb went off."

Penny freezes. "How can you possibly —"

"That isn't important. What matters is, that isn't *all* I know." Melek's voice remains gentle. "I know Zachary's secret. And that means I know yours, too, my dear."

"My secret?" Penny's heart is pounding. "Melek *Hanım,* I swear I don't know what you're talking about."

Melek is perfectly still for a moment. Then she laughs, a polite, garden-club-lady laugh. "Oh, Penny. Is that the best the CIA could teach you?"

Penny forces herself to sound as normal as she can, but her voice still comes out shaky. "I'm not a spy, Melek *Hanım.* I'm a college student."

Melek's expression is stony.

"I don't know what Zach was doing," protests Penny. "He told me to put Mehmetoğlu on the guest list, but I don't know why. I don't know whether he was really a spy or not. I don't know anything. I know you don't believe me, but it's true. *It's true.*" Despite herself, she can hear the catch in her voice.

"I take it back, my dear." Melek observes her calmly. "That *was* convincing. It might work on a man. *I* might even believe you, if I didn't have proof that you're lying."

Penny looks at her, horror-struck. Melek's got to be bluffing. She *must* be. "How can you have proof of something that isn't true?"

"Just before the party, Davut Mehmetoğlu, the man you and Zachary were talking with, sent a message to an unknown contact. Someone we believe to be affiliated with a Kurdish terrorist group. I have seen this message. Do you know what it says?"

Penny pulls her knees up to her chest. "Of course not."

"Take a look." Melek holds out her phone. There is a screenshot of a phone, with a short text message visible, in English, sent at 19:48 p.m. on July 4. "What does that say, Penny? Go on."

Penny swallows. "It says, 'Good luck to the girl with the flag.' "

Melek looks grimly triumphant. "The girl

with the flag. Now, who do you think that is?"

Penny doesn't dare meet Melek's eyes.

"Good luck with *what?*" Melek's fingers clamp painfully tight around Penny's upper arm. "Mehmetoğlu never mentioned you in any of his other messages. Neither did Zachary." There is something almost frightened in Melek's intensity. "Just what did Zachary have you doing? And before you lie to me, remember where you are, and who I am."

"I've told you everything I know," says Penny hoarsely.

"Mehmetoğlu received another message fifteen minutes after this one. A reply. Just one word. 'Delivered.' *What* was delivered? The bomb?"

"I don't know."

"You must know."

"But I don't." Penny is shaking.

"Who are you?" Melek's eyes narrow. "Did Christina send you?"

"I don't know who that is." With the numbness of terror, Penny can see every stray speck of Melek's mascara, the faint lines at the corners of her mouth, the flare of her nostrils. There is no cruelty in the President's daughter's face. If anything, she looks confused.

"Maybe you don't." Melek releases Penny's arm and frowns. She walks over to the window and closes it firmly.

Penny rubs her sore arm; Melek's gleaming French manicure is sharp. "May I please make a call?"

"To whom?"

"My supervisor. Brenda Pelecchia."

"Why?"

A deep chill creeps up the back of Penny's neck. "She was going to bring me some clothes."

"I really don't think you're well enough for a long chat, my dear. The doctor said you might take a turn for the worse. It was a bad head injury. They're very unpredictable."

Penny's headache has clanged painfully back to life. "Are you . . . *threatening* me?"

"I don't want to." Melek is visibly upset. "Truly I don't." She sounds sincere enough. "Please help me, my dear. Otherwise, I won't have any choice. Believe me, I'm the best friend you'll find here."

"What do you mean?"

Melek looks away. "This isn't personal, Penny. But you are making things very difficult."

"You don't dare hurt me." Penny tries to sound much braver than she feels. The rumors about Palamut's Presidential Guard are ugly. Political prisoners have been tortured. A few have simply disappeared. "Everybody knows I'm here."

Melek gives her an almost pitying look. "Everybody knows you came here in an ambulance. It would hardly be shocking if you leave in one."

Penny brazens it out. "That won't look good for your father."

"My father isn't the one who came to the hospital in front of all the TV cameras."

"So you'd throw Prime Minister Bolu under the bus?"

Melek is unmoved. "That is not your concern."

"It's still your father's palace! Do you think he won't be blamed if you murder me?"

"Your brain damage was not fully assessed. Perhaps it's worse than the doctors believed. It would be tragic. You have so much potential."

Penny can feel the blood throbbing in her neck. "As you say, I had a concussion," she says, deliberately allowing her speech to slur a little. "I'm — really not thinking very clearly. I'm still dizzy. I don't want to do anything stupid."

"No," agrees Melek softly.

"Maybe — maybe if I rest for a while, I'll remember something. About Zach."

"A very good idea." Penny could swear Melek looks almost amused. "Ünal *Bey*!"

A beep, and the door swings open. Ünal makes a deferential bow of the head. *"Efendim, Melek Hanım?"*

"Penny is going to rest a little while. I'll come back in twenty minutes." Melek gives Penny a sharp look. "I hope by then your memory will return. Meanwhile, Ünal *Bey* will keep you company."

Penny's face falls. "Oh."

"And," Melek continues sharply, "two guards will remain outside the door. In case you need any assistance."

"Thank you," says Penny lamely.

Melek smiles. "Have a good rest, my dear. Think things over."

The door closes behind her.

Twenty minutes.

Penny looks around the room. She *has* to escape. The window is her only chance. But how can she get rid of Ünal? There's no way he'll leave her alone. There's really only one option.

She's going to have to knock him out.

The thought is absolutely, comically absurd. She's never even slapped somebody. She doesn't even swat flies — she always

108

tries to trap them and carry them to a window.

Ünal has pulled a poufy armchair up to her bedside. "You've taken out your IV drip, Penny."

"It hurt."

"You'll get dehydrated." He waggles his finger. "We have to take good care of you."

"I *am* kind of thirsty." An idea crosses Penny's mind. It'll never work. But what other chance does she have? She points to the heavy silver ewer. "Could I have a little water?"

"Of course." He gives a courtly nod, walks over to the little table, pours a tiny golden *zemzem* glass of water, and sets the pitcher back down.

Damn.

Ünal hands Penny the miniature glass and leans back in his armchair.

Penny knocks the water back in two gulps. "It's so nice and cool." She tries to slur her words. "Can I please have some more?"

Ünal looks mildly irritated, but he stands up. "Maybe you shouldn't have taken out your IV drip."

Penny bows her head meekly.

"Here." Ünal slams the pitcher down on Penny's bedside table. "Help yourself."

"Thank you, Ünal *Bey."*

Ünal just nods, lips thin. As he sits down, Penny notices the outline of a holster at his generously padded waist.

Now or never. Penny reaches out and picks up the pitcher. Her stomach feels like it was tying itself into pretzel knots. "My grandma always said that when you're dehydrated, the best thing is lemonade." The handle of the pitcher is getting hot under her palm. She's got to do it. She's *got* to. But how can she? Ünal's basset eyes are fixed straight on her face. His benign expression has grown taut; he must be getting suspicious. She licks her dry lips.

"I'll have the guards fetch the doctor. He'll put your IV back in."

"Oh — good." Penny swallows nervously. "Oops. Oh, I'm so sorry —"

Ünal shakes his head, and his waxed mustache quivers. Clearly, he thinks she's an idiot. "I'll get it." He stoops to pick up her *zemzem* glass, which has rolled under the bed.

He's down on his hands and knees.

Do it! Penny tells herself furiously. *Just — goddamn — DO it!*

"Got it," announces Ünal, his head emerging from under the bed skirt. His hair is thinning just at the back, like a worn patch of carpet.

"Great!" says Penny brightly. With both hands, wrists trembling at the weight, she brings the heavy silver ewer down on the back of his skull.

There is a soft *clonk,* barely audible, like a teapot being set down on a thick tablecloth.

Ünal doesn't look surprised or pained. His jaw simply slacks open as he falls face-first into the Hereke carpet.

9
INCHWORM

For a moment, Penny just stares at him, too stunned to move.

Did it actually work?

It actually worked!

"Yes!" She beams, then feels guilty. "Sorry." She's still holding the silver ewer, but her palms are getting sweaty. She leans over the side of the bed. Ünal is absolutely still.

Oh, Jesus, has she killed him?

No, the back of his suit is moving slightly up and down. He must be breathing. Good.

She plonks the ewer on the bedside table and slides out the other side. She pads around the bed to the window, glancing nervously back at Ünal's prone form. His suit jacket has hitched up, revealing an inch of pallid muffin-top. His holster is sandwiched between his thigh and the floor — no way to extract it. He hasn't moved.

Penny steps toward the window and feels

for the catch in the side. She slides the window open. It's a lot heavier than she expected.

Two, four, six, eight, ten, twelve inches — wide enough for her to squeeze through.

She takes a deep breath of the dusty outside air. It's flatteningly hot even this late in the afternoon. She steps up to the wrought-iron railing. It's a forty-foot drop straight down to the marble pavement. There isn't even a convenient climbing vine, or a drainpipe.

The room to her left has a balcony — a real one, nor just the ornamental railing. She'd have to leap about five feet. It's a stretch, but it beats waiting for Melek to come back.

She tightens the red bathrobe around her waist. Right. She can do this.

A huge burst of sound sends her lurching back into the room.

A man's rich voice, soaring and swooping in the call to prayer, an everyday act of startling beauty, made tooth-achingly loud by the loudspeaker. Penny can feel the vibrations in her jaw. It's the late afternoon *ezan.*

"Allahu akbar, Allahu akbar . . ."

She looks fearfully over her shoulder. Ünal *Bey* is still out cold.

The summons grows louder, and more yearning. Some muezzins sound about as musical as bawling fishwives; this one could sing Wagner at the Met. Of course President Palamut would have the best. Every word floats in the air, as pure and haunting as the church bells in Petoskey. Penny can remember the first time she heard the *ezan* reverberating through the concrete streets, badly distorted by a hundred speakers. Fatma, Penny's square-jawed, proudly secular, never-married landlady, had been baffled why the American girl was getting misty-eyed over the call to prayer. "Just you wait till it comes on when you're trying to watch the news," she'd told Penny darkly. Sure enough, within a couple of weeks, the magic had worn off. But right now, in its transcendent, deafening music, the *ezan* feels like a gift.

"Ash-hadu an la ilaha illallah . . ."

Penny perches on the wrought-iron railing and slides first one leg, then the other, onto the outer side. The metal is sun hot on her bare feet. She's still dizzy. But she can't afford to miss.

She takes a steadying breath of hot air. Nope nope nope. Don't look down.

With every scrap of strength, she flings herself across the empty space, toward the balcony, eyes squeezed shut.

A moment of fearful weightlessness, and the railing catches her like an iron punch to the gut. For a second, she hangs there, panting, clinging to the burning metal, the red bathrobe fluttering. She opens her eyes. She made it. Awkwardly, she pulls herself onto the balcony. The curtains to the room are closed, and the door is locked.

What now? Her blood is throbbing. Is anyone chasing her? She looks back.

No sign of anyone. Far below, the guards are facing outward; no one's looking at the palace itself.

She inches across the hot marble, toward the next balcony.

It's over twenty feet long, with a half-finished marble fountain rising amid dust and broken fiberglass. It looks — familiar? Yes! There's that giant yellow tube leading down into the dump truck. This is the balcony she saw as she came in.

The one with all the workmen.

She ducks down and peers through the railing, breathing hard. What if someone saw her? There's no sign of the neon-orange vests. None. Maybe the men have gone to pray?

"Ash-hadu anna Muhammadan Rasul-Ullah . . ."

Penny glances towards the gate. The soldiers are marching; no one looking her way. She stands up. The balcony with the fountain is only a four-foot leap. She needs to move fast. She hops on the railing and swings her legs to the other side. Her muscles are screaming at her. She pushes through the pain. Better than whatever Melek was going to do, she tells herself. She's done the jump once — she can do it again. It's almost fun.

Eyes open this time, she leaps.

She reaches out for the next railing. Her hands graze the marble, scraping uselessly against the stone as she starts to fall. She manages to grab one of the marble struts that holds up the balcony railing. Slippery. Her fingers lock around the marble. Her shoulders feel like they're about to rip out of their sockets.

Hold on. Just hold on.

Except she can't.

The muscles in her shoulders start to burn, then quiver uncontrollably. Sweaty fingers are losing their grip.

Physical terror, deep in her gut. She'll fall. Crack her spine. Her skull if she's lucky.

"Haiya 'alas-Salah . . ."

The sun reflects off the marble paving far below, half blinding her.

She feels a hot surge of defiance. She survived the bomb. She's sure as hell not going to die as a splat on Palamut's driveway. She swings her left leg back and forth, gaining momentum.

"Haiya 'alal-Falah . . ."

"Ooph." Penny snags her left foot up onto the outer edge of the marble balcony. She hugs herself closer to the railing, gasping. The fluffy red bathrobe feels as if it's run through with heating coils. Suffocating. Penny drags herself between the marble struts and onto the main balcony. Her arms are burning, useless. The scabs are scraped clean off her bleeding knees. She can feel the wetness of fresh blood pumping in the wound on her head.

But she's up.

Too weak to crawl, Penny rolls onto her back. She can feel her heart hammering against the dusty stone. Her lungs ache, and the dust isn't helping. How the hell did she think she was going to get past the guards? Running is unthinkable. *Walking* is pretty much out of the question. She might as well just lie here. Nothing Melek can do to her is going to hurt more than this.

"Allahu akbar! Allahu akbar!"

Squinting into the sun, Penny's eyes fix on the yellow garbage tube bolted to the side of the railing. It's wide enough for a person to fit inside.

A person.

A faint hope flickers, insubstantial as an itch. But she shoves herself upright. Yes, the tube runs straight down into that red dump truck. Penny drags herself toward the tube, blood from her knees smearing across the dusty marble. She pulls herself to her feet, still panting as she leans on the marble railing for support. She peers down the darkening yellow tunnel and recoils.

No. She can't.

The dark, narrow tube smells sick-sweetly of half-melted plastic and broken fiberglass. It funnels two stories down to a truck full of jagged stones.

"I *can't*," whispers Penny.

She looks down at the tube. Then over at the guards, marching in crisp formation by the gates.

The last haunting notes of the *ezan* hang in the heavy air.

"La ilaha illallah!"

Penny sits on the edge of the balcony. She slides her feet gingerly into the tube, up to her knees, then her midthighs. It's like climbing into an oven. She inches her behind to the edge of the tube and gulps. She can't just slide. She'll kill herself. She's got to go slow. She presses her bare feet against the sides of the tube, ignoring her stinging cuts, and eases her body down into the weird yellow dimness, arms flat against her sides, palms tight to the tube wall. She lurches a few inches down, and a few inches more. One last deep breath of fresh air. Now her head is inside, too.

It's horrible, much worse than she'd imagined. The light glows highlighter-yellow through the thick plastic. The heat is already soaking her in stinging sweat. She can barely breathe. The fiberglass fragments are making her itch uncontrollably.

What if she gets stuck in here? What if she *dies* in here?

Shut up, she tells herself. *You just have to inch down slowly.* Inch by inch by inch. Another memory comes. Holding Grandma's mitten in the sleety February wind on the way back from ice-skating, too big to be carried and too little to walk the whole half mile easily. Grandma urged her toward the warmth of the house with a chorus of "Inchworm, Inchworm."

Penny finds herself humming the words as she slides slowly, slowly down the construction tube. Foot over foot, hand over hand.

" 'Seems to me you'd stop and see' — *ouch*" — she grits her teeth — " 'How —

beautiful' — *damn!* — 'they — are.' "

Almost there, almost there! She can feel fresh air on the soles of her feet. She slides her legs down and lets herself fall the last two feet onto the dusty truck bed, trying not to cut herself on the jagged pieces of stone and concrete. Soaked in sweat, the scrapes on her face feel like they're on fire.

Penny crawls out from beneath the chute and lies flat on her back, gulping in fresh, garbagey air.

The balcony is high above her. There's no sign of movement — they don't even know she's gone.

She hears a young man's voice call, *"Kolay gelsin, kanka!"* — *Take it easy, bro!* — and the truck door slams.

Penny holds her breath, hardly daring to hope.

An engine sputters to life, and the contents of the truck bed begin to shake. Then the dump truck, the magnificent, beautiful dump truck, begins to move.

It rolls to a momentary stop at the gate, and the stones slide dangerously around Penny. She can hear the dogs barking. And then the truck pulls out, and into the piney air of the grounds.

Bouncing down the road, Penny looks up at the overhanging branches of the evergreens. She's smiling so wide it hurts. She's out. *She's free!*

Now, she just has to find Zach.

And Brenda.

And the first goddamn plane back to Michigan.

But first . . .

She props her exhausted head on a cracked marble pilaster.

Her eyelids feel like they're made of marble, too. It won't hurt if she closes her eyes for just a second. Okay, two seconds.

The truck pulls onto the highway, toward the Çalışkan Yapı construction yard.

10
KEEP YOUR SPIES CLOSE

Langley, Virginia
10:12 Local Time

In the STAB OPS Center break room, Christina presses the ice water tab on the cooler. On the bulletin board, photos from December's gingerbread cookie contest are starting to curl. Omar from the Erbil desk won with a toppled statue of Saddam Hussein, with buttercream mustache. Taylor nabbed second place with an edible replica of the *Kryptos* sculpture — cracked, unlike the real one.

"Ma'am?" Taylor herself hurries through the door. "It's Ankara Station. There's an emergency signal from FOXFIRE? I can't locate the record. . . ."

Never, not once, has Melek used the emergency alert system. This can't wait the twenty minutes it would take to get off-site. Christina locks her office door, cranks the AC up to its noisiest, and dials.

"Melek. I got your signal —"

"You told me she was a civilian with no specialized training." Melek's mellow voice is husky with anger. "I handled her accordingly. But it appears that you haven't been honest with me."

"You interrogated her?" Christina stiffens in her ergonomic chair.

"What do you expect, when you won't tell me the simple truth?"

Christina doesn't let her anger show. "I take it you lied to me about Prime Minister Bolu?"

"Bolu? The man would lose at chess to a stuffed pepper. If you don't know that by now, I recommend you get better spies."

"Melek, allies have to trust each other."

There is hurt, as much as anger, in Melek's voice. "Is that why you told me the girl was just some State Department intern?"

"What makes you think she's not? What *exactly* did she tell you?"

"Tell me?" Melek gives a furious laugh. "Don't her actions speak loud enough? She gives my father's Chief of Staff a concussion, sneaks past hundreds of armed soldiers, rides straight out through the gate . . ."

Melek's lies hardly rattled Christina. Even the kidnapping she could overlook — Melek hadn't actually managed to acquire any compromising intel. But this is beyond the pale.

Christina's outrage breaks the surface. "You mean you let her *escape*?"

"Who is she?" demands Melek. "She denies you sent her. Was that another lie?"

Christina lowers her voice. "What have you done?"

"What have *I* done? You didn't even warn me about Zachary Robson and that Kurdish terrorist!"

"Diplomats talk to sources, Melek."

"Diplomats? Davut Mehmetoğlu is affiliated with known Kurdish separatist groups."

"He's a former politician in your parliament."

"*Former.* You may pal around with those people in Syria. But in Turkey, we call them terrorists. Mehmetoğlu was at that party to sell your spy Zachary Robson secret information. I have evidence that proves Penny Kessler was involved. I also know you told me *none* of this. So you tell me. What is the CIA playing at?"

"I thought you were too smart for this, Melek. Is your father's paranoia contagious? We want Turkey stable as much as you do. I'm just trying to help. But you're making that almost impossible."

"What a convenient excuse for you."

"I don't like your attitude, Melek." Christina's tone sharpens. "How do I know you didn't deliberately release the girl, as a childish threat to me? A kind of plague rat, to spread inconvenient rumors? Have you grown tired of my help, Melek? Are you such a big girl now that you think that you can act alone? Do you want to see how fast you'll fail without me? What *would* your father say, if he finds out?"

"Your condescension is as unbecoming as it is unwise." Melek is keeping her composure, but only just.

"I'm a realist, Melek. I thought you were, too."

"You're trying to provoke me." There is a rustle as Melek straightens a stack of papers on her desk. "But I won't be so easily distracted. The girl is gone. And now I begin to wonder: Was Zachary Robson the loose cannon you claimed? Or was he acting on your orders all along?"

"Don't be ridiculous," hisses Christina. "You should be sweating bullets to help bring the real terrorists to justice. Instead, you kidnap Flag Girl and illegally interrogate her *in the Presidential Palace*!"

"My father said I could invite her here as a humanitarian gesture. He has no idea about the interrogation!"

"I believe you. But we both know no one else will."

"Would you undo a peace so many have died for just to get the upper hand?"

"That's a lot of moralizing, coming from a kidnapper."

"I only scared the girl!"

"You've screwed this up, Melek. I'm going to give you just one chance to put it right."

Melek says nothing. But they both know she can't afford to hang up now.

"Do you have any idea where Penny Kessler is?" asks Christina.

"We know where the vehicle she's in is probably headed. But —"

"Where?" Christina has already pulled up the map on her computer.

"What are you going to do?"

"Tell me where to find Penny Kessler."

"Tell me what Zach Robson was digging for."

"Let me help you, Melek. I can make this whole problem go away."

"I wonder" — Melek's voice is quiet with stifled rage — "what is in this for you?"

11
ORDERS

Ankara, Turkey
17:12 Local Time

"Thank God that's fucking over." Frank Lerman leans back in the only chair in room 754 of the Rixos Grand Ankara (the budget section, commanding views of a nearby fire escape) and props his oxfords on the bedspread. "I hate seeing injured people, you know what I mean? That guy with the burns on his face gave me the creeps. I'd make a really shitty doctor. Thank God for law school." He rubs his eyes. Stretches. "Teleconference is five thirty, right?"

Connor nods, still at attention. "Yes, sir."

"No time for the spa, I guess." Frank jabs his finger at the glossy model on the cover of the hotel-amenities brochure. "Why's she got a bunch of little rocks lined up on her spine? What's that gonna do for you?"

Connor shrugs. "No idea, sir."

"Nice ass, though."

Connor gives a noncommittal mumble.

Frank drums his fingers on the chair. "What are they doing down there, inventing the coffee bean? Milking the little coffee cows?"

Connor shifts uncomfortably. His shoes are too new, his feet are getting sore, and Frank Lerman is growing dangerously punchable. "You want me to go down and check on it, sir?"

"Coffee detail? Nah. I'm not that kind of boss."

Connor keeps his expression carefully neutral. "No, sir."

Frank's eyebrows arch toward the shiny pink dome of his head. "Yessir nosir. What was it, the Marines?"

Connor laughs. "Fourth-generation Navy, sir." It's been ten years since he got his acceptance letter from the Naval Academy, and he still loves being able to say it. He remembers Pop's beaming face and crinkled eyes, the first time Connor came home to Peachtree City in uniform — the closest he'd ever seen his father to tears. Back when Pop still knew how to be proud of him.

"Should've guessed it," says Frank. "You stand like you're about to salute. Sailing the ocean blue, huh?"

"I sailed a computer, sir. Naval Intelligence. 'In God we trust. All others we monitor.' "

"Ha." Frank rubs his shadowed eyes. "You ever been to Turkey before?"

"No, sir. First time in the Middle East. They had me learning Russian before this."

"Borscht patrol?"

"Not yet, sir. Navy had me in Florida, then the Med."

"Lucky bastard. You surf?"

"Not really, sir. I play a mean Marco Polo, though."

"Ha. Funny guy. Me, I run. Did the DC Rock 'n' Roll Half Marathon this year. I've got these toe-shoes — it's just like running barefoot. Back to nature. Like organic bourbon." Frank loosens his tie. "When that goddamn coffee comes, it better be made of Buddha's piss, I'm telling you." His beady eyes fix on Connor's face. "So. They've got you on the Turkish Agricultural Policy and Food Security desk?"

"That's right, sir. Good old Foggy Bottom. They've still got me down on the third floor, though."

"Agriculture." Frank grins crookedly. "And for the biggest terrorist attack of the decade they just thought it would be fun to reassign my usual aide and send you instead. Take Your Farmer to Work Day."

Connor shrugs. "Guess so, sir. State moves in mysterious ways."

"Agriculture."

"About seventy-five percent of the world's figs come from Turkey," says Connor with well-simulated enthusiasm. "That's a lot of Fig Newtons. America's favorite fruit cookie."

"Hate figs. Seeds get in your teeth."

Connor's phone beeps.

"That'll be your girlfriend, huh?" says Frank. "The one you keep texting when you think I don't see you?"

Connor grimaces theatrically. Better to play it broad for a jerk like Lerman. "She's the clingy type."

"Sure." Frank rolls his eyes. "Because I'm as dumb as Brenda Pelecchia looks."

Connor tries to match Frank's tone. "That blazer of hers was a little grim."

"Listen, buddy." The jollity slides out of Frank's voice. "This belongs to State. Do you get me?"

"Sir?"

"Don't *sir* me, my friend. You just tell your real boss, whoever he is, to keep his chips out of my guacamole."

Connor shakes his head. "Sir —"

"Go check on my coffee. I don't want to snore in Secretary Winthrop's digital face.

Wouldn't look good, you know? We're supposed to be on high alert here."

"Yes, sir." Connor rolls back on his heels. "Skinny macchiato, right?"

"Hell, make it soy. Knock yourself out. And leave my briefcase here."

Connor sets it down on the bed. "I think you've got the wrong idea, Mr. Lerman. We're all on the same team."

"Yeah, buddy?" Frank leans forward. "You know what I think? I think it's weird that a hundred and eighty-nine Americans are murdered, and CIA tries to send some undercover Boy Scout to deal with it. What are you, twenty-six? Twenty-seven?"

Connor takes a deep breath. "Sir, as you know, Martin MacGowan, CIA's Ankara Station Chief, was killed in the explosion, along with both his aides."

"So? MacGowan doesn't have a deputy?"

"That would be Zachary Robson, sir."

"Fuck."

"Sir, Istanbul Station's working round-the-clock to protect the NATO Summit. We needed more officers on the ground. I'm honored to serve."

"Well, I'm honored to tell you to fuck off. This isn't the place to get your training wheels. And why lie to me about it? It's bad enough having you assholes second-guess

131

our every move. But this is over the line. And Secretary Winthrop isn't going to like it."

Connor blanches. He can imagine Christina's reaction; he'll spend the next decade handcuffed to a desk in Langley. Not even a nice desk near the window. He tries to sound suave. "What makes you think Secretary Winthrop didn't personally authorize it, sir?"

"Nice bluff, son. What makes you think I have the IQ of a zucchini?"

"Very funny, sir."

"You know what I think?" Frank's eyes narrow. "I think this smells like a cover-up. Zachary Robson was one of your guys. I think somebody at CIA screwed up something big. And that somebody doesn't want to get caught."

"Would that be before or after we faked the moon landings, sir?"

"Sassing me, huh? That's *real* professional."

"Sorry, sir. Soy macchiato, right?"

"I don't want to know what your boss is up to. You're too junior to have a clue, anyway. But let me let you in on a little secret. The preliminary forensics report came in. And whoop-de-do, it *was* a bomb. A big fat bomb, inside the soft-serve ma-

132

chine in the ice cream truck. Not home-made. No TATP. Military-grade. *Expensive.* And made in the US of A."

"What?" Connor doesn't even try to hide his exasperation. "Why didn't you tell me?"

Frank smirks. "So State isn't always the dumb older brother, huh? Well, let me tell you something else. Security cleared that truck when it came in. No K9s, because of food safety. So whoever put that bomb there did it before the party. And they hid it plain sight, where a doggy could've sniffed it out, but human security missed it."

"Security didn't X-ray the soft-serve machine?"

"It was bolted into place."

"So the company that owns the ice cream truck must have known!"

"Nope. Apparently, those stupid fuckers keep the truck parked on the side of a street. Anybody could break in."

Connor's phone beeps.

"Our analysts are saying this attack has Hashashin written all over it," says Frank. "And if *that's* true, maybe you could tell me what the fuck the Hashashin are doing with state-of-the-art, military-grade American bombs?"

Connor's phone beeps again.

"I'm glad somebody out there wants to

133

talk to you. 'Cause I sure as shit don't."

"Sir —"

"Listen, buddy. As soon as Secretary Winthrop talks to me, he's going to talk to the President, and the President is going to make a statement to the press. And let me tell you something. If it turns out the terrorists piggybacked in on some cockeyed CIA mission, heads will roll. Important heads."

"Sir —"

"The point," says Frank, "is that I want no part of your shitstorm. I'm clean, and Secretary Winthrop is clean. And I'm going to keep it that way. You go take that back to your boss like a good boy, huh?"

"Your coffee —"

"Fuck the coffee. Get the hell out of my room."

"Sir." Connor steps outside. The muscles in his jaw are as tight as guitar strings. He pulls out his phone. Christina's sent him three pings to call her on the secure line. He opens the doors to the stairwell. Empty. Good. He leans against the wall and dials.

A momentary pause, and Christina's voice comes through. "On what planet does 'red star alert' mean 'call me when you feel like it,' Connor?"

"Sorry, ma'am. Lerman's not happy. He

says the bomb —"

"We know. If you answered your phone, I could have told you."

Connor squares his shoulders. "He's guessed my true affiliation. He thinks I'm on some crazy cover-up —"

"Never mind that. The Penny Kessler situation has gone critical."

"It's bad," Connor agrees, eager to show he's at least up to speed on this. "Official update from the Presidential Palace about ten minutes ago said Palamut's doctor had seen her, and she's resting up. They're not letting us anywhere near her —"

"That's because she's gone."

Connor can see Penny's face so clearly: ashen and fearful, desperate for someone to trust. And he sent her into enemy territory stuffed with tranqs. Guilt twists in his gut like a broken bottle. "Is she — dead?"

"Hardly." Christina snorts. "She escaped from under direct surveillance at the Presidential Palace in broad daylight. Knocked out the guy guarding her and hitched a ride out of the compound."

"She *what*?" The three premature creases across Connor's forehead deepen. He must have misheard. "How?"

"You tell me, Connor." Christina sounds way too nice, which means she's livid.

"Are we talking about the same girl? 'Cause the one I saw looked like a babysitter who'd been run over by a truck."

"Fortunately," continues Christina's dry voice, "we're pretty sure where she's headed. Ditch Lerman. I've set up a driver — he should be in the lobby dressed as a chauffeur, holding a sign with 'Eagle Eye Tourism' on it. His name's Faruk. He's seen your photo. Doesn't speak English, but he's been instructed where to go."

"I'm on my way down." Connor pounds down the stairs three at a time.

"Stay alert. Given her association with Mehmetoğlu, we're now treating Penny Kessler as the primary suspect in the bombing."

"Penny?"

"Penny."

"I don't believe it," Connor mutters. "She just seemed like a normal college kid!"

"Do you know how many 'normal college kids' ran off and joined ISIS? Babysitters can be terrorists, too."

"Ma'am." Connor tries to cram as much respect as possible into the syllable; Christina is no fan of being contradicted. "Are we absolutely sure? Penny just seemed scared. And . . ." He races down the stairs. "You know. Young. Innocent."

"Innocent? Would you say that about a twenty-one-year-old male who fraternized with known terrorists and punched out a Turkish government official?"

"Ma'am, I didn't —"

"I didn't expect that kind of sexist crap from a guy like you. How fucking naïve are you, Connor?"

Connor feels an acid wave of shame burn in his stomach. He'd felt terrible for Penny in the hospital, with her big scared eyes and shaky voice. He believed her. Now Christina thinks he's weak. Connor knows where that leads for *a guy like him.*

It happened in the Navy after he came out. Buddies he'd survived plebe summer with, guys who'd have died or killed or been best man for him, suddenly went cold, as if his being gay erased everything else they knew about him. They scrutinized every friendly word. Called him a coward when they used to joke about how nobody could get him riled up. Sabotaged his work just to see him fail. Not everybody — but enough to sour the whole ship's morale. Connor had faith. He held on for two more years, determined that he could change their minds. He couldn't. He'd joined the Navy to serve, not to hide. The day he served out his enlistment, he applied to the CIA.

Connor had been out at the Agency from day one — he even kept a photo of his and Alex's engagement party on his desk. CIA genuinely makes an effort: during Pride Month, Connor smiled resolutely through half a dozen Agency pride events, those living Venn diagrams of awkwardness, good intentions, and colorful ties. But regulations don't change a culture overnight, and at CIA more than a smidgen of paramilitary hypermachismo was still sloshing around. His years in Naval Intelligence didn't matter. He'd have to prove himself all over again. So far, he hadn't had much of a chance. Fresh off the Farm and raring to hit the field, he'd gotten stranded with almost a year of office work. He'd been stunned and grateful when Christina Ekdahl — *the* Christina Ekdahl — chose him personally for this assignment. "There's a dozen Turkey specialists I could send," she'd told him. "But they're so sure they know the patterns, they don't see what's right in front of them. You'll be my fresh eyes." Connor knew a big break when he got one. And now, thanks to Penny freaking Kessler, Christina thought he was a weakling and a dupe.

And yet.

He remembers the catch in Penny's voice.

The way she looked when she found out her friends were dead. He's seen that look before. Back in the Navy, his ship once rescued a boatload of refugees off Lampedusa. Half of their group had already drowned. The survivors' faces had that same uncomprehending grief.

"Ma'am, Penny had just come out of sedation. She's got to be in shock. Half the people she works with were just murdered. Her boyfriend's missing. Her record's cleaner than clean. Don't you think there's a chance —"

"Listen to yourself." Christina's voice comes through calm as a 911 operator. "She secretly helped a terrorist gain access to the U.S. Embassy, lied about her relationship with Zach Robson, got rid of the pills you gave her, gave President Palamut's Chief of Staff a concussion, and is currently on the run from the Turkish police. Is that what you call clean?"

"No, ma'am."

"Just get her into the car. Faruk will take you both to a secure location. Do *not* attempt interrogation on your own. Be careful. Treat her like you would any other terror suspect."

Connor swallows. "Yes, ma'am."

"Have you got your ECRP with you?"

"My ECRP?" Connor balks. Emergency Combat Readiness Packs are a highly controversial last resort, first developed for fieldwork in Yemen and almost never authorized outside war zones. Connor had to sign three extra forms just to transport this one; he never thought he'd have to use it.

"I'm not saying you're going to need it. But I need you prepared."

"Yes, ma'am." Connor races out along the second-floor corridor, swipes into his hotel room, and digs into his suitcase. In its plain dark gray bag, the ECRP looks like a boring men's shaving kit — the kind that makes for a half-thoughtful birthday present. "Got it."

"Keep it on you at all times. Connor?"

"Ma'am?"

"I know it's your first time on the ground. But you got this."

It's the kindest thing she's ever said to him; Christina doesn't do praise. Connor glows. "Thanks, ma'am."

"Move it. She's ten minutes away, and you've got fifteen, max, before the Turkish police get there."

Connor's already in the lobby. "Ma'am, can I ask who our source —"

Plastic stillness on the line. She's already gone.

A tan, bored-looking man with a beer belly bulging under his blue suit is standing by the door, munching a chocolate bar. The sign he's holding bears the logo of a cartoon eagle, with an incongruously toothy smile.

Langley, Virginia
10:28 Local Time
Christina clicks the aerial stream from Ankara. The loading icon spins like a forlorn satellite; CIA's office desktops are slow as they are crappy.

Christina takes a deep breath.

She looks at Elastigirl, clinging to the desk lamp. Isabel's last gift.

It's twelve years since Isabel died in Helmand Province. Christina's first mentor at the Agency. Her role model. Her best friend.

Christina was Chief of Station in Karachi then. She got Langley to send her the report. The suicide bomber who attacked Isabel's convoy had been scooped up for questioning two weeks before at another CIA station. He'd been released: insufficient evidence. The location was redacted.

Christina was livid. She dialed Langley, demanding to know whose fuckup had cost Isabel her life. "Which station?" she'd screamed. "Who let him go?"

"Nobody blames you," her chief had

begun. "You were just following proto-col. . . ."

There's only so far you can stretch before you snap.

Never again. No more squeamish qualms. All our enemies fight dirty. Why should we follow rules that make us weak? You crush the bastards hard, when you still can. Let others wring their hands about legality. Any methods, any cost, any sacrifice. As long as it worked.

And it *did* work.

Until Zach Robson threatened everything she'd built.

Christina watches traffic crawl fifty-four hundred miles away. The white pulse of Connor's tracker is easy to locate. He should be confirming pickup of Penny Kessler any minute now.

One thing is certain: if Zach Robson had proof, he'd have made his move by now.

Good luck to the girl with the flag.

And then, *Delivered.*

The Kurds brought the proof to the Embassy party. They delivered that proof.

Zach doesn't have it.

Which means someone else does.

Christina thought Penny Kessler could help lead her to Zach. But if what Melek says is true, Christina has only one option.

She'll do what she has to do.
She always has.
Good luck to the girl with the flag.
A tense smile flickers on Christina's face.
Luck isn't going to cut it.

12
SAFETY

Ankara, Turkey
17:35 Local Time
The dump truck slows to a crawl outside a convenience store in Ulus, near Ankara's ancient citadel, a hodgepodge neighborhood of sloppy new construction and crumbling early-twentieth-century buildings too un-picturesque for tourists. Here and there rise the rusting steel and stained concrete of government buildings from the dawn of the Turkish Republic, manifestos made manifest in glass and steel, hopeful declarations of modernity and secularism eighty years out of date.

A marble slab heaves against the inner wall of the truck bed, waking Penny with a jolt. For a moment, disoriented, she wonders why she's lying on rocks. Memory kicks back in, and she sits up painfully. The red bathrobe is dusky with debris; by the strange, dry feel of it, her face is, too. Her legs itch with dried blood and crumbled fiberglass. At least her head isn't throbbing quite so much.

"Hey, Recep *amca*!" shouts the driver. "Toss me an Efes!"

"Shouldn't that be an *ayran*?" replies what sounds like an older man; you can tell he's grinning.

The driver groans theatrically. Penny hears him catch the beer bottle and pop it open on the edge of the window.

The older man says, "Tough day at the palace?"

"My brother-in-law cut us down to four tea breaks!"

The older man tsks sympathetically.

"And I had to drive halfway to Batıkent to get back — they've closed off every road into Çankaya!"

"Still?" The old man sounds incredulous.

"That bomb, I guess. I think it was those Syrians. 'Refugees' — yeah, right."

The old man gives a knowing tut and says *he's* sure it was the Israelis.

"No way, *amca*," protests the driver. "The Israelis love the Americans. I hear the U.S. president is secretly an Israeli."

That, says the old man confidently, just proves his point.

Chat turns to the soccer match that night

— both men are rooting for Galatasaray, but the driver thinks Arsenal's new striker could be a threat.

Penny shifts uncomfortably in the truck bed. Finally, the driver sighs, takes his leave, and the engine fires up again. A few minutes later, the truck pulls under a battered metal arch that bears the rusting legend Çalışkan Yapı. This must be the construction yard; he's dropping off the truck for the night.

A terrible thought occurs to Penny. What if he empties the truck? She holds her breath.

The engine cuts. Thank God. Penny hears the driver slam out, humming the summer's mega pop hit. They were blasting the buzzy synth on infinite repeat at that club Ayla dragged her to last week.

"Bebby, bebby, ooh," he hums, his voice getting farther away. "Oowah loveya, bebby . . ."

"You're late!" croaks a four-pack-a-day voice from across the yard.

Trafik," the driver replies unrepentantly.

"You've still got junk in the truck?" Four-Pack sounds ballistic. "How many times I got to tell you? Don't leave trash in my trucks overnight!"

"The D200 to Mamak is all blocked, *abi*. I'll dump everything in the morning."

"Your head is all blocked," mutters Four-Pack. "I told Ece we shouldn't've given you a job. But *no*. Mehmetçik can do no wrong. You lazy son of a . . ."

Lying as flat as she can in the truck bed, Penny can make out the metallic, angry-lawn-mower rattling of a motorcycle revving to life and then roaring away.

For a full minute, Penny lies still and sore in the bright heat, just listening. She can hear the low thrumming melody of impatient horns and rush-hour city traffic, and a tinny, squawky soap-opera catfight. She pushes herself to her knees and peers cautiously over the edge of the dump truck, into the wide and badly paved lot. It's empty. Through the grimy office window, she can see a bald guy — Four-Pack — with his feet propped on a table, apparently engrossed in the tiny television screen. Penny recognizes the theme music — her Turkish teacher in Ann Arbor used to make them watch this show for vocab practice.

Slowly, agonizingly, Penny stands up and swings her sore legs over the back wall of the truck bed. She slides her feet down to the bumper and jumps to the ground, with a billow of the red bathrobe. Her legs almost give way beneath her. The pebbly, broken asphalt cuts into the soles of her feet. She crouches low to the ground, breathing raggedly.

She can hardly believe how weak she feels. She won't get far in Ankara, especially not in this getup. But she *must* find Connor — it's her only hope of helping Zach. With luck, he might still be at the hospital. She glances in the direction of Four-Pack in the office. Should she knock on the window and throw herself on his mercy? What could she say? The truth is out of the question. She could pretend to be lost and ask him to take her to the hospital. And then what? How could she explain what she was doing in his construction yard, covered in blood and grime, in a bathrobe with the presidential seal emblazoned across the shoulders? At best, he'd think she was crazy. At worst, he might recognize her from the news. Either way, he'd be sure to call the police.

Penny leans against the side of the dump truck. A plan. She needs a plan. Okay. She'll get out of the construction yard, find a cab, and get to the hospital.

Her face falls. She has no money, no cards. Well, *somebody* from the Embassy is bound to be at the hospital — they can lend her the fare when she arrives.

Buoyed by a new sense of purpose, she edges along the truck to the cinder-block

148

wall of the construction yard and heads for the gate, as quickly as her sore legs will allow.

A cry of rage from the direction of the office. "You bitch!"

Penny flinches. Every muscle tenses to bolt.

"You cow!" cries the furious manager in Turkish. "You lying cow! You knew Betül was pregnant all along!"

Penny is so relieved she almost laughs. She limps quickly toward the gate and out into the road, which an optimistic sign identifies as Beauty Street. It's obviously a poor neighborhood, not like green, suburban Batıkent, where she's been subletting a spare room in a row house near the metro stop, and her landlady, Fatma, even nurses a few willful rosebushes. The asphalt here is cracked and concave, like a dusty riverbed. This neighborhood must not have voted for Palamut's party. Decrepit, pastel-plastered three-story apartment buildings line the road. No stores, just one basement *bakkal* — a dinky mom-and-pop store for buying bottled water, gum, bags of toasted chickpeas, and cheap ice pops.

The low, brilliant sun flares in Penny's eyes. Out of the shaded yard, the heat presses into her. Light and heat. The terrible dry boom of the blast in the Embassy garden. And just like that, the memories choke her. Vertigo. Nausea. Rising panic strangles her breath. She can't fall apart now. She can't. *Can't.*

Penny's nails dig into her palms. Her eyes fix on a sign in the window of the *bakkal,* advertising those splintery sunflower seeds that Turkish farmers and their city cousins like to chew and spit, until the papery gnawed pods heap up around their ankles. Fatma hates them — calls them "peasant garbage," which Penny had found kind of offensive. Now, she'd give anything for the ordinary, comfortable irritation of Fatma's nagging offers of sage tea and unsolicited opinions on Penny's love life, choice of shampoo, failure to starch her underclothes, and method of making coffee.

The street is still — too still. No sign of a taxi. A stripy cat suns itself in the dust. A head-scarfed woman hanging undershirts off a balcony fixes Penny with a disapproving stare.

Penny can feel her cheeks turn red. She feels terribly exposed, painfully conscious of how alone she is. The woman is watching her with alarming intensity.

Oh, God, why aren't there any taxis? There's just one car on the street — a shiny charcoal-gray BMW parked near the *bakkal.* That's much too expensive for this neighborhood, isn't it? The windows are tinted; she can't see in.

Penny limps toward the corner. There's got to be a taxi rank somewhere nearby.

The gray BMW starts pulling out. It's headed in her direction.

Penny backs away, toward the stairs of a dilapidated pink apartment building.

The door of the car opens, and a familiar blond crew cut appears.

"Connor?" Penny gasps.

He looks haggard and tense; deep worry lines across his forehead make him appear suddenly older, and a lot less flip. But it's him, all right.

"Oh, my God." Tears sting suddenly in Penny's eyes. For a moment, she's too stunned even to smile. It's a goddamn miracle. All he's missing is a white steed and a suit of armor. "It *is* you," she croaks. How could she ever have been cross with him? After so much fear, the relief makes her dizzy. "How did you find me?"

"Are you alone?"

Penny glances nervously over her shoulder. "I . . . think so." She steps toward the car.

"Don't move." Connor stares suspiciously

at her robe. "What's that?"

Annoyance sidles like a crab through her wave of gratitude. Who the hell cares what she's wearing? "A . . . bathrobe?" The woman on the balcony has pulled out a cell phone. Penny's heart thumps. "Connor, can we talk about this in the car?"

He pauses a beat too long before he says, "Get in."

"Nataşa!" spits the woman on the balcony.

Penny slams the door and leans blissfully into the cool, plush upholstery as the BMW pulls away. The broken stones have left bruises all down her back. Now that she's safe, exhaustion is already sweeping over her.

Connor is frowning. "Why did she just call you Natasha?" He still sounds more like a cop-show interrogator than a friend.

"It's a slang word."

"For?"

"Foreign prostitute." She looks up at him. No reaction; he's texting. He unzips his briefcase and tucks the phone into a specially shaped compartment. There's something furious in his precision. And he still won't look her in the face. *"Merhaba,"* she calls up to the driver. *"Ben Penny."*

The driver smiles warmly at her in the rearview mirror. "Faruk."

"Don't talk to him," orders Connor.

Penny frowns. "Why not?"

"Just don't."

His pale eyes are hard, expression guarded; he's sitting bolt upright.

"Thank you for finding me."

"Just doing my job, Miss Kessler."

Penny draws back. Didn't he call her Penny back at the hospital? Maybe formality is the way he handles fear. She just wishes he'd stop glaring at her. He obviously doesn't want to talk, but she has to know. "How did you know where I was?"

She hadn't thought it possible for Connor to look less friendly, but he does. "That information is classified."

"Oh." Penny swallows; her mouth is so dry. "Okay." She glances up at the driver as they turn down off Beauty Street. "Are you taking me to Frank Lerman?"

Connor shakes his head. "We're going to a safe house."

"Oh." In the stuffy stillness of the car, Penny's headache is blazing back to life behind her eyes. "Do you have any more of that aspirin?"

"Aspirin?" Whatever has been simmering beneath Connor's forced calm explodes. "Is that supposed to be funny?"

"No." Penny gives him a puzzled look.

Connor's voice is low and tightly controlled. "I'm not in charge of interrogating you, Miss Kessler. We have specialists for that —"

Penny blanches. "Interrogating me?"

He steamrolls over her interruption. "— but there's one thing I'd like to know. Just one thing. Professional interest, you might say."

Penny wishes he didn't sound so angry. What does this starched twerp have to be angry about? Stupid, tired tears are prickling in her eyes. She tries to sound professional. "What's that, Mr. . . ." She can't remember his last name. Did he even tell her? "What?"

"Just how, exactly, did you become immune to sedatives?"

"Sedatives?"

"Don't play stupid." His ears are bright red. "I saw you swallow them. I s*aw* you. And next thing I hear, you're punching out Turkish officials!"

"It was one guy!" she protests. "And how did you even know I —" His words suddenly slide into place. The pills she threw up in the ambulance. "Did you —" Penny stares at him in horror. "Did you *drug* me?"

"Fine." Connor straightens his narrow charcoal tie, which doesn't need straightening. "You can tell them at the safe house."

"You drugged me," Penny repeats; she can hear her voice getting thin with fury.

Connor is watching her with an expression of consternation. He puts on a voice clearly intended to sound brusque. "I'm hardly the one at fault here, Miss Kessler."

Penny's getting nauseous. "Why? Why would you do that?"

"To be sure they couldn't question you" is Connor's pat reply.

He doesn't even bother to deny it.

"It was for your own good as much as the Agency's," Connor adds defensively. "Standard procedure. They could've tortured you."

"So you thought I'd be safer unconscious?" Penny is so angry, she can barely speak. "With people you thought were probably going to torture me?"

Something that could be guilt, or just embarrassment, flickers across Connor's face. "Keep it down."

Penny's breath is coming faster now. "How *dare* you?"

"How dare *I*?" Connor's cheeks are blotchy. "You play with terrorists, Miss Kessler, you get hurt. You're lucky you're not in cuffs on your way to prison. And if you're what I think you are, you will be soon."

Penny stares at him.

Now that Connor has started talking, he doesn't seem to be able to stop the machine-gun rattle of his rage. "I don't get it," he splutters. "I just don't. You don't *sound* like a sociopath. You remind me of my kid sister. What happened to you? How do you work with people every day and then decide you're going to blow them up?"

Faruk turns around with a kindly, questioning look. "Okay?" he asks in heavily accented English.

"Okay," says Connor firmly. He draws a deep breath. "You know what, Miss Kessler? Never mind. I'm not even supposed to be talking to you. You just sit tight. You just sit tight till we're at the safe house."

"You think I'm a terrorist." An awful numbness makes Penny's voice almost robotic. This can't be real.

"You sure aren't behaving like some innocent little intern from Michigan."

Penny sucks in her breath. "Does trying not to get killed make me a criminal? I'm sorry, was I supposed to wait in the palace so you and Frank Lerman could ride in on your fire-breathing eagles or something?"

"What about inviting Mehmetoğlu?"

"It was a *mistake*," says Penny hoarsely. "Zach asked me to add Mehmetoğlu's name to the guest list. That's it. That's all I did. I typed one name. I didn't know who he was." Her voice cracks. "If I did anything wrong, I'm sorry. I'm not a terrorist. I don't want to hurt anybody. I just want to go home." She's full on crying now. She's got no energy to fight it down or care what Connor thinks. "I just want to go home."

Faruk turns around again, obviously concerned. "Okay?"

"Okay!" snaps Connor.

"Çikolata?" Faruk holds a half-eaten candy bar toward Penny.

The BMW has veered into the neighboring lane; a chorus of horns sounds.

"Just drive, Faruk!" snaps Connor, gesturing at the road. "Okay?"

"Okay." Faruk squares his padded shoulders. He's clearly placed Connor in the mental file marked "Assholes."

Penny feels a surge of fellow feeling for the driver. She breaks a square off the chocolate bar. It's salty-sweet, studded with pistachios. She's startled to realize that she's ravenous. How long has it been since that ice cream in the Embassy garden? She scrapes the last traces off the wrapper. "You really don't believe me," she says quietly.

Connor stares straight ahead.

Her mind is racing. "If I were a terrorist

157

and I escaped, why the hell would I get into the car with you? It doesn't make any sense!"

She can see the words hit home.

Connor hesitates. She senses his doubt. His kindness from the hospital almost resurges; she can see it in his face. But no. It's not enough. He stares ahead. "I have nothing further to say to you, Miss Kessler."

Penny's heart is hammering. "I want to get out of the car."

"That's not an option."

"Am I under arrest?" The words taste funny in her mouth. Dad used to accuse her of being an approval junkie; she always tried to follow the rules. She remembers last semester, when an unexpected B- on her statistics midterm reduced her to ugly tears in the Michigan Union ladies' room. It seems very far away.

Connor replies stiffly, "I'm not a police officer."

"Then why can't I leave?"

"We're going fifty miles an hour."

"Where's Brenda?" demands Penny in a low voice. "I want to talk to Brenda Pelecchia." He doesn't answer. "What about the media? What about the people at the Presidential Palace? Don't you think they'll all be wondering where I've gone?"

"I'm taking you to the safe house."

"I promised I'd help you find Zach," says Penny furiously. "If the Hashashin have got him, every hour we wait is going to put him in more danger. He's one of your people, isn't he? Are you going to let me help him or not?"

"Miss Kessler, right now my orders are to take you to the safe house. Nothing else."

They sit in furious silence as the gray BMW weaves down the D200 highway, past the ANKAmall, out toward Middle East Technical University, on the low-rise western fringe of the city.

Penny's evil eye bracelet glints in the golden light. Some good luck charm. She leans her throbbing, exhausted head on her dusty knees. She badly needs the rest — and this way, she doesn't have to see Connor's snub-nosed, self-righteous face, his perfectly side-parted baby-blond hair.

For his part, Connor sits rigidly upright, arms crossed over his spotless suit jacket, eyes suspiciously on Penny. He takes a swig of blue Gatorade. "You want some? It's got lots of electrolytes."

Penny glowers at him. "Would that be their new knockout-drops flavor?"

Connor rolls his eyes. "That was to stop you from being tortured. You could try a little gratitude. You thirsty or not?"

Penny's lips are cracking, but she shakes her sore head. "No thank you."

Connor shrugs. "It's your funeral."

Penny swallows hard. That's just an expression, isn't it? A CIA "safe house" could mean almost anything, especially if they think she's a terrorist. Why won't they let her talk to Brenda? Is she really any safer than she was in Palamut's palace?

What would Zach do? Penny bites the inside of her cheek, willing her mind to focus. For the second time in an hour, she's got to find some way to escape.

This time from a moving car, with an angry (and presumably armed) spy sitting next to her.

She watches Connor drain his Gatorade and fiddle with the lid.

Why should *he* be nervous? Because of what is waiting at the "safe house"? Penny's mouth is painfully dry. She's got to find some way out of here.

Obeying the canned voice of the GPS, Faruk exits the D200 onto Mevlana Boulevard, heading south toward the Middle East Technical University's man-made forest: hundreds of thousands of scrubby trees in tidy rows, used mostly by students for picnics and privacy. There's hardly another car on the road, except for the enormous Eti biscuit truck lumbering in front of them.

Penny slides her fingers over her seat-belt buckle. She presses it slowly, to muffle the click. The forest — rows of skinny evergreens — runs all along the right side of the car. She'll only have to make it about ten feet to gain the cover of the trees. She just needs the car to slow down.

They're coming up to a traffic light. Green. Dammit.

The Eti truck rolls through, and the light turns yellow. Faruk hits the brakes.

"It's just a yellow light," grouses Connor. "It's not like there's anybody on the road."

The light turns red.

Shielded by the bulk of her red bathrobe, Penny grips the door handle. If she waits till the red light is almost up, there's a chance Faruk will already be accelerating as she jumps, making it harder for Connor to follow. It might buy her a few extra seconds.

Three, two, go.

Penny flings open the door and hurls herself onto the asphalt, just as Faruk accelerates. The bitter smell of sun-melted tar stings in her nostrils. The black goo burns as it gloms on to her bare feet. Her knees threaten to buckle as she staggers toward the forest.

This was a stupid, stupid idea.

Faruk hits the breaks and turns around, confused. "Mr. Connor —"

"Jesus!" Connor may be stunned, but he's well trained — and wearing shoes. He clicks off his seat belt and lunges after her.

Penny struggles onto the spiky, desiccated grass off the shoulder. Only two feet to the shelter of the trees.

"Stop!" Connor has drawn a small black gun. He's only ten feet away now, on the edge of the road. "Stop now!" His voice is shaking, but his hand is steady. "I'll shoot you if I have to!"

Penny turns around. "Please, I —"

The force of the explosion knocks them both to the earth.

13

THE QUICK AND THE DEAD

Penny never thought she'd have to feel it again. That boom, like a punch to the chest. That singe of heat. That tingling roar in her ears.

Time stretches.

The flaming shell of the BMW has blown itself upward, almost fifteen feet in the air.

Beneath it, Connor's lanky form sprawls on the edge of the road.

The car, thinks Penny numbly.

And then, *Connor.*

She realizes she's screaming his name, almost ripping his suit jacket as she drags him onto the grass, out of danger. The flaming BMW crunches back down on the road in a spray of glass, upside down, crackling like an acrid bonfire.

"Run," gasps Connor. He tugs her toward the trees.

"Faruk —"

"Gas tank!"

Penny fights him. "But —"

Hell heat. A riptide of sound.

A twenty-foot inferno engulfs the BMW as the gas tank explodes. The fat column of black smoke soars into the clouds.

Penny is shaking uncontrollably.

"Come on!" Connor has her by the wrist. His gun is back in its holster, and the chill is gone from his voice. "We've got to get out of here!"

"But Faruk —" She stops herself. She knows there's no way he survived.

Connor shakes his head. "Come on."

"We need to call an ambulance!"

"Hell no, we don't." Now that he's agitated, his Southern accent is a lot more noticeable. "Move it, before somebody sees us!"

Over her shoulder, as Connor pulls her into the woods, Penny sees a battered blue Peugeot pull up. The driver jumps out and runs toward the wreck.

Connor yanks her arm. "Hurry!"

Penny limps barefoot through the undergrowth of coarse grass, struggling to keep pace.

When they're a few hundred yards into the forest, Connor stops and raises a finger to his lips. Penny sits down heavily, gasping. She leans against one of the narrow trunks.

Connor leans over her, panting. "You okay?"

She nods.

There's no sound but the slight creaking of the branches in the warm breeze. It must be around six; the golden sun is sinking toward the horizon.

"I'm going to make a call," Connor says. "You try to run away, I swear I'll shoot you. Got that?"

Penny nods again, still trying to catch her breath.

Connor reaches in the pocket of his suit, and his face falls. He pats his trouser pockets. He pulls his jacket off and shakes it upside down.

"It's in your briefcase," says Penny. "In the car."

"Thank you, Captain Obvious." Connor glowers.

"Don't you have a secret radio in your shoe, or something?"

Connor rolls his eyes. "Yeah, 'cause *that* wouldn't look suspicious coming through airport security."

"Haven't you got anything?"

He feels his belt. "My Swiss Army knife."

Penny's hands are still shaking. "Did you bring marshmallows for the campfire, too?"

"My equipment was in my briefcase," says

Connor through his teeth.

Penny looks up at him. "So what now? You going to march me to your safe house at gunpoint?"

"Can't." Connor rubs the back of his neck. "My boss sent the directions directly to Faruk."

"You mean *you* don't even know where you were taking me?"

"It doesn't matter!" snaps Connor, rolling up his shirtsleeves. "Don't you get it? The explosion came from *inside* the car. That means one of three things. Option one, someone put a bomb in the car before Faruk got into it. Which means the safe house may be compromised. Option two, Faruk was some kind of suicide bomber — which I seriously doubt, seeing as he works for the Agency —"

"And seeing as he just gave me his candy bar." Penny's breathing raggedly. Her ears are still ringing. "What's option three? Are you going to blame me for this one, too?"

"Physically impossible for you to have done it." Connor crouches down next to her and meets her eyes. "Besides. Your first instinct was to drag me away from the wreck."

Penny swallows. "So what's option three?"

Connor looks embarrassed. "I had an

ECRP in my briefcase."

"A what?"

"A kind of emergency kit."

"Like matches and a whistle?"

He won't meet her eyes. "And a certain quantity of plastic explosives."

"Hang on." Penny's voice is hoarse. "You were walking around with a *bomb*?"

"Not a bomb," Connor objects. "More like a code-activated grenade."

"You accused me of blowing up the Embassy." Tears sting Penny's eyes. "You accused me of murdering my friends. But you're the one with the bomb and the knife and the gun! How do I know *you* didn't blow up the car?"

"Are you insane?" Connor stares at her. "Look, I'm sorry. Maybe my boss was wrong about you. Bad intel happens —"

"Is that supposed to make it okay that you drugged me and called me a terrorist?"

"I don't know what you are," says Connor flatly. "And until I get in touch with my boss, unless you try to run away or kill me, I don't care. The point is, there's a chance the bad guys may have hacked and remotely detonated my equipment. It's not supposed to be possible. . . ."

"None of this is supposed to be possible." Penny hears sirens in the far distance, from the direction of the wreck.

"There's a thermal sensor in my phone. My supervisor will know it's been destroyed. I've got to contact Langley ASAP."

"Langley." Penny looks at him. "You really are a spy."

Connor gives her a funny look and starts to untie his shoelaces. "You're pretty new to this, aren't you?"

Penny crosses her arms. "I'm a fast learner."

"Here." Connor slides his shoes back on and hands Penny his socks. "They'll be big on you, but you can't walk barefoot on pine needles."

"Thick wool socks in Turkey in July?" She pulls them on.

Something almost like a smile flickers on his face. "Maybe my last posting was in Siberia, hunting down corrupt oligarchs and caviar smugglers in big furry hats."

"For real?"

"I'd tell you, but then I'd have to kill you."

"Okay, now you're just trolling."

He reaches out a hand to help her up.

She hesitates a moment, then takes it.

"Right," he says. "The last buildings we passed were to the west. We haven't got a compass, but my dad used to take me hunting, and he taught me a little trick for this."

Connor snaps a small twig off the nearest tree. "We're in the northern hemisphere, so if I align the shadow of the twig on my watch halfway between the hour hand and twelve, we see that west is —"

"That way." Penny points up toward the narrow trunks of the pines.

Connor lowers his watch, frowning. "How do you know?"

Penny gestures at the sinking sun.

"Just as well." Connor shakes his watch. "It's stopped."

Ankara, Turkey
18:20 Local Time

Frank Lerman steps out of the revolving door of the Rixos Grand Ankara into the red twilight. "Where is she?"

The dark-suited bodyguard gestures him across the driveway. Dust spatters the armored black SUV, half obscuring the telltale green-and-white diplomatic plates.

Frank climbs into the SUV and grins. "Ms. Pelecchia. We meet again."

Brenda peers behind him. "Where's your assistant? We could use another hand on deck."

"C-3PO had to step out. It's just me."

Brenda doesn't return his smile. "Close the door." She calls up to the driver, "Please

169

go as fast as you safely can."

The SUV pulls out onto Atatürk Boulevard.

"I gather congratulations are in order," says Frank, angling to get a better look at her. "Chargé d'Affaires, huh? Our acting Ambassador. That's a big step up for you. I guess the mushroom cloud has a silver lining."

Brenda eyes him with obvious distaste. "Mr. Lerman, almost two hundred of my colleagues — *our* colleagues — have just been murdered. Secretary Winthrop seems to feel I'm the only senior diplomat with sufficient area knowledge to take charge in this time of crisis. Congratulations are the last thing I want from you. What I need is complete cooperation, and an open line of communication to Secretary Winthrop."

"Call me Frank. You're sixth-floor level now."

"Well, *Frank,* non-emergency personnel and families are obviously being evacuated to Oakwood. Except for a skeleton staff to keep an eye on the wounded and the Embassy building, everyone else is being transferred to the Consulate General in Istanbul."

"I know." Frank nods. "Secretary Winthrop has directed me to come along as special adviser."

Brenda's lips press to a thin line. "So I hear."

Frank raises his eyebrows significantly. "The NATO Summit will be the *defining* moment of Secretary Winthrop's legacy. You're going to need someone experienced helping you out."

Brenda's expression is tight.

"So." Frank puts his feet up on the opposite seat. "Straight to the airport?"

"We need to make a stop at the hospital. I just got a call from a Mr. Ünal Kuyu, President Palamut's Chief of Staff. He said Penny Kessler told them she was feeling dizzy. Their doctor was worried about some kind of internal bleeding and sent her back to the hospital for tests, just to be sure. Mr. Kuyu seemed to think it was *my* fault that Penny wasn't all bright eyed and bushy tailed and ready to tap-dance." Brenda makes a face. "He accused us of trying to make President Palamut look bad."

"Weird to let her go so fast, when they fought so hard to get her. Didn't want her dying on their watch, I guess."

Frank Lerman may be an asshole, but that has the ring of truth. "Penny seemed perfectly lucid." Brenda grimaces. "I don't like the smell of this."

■ ■ ■ ■

It's a shame, thinks Christina Ekdahl, that security banned CIA's private branch of Starbucks from giving out loyalty cards. She'd be due a bathtubful of skinny double-shot lattes by now. She steps up to the high Formica counter. "Grande vanilla Frappuccino and a peanut-butter-cup cookie."

The barista grins. "Going straight for the hard stuff?"

Christina drums her fingers. No need to slap him down; he doesn't count. "It's one of those days."

"You're telling me, ma'am. We ran out of cheesecake by eleven."

Christina watches the barista clip the beans into the coffee grinder. After a couple decades, the Threat and Allegiance Assessment is so automatic she can't turn it off. This guy's less an open book than a giant flashing billboard. Corpse-white upper arms and an unironic necklace of cuboid white plastic beads that spell out *J-E-S-U-S-I-S-M-Y-W-I-N-G-M-A-N*. He's even got the strip-mall crew cut to match. Prospectless loser, clinging to God and country as his last

172

lifeline. If he worked for an enemy, she'd have him geysering intel in two days. Maybe she *should* talk to HR.

The military haircut makes her think of Connor.

Official confirmation should come through any minute now.

Tension twinges between Christina's shoulder blades. Annoying, distracting. Maybe she *should* go to the yoga classes at the Y that her PTA-and-polyester sister-in-law Alice keeps proselytizing about. But when the hell is she ever out of the office before eight p.m.? Anyway, Alice keeps passive-aggressively forwarding her articles about work/life balance and the greatest regrets of the dying. Screw her. Christina does what she has to. Period.

There *must* be something from Ankara by now.

It reminds Christina of the bad old days, when she ran surveillance ops and had to wait for hours in that loaner station wagon that smelled like egg salad, just watching. Even then, the waiting drove her nuts. You can't listen to the news or an audiobook on surveillance — too engaging. Christina used to sing along to Dolly Parton. To this day, "Jolene" still makes her think of the KGB.

She scans Starbucks for an empty table.

No hope — the place is jammed. But instead of the usual buzzy busyness and ambitious, nerdy maneuvering, there's something else. Guilt. Terrorists blowing up a U.S. Embassy on the Fourth of July? How did we fuck up this big?

Good. Let them feel it, too, for once.

Christina can sense something else as well. A new electric charge of energy, crackling like lightning in a puddle. The good old tragedy boost. Nice while it lasts.

Why the hell hasn't she heard from Ankara?

She spots a junior weapons analyst from the "Women in the Intelligence Community" panel she finally browbeat HR into organizing last week.

The young analyst lurches to her sensible pumps. "I was just leaving, ma'am." She adds, with audible pride, "Got to go drill down on the Ankara situation."

"Deepika, right? How're you liking the manatees?" Joe Weinberger, chief of MENATI (the Middle East Nonstate Actors, Terrorism, and Insurgency group at the Mission Center for Weapons and Counter-proliferation), hates the nickname. Christina uses it every chance she gets. Weinberger is a sanctimonious bleeding heart; Stare Kiejkuty could've been a gold mine, if he hadn't started squealing about enhanced interrogation.

Deepika glows. "It's an amazing opportunity, ma'am. Thanks again for recommending me."

"We can't have our best young analysts on Serbian junkyard patrol. Weinberger's a slave driver, but you'll learn fast."

"He's got me writing up the Hashashin weapons holdings for the PDB." Deepika speaks in the hushed, portentous voice of someone fresh enough that putting words in the President's daily briefing feels like a thrilling brush with power, rather than an exercise in futility worthy of a sandcastle zoning board. "They need the *highest* possible granularity."

"Anything interesting?"

Deepika looks embarrassed, but Christina's a mentor she can trust. "It's bizarre, ma'am. There are so many gaps. Almost nothing on Hashashin weapons acquisition from before this year. Like we were barely even monitoring them. SIGINT really fell down on the job."

"Here you go, ma'am." The slug-chinned barista hands Christina a plastic cup, fogged slick with icy condensation. No name on it, of course.

Christina slides into Deepika's abandoned

chair, breaks the cookie in half. No snap; like most things at CIA, it's gone flabby. "Here. Got to keep up your strength."

The young analyst cradles the broken cookie like a trophy.

"Thank you, ma'am." Deepika glances slightly behind her, toward a group of hawk-eyed, pasty-faced young men — the rest of the MENATI weapons analysis group, who greedily observe the mark of favor.

Christina's no D/CIA — give it another few years — but she knows the rep she's built: Christina Ekdahl makes things happen. She can make *you* happen, if she wants. Plenty of new hires, especially the ex-lawyers and consultants, try to schmooze her. Connor never had, though she could tell he yearned to prove himself. The trick to recruiting case officers is to find the bowling balls: hard, smooth, almost flawless, but with enough holes in their shell for one person to grip tight and control.

"Ma'am!" Taylor's tight ponytail wags as she clatters toward Christina's table.

"It's about time —"

Taylor's too-high voice is quivering. "It's an emergency."

No heads turn. No eyes flicker. But the attention amps up. Everyone here is a professional watcher. Except the Christpiloted barista.

"Not here." Christina clamps onto her PA's arm and steers her out the door. "Taylor," she begins in a strained voice, "we have procedures for a reason. You do not go clomping across Starbucks —"

"It's Connor." Taylor looks shell-shocked. "The signal from his phone and his laptop just terminated." She swallows. "The sensor data suggests sudden, extreme heat, consistent with an explosion."

Christina quickens her pace. "What about his tracker watch?"

"That's gone dead, too." Taylor looks stricken. "All within the same three-second interval."

Christina keeps her voice level. "Location?"

Taylor brandishes her tablet. "The last tracking data has him on a highway on the outskirts of Ankara."

"A highway? He's supposed to be gofering for Frank Lerman. What's he doing on a highway?"

"Audrey is liaising with State now. Ma'am, should I instruct Istanbul or Adana Station to dispatch someone to the accident? If Connor's wounded . . ."

Christina bypasses the crowded elevator and runs up the stairs. "The site isn't secure. We're down too many officers already."

"Turkish Intelligence?"

"As far as the Turks know, Connor's just another diplomat. This has to come through State."

"But, ma'am . . ." Taylor falters, her voice shrill with a fear she can't hide. "Connor — what if he . . . he's . . ."

"Connor knew the risks. This isn't UNICEF, Taylor. And if he strayed off target . . ."

Christina can see her assistant fighting back tears. "It's just —" Taylor swallows. "I got the Save the Date. Connor's supposed to get married in April."

Christina puts a steadying hand on Taylor's shoulder. "Emergencies are when we need our routines the most. The best thing we can do for him is to follow protocol. Get me Secretary Winthrop on the phone. And mark Connor as gray."

14
FOREST FOR THE TREES

Ankara, Turkey
18:48 Local Time

Dry undergrowth crunches under every step. With each sharp breath, Penny tastes pine in the air. And salt.

Blood in her mouth. Dizziness surges around the curve of her skull. She's getting really sick of this confusion.

Conclusion.

Concussion.

That's it. One more step. One step closer to finding Zach.

Connor must be tired, too, he *must.* His white shirt back is splotchy-clear with sweat, but he never stops to catch his breath, and she's not about to ask him to slow down. He plows uphill between the narrow trunks, aerodynamic and relentless as a drone, eyes straight ahead, jacket over his arm, his silence like a wall.

Penny's feet slip in Connor's woolen

socks. Hot blisters bubble across her soles. The temperature is dropping with the sun, but sweat glues the heavy bathrobe to her back. Thank God for the exhaustion. It crowds out most everything else.

Connor's voice startles her.

She licks her lips. "What?"

"I said, it all comes down to one question." He sounds like he's in a seminar.

Her voice comes out raspy. "You've only got one?"

Connor doesn't break stride. "Which of us were they trying to kill?"

"*That's* your question?" Penny laughs. "How about, where on earth are we going, once we get out of the woods? 'Cause I've been thinking." She ticks off on her fingers. "We don't have an Embassy to go to. We can't go to your CIA safe house. We can't go anywhere Palamut's people can find me — so no hospitals or police stations or friendly embassies. I'm sure they're watching my landlady's apartment. Hotels and planes need passports, which we don't have. Neither of us has a phone, and between your tux and my bathrobe, we're not exactly inconspicuous. So what are we supposed to do?"

"It's a suit." Connor glances back at her. "Zach didn't teach you much about intelligence, did he? First you have to know your enemy's rationale. His goals."

Penny pushes up the bathrobe sleeves. "Right now I'd settle for a name, an address, and a grenade launcher."

He chuckles. "Have you ever even *seen* a grenade launcher?"

"Have *you*?"

"That's beside the point," he says stiffly. "If we know our enemy's motivation, we can infer what he'll do next."

"What do you mean, *next*?"

"Someone set off that bomb. What's he going to do when he finds out there was only one body in that car?"

Penny shoves past a dried-out patch of scrub.

"So the question remains," says Connor. "Was the bomb meant primarily for you, or for me?"

Penny shakes her head, which makes it hurt more. "It was in your briefcase. It must've been meant for you. How could anyone possibly have known that you were going to find me at the construction yard? Speaking of which" — her eyes narrow — "just how *did* you find me?"

Connor ignores this. "If my phone was compromised . . ." He frowns. "It's possible they knew I was coming to get you. And frankly, between the two of us, you're a much more plausible target."

"Why?" Penny catches up with him. Frustration catalyzes pain into emotional rocket fuel. "You're the spy, not me!" A blister on her right heel pops, and she staggers, cursing.

Connor glances back. "You need a hand?"

She grits her teeth and limps uphill. "First I get kidnapped. Now someone's trying to kill me? *Tell. Me. Why.*"

"Zach Robson is missing. He may be dead. He was buying secret information from Mehmetoğlu — information important enough to kill for. You're our only link to what he found."

"I don't even know what Zach was looking for!"

"Obviously, Palamut's people think you do. So does Frank Lerman. So does my boss."

"What is it then?"

"You tell me."

"Hang on," says Penny. "Are you saying the CIA doesn't know what Zach was doing with Mehmetoğlu?"

"I didn't say that."

"Yes, you did. You said I was the only link."

Connor scowls. "You're so sharp, you'll cut yourself."

"How can the CIA not know what Zach was doing with Mehmetoğlu?" demands Penny. "At the Embassy, there's paperwork for *everything*. Are you telling me there isn't some kind of form that Zach filled out for his new" — she waves her hands — "I don't know, secret terrorist spy contact?"

"Sure. There are forms, safeguards, cross-checks, you name it. We've got a whole procedure. Your boyfriend is — pardon my saying so — an entitled jerk who thinks he's Jason freaking Bourne and the rules don't apply to him. Sure, he filled out lots of forms. But he never mentioned Mehmetoğlu on any of them."

"Zach Robson is my *friend*." Penny hoists herself uphill, grabbing narrow trunks like monkey bars. "And since when is not doing paperwork a crime?"

"In Zach's job? It's a fricking felony. He used you to circumvent procedure to get Davut Mehmetoğlu into the Embassy party the very night it was bombed. If you look up suspicious in the dictionary, that's pretty much the definition."

"What makes you think Mehmetoğlu even had anything to do with the bomb?"

"He wasn't just some Kurdish politician. He was a Kurdish independence activist." Connor raises his eyebrows. "There's a reason he was on the terror watchlist."

"Kurdish terrorists don't target Americans! America is the Kurds' best ally. It's the Turkish government they hate. They go after Turkish army barracks, police stations — stuff like that."

"Maybe the Kurds aren't huge fans of our new NATO peace deal that's going to give away half of their territory in northern Syria, huh?"

Penny protests, "Even Palamut's people said they thought the Hashashin were involved."

"So do we. But how many other terrorists do you think were at that party?"

"So maybe Zach was trying to catch Mehmetoğlu!" Penny leans against a stump, trying to catch her breath.

"Zach bought a burner phone two weeks ago. He's been using a second laptop we can't trace. We know Zach was hiding something. We just don't know what."

"If Zach was hiding something from the CIA, I'm sure he had a good reason," says Penny fiercely. "For all you know, he could be a whistle-blower!"

Connor sighs. "You know, I honestly believe that you believe that."

Penny sticks out her chin. "I believe in Zach."

Connor turns to look at her. "Sometimes people we care about aren't who we think they are."

"That's rich, coming from the guy who thought *I* was a terrorist."

They emerge from between the thin, scrubby evergreens onto the edge of a small valley, carpeted with knee-high dry grass.

"Okay." Connor slows down until she can keep pace. "So you know the *real* Zach Robson, huh?"

"I know I can trust him."

"Really. Did he tell you he was about to lose his job?"

"What?"

Connor lopes down the hill. "Zach was supposed to transfer to Geneva last January. Huge promotion. Ridiculously plushy gig — unofficial cover as some banker playboy who could pal around with Qatari princes. Now, that's not normal — Zach hasn't earned that. Never even served a hardship tour. Somebody in Washington must think he walks on water."

"Zach's special."

"Well, anyway, he got promoted. Right over his Chief of Station's head." Connor sounds grim. "Except a month before Prince Charming was supposed to leave for Geneva, you know what he did? He screwed

185

his Chief of Station's *wife.* At CIA's Ankara Station St. Patrick's Day party. In the Chief of Station's house. On the breakfast banquette."

Penny struggles back uphill through the tall dry grass, suddenly nauseated. "What?"

"Oh, my boss told me *all* about it. Zach almost lost his clearance — "recklessness and poor judgment." They took the Geneva post away. By the rulebook, Zach should've been fired immediately. But his language skills are hard to replace, so they're letting him stay here through the summer, on probation. Under the direct command of the guy whose wife he screwed."

"I don't believe it." Penny's cheeks are burning. She follows Connor back into the shadow of the woods.

"Why would my boss lie about that?"

"Yeah," says Penny drily. "Why would the CIA try to smear a whistle-blower?"

"Zach's not a whistle-blower."

"What makes you so sure? If Zach did uncover something, isn't this just the kind of mud they'd try to sling? What kind of proof do you have?"

"For God's sake." Connor stops and looks her full in the face. "Don't you understand what's at stake here? Our alliance with Turkey is so frayed, it's about to snap. Now, because of the Embassy bombing, the Syria peace deal is on the line as well. If anything else happens before the NATO Summit, the whole region could implode, and we all get dragged into a war. Penny, I'm asking you. If you know anything at all about what Zach was looking for, you've got to tell me now."

Penny hits her limit. "I told Melek Palamut, and I'll tell you. *I don't know what Zach was doing!*"

"Whoa, whoa, whoa." Connor comes to a sharp halt, tense as a terrier. He looks more shocked than he did after the car exploded. "You told *Melek Palamut?*"

15
PIGS, DOGS, AND RATS

Penny sinks gratefully onto the prickly carpeting of dry pine needles. "Melek showed me a text Mehmetoğlu sent to his Hashashin contact that said, 'Good luck to the girl with the flag.' And then a text the contact sent back that said, 'Delivered.' "

" 'Delivered'? What was delivered?"

"I don't know!"

"What did you tell Melek?"

"The truth. She didn't believe me."

Connor's voice is grim. "Our records say Melek met Zach *once* in passing. She shouldn't even remember he exists."

"She acted like they were really close. But I'm sure she was lying."

"Why exactly?" Connor crouches down beside her.

"She kept calling him Zachary, and he hates that."

"What else did she say? Penny, this is extremely important."

188

Penny closes her eyes. Her head is swimming. In the branches overhead, a red squirrel begins to chatter. "She knew I'd been talking to Zach and Mehmetoğlu just before the bomb. But she can't have seen me — she and her guards left like fifteen minutes before that. So how did she know?"

Connor looks grim. "Melek Palamut was at the party, and she conveniently left right before the bomb went off?"

Penny takes a deep breath of piney air. "Do you think she knew?"

"The only way she'd know is if she's implicated."

"The Turkish President's daughter blowing up the U.S. Embassy?" Penny shakes her head. "Bullshit."

"She wouldn't have had to organize it — she could have just known and let it happen."

"No. Melek didn't seem evil."

"Oh, well, in *that* case . . ."

"Well, she didn't. Not even angry. She was like a — a fancy lawyer or a fashion executive or something. But something was really wrong. She was — desperate. Like she was protecting someone."

"Her father?"

Penny meets his eyes. "I know Palamut's crazy, but . . ."

"Plenty of people think he tangoed with ISIS when he wanted the oil revenues. Maybe he got involved with the Hashashin as well."

"That's crazy." Penny runs dry pine needles through her fingers. "Some weird business deal between Palamut and ISIS, okay, I can see — at least they're both some kind of Sunni. But Palamut hates the Hashashin almost as much as he hates the Kurds, and he really, *really* hates the Kurds. I translated a speech last week where he called the Hashashin 'Shia pigs,' 'Iranian dogs,' and 'traitorous rats.'"

"Not awesome at metaphors, our Palamut."

"Not awesome at democracy."

"But pragmatic," says Connor. "Or he wouldn't still be in power. Palamut kept going back and forth on the NATO deal before he agreed, trying to extort more money for his government. He can't back out now. But if he wanted to scare the U.S. into defaulting on our side of the agreement, 'accidentally' letting the Hashashin blow up our Embassy wouldn't be a bad strategy."

"I'm telling you, it's crazy."

"But not impossible."

"If Palamut *is* mixed up with the Hashashin . . ." Penny's pulse quickens. "It could explain why a Kurd like Mehmetoğlu wanted to talk to Zach. Palamut's bullied the Kurds for decades. If they could catch him involved in terrorism against the United States . . ."

"It would destroy Palamut." Connor nods. "America forgives a lot, but we can't be allies with a guy who just let terrorists blow up our Embassy. Palamut knows that. His enemies do, too."

"If Zach thought he'd found something that big . . ."

"If Zach found something that big, he should have reported it!"

"What if he couldn't?" says Penny slowly. Her heart pounds. "Was Zach's Chief of Station Martin MacGowan?"

Connor's face goes suddenly blank. "What makes you think that?"

"Zach said MacGowan was stalling the paperwork for his meeting with Mehmetoğlu. That's why he needed my help to put him on the guest list. I thought it was some bureaucratic thing. But what if MacGowan is crooked? What if Zach found something MacGowan didn't want him to find? What if MacGowan tried to get him fired, and it didn't work, and Zach kept digging?"

"But then why meet with Mehmetoğlu at the party? Right in front of MacGowan?"

"The guy's a Kurdish separatist. You said yourself, he's on the terror watchlist. It's not like he can just waltz around Ankara, meeting with American spies. At least if he meets with Zach at the U.S. Embassy, he knows Palamut's secret police can't just scoop him up."

"But why meet in person at all? Zach had a burner phone — why not use that?"

"Delivered," Penny whispers. "The text Mehmetoğlu received said, 'Delivered.' " She looks up at Connor. "Maybe Mehmetoğlu and Zach weren't just *talking* about Palamut and the Hashashin. Maybe Mehmetoğlu had proof."

"If Melek knew that, and Palamut's in bed with the Hashashin . . ."

Penny draws a sharp breath. "You think that's why they kidnapped Zach?"

"Let's go." Connor stands up and dusts pine needles off his trousers. "We've got to get hold of my boss."

16
THE ONLY THING BETTER

Ankara, Turkey
18:56 Local Time

The black SUV with diplomatic plates pulls up outside the Ulus State Hospital. Brenda and Frank hustle past the mic-thrusting journalists, up to the emergency room triage station. Eight armed Diplomatic Security agents hulk behind them; Brenda rounded up the toughest-looking ones she could find.

"Brenda Pelecchia. I'm looking for Penny Kessler?"

A fortysomething doctor steps briskly up behind her. Expensive glasses, careful makeup, an inch or two taller than Frank. Her badge identifies her as deputy director of the hospital. "You are from the American Embassy?"

"I'm Brenda Pelecchia. Acting Ambassador. I need to see Miss Kessler immediately."

"We had to rush her into surgery. A catastrophic cerebral hemorrhage. It's not uncommon in the aftermath of an explosion." The doctor's penciled-on eyebrows slope in sympathy. "I'm sorry."

Brenda's voice cracks. "Is she dead?"

"She received the best possible care."

"Not good enough, clearly," Brenda snaps. She clutches her head. "I'm sorry. It's not your fault. But I'm going to need to see her."

"I'm afraid that she, and the rest of the bombing victims, have already been transferred to the morgue."

"Then take me to the morgue."

The doctor's face is set. "The city morgue couldn't cope with the sudden influx. There's a military hospital nearby — we're using theirs. But I'm afraid it isn't open to civilians."

"That's unacceptable. Why wasn't the Embassy consulted?"

"Madam Ambassador, we're in the middle of a heat wave. Hundreds of bodies in the hospital constitute a public health risk. We had to move them. When Penny's family comes to collect her, the morgue will release the remains."

"I am accountable for every single one of my staff. I leave for Istanbul in less than an hour. I need to see Penny Kessler's body.

Now."

"Legally, I'm afraid that isn't possible."

"This is an emergency."

"I'm sorry. It's a military base — the headquarters of the Presidential Guard. There's really nothing I can do. I understand she was important to you. . . ."

Brenda says in a hollow voice, "I was responsible for her."

The doctor nods.

"Can I at least speak with the surgeons who attended her?"

"They're still in the operating theater. We have over a hundred victims still in intensive care."

"Brenda. Let's huddle." Frank smiles at the doctor. "Hang tight a sec, okay?"

Brenda and Frank walk fifteen feet down the hall. Diplomatic Security forms a wall around them.

"Just delegate someone to liaise with the morgue," Frank hisses. "We have to get to Istanbul."

"They can't just seize the remains of U.S. citizens!"

"Brenda, the kid is dead. Secretary Winthrop is arriving in Istanbul tomorrow morning, and then we've got the fucking NATO conference. Is *this* the hill you're going to die on?"

"You really don't care, do you, Mr. Ler-man?"

"I know my priorities. So should you."

"Doesn't this look wrong to you?"

"I get sent to all the crises, Brenda. And you know what? After an attack, a natural disaster, a coup — things are chaotic. Messy. You just get through it as best you can. You're the acting Ambassador now. Your job is to hold things together. Not to go trawling for another crisis."

"Even if you feel nothing for Penny and her family, how do you think the press is going to play this? She was your symbol of resilience!"

Frank shrugs. "The only thing better than a pretty girl with a flag is a pretty, dead girl with a flag."

17
METU

Ankara, Turkey
19:08 Local Time

Twenty minutes later, Penny and Connor emerge from the woods onto the brown, baked-grass shoulder of a busy intersection. Across the highway rise the angular concrete buildings of METU, the Middle East Technical University, and the narrow minaret of a small mosque, whose shiny dome looks as if it were coated with aluminum foil. Cars shush past in the soft twilight, yellow headlights pointing homeward.

Penny and Connor are about to cross when a car honks. Then another. A truck driver hisses through his teeth.

"Hey, baby!" One guy leers out the window at Penny. "Take off the robe!"

Penny lurches back behind a tree, cheeks burning. "Assholes." She pulls the red bathrobe tighter around her. "What are we going to do? We've got to be inconspicuous.

We won't make it ten feet!"

"Not with you in that getup." Connor follows her back into the trees. "We need to get you some real clothes." He squints. "If you wore my shirt like a dress . . ."

Penny shakes her head. "Nothing says inconspicuous like a bleeding foreign *nataşa* in a man's shirt, woolly socks, and no shoes."

Connor unbuttons his shirt anyway. "Put it on. Hide the bathrobe and the hospital gown." He tucks in his undershirt and hands her his Swiss Army knife. "It has a small pair of scissors. Cut yourself some bangs — long enough to cover that cut on your eyebrow. I'll be right back."

"Where are you going?"

He sounds evasive. "Just wait here."

Eight minutes later, just as Penny has finished cutting her hair, Connor returns.

He nods approvingly at her new bangs. "Good."

"Crooked."

"Trendy. And . . ." Connor reaches triumphantly into his jacket pocket and removes a small pair of knockoff Nike sneakers and an ugly yellow cotton shawl — the kind mosques keep by the door as spares.

A mosque.

"Oh, my God." Penny stares at him. *"You stole shoes from the mosque?"*

"The lord helps those who help themselves."

"Some poor guy is going to finish praying, go to put his shoes back on, and —"

"— find enough money to buy *real* Nikes. Hurry up and put them on. You can tie the shawl like a skirt."

Penny knots the unyielding cotton around her waist and looks warily across the road. "What if someone recognizes me from the news?"

"No one's going to recognize you because no one expects Flag Girl to be wandering the METU campus." He adds sharply, "You stay where I can see you."

"I didn't run away before, did I?"

"Let's just find the library."

Penny gives a mock salute. "Aye, aye, Cap'n."

Connor's head snaps around. "How'd you know I was in the Navy?"

"Well, I guess you just told me. Come on. Damn the torpedoes."

The METU campus isn't as deserted as it looked from across the road. T-shirted summer school students lounge in the warm half-light, laughing over their phones and straggling to evening classes.

"Kütüphane." Penny nods at a sign. "Here we go."

As they head down the path toward the library, a faint chant becomes audible. Hundreds of candles flicker in the gathering dark, illuminating hand-daubed doves and peace symbols. Students bang pots and pans and hold up blotchily printed photos.

Connor is instantly on the alert. "A protest?"

Penny scans the signs and faces. "A vigil, I think."

"What are they chanting?"

"Yurtta sulh, cihanda sulh." Penny swallows. "It's one of Atatürk's most famous sayings: 'Peace at home, peace in the world.' "

Connor is staring at the students, unnerved. "Penny, keep back."

"But look. They're holding American flags."

"Exactly." Connor's voice is grim. "And a lot of candles to burn them with."

"Oh, *please.*"

He squares his jaw. "I've seen the stats. America has a lower approval rating in Turkey than we do in Iraq."

"On paper, maybe," Penny retorts. "Everyone's been very kind to me."

"Oh, really?" Connor's talking a little too loudly. "Everyone? Now who's overgeneral-

200

izing? Who do you think blew up the Embassy?"

"Terrorists!"

"You think they were a bunch of Episcopalians from Vermont?"

"Who saved me at the hospital? Who do you think the first responders were? Do you know how many people in the Embassy are Muslim, Turkish local hires?"

"Who do you think set off a bomb in our car?"

"I don't know, and neither do you. But I know who got murdered. Faruk!"

A bearded young guy in a dark hoodie grabs Connor's shoulder. "You are American?"

Connor's hand rests lightly where Penny knows his holster is. Without her realizing it, he has positioned himself protectively between her and Hoodie Guy.

"Yes." Penny replies, stepping out from behind Connor. "We are."

"Başınız sağolsun," says Hoodie Guy, squeezing Connor's shoulder. It is the ritual Turkish expression of well-wishing for the bereaved: *may your head be healthy.* "My brother and I drove back to school from Trabzon for this." He gestures at the chanting students. "Attacks like this are a scar on the world. We all feel the pain with you."

Penny finds her voice first. "Thank you."

The guy in the hoodie nods to the hundreds of photos the students are holding up. Candlelight shines in the wetness of his eyes. "May they rest in the light."

When the young man is gone, Penny and Connor stand silent for a moment.

"Connor." Penny can barely speak. "Those photographs they're holding . . . they're the people who died."

"Yeah." His voice is husky. "Lerman said State was going to release official photos of all the deceased."

"Connor," says Penny, her heart shuddering, *"Look at the one that guy is holding."* Penny's mouth is dry. "And that guy. And those girls . . ."

Connor's only reaction is one long, sharp breath. "We've got to get out of here."

18
THE SECOND PHOTOGRAPH

"That's my official State Department ID photo," says Penny, trying to rub down the chills on her arms as they weave through the crowd. "It's not online anywhere — *nobody* has that but the Embassy."

"Just keep moving."

They duck through the glass doors of the library.

"Connor, why would State release a photo of me with all the people who died?"

His face is unreadable. "Probably just a mistake."

Penny feels nauseous. "You think?"

"Let's just find a computer."

They find an available computer by a window in the second-floor computer lab. Pale wood, white paint, stainless-steel shelves, the panicked typing of a few desperate deadline crunchers, the high-pitched nattering of a talk-show clip through somebody's headphones — it could be any college library, all but empty on a summer evening.

"Hang on." Penny strolls up to a cluster of girls. She lets anxiety spread across her face. *That* doesn't take much pretending. "Excuse me — *affedersiniz . . .*"

A girl in a green head scarf smiles at her and says, in careful English, "What is up?"

"I'm so sorry to interrupt, but the registrar hasn't processed my visiting student log-in yet, and I can't print my essay, and it's like thirty percent of my grade —"

"That freaking sucks," says the girl in the green head scarf earnestly. Her intonation is pure late-nineties Cartoon Network.

"The registrar is the *worst,*" adds the girl's round-faced friend. "Here, I'll log you in. . . ."

Connor's back goes rigid as the cluster of girls follow Penny back to the computer terminal.

"*Haydi, bakalım. . . .* There!"

"*Sağol.*" Penny smiles.

The girl in green notices the cuts through Penny's eyebrow. "*Geçmiş olsun!* What went down?"

"Just . . ." Penny's mouth goes dry. "Soccer practice."

"Come to volleyball club tryouts." The round-faced girl tucks a strand of hair back into her rainbow-striped head scarf. "To-morrow at the gym at four. We're not so violent." She looks through her eyelashes at Connor and smiles. "There's a men's team, too."

"Zach Robson trained you pretty well," says Connor, as the girls wave aside Penny's thanks and wander toward the vending machine.

"Zach didn't train me at all," Penny retorts. "I know how to lie. I just don't like doing it."

Connor rolls his office chair up beside hers at the computer station. "What are you doing? I need to contact my boss!"

"Just a minute." Penny types ferociously. "All social media's blocked. Every major site. Let me check the newspapers."

"What are you looking for?"

Penny types faster. "I want to know what my ID photo is doing on a list of dead people."

Hürriyet Daily News, Turkey's most reliable English-language daily, finally loads.

Penny swallows hard.

**BREAKING: U.S. EMBASSY BOMBING
'FLAG GIRL' SUCCUMBS TO INJURIES**

For almost 24 hours, U.S. Embassy

intern Penny Kessler, 21, became a symbol of hope to millions in the wake of the worst terrorist attack in Turkey's history, and America's greatest loss of civilian life since the September 11 attacks. The Ulus State Hospital has confirmed that shortly before 6 p.m. tonight, Kessler died of complications of a catastrophic cerebral hemorrhage received in the bomb blast. This makes her the 287th victim of yesterday's terrorist atrocity. The death toll continues to rise.

"Penny Kessler represents everything America is most proud of, and everything we'll always fight for — our courage, our determination, and our patriotism," said U.S. Under Secretary of State for Management Frank Lerman. Brenda Pelecchia, acting U.S. Ambassador in Turkey, added, "Penny was a credit to her family, her university, and the Foreign Service. We extend our deepest condolences to her loved ones at this tragic time."

President Palamut, who returned this evening from a state visit to Moscow to handle the growing crisis, has also issued a statement: "I mourn Penny Kessler's heartbreakingly early death. When I sent my Prime Minister to meet with her today, she begged him to ask me to find the terrorists who destroyed her beautiful young life. I have sworn we will not rest until we have avenged the honor of Turkey and destroyed these traitors and enemies of our nation."

President Palamut's office confirmed earlier today that both Turkey and the United States are now treating yesterday's U.S. Embassy bombing as an act of international terrorism. The two countries will be collaborating in the investigation. No suspects have yet been named, and the widely suspected involvement of the extremist Hashashin group remains unconfirmed.

Penny sits back numbly.

"Oh, boy," says Connor.

Penny is shaking her head. She twists the evil eye bead on her wrist, her breath coming in shallow gulps. "I have to call Brenda."

"Penny —"

"Why would she say that, Connor? Why?"

"Penny." Connor takes her wrist, speaking so quietly he's hardly audible. "I need you to stay calm."

" 'Catastrophic cerebral hemorrhage'?"

"Obviously, whoever tried to kill us thinks we're dead. If we use a phone that's not secure, they'll know we're alive — and exactly where we are." Penny opens her mouth, and he adds, "That goes for email, too. It would take about a minute to match our IP address with this location."

"Just use a VPN!"

"A VPN." Connor raises his eyebrows in triumph. "And you say Zach didn't train you?"

Penny barely masters her frustration. "Palamut blocks any site he thinks might threaten his authority. Half the time, you need a VPN to watch cat videos!"

Connor shakes his head. "Even if they can't find us right away, they'll still know we didn't die."

"How about we go straight to the hospital? Or the nearest TV crew? I'll show them how dead I am!"

"If Palamut's the one who wants us dead, that could be the last thing you ever do. Right now, the only reason nobody's trying to kill us is because they think we're already dead. And until we can get some help from my boss, that is literally the only card we hold."

Penny lets Connor nudge her chair aside. He pulls up a familiar site.

"*Please* tell me the CIA doesn't use Gmail."

Connor gives a half grin. "We're not all as

dumb as Petraeus. You should look away. This is classified."

Penny crosses her arms. "No."

Connor shrugs and logs into an account for D. J. M. Cornwell.

"Is that your real name?"

"Nope."

"Is Connor your real name?"

"What makes you think it's not?"

Connor clicks on an email, dated this morning, with the subject line **Re: Mom's banana fritters.** The text reads simply, Hi honey. This is the one I usually use — just double the nutmeg. There's a link, leading to what appears to be a Culinary Institute of America baking blog.

Penny stares. "You've got to be kidding me."

"When we can't access a secure connection, we have to do it the old-fashioned way. Send a message in plain sight. In the old days, they'd take out a classified ad in the newspaper or chalk a cross on some back-alley wall. This is a lot faster and more secure. We just use the comments section. Do you have any idea how many cooking blogs there are?" He sounds defensive. "It's a lot more secure than you would think."

"Plus all those great recipes."

"I'm more a take-out kind of guy. All

those years of wardroom food."

"What's a wardroom?"

"Officers' mess. But in the Navy."

"Culinary Institute of America." Penny shakes her head. "Nice initials."

"We used to use the chat function on *Gem Crunch*. You know, the game? But people kept getting distracted."

"I'm getting dizzy again."

Hi, Connor types, *I've been doing Paleo for a month. Do you know if I can substitute coconut sugar? I have some extra bananas, but my doctor says I have to keep things healthy. Blessings.*

"I *really* hope that's a code."

"Nothing wrong with a guy looking after his cholesterol." Connor checks over his shoulder.

"I hate when people sign their emails 'blessings.' " Penny crosses her arms. "*Blessings.* Do you think you're Zeus?"

Connor gives her a funny look. "Somebody sounds a little punchy."

Penny takes a deep breath. The chants outside are getting louder. "So now what? We wait for our banana fritters?"

"My boss monitors this directly. We should get a reply within ten minutes."

■ ■ ■ ■

"Absolutely, Secretary Winthrop. I wanted to dialogue with you soonest." Christina's voice is warm, all-American, dependable. Federal Service Barbie. "That's right. Diplomatic cover. Turkish Agricultural Policy and Food Security desk." She leans back in her ergonomic office chair. "That's very thoughtful. I'm sure Connor's parents would be honored." She laughs. "Yes, sir. Every vote counts. We'll send their number over when the time comes." She smooths her frosty highlights back into place. "Of course. We'll let your people know as soon as we get confirmation." A pause. "Brain hemorrhage?" Christina's voice turns grave. "That poor young woman." She listens. "I couldn't put it better myself, sir. You, too. Safe landing in Istanbul."

In her sunlit corner office in Langley, Christina pops open a can of lemon-lime seltzer with a sigh of relief.

Melek's already ensured an acceptable explanation for Penny's death. It wasn't easy getting Melek to cooperate. Christina had to assure her the girl's death was already

211

confirmed before Melek would call the hospital. But that's water under the bridge. Soon, Connor's accidental death will be official, too.

Then Christina can finally close the drawer on this whole mission malfunction.

It had seemed so promising. But then, doesn't it always?

The concept had been controversial from the instant Christina proposed it. Still, she'd made a damn good case. The then-President had refused. Fortunately, the CIA Director took a longer view. Administrations come and go. Maybe, he'd hinted to Christina, she could look into things, just a little more. Just scope out the situation quietly. He'd be happy to look the other way.

Christina had done more than scope. She'd covertly approached a powerful friend at State. Robert Winthrop, she'd said, could be the Secretary of State who fixed Syria — maybe even the whole Middle East. When she said that, she could practically see the tiny White Houses in the pupils of his eyes. She didn't offer too many details, and he didn't want them.

But then, about a year ago, everything started to go wrong.

"We didn't, did we?" the Director had asked Christina.

And she'd replied, "Of course not, sir."

And as far as anyone could ever prove, they hadn't. Nobody even seemed to suspect it.

At least until Zach Robson started digging.

And apparently started talking to Penny Kessler.

But Christina has fixed it. As soon as Connor's Turkish death certificate comes through, the well-greased procedure can kick into gear. A knock on his parents' door with the tragic news. A flag-wrapped coffin in some muggy Georgia cemetery. Get out the chisel and pneumatic hammer and carve a new star on the Memorial Wall of the Original Headquarters Building lobby. Stay at CIA as long as Christina and you'll bury a few.

Christina glances down at Elastigirl, clinging to the lamp.

A ping from the computer.

Christina leans forward. What she sees makes every muscle in her body tense.

Impossible.

But there it is. A code nine.

They're alive. Both of them.

"Ma'am?" Taylor's heels clack an approach.

Christina snatches up the phone before

her assistant can round the door. "Yes, Mr. Secretary," she says loudly into the empty plastic. "We value your optic. Did the President mention anything else?"

Taylor mouths, "Sorry," and backs away.

Christina stares at the screen.

For a moment, she can see everything she's worked for spiraling into nothingness. But her composure is soldered in place. She's not about to lose now.

Time for some damage control.

Melek answers on the fourth ring. "I did what you asked, Allah forgive me," she hisses. "What more do you want?"

19
LIBRARY

From the reference desk, a librarian calls out, "Half an hour to closing!"

Across the stacks, in the computer lab, Penny watches Connor click refresh for the twentieth time. "Still nothing?"

He shakes his head.

"Can we go back to *Hürriyet*? I want to see if they have anything about Zach."

"I seriously doubt it." But he clicks back. "Nope. It's all stuff about the Embassy. And this." He leans toward the screen, visibly tensing. "Hashashin Fighters Capture Fourth-Century Mor Samuel 'Border' Monastery."

The photo of Mor Samuel, familiar from her sophomore Ancient Civ lectures, shows an ancient golden fortress, built around a huge central hexagonal tower. Founded by Saint Samuel in the fourth century after Christ, Mor Samuel, a UNESCO World

Heritage Site, houses the second-oldest Syriac church in the world. In Ottoman days, Grand Tourists flocked there; a *National Geographic* cover story twelve years ago drew their modern counterparts. But Mor Samuel hasn't seen visitors in years, not even pilgrims: it sits just a few miles outside Turkey, across the border with Syria. This accident of geography rankles deeply in Turkey; ten years ago, a coalition of Turkish academics, executives, and expats raised $15 million to restore what many Turks insist is part of their cultural heritage.

"The Hashashin have Mor Samuel?" Penny peers over Connor's shoulder. "But that's in Rojava — Kurdish territory!"

"Not anymore." Connor makes a face. "My boss is not going to like this."

"So now the Hashashin are within spitting distance of the border?" Penny stares at the screen. "What's the Turkish army even doing?"

Connor skims the article. "Palamut can't exactly bomb one of the world's oldest working Christian monasteries. Not with the monks still inside." Connor's voice drops. "And if we're right, and he's cooperating with the Hashashin . . ."

"Connor," says Penny in a low voice, standing up, "why is everyone leaving?"

Around them, agitated students sweep their belongings into purses and backpacks and run toward the door.

Penny taps the arm of a Circassian-looking girl with sharp cheekbones and a long chestnut ponytail, who's hurrying toward the door. "Where's everyone going?"

"The police are here." The girl is hyperventilating. Her narrow face is as white as Kütahya clay. "It's not safe. My big brother lost an eye in the Gezi protests. My mother made me promise —"

A loud, dry pop comes from outside, followed by howls of pain as a huge, stinging white cloud engulfs the crowd.

Penny's hands are shaking. She can feel the cold sweat down her back.

The Embassy.

Limbless bodies in the smoke. Bloody grass. Her own hoarse screaming.

Penny stumbled through the Embassy garden until she saw that stocky body in the grass, dark stains on her purple dress. Eye shadow glittered around Ayla's dead brown eyes. Beside her slumped her handsome Marine, all broad shoulders and smoldering gold braid.

Ears ringing. Choking now. Her head. The sirens . . .

Police sirens scream to life outside the library.

"Tear gas." Connor's Georgia twang pulls Penny back to earth, as a series of spuming canisters explode outside.

Plastic-helmeted riot police charge the clustered students. Fallen candles roll on the asphalt. Water cannons soak the peace banners. The cheap poster paint starts to run. Penny hears screams as bloodied students crumple under police batons.

"Hey!" The round-faced girl in the rainbow head scarf, the one who loaned Penny her password, hurries toward them. "You're foreigners, aren't you?"

Penny is careful. "We . . ."

"They're saying 'foreign agents' started the demonstration. The police are looking for foreigners. You've got to get out of here!"

Connor looks up at her. "Is there a back way out?"

The girl nods and beckons them through the stacks.

Connor's hand is warm and solid on Penny's arm. "Penny?"

"Coming." All the soreness of her muscles returns as she tries to keep pace with him through the stacks. Fear and adrenaline are sputtering out, leaving nothing but a terrible gray weariness.

The girl with the rainbow head scarf shoves open a small metal door with a red sign that reads YANGIN ÇIKIŞI.

The fire alarm bellows to life as they tumble out onto the fire escape.

Penny wrenches at the ladder. "It's stuck!"

Behind them, people scream and bookshelves crash to the floor as the police storm into the library.

Connor grips the ladder with both hands. "It's rusted into place!"

"There's no time!" The girl in the rainbow head scarf leaps into the bushes below, landing with a crash of branches. She dusts herself off and beckons them. *"Haydi!"*

"It's okay!" shouts Connor "Don't wait for us! Just run!"

The girl raises her eyebrows and clicks her tongue, the Turkish equivalent of a head-shake no. "I know a shortcut. Come on!"

Connor meets Penny's eye. "Together, on three?"

"One, two . . ."

A short rush of summer darkness, and the bushes scrape their legs.

"Haydi, come!"

Connor and Penny follow the girl down an illuminated path. No more lazy sprawlers and flirting coeds. Coughing, choking,

219

crying, spitting students stagger down the white gravel, clutching their eyes or supporting blinded friends. Police sirens compete with screaming. The scattered *pop-pop-pop* of tear-gas canisters fills the darkness. The noises don't feel big enough for the towering acid clouds that come billowing out.

"What kind of crazy bastards gas a memorial vigil?" sputters Connor. He turns around. "Penny?"

She's on the gravel, gasping and hacking as the burning tear gas closes around them. The screaming is getting closer. A stitch blazes in her side.

"Come on!" Connor doubles back for her. "Do you know what's going to happen if Palamut's police get their hands on us?"

Her eyes are streaming. "Nobody's asking you to stay!" She tries to stand and lands painfully on her knees. Coughs rock her sore shoulders. She's so frustrated she could scream.

"C'mon." Connor crouches beside her and presses his suit jacket into her arms. "Breathe through this. Grab my arm. Up we go. That's better. One step at a time."

They come to a road.

"This way," calls the girl in the rainbow

head scarf. "Good luck! May God protect you!"

"Buraya! Çabuk, çabuk!" The elderly driver of a battered minibus, the university's shuttle service, beckons them aboard.

Penny and Connor crush onto the minibus with at least twenty other students. Penny wedges herself between four other girls on a seat meant for three people; Connor crouches on the floor. Everyone is sniffling, rubbing sore eyes, or gasping between coughs.

Tear-gas residue soaks everyone's clothes. Penny's eyes and nose sting and stream. Dabbing at them just doubles the pain. Someone shouts to open the windows as the minibus rattles onto the highway.

The bleached-blond girl wedged to Penny's right offers her a bottle of bubble-gum-pink antacid to rub into her arms. "Look at you!" she exclaims in Turkish, clicking her tongue in disapproval at the cuts on Penny's face. "Those monsters."

A waterfall of electronic trills, as everyone simultaneously receives the same text.

"They're closing the university until further notice," a clean-shaven guy in a penguin T-shirt says in English. "For harboring terrorists. Effective immediately."

"Palamut thinks everyone who won't kiss

his ass is a terrorist," says the bleached-blond girl.

In the back row, a boy with a weedy mustache is hysterical, clutching at his eyes and howling. His friends hover around him, terrified

Connor's voice comes from the floor. "What's wrong with him?"

Penny grimaces. "He says his eyes are burning. He can't see."

Connor crawls back along the dirty carpet of the minibus to the boy. "Hold still a second, buddy. Let me take a look. Penny, can you make sure he knows what I'm saying?"

She translates, and the boy stops thrashing, though he can't stifle a moan.

Connor pries open the boy's tearing eyes. "The tear gas is trapped under his contacts. We've got to flush them out. Has anybody got a bottle of water?"

A bottle is passed up.

"Awesome." Connor squirts the water over his hands. "Hang in there, buddy. Slow breaths. Slow."

"Sakin ol," Penny calls to the boy.

Connor turns to one of the boy's friends. "You tilt his head back. Hold it really still, okay?" Connor flushes water into the corners of the boy's eyes. With two swift movements, he pinches the warped contact lenses and pulls them out. "Keep your eyes open, buddy. We're going to wash some of this crud out of there. There we go. You're doing great."

The boy's breathing grows less ragged. His face is shiny with sweat and snot and tears. Everywhere his eyes should be white is veiny scarlet.

Connor leans back. "Penny, ask him if he can see me okay."

She does, and the boy nods.

"Good man," says Connor. "You'll be fine. You're gonna want to flush your eyes out in the sink as soon as you can. Clean water. Ten minutes at least."

"Fuck Palamut and fuck his fucking fascist janissaries," croaks the boy in Turkish. "They can beat up students. Why can't they beat up the fucking Hashashin?"

Connor looks to Penny. "What was that?"

She tells him.

Connor shakes his head. "Tell him it's a good fucking question."

Penny raises her eyebrows. "So you do swear."

"My momma taught me to save my cussing for special occasions."

The minibus is quiet, except for the pony-tailed Circassian girl, tearfully snuffling into her phone.

The minibus rolls down out of the red-dening sunset, into the darkness of a tun-nel. In the pale flash of passing lights, Penny can only make out the silhouette of Con-nor's shoulders, where he crouches back down on the floor. She wishes she could talk to him. What the hell are they supposed to do now?

20
PEPPER FLAKES
AND GUMMY BEARS

11:40 Sokak, Ankara
19:49 Local Time

A few minutes later, the minibus driver pulls over at a bus stop, beside a row of pastel tower blocks. "I'm going to go back and see if I can get anybody else. Are you kids okay to get home from here? Anybody need bus fare?"

Twenty young people straggle out of the minibus, into the hot evening air.

"Allah, Allah!" The bleached-blond girl fixes Penny with an appalled stare. "*Tatlım,* you need a doctor."

Penny looks away. "I'm just a little carsick. . . ."

"No, your legs — your head! What did they *do* to you?"

A city bus pulls up at the stop.

The students who haven't boarded yet are starting to turn.

"It's no big deal." Penny shakes her head,

trying to keep the girl from getting a better look at her face. She latches onto Connor's hand. "My cousin will take me home. I live near here." Connor's expression is carefully neutral. Of course — he can't understand a word. Penny silently wills him to play along. Connor nods convincingly.

"You look familiar." The blond girl squints harder. "Are you in Öztürk's microbiology lab?"

Penny's heart bottoms out. Somehow, her voice stays even. "I think I saw you at the canteen."

"Maybe." The girl glances uncertainly back toward her friends, who are gesturing from the door of the bus.

"Go ahead," urges Penny. "I'm okay. Go home. Be safe."

The bus heaves away. Penny exhales.

"You look like death in a microwave," says Connor.

She turns. "It's *your* shirt, pal."

"Come on. Hold my arm. You'll feel better once you sit down and get some food in your stomach."

"Food?" Penny's hopes shrink. "I don't have any money."

Connor grins and pats his wallet. "The Agency always sends us with plenty of cash. What do you say to a falafel?"

"Wrong country."

"Close enough."

Penny makes a face. "Who do you work for, again?"

But there are no restaurants on that street, or the next. Just row after row of identical apartment blocks, unnaturally even-spaced in the bald concrete like giant hair plugs — the kind balding Arab businessmen fly to Istanbul to get implanted on the cheap.

The tower blocks thin out to shabby one-story buildings: a shuttered tailor's shop, a secondhand hardware store with smoke alarms stacked in the window, and — finally — a little neighborhood *lokanta*.

Penny and Connor duck through the *lokanta*'s open door. The restaurant is a garishly lit, white-tiled room, lurid with cheap Orientalist prints. Near the cash register looms a blurry skyline of the Golden Horn, complete with incongruous yellow camel. A calendar illustration of Osman Hamdi Bey's *The Tortoise Trainer* has been taped to the kitchen door. The TV in the corner singsongs tomorrow's weather report: blisteringly hot everywhere, with light rains in the mountains along the Black Sea coast. The only other customers are a couple of old men playing backgammon and a young construction worker slurping lentil soup.

Near the counter, the waiter's elderly mother (same upturned nose, same shock of curly hair), airplane-feeds caramelized *sütlaç,* rice pudding, to a sticky toddler. They all look up to stare.

"I'd better do the ordering," Penny mutters. "We're conspicuous enough already."

"Try and keep it under twenty bucks, okay?" whispers Connor, sliding into a table in the corner. "Otherwise I'll have to file a reimbursement claim."

Penny tries to raise her eyebrows; the gash above the right one smarts. "I'll bear that in mind, Double-O-Seven."

"Ne arzu edersiniz?" demands the waiter, with a challenging stare at Connor.

Speaking quickly, in hopes that her accent will pass unnoticed, Penny asks for two orders of lamb shish.

"Yok," snaps the waiter, still glowering at Connor. It's one of the most starkly expressive words in Turkish — "all gone," "nope," and "it doesn't exist" rolled into one.

"Grilled lamb chops?"

"Yok."

"Chicken?"

"Yok."

"What *do* you have?"

"Wait." The waiter stumps into the kitchen.

Connor reaches into his pocket and pulls out a pink smartphone. A moody portrait of the Turkish pop idol Tarkan smolders on the back, surrounded by a flotilla of tiny rhinestone hearts. "Let's see what my boss has to say."

Penny stares. "Where did you get that?"

Connor all but preens. It's the closest you can get to a swagger while sitting down.

Penny is impressed, despite herself. "Did you steal it?"

"Let's just say the minibus was dark, and your blond friend had her hands full with the Pepto-Bismol."

"You stole her phone?"

He crosses his arms. "I slipped a hundred lira in her pocket."

"You know that's only thirty bucks, right?"

"No good deed . . ." He frowns at the phone. "That's weird. Still no response."

"Should we send another message?"

"We can't." He shakes his head. "We have to follow protocol. At least if I keep checking, she'll be able to track our location."

The waiter reappears with two steaming brown plates of eggplant sautéed with minced lamb, each crowned with a dollop of runny white yogurt. He slams down a basket of crusty bread and a ceramic bowl of golden-crusted, jiggly rice pudding. *"Afi-*

yet olsun," he mutters, and stumps back behind his counter.

"Brown mush." Connor stares down at his plate. "My favorite."

"It's musakka." Penny grabs a hunk of bread. "Sprinkle some red pepper flakes on it. It's better spicy."

"You sound like my fiancé." Connor grins. "Alex would put sriracha on a cantaloupe."

"Is she a chef?" Penny swipes the bread through the musakka. The meaty savor of sautéed eggplant swirls with the cool creaminess of the yogurt. God, she's starving.

"He." Connor steers clear of the red pepper, but gives the saltcellar a vehement shake. "And no. Latin teacher. Lived above a Szechuan restaurant in college. Burned most of his taste buds off." He meets Penny's eyes. "What?"

"It's just . . ." Penny shakes her head. "I didn't picture you —"

"Picture me what?"

"With a Latin teacher." She swirls the yogurt. "A Navy SEAL, maybe . . ."

Connor visibly relaxes. "Alex's tougher than I am. Never mind Navy SEALs — classicists are *crazy* hard-core."

"Does he know you're here?"

"Just that I'm overseas."

Penny leans on her elbow. "That's got to

be hard."

Connor shrugs. "We're honest about everything else."

Penny sprinkles more pepper. "So how does a spy end up with a Latin teacher?"

"We met when I was in the Navy. I was posted to a base called Sigonella, in Sicily. Alex was in college, working on an underwater dig off Taormina — a Roman shipwreck. Well, one night, there was a break-in. These guys packed a speedboat with antiquities and headed for Tunisia. Italian coast guard wasn't fast enough. But my ship, the *Mount Sugarloaf*, was doing exercises off Siracusa. We nabbed them. Got everything back." Connor smiles. "That's how I met Alex."

Penny cracks a smile. "That's ridiculously romantic."

Connor stabs his musakka. "Wish my parents agreed with you."

"How could anyone not like that story?"

Connor rubs the back of his neck. "My dad flew helicopters for the Navy for twenty years. Taught me to fly when I was twelve, on this tiny old Bell 47G he pretty much rebuilt from scrap." Connor drains his little plastic water glass. "He's not a big fan of change."

"Oh."

Connor drums on the table. "I always told

231

myself I wasn't scared to come out. I was just waiting. That as soon as I met somebody special, I'd tell Dad. I knew Alex was special. So, on my next home leave, I got my family together, and I told them." Connor shifts his shoulders, as if he's trying to shrug it off. "They haven't spoken to me since."

"Jesus."

"Jesus has nothing to do with it. Dad's just embarrassed about what his fishing buddies will think."

Penny doesn't know what to say. She leans forward. "When I got sad, my grandma used to make me vanilla pudding with gummy bears." She nudges the little ceramic bowl toward him. "You — want some *sütlaç*?"

Connor grins crookedly. "Do I get gummy bears?"

"Try it. It's like lumpy crème brûlée."

Connor takes a spoonful and makes a face. "Ever the optimist." He checks the phone. "Let's see if we've heard from my boss."

Penny leans forward. "Anything?"

"Something's not right." Connor shakes his head. "It shouldn't be taking this long."

"Check the news. Anything about the car bomb?"

"No." Connor scrolls. "But . . ." He looks

grim. "It's official. The Hashashin just claimed the Embassy attack. With a mass decapitation video."

Penny's voice shakes a little. "Let me see."

Connor holds out the phone.

Beneath the headline is a still photograph, taken in front of the tower of Mor Samuel. Six masked Hashashin fighters stand in a row. Each holds a severed head up to the camera. Most of the victims look old — gray beards, dripping blood. Monks? Sickened, Penny is about to look away when she notices the last head in the row. A dark-haired, bearded man, his dead blue eyes still staring.

The cold pudding feels like wet cement in Penny's mouth. She can't force it down. She spits into her napkin.

"Penny?" Connor looks worried.

"Mehmetoğlu," Penny chokes. "That's him."

Connor is perfectly still. "You're sure?"

Penny nods and squeezes her eyes shut. Doesn't help. She won't ever unsee that. She can still hear his dry voice in the Embassy garden.

"You said the terrorists loaded two men into the van." Her face is wet, but she doesn't remember crying. "If the Hashashin have Mehmetoğlu, they must have Zach, too."

Connor's voice is quiet. "Trust me, if they'd beheaded an American spy, we'd be hearing about it. Zach must still be alive."

"Which means they're probably torturing him."

Connor puts a hand on her arm. "I'm sorry."

"Mor Samuel . . ." Penny traces her finger on the screen. "We have to tell someone. The State Department, the army, the media — *somebody*!"

"We can't."

"They'll kill him!"

"Whoever blew up our car hacked a secure Agency line. Do you have any idea how impossible that's supposed to be? We've got the Turkish police against us. Palamut said you were dead. Frank Lerman said you were dead. Brenda Pelecchia said you were dead. How high up does this go? There's no one left to trust, except my boss."

"So you think we should just hide and let those bastards murder Zach?"

"Until we get through to my boss, there's nothing we can do."

"Why can't we just go to the media?"

"You'd be putting anyone you contact in danger. These people already blew up our car. Are you prepared to bet they won't blow up a newspaper office? A TV station?"

"So we put it online. Tell the whole world!"

"Put what? That Zach's a diplomat? A CIA officer? If that goes public, our government will pressure Turkey to attack Mor Samuel. I don't see how Zach survives that."

Penny clenches her fists so tight her fingers ache. "Zach has a little girl," she says hoarsely. "She's almost six. Zach gets up at three a.m. every single day so he can blow Mia kisses at bedtime. Zach was counting down the days until she comes to live with him in Ankara." Penny's voice gets stronger. "If there's anything I can do to save Zach's life, I'm going to do it."

Connor exhales. "Zach Robson is a trained officer. There's nothing you can do for him he can't do twice as well for himself."

She nods, throat tight.

"You've just got to have a little faith. If anyone can save Zach, it's my boss."

Penny picks up the sparkly phone. "There's a new comment. From 'BuckeyeBuckwheat'?"

"That's her." As Connor decodes the message, relief spreads across his face. "Get the bill. My boss is sending help."

21

OKYANUS

Near Bişkek Caddesi, Ankara,
Turkey 20:36 Local Time

Fifteen minutes later, Connor and Penny step out of a taxi on a deserted side street in Emek, on the other side of Ankara, just a few blocks from the central bus station. The untidy backs of shops make the street dingy, all pipes and wiring and dirty windows. Behind a photocopy store, a family of black-and-white kittens nurses in an old printer-cartridge box. The side of a purple van proclaims OKYANUS DÜGÜN VE SÜNNET SALONU.

"This is it," Connor says, checking the location on his phone.

Penny looks up at the back of a two-story concrete building, to all appearances a re-purposed warehouse. "Are you sure?"

"Matches the coordinates." Connor taps the phone. "Okay, my boss posted the security code." He squints at letters stenciled on the back door, in the same swirly typeface as on the van. "Huh. *Ok-ya* —"

"Okyanus Düğün ve Sünnet Salonu." Penny crosses her arms. "The Okyanus Wedding and Circumcision Salon. The little paper sign says 'foreclosed.' "

"Wedding and *Circumcision* Salon?"

"Circumcision's a big deal in Turkey. They wait until the boys are about seven or eight, then dress them up like little princes with sparkly capes and scepters and have a huge party for everyone they know."

"Sparkly *capes*?" Connor steps up to the door and dials the four-digit security code.

The tiny white box emits a fusillade of loud, shrill beeps.

"What's happening?" hisses Penny.

"I must've got the code wrong!" Connor scrolls frantically on the rhinestone phone, as the beeps increase from alarm-clock to fire-alarm loud.

"It's counting down from ten." Penny looks frantically for an electric cord to cut, but the alarm box is cemented in place, cord sheltered deep in the wall. "What happens when —"

"Seven to eight tablespoons, five cups — *four*!" Connor pounds frantically on the little box's keypad. "Seven — eight — five — four."

The beeps subside. Connor exhales. Penny wipes her stinging forehead.

The stillness seems to throb.

The door swings open.

The narrow hallway opens into a huge, dark celebration hall.

Connor fumbles for the light switch.

Suddenly, a galaxy of pinprick lights illuminates the low, pillared hall. Water stagnates in a still fountain. Tall-backed chairs — wrapped like mummies in white canvas and blue gauze bows — circle dozens of tables with dubious dolphin centerpieces, crowding the hall to the edge of a shimering dais. On the dais, two irridescent clamshell-backed thrones sit empty, ready for bride and groom to intone their vows into two large microphones bolted to a conference table.

"*Little Mermaid* meets regional sales conference," says Connor, pulling up a mummy chair at a table near the wall. "Got to admit, it's an original theme."

"It this *normal*?" Penny rubs her eyes. "When you said 'deserted location' . . ."

"It's a bit unusual." Connor shakes his head. "Typically, if a safe house is compromised, we'd meet in a neutral high-traffic location. But Palamut's people won't be looking for us here." He checks the time.

"T minus two minutes. You'd better get under the table."

"What?"

"Under the table. The bad guys hacked my comms once. We can't rule out that someone might know we're coming. If there's going to be a mess, I want you out of the way."

"Connor . . ."

"Indulge me."

"This is ridiculous." Penny crawls under the tablecloth and kneels uncomfortably on the cold tile. "Isn't your boss's guy supposed to be here already?"

"We're a touch early."

"Connor?" Penny swallows hard. "You really think he can help us save Zach?"

"First, let's worry about getting *us* out of this alive." Connor's eyes fix on the door. "Hush."

Penny hears footsteps approach on the tiles. She holds her breath. From under the tablecloth, she sees Connor pull back his chair to stand up.

"Hey," says a woman's cheerful voice, with an unmistakable Boston accent. "You know a decent sports bar this side of Sakarya?"

Connor answers, "If the Braves aren't playing, I'm not watching."

Connor and the woman both sit down.

Penny sees the woman's long legs stretch wide, as if in a La-Z-Boy. There's something so American, so harmlessly lady-on-a-jog normal about her white sneakers and black cargo pants that Penny almost smiles with relief. Her legs are getting uncomfortable. Can't she just crawl out already?

"Name's Liza," says the cheerful woman.

"Connor. Boy, am I glad to see you."

Penny hears their hands clasp.

"I bet." Liza chuckles. "The way Christina told it, I thought I might be scraping you up off the floor."

Then, to Penny's disbelieving horror, she sees Liza's muscular left hand open the knee pocket of her cargo pants and silently draw out a small black pistol, followed by a thick metal cylinder.

"So" — Liza twists the cylinder onto the muzzle — "where's the little lady?"

22
LIZA

Penny freezes.

That thing's a silencer.

"Well," Connor begins, "actually . . ."

Penny looks desperately around. A fallen steak knife? *Anything?*

". . . she's . . ."

There's no time.

Penny presses her palms to the underside of the table. In one swift, muscle-jarring movement, she stands up.

The table cracks up against Liza's jaw, sending her sprawling across the tiles.

"What the hell?" Connor lurches to his feet.

"Ow!" Penny rubs her smarting wrists.

The table rolls on its side, place settings and cutlery crashing to the ground.

Liza lies motionless, blood dribbling from her sagging mouth every time she exhales, her ponytail a brown crescent against the tiles. Her jaw sits at a strange angle.

"Are you insane?" Connor rounds on Penny. "She's on *our side*!"

"She was going to shoot you!"

Connor turns. The gun still rests in Liza's limp hand. Connor drops to his knees. "No," he mutters, "this isn't possible. A Makarov?" He examines the gun. "PB silent pistol. This is Russian."

Penny's heart is pounding, her arms still stinging from the effort. "Is she — some kind of assassin?"

Connor's cheeks are blotchy red. "What do you think, the CIA has teams of assassins waiting in vans all over the world, ready to deliver like Domino's pizza?"

"I don't know!" Penny shouts back. "*Do* you?"

"This —" Connor points furiously at Liza and her silenced gun. "This is *not normal.*"

"Did you say the gun was Russian?"

"Let's just say it's the gun you'd carry if you wanted Russia to get blamed." Connor rubs the back of his neck. "Real GRU officers don't walk around with name tags that say, '*Privet!* I'm a Russian spy!' " Connor pulls up the lids of Liza's eyes. "Out cold. I think you broke her jaw."

Penny crouches down beside him on the tiles. "What now?"

The veins stand out in Connor's neck.

"Let's see what else she's got." An empty holster for the Makarov is clipped to Liza's belt. Connor checks every pocket of her cargo pants, making a careful row on the tiles: a coil of what looks like a guitar string but with grips at each end, a cheap prepaid phone that still has plastic wrapping on the screen, an eight-round Makarov magazine, and a pack of what looks like breath mints. Connor sniffs it cautiously and makes a face.

"What is it?" Penny leans closer.

"Cinnamon."

Penny's hands are clammy.

Connor rocks back on his heels. "She's not Russian. And she's not Turkish intelligence. I'd almost say we're looking at some kind of private contractor. Except —" He shakes his head. "She knew the sign and countersign. She knew the location, which means she read and decoded the messages. She knew Christina's *name*!"

Something clicks into place.

"Christina?" A cold weight sinks through Penny's chest. "Christina is your *boss*?"

Connor turns to her. "You're scaring me."

"At the palace, Melek Palamut asked if Christina sent me."

"She *what*?" Connor stares. "No. That can't be. No one outside the Agency should even know who Christina is."

Penny's voice shakes. "You knew I'd knocked out Palamut's Chief of Staff. But no one could have known that except Melek and her people. Who told you? It was Christina, wasn't it? Who told you where to find me? Who knew what junkyard I'd be at? Was that Christina, too?"

"That doesn't prove anything."

"It proves Christina is cooperating with Melek. How else could she have known?"

Connor looks sick.

"Who told you I was a terrorist? Christina, right? Did she even tell you why?"

He hesitates. Then, "No."

"Connor." Penny feels a terrible certainty, even as her mind forms the question. "Was your boss the one who told you to get into that car?"

Connor's face goes perfectly blank.

"She was, wasn't she?" Penny feels a deep chill scrape down her arms. "Did she have the access code for your ECRP?"

He is motionless.

Penny swallows. "Did anyone else even know?"

For a moment, neither can speak.

"When I sent the message to Christina from the library," says Connor slowly, "the police arrived . . . what? Less than ten minutes later?"

"Looking for foreigners." Penny's heart pounds.

"A bomb. The Turkish police." Connor looks down. "And then she sends us Liza."

"I can believe that Melek Palamut would do anything to protect her father. But why would *Christina* want us dead?"

"It's Zach. It all leads back to Zach Robson. Christina sent me to interrogate you because you were our only link to him."

Penny slides onto her knees. "If we'd died like we were supposed to, it would have been a dead trail."

"Whatever Zach was looking for, whatever he found, Christina wants every trace destroyed."

"Including us."

They're both quiet for a moment.

"We've got to run." Penny's head throbs. "The Canadian Embassy's on the other side of town — or there are the Brits —"

"Christina probably has eyes on all of them." Connor shakes his head. "So will the Turks. We'd be dead before we got in the door."

"If we could just get out of Turkey —"

"Palamut's people will be watching all the airports, all the borders." Connor snorts. "Except maybe Syria. They don't seem too good at that."

"What could be worth all this?" whispers Penny.

"The only person who can tell us that is Zach Robson."

Their eyes meet.

"Well?" says Penny.

"No." Connor's forehead creases. "Absolutely not."

"Think about it! You said they'll be watching all the other borders. What's the one place nobody would ever expect us to go?"

"Because it's *suicide*!"

"We'll die anyway if we stay here!"

Connor makes a face. "I'd rather get shot than have my head chopped off."

"At least if we run, we might buy a little time. And Zach's the only person who can help us!"

"How do you figure that?"

"Whatever information Mehmetoğlu gave him, Christina and Melek are so scared of it, they're prepared to do *anything* to stop it getting out. What's big enough to scare the President of Turkey's daughter *and* your boss?"

"Even if that's true, how exactly are you planning to break Zach out of Mor Samuel? We've got two lousy guns!"

"Maybe we don't have to actually get Zach." Penny's breath is coming fast now.

"Maybe the Hashashin will bring him to us."

"If they bothered to drag him all the way to Mor Samuel, they're not just going to let him go."

"Do you know how to contact the Hashashin?"

"Why? You got ten million bucks' ransom to spare?"

"Do you or don't you?"

He shrugs. "They recruit a lot on ExciDox."

"That disgusting app?"

"That disgusting app."

Penny makes a face. "So be it." She picks up the assassin's prepaid phone.

"What do you think you're doing?"

"It's our only chance." Penny hits download. "We tell the Hashashin that we're prepared to make a deal. They give us Zach. We give them something they want even more."

"More than a captive CIA officer? Like *what*?"

Penny hands him the phone. "I can think of one thing."

Ten minutes later, the yellow-and-black graphics of the ExciDox app glow on the prepaid phone. A beep, as the Hashashin's message decrypts.

Penny exhales shakily. "They sent the address. Mardin, tomorrow. The nearest town to Mor Samuel on the Turkish side of the border — neutral ground. Nine a.m."

"Well," says Connor, "either they just took the bait, or we just did." He snaps out the SIM card and tosses Liza's phone into the fountain. He walks over to where Liza still lies sprawled on the tiles and picks up the PB pistol.

"Connor, don't!" Penny hurries over. "It's not like she's going to talk. And if the cops find a dead body, they'll come looking for a murderer."

Connor unclips the empty holster from Liza's belt, fixes it to his own, and tucks in the PB pistol. "That's why we're going to make it look like a burglary. Help me put her in recovery."

"What?"

"Roll her on her side, so she won't choke on her own blood. We don't want her to miss all the fun she's going to have with the Turkish police. There we go." Connor picks up the contents of Liza's pockets and shoves them in his own. "Come on."

Penny glances back at the illuminated clamshell thrones and shakes her head.

Connor grabs a painted concrete dolphin

centerpiece and lifts it speculatively. "Should do."

"Souvenir? You know, most people just buy a carpet."

"You'll see."

They jog down the little hallway to the door, which Connor leaves ajar. "Now," he says, "run."

He hefts the dolphin and sends it smashing into the alarm box.

The alarm system howls back to life, beeping like hysterical sonar.

"Score." Connor grins and takes off.

A moment later, he has caught up with Penny. They run through the warm darkness, toward the steep dirty glass of Ankara's central bus station.

23
CONSPICUOUS

Penny and Connor shell out cash for two tickets for the 21:35 to Mardin. Penny leads the way across the terminal, toward the Lost Luggage counter.

"I don't like all these policemen," Connor mutters.

"There are always more after an attack. These guys look practically asleep. That one's even got a glass of tea."

"If you'd just let me grab a suitcase —"

"What are you, a kleptomaniac?"

"It's tradecraft!"

Penny leads him up to the grubby white Lost Luggage counter. "At least these ones are already lost."

The counter attendant, a slight young man, pushes thick hipster glasses up his nose. "Tourists!" He regards Connor and Penny with the bug-eyed enthusiasm of a keen student who has finally, wondrously found someone to practice on. "Welcome, hello, yes, please?"

"Bonsoir!" Connor booms in a cheery voice thoroughly unlike his own. "We lose bag. Big bag. You find?"

Penny and the counter attendant both stare at him.

The counter attendant speaks in slow mo. "Is your name on the bag, sir? Your *name*?"

"No name." Connor wags a finger at Penny in pantomime reproach. "Silly girl."

Penny glowers.

"Ah." The young man's smile is growing fixed. "What color, sir?"

"Big bag," repeats Connor with conviction.

"Okay." The young man beckons them through the door behind the counter. "Follow me." They pass shelves of tidily stacked luggage. The young man opens the door to another, much dingier room. "Here, sir, miss. Bags without name."

A single bulb lights a heap of twenty suitcases on the bare concrete, mostly battered black or faded plastic. A plate-size blue-and-white evil eye has been nailed to the far wall.

Connor kneels by one of the least shabby looking suitcases, a black duffel bag. It offers a fuchsia evening gown, several bikinis, a Qur'an, and a brochure for hoverboards. Connor clicks open a tattered maroon canvas suitcase, revealing several men's suits, a pair of blue pajamas, and a well-thumbed stack of *Playboy*s. He grabs a clean white shirt.

"Sir, you cannot —"

"Un moment!" Connor lunges for a dusty plastic roll-along adorned with cartoon apples and bananas. *"Alors . . ."* A couple of flowery blouses spill out.

"Connor," says Penny through her teeth.

"Sir!" The attendant darts forward. "You can't —"

Connor stands up with the fruitcase and presses a fifty-lira note into the young man's hand. *"Merci."* He beckons Penny. *"Allons-y."*

"You want more? Only twenty lira, sir? For the one with the magazines?"

With one hand on her shoulder, Connor propels Penny out the door, tugging the suitcase along behind.

"What in *Dieu*'s name was that?" she whispers.

"Old trick," says Connor in his normal voice. "Keep it in mind. Being conspicuous makes you *less* suspicious. If you're colorful enough, they'll remember the act, not your face. Here's the ladies' room. Change fast."

In the bathroom stall (an honest-to-goodness Western-style toilet, thank God, not pit-style), Penny wipes a damp paper towel across her head and neck. She perches on the closed lid and unzips the fruit-print suitcase. It's like a time capsule. Stale jasmine perfume rises from the neatly folded, eye-wateringly colorful clothes — what the stylish middle-class conservative girl was wearing ten years ago. Everything that can be ironed has been, down to the flowery underpants and black sports bra, neatly creased into quarters. What is it about Turkish women ironing their underwear? Fatma does it, too. Penny yanks on a pair of black leggings, only a few sizes too tight. "Shirt." Penny digs down in the luggage. She pulls a green tunic over her head, and a faded blue-jean jacket over that.

In the outer pocket of the suitcase, she finds four head scarves: three wallpapery cotton prints, and one clearly for "best": blue Bursa silk, brilliant as a Bukhara dome, nearly six feet long.

Her fingers curl around the rough coolness of the scarf. It's the obvious, practical disguise. But she never wears a head scarf in Turkey, unless she's sightseeing in a mosque. Fatma doesn't. Plenty of the Turkish women she worked with at the Embassy didn't "cover," even the devout ones.

These days in Turkey, the choice to hide your hair sometimes has as much to do with politics and what the Turks call *mahalle baskısı* — neighborhood pressure — as it does with God or private piety. It's as coded, as loaded, as black lipstick, a gold cross, or a six-gallon cowboy hat. Choose to cover a certain way, and strangers assume you're a *gözleme*-frying, *mantı*-pinching housewife loyal to Palamut, and his party's trademark middle-class, Sunni Islamist conformity. Even if you're a physicist with a PhD, an engineer, a professional cellist, a single mom. A scrap of polyester can surround a multitude of thoughts.

Don't cover, and — though you pray five times a day, give alms, and fast for Ramadan — plenty will call you godless or just treat you like a slut. It used to drive Ayla crazy. Penny can remember Ayla ranting over sugary midnight Turkish coffees on Tunalı Avenue, "Palamut doesn't own *my* Islam! He doesn't own *my* faith!"

Seconds are slipping away. Hand-wringing is a luxury she can't afford. Penny loops the blue silk around her head as best she can. Ayla showed her how, but Penny hasn't mastered the art of draping a head scarf gracefully. Like tying a scarf *à la Parisienne,* which she also can't do, it's trickier than it looks.

"What were you *doing* in there?" snaps Connor when she emerges. "We have to run. The bus leaves from Bay 14."

They hustle through the crowded station. Connor buttons his new shirt up to the neck and makes to loop his tie.

"Hey." Penny touches his arm. "I think the night bus to Mardin is business casual."

"Point taken." He stuffs the tie into his trouser pocket.

They step outside at Bay 3. The heavy, warm darkness of the night folds around them like a feather duvet, soaked with the sweet reek of gasoline fumes. They hurry onward.

Across the floodlit parking lot, three police vans pull up. At least thirty armed policemen file out.

Penny freezes.

"Keep walking normally," hisses Connor. "It could have nothing to do with us."

They walk as fast as they dare. Bay 8, Bay 9, Bay 10.

"Come on!" Connor urges. "Almost there!"

Bay 14. Pacing beside the wheezing orange

Peygamber Otobüsleri bus is a ticket collector with a face like a malevolent walnut.

"Geç kaldınız!" he rebukes them — you're late! His husky eastern accent turns the *k* into a phlegmy fricative. He marches them to their seats at the back of the close-aired bus, apparently last upholstered in the seventies. Connor takes the window seat and immediately stoops down below window level, as if adjusting his shoelaces.

Penny moves to sit beside him.

"Bi dakka," says the ticket collector suspiciously, holding up a finger. "Is the *yabancı* your husband?"

"He's my cousin," Penny replies. She's never had any problems moving around Ankara with Zach or Matt, or any of the other guys from POL. But then she was an obvious foreigner. Her Americanness won't protect her anymore.

"Cousin?" The old man is clearly reveling in his tiny dictatorship. "Oh, no. Not on this bus, my girl. You cannot sit with him."

"But —"

Penny catches Connor's eyes. His message couldn't be clearer: *Do not make a scene.*

Through the tinted window, Penny can make out police running into the terminal building.

"You sit *here.*" The old man points Penny to an empty seat beside a woman with a shiny black bob. She could be a bureaucrat or an academic — plump, tidy, middle-class. The woman nods cordially. Penny flings herself into the seat and slides as low down as she can.

The bus rolls toward the exit, and Penny starts to relax.

A policemen runs up, shouting. The bus creaks to a stop.

Penny's nails dig into the seat cushion.

"I'm late already," grouses the bus driver. "What do you want?"

"It's a red alert, *abi*!" calls the young officer; he looks all of eighteen, a beanpole schoolboy. It's ingratiating of him to give the driver the honorific *abi* — "big brother" — when *amca* — "uncle" — is so obviously more appropriate. "We're checking all the buses for terrorists."

"You think I let terrorists on my bus?"

"I have to ask, *abi,*" protests the young officer. "Have you seen anything suspicious?"

"Trust me, son. If anyone tries something suspicious on my bus, they'd be dead before the police got them!"

The young officer chuckles and waves him on. "*Sağol, abi!*"

257

The lights switch off overhead. The darkened bus accelerates eastward along the headlight-spangled highway.

24
THE HOUSE ON THE CLIFF

Istanbul Atatürk Airport
21:15 Local Time

A black, armored SUV with green diplomatic plates is waiting for Brenda and Frank at Istanbul Atatürk Airport. Four new bodyguards hastily stub out their cigarettes and climb into the follow car.

As the seagull flies, it's only fifteen miles through central Istanbul from the airport to the residence of the U.S. Consul General in a waterside neighborhood on the European shore. But it's a clear night in July, and the traffic hardly budges. Buckled into the cavernous, bulletproof backseat, Brenda chews up half a pack of gum. The gum's a common Turkish brand, Falım — "my fate" — left in her pocket from before the Fourth. Each minty stick comes wrapped in a fortune-cookie-like prediction. Brenda crumples one after the other.

> You will meet a tall dark stranger.

No, thanks.

> True love and passion await you.

Steve is already on the plane back to DC with the kids, thank God. She barely had time to hug them. At least they're out of here.

There's no gum prediction that says, *You will lose every friend you've made in the last two years, every colleague who's ever gotten on your nerves and sourced limes for Margarita Night and made Ankara bearable. And then you'll have to clean up the mess.*

Candy doesn't tend to tell you stuff like that.

The black SUV inches along the coastal road, past the immense parade ground for political rallies that Palamut dumped thousands of tons of concrete on a Byzantine harbor to build. Beyond the road, oil tankers lurk in the dark waters, waiting for permission to churn up the Bosphorus Strait to the Black Sea.

Brenda scrolls through the latest press

summaries on her BlackBerry. A shrill op-ed in *Slate* wants to know why the death of Flag Girl is getting so much more coverage across the international press than the deaths of dozens of Turks, or the other bombings this week in Mogadishu, Basra, Karachi: "Why do people only care when the person who dies is a photogenic white American?" #NotOnlyFlagGirl is inching up alongside #PrayforAnkara and #Stand-StrongUSA in global trends. The trolls from 55 Savushkina Street are blasting every comments section with Russian-accented conspiracy theories. The Democrats are blaming the Republicans, the Republicans are blaming the Muslims, and the rest of the world is blaming American foreign policy — except for the Brits, who are blaming each other.

Brenda clicks the little screen black. No point giving herself an aneurysm. *Flag Girl.* Two days ago, Penny was just the summer intern who jammed the photocopier twice a week and got in much too early every morning, trying so hard to do the right thing. Now that she's lying in a Turkish military morgue, the whole world acts like she was Joan of Arc. At least Joan of Arc chose her battle. Penny wasn't even in Turkey to fight. When Brenda was picking up her luggage at the baggage carousel, she got a text message from Greg, the FSO liaising with the hospital. The death count is up to 294.

Frank Lerman is clipping his fingernails over the SUV's carpeted floor. Brenda tries to pretend she hasn't noticed.

They round the beaked nose of Sarayburnu point and the faintly silhouetted chimneys of Topkapı Palace. Slowly, they roll up to the mouth of the moonlit, ferry-studded Golden Horn. The familiar postcard skyline of slim, balconied minarets and apple domes appears through the back window as the car crawls across the Galata Bridge. They move slower than the boys selling cups of milk-sweet boiled corn, but faster than the handful of photo-snapping tourists from the Gulf, obvious outsiders in their robes amid the blue-jeaned Istanbullus, who don't look much different from the nighttime crowd in any Mediterranean port. There never used to be so many beggars on the bridge. The ones Brenda can see look like dolls left at the mercy of a vicious child, with limp heads and missing limbs.

The SUV quickens to a walking pace as they head north up the European bank of the Bosphorus, under victory arches of traffic lights and Palamut's electoral slogans. Brenda is wound too tight to feel exhausted.

Danger feels surreally far away tonight, as the car climbs past the intricate wooden Ottoman façades of the old waterfront neighborhood, a stronghold of the beleaguered secular elite that, once upon a time, was Turkey's ruling class. Up the car spirals, to the high steel gates of the Consul General's residence on its rocky outcropping.

The CG, Moe Sokolof, is waiting in the doorway, a mountain of a man in a black T-shirt and khaki shorts, his graying beard only half-masking a double chin. He's a career Foreign Service officer like Brenda, and a gifted amateur chef. He used to fry up goat tacos when they served their first tours of duty together in Almaty, fresh out of A-100. Rachel from the ECON Section used to make "crack rice" (butter *and* oil) as a side. Brenda had to identify her body this morning. There were no legs below the hem of her twinset.

Moe folds Brenda into a bear hug. "We'll get them, Bren. We'll goddamn bring them down."

When he releases her, Brenda asks, "Where's Carolyn?"

"Triaging new arrivals at the Consulate — she might have to stay till late. She sends her love."

Frank sticks out his hand. "Mr. Sokolof?

I'm Frank Lerman."

Moe clasps his arm. "Thanks for being here. Let me get you guys a drink."

Brenda and Frank settle in cream-colored Drexel couches, a familiar sight in pretty much any Foreign Service home at any post in the world. The familiarity just makes it worse. French windows face onto the dark waters of the Bosphorus, a wide panorama of the fifteenth-century Rumelihisar fortress and the great steel transcontinental bridge, stretching across to the twinkling Asian shore. "So," Frank says, "Secretary Winthrop arrives at seven a.m. How's the prep going?"

"My team is taking care of everything," says Moe. "We've got extra security coming up from Adana. I spoke to CIA — the threat level is holding stable. The NATO Summit is going forward."

"Any updates on Zach Robson and Mehmetoğlu?" asks Brenda.

"That's not the priority here," says Frank. "Let's try to focus, huh?"

Moe gives him a stern look. "I'm sorry, Bren. I haven't heard anything."

"Something just feels wrong," says Brenda. "I know Zach Robson. He's been here three years — he knows the ropes. He'd never invite someone like Mehmetoğlu into the Embassy without checking him. He must've known the guy was shady. So why sneak him in?"

"What are you implying?" says Frank. "Zach Robson's an intelligence officer. One of our own."

"Since when has that ever meant we shouldn't play it safe?" says Moe. "I'm not accusing Mr. Robson. I don't even know the guy. But if Brenda thinks we should check —"

"I'm telling you, you're barking up the wrong tree," says Frank.

"You seem mighty sure," says Brenda.

"I have my reasons."

Brenda's hand tightens around her phone. "Mr. Lerman, I know when I'm being lied to. I can tell you're hiding something. So give me one good reason why I shouldn't go straight over your head with this."

"Maybe we should take a selfie," Frank says, smirking. "You're going to want to remember this. Because this is the moment when Frank Lerman saved your fucking careers." He reaches into his jacket and pulls out his BlackBerry. He pulls up a scan of a passport photo page.

Zach Robson must've been a few years younger when the photo was snapped, but he's instantly recognizable. Brenda's eyes skim across.

Surname/Nom/pellidos
CABOT
Given names/Prénoms/Nombres
JOHN WINTHROP

"Oh, Christ."

"Jack is the Secretary's first cousin," says Frank. "We know everything about him back to the day he was born."

"Why didn't you tell me?" demands Brenda. "This is a huge security issue!"

"We believe the Hashashin targeted Jack because of his work for CIA. If they find out they've got hold of the Secretary of State's cousin . . ." Frank shakes his head.

"And we really have no idea what's happened to him?" says Moe. "No idea where he is?"

"Secretary Winthrop spoke to Christina Ekdahl," says Frank. "He assures me she's doing everything in her power to find him."

Brenda shakes her head. "I hope to God she's in time."

25
A VOICE IN THE NIGHT

Langley, Virginia
19:59 Local Time

It's late enough that no one but Christina and the night teams are left in the Original Headquarters Building.

It's been too long.

Much too long.

Connor's signal showed up at the meeting point on schedule. Soldier boys like him don't disobey commands.

The signal terminated quickly. That was good.

But still no word from Liza.

Did they kill each other? That would spare her the inconvenience of camouflaging Liza's contractor's fee in the maintenance budget.

Except that would mean three bodies waiting to be found. Connor and Liza could be explained away. But Flag Girl, bleeding out on the floor of some foreclosed Turkish

267

wedding salon, hours after she was supposed to have died in the hospital?

There's no avoiding it.

Christina reaches for the phone.

Ankara, Turkey
03:05 Local Time
Melek is already in her morning yoga clothes, no makeup, hair pulled up in a soft ponytail. She looks without seeing at her untouched breakfast: tiny ceramic pots of perfectly sliced cucumbers and tomatoes, black and green olives sparkling with oil, sesame-studded *simit* rolls, nutty *kaşar* cheese in every shade of yellow, a reddish-dark rainbow of syrupy fruit *reçel*. A peace-time breakfast. But Melek doesn't feel at peace. She can smell the acid sweetness of the tall glass of fresh-squeezed orange juice. Melek doesn't care much for it, but it's always there and always has been. Back when he had nothing going for him but ambition, guts, and gravity-strength charisma, her father got his start selling little plastic cups of orange juice outside the mosque in Bayburt, squeezing a few drops from the rotten fruit the local greengrocer couldn't sell.

Her father. That strong, magnificent, blinkered man.

Her father, so messianically certain of his righteousness that he divided his people into acolytes and apostates and wouldn't acknowledge any middle ground. He refused to see the Americans subtly realigning their support to the milder one, that tame monkey, the grinning Prime Minister.

Her father, who played secret games with Daesh and didn't seem to notice his black dogs were losing ground to the Hashashin by the minute.

Her father, who raised her incompetent brother to be his heir.

Her father, who told Melek to stay out of it.

The phone rings.

Christina doesn't bother with pleasantries. "They got away. I need the CCTV since eight p.m. from every camera in the Emek neighborhood. And the central bus station, too."

"Emek." Melek's voice is dry. "You know, we had the strangest report from Emek. A very muscular, unconscious female burglar. American clothes. Absolutely nothing in her pockets. In a foreclosed wedding salon, of all places. The local police were *very* puzzled."

"What does that have to do with me?"

"Is this your idea of 'making it all go away'?"

"Melek, I don't have time to waste. Send me the footage. Now."

"What are you so afraid of? So what if Penny Kessler escapes? You'll deny everything. We'll deny everything. Who will believe the little intern with a concussion? Yet you're so terrified of what this girl might know, you're prepared to blow up two of your own citizens, and one of ours? Just what does Zachary Robson have on you?"

"That is not your concern."

"If you will tell me nothing, I have nothing further to say to you."

"Melek, I urge you to reconsider."

"No. Not until you tell me what is going on."

A pause.

"Have it your way." Christina's voice is eerily calm. "I have a feeling you may change your mind."

26
PATRON SAINTS

Highway D-52, Outside Osmaniye, Turkey
03:08 Local Time

As the bus jostles along the lonely eastbound highway, Penny's thoughts slide into dreams.

A sunlit memory.

The day Brenda chewed her out in front of everyone. Penny was still hiding at her desk when Zach found her.

"She won't let me wear braids, either," he said. "It's tyranny, I tell you."

She looked up to find him in shirtsleeves, grinning.

"I enjoyed your op-ed gists," he added, perching on her desk. "I'd like to hear your thoughts on the youth groups data. Have lunch with me?"

They bought shiny *poğaça* rolls from a little red cart, the salty feta-stuffed kind that crunch with nigella seeds, and strolled to Kuğulu Park to watch the swans. Neither mentioned the youth groups data.

Zach was charming, but it never felt like an act; he was comfortable, and disarmingly quiet. He joked about his failed attempt to start a ski club in Ankara ("some weird guy from the German Embassy, bored expat wives, and me") and about his photography.

"Portraits. It's a rush — the moment when you really *see* someone for the first time." Zach leaned close. "I've got this one pet project. Promise you won't laugh?"

Penny smiled. "Not if it's not funny."

"Shake on that?" His hand was surprisingly calloused. "Okay. *Eskiciler.*"

"Eskiciler?"

"You know, those guys who sell old junk on street corners? I bought so much crap from them, trying to win them over to pose for me. You ever want a broken toaster, hit me up."

"Waste not, want not."

"Said no twenty-one-year-old ever."

"I can't help it." Penny smiled. "I grew up with my grandparents." She shifted on the grass. "I was the only kid in school who'd seen every Ginger Rogers musical."

His eyes were intent. "How'd that happen?"

"Grandma had a thing for Fred Astaire."

"Okay." Zach screwed the top back on his

water. "You don't have to tell me."

"No, it's just —" She shook her head. "I just don't usually talk about it."

"I'm good at keeping secrets, Penny."

"It's not a secret. No sob story. My parents are both fine. My dad's a sculptor. My mom used to pose for him. That's how they met." Penny crumbled the last of her *poğaça*. "She's really beautiful."

"That's easy to believe."

"I look like my dad." Penny looked down at the grass. "Anyway. She dropped out of college and had me, and they ended up back in Michigan. She felt trapped. They split. Dad traveled. She left." Penny tossed a fistful of crumbs into the water. "I stayed."

The next day, after work, Penny and Zach climbed up to the citadel with spicy *dürüm* wraps. He told her about Mia for the first time. They dangled their legs over the edge of the medieval fortress walls and looked down at the red rooftops of the old city, almost pretty from up here. "You can see the little town Ankara used to be, before Atatürk made it his new capital," says Zach. "You been to his mausoleum?"

"Not yet."

"We should go sometime." He gave her a warm smile. "It's amazing. No wonder Palamut's so jealous of the guy. Dead more than eighty years, and people still revere him. Can you imagine?"

"My landlady talks about him as if he were a saint."

"Patron saint of Scotch and cigs." Zach clasps his chest with mock sincerity. "Man after my own heart." He dug a pack of cheap Turkish cigarettes out of his pocket and lit up. He held the pack out to Penny. "You smoke?"

She shook her head.

"Course you don't." He sounded sardonic. "Don't you ever break the rules?"

"When I was ten, my dad had me try one of his joints. I got so sick, Grandma almost had to take me to the hospital." Penny kicks her heels against the wall. "It kind of put me off smoking."

Zach stubbed out his cigarette.

"You don't have to do that."

"Yes. I do."

As the sun sank lower, he started to open up. He told her about how his family never let him live down "only" getting into UVA, when every other lacrosse captain in Groton's history went to Yale.

"Are they insane?" said Penny.

"They practically disowned me when Jess got pregnant — she wasn't *their kind*. And even after Jess died, they acted like Mia was second-class. Not really a member of the family."

"That's horrible."

"I learned to be my own man." Zach shrugged. "They wrote me off as a failure a long time ago."

"Why?" Penny protested. "You're providing for your daughter, aren't you? You're serving your country!"

"Serving my country." Zach shook his head. "My family's been in public service a long time. Senators. Generals." She could hear his pain, his bitterness. "I'm almost thirty. Information officer in Ankara isn't going to impress anybody. My cousin — *he's* their golden boy. You'd know his name, if I told you. But he doesn't know squat. He just coasts along his golden-brick road. And it's all built on a lie." There was a hoarseness in his voice, a vulnerability she didn't expect. He squared his shoulders. "Sorry. I shouldn't . . ."

"No." Penny put her hand on his shoulder. "Tell me."

"My grandfather had a house up in Maine, on Mount Desert Island. In Northeast Harbor — the most beautiful place you've ever seen. We called it the Cottage. Aunts, uncles, cousins, nannies — we'd all go stay there, every summer, all thirty of us."

"Pretty big cottage."

"Yeah, well — my grandfather was a war hero. Understatement was kind of his thing." Zach squinted at the sunset. "We would have picnic suppers on his boat. Lobster rolls and watermelon. My grandmother — she's very theatrical — she used to make us all play charades. I was fifteen. I thought I was in hell." Zach grinned. "I was a real little asshole."

Penny laughed. "Poor Zach."

"One weekend, my cousin — our golden boy — drove up from Harvard Law with some friends. He said he was going to take them out on this catamaran the family owned, but I knew they were planning to stay back at the Cottage and have a *real* party. He was my idol. I begged him to let me come. Of course he didn't want me there. But his buddies had some . . ." Zach pantomimed snorting cocaine. "And they thought it would be *hilarious* to get me high. Anyway, they got some girls and a few bottles of Scotch. We were all at the Cottage. I was upstairs, pretty much wrecked. And apparently, my cousin accidently dropped one of my grandfather's lit cigars onto my grandmother's heirloom curtains."

Zach shrugged. "Old houses catch fire fast."

"Oh my God."

"My cousin and his buddies and the girls, they panicked. They jumped in their cars and drove away. I was so out of it upstairs that I didn't even realize what was happening. My cousin called 911, pretending he'd seen the flames from the catamaran. The fire department showed up. My whole *family* showed up. My cousin ran in and *saved* me — from the fire he started. The big hero. I got blamed for everything. Kicked out of school. I could barely get into UVA. The official family screwup for the rest of forever."

"The other guys just let you take the blame?"

"They couldn't afford to get caught — they all wanted to go into politics. My cousin told me, he figured I was just a kid — I'd get past it." Zach shook his head. "My grandfather sure never did."

"But why didn't you tell the truth?"

"Oh, I did. But I'd been suspended at school that spring for sharing my Adderall. Dorm parties — you know, kids trying to be cool? We all did it. But I got caught. So when my cousin said I started the fire all by my little coked-up self . . ."

"They believed him."

"Yup."

"But that was years ago. Look at you now! You're a diplomat. You've lived all over the world. You have Mia. . . ."

He grimaced. "I wish I could do better for her."

"You'll be there for her. That's the best any dad can do."

Zach leaned back on the warm rock of the citadel wall. He was quiet for a minute. "You're sweet. Do you know that?"

"I'm right."

"We'll see."

A one-eyed orange kitten hopped up between them on the stone wall, meowing hopefully.

"Oh, really? You've never been fed in your whole life?" Zach scraped leftover ground lamb from his *dürüm* wrap onto the stone wall. The tiny creature purred. "Yeah, yeah. I'm a soft touch." Zach rubbed the kitten's head and looked up at Penny, smiling. "So. Did it go better with Brenda the Bad Witch today?"

"I wish I knew how to make her happy." Penny stroked the kitten's back. "I've tried everything —"

"Stop trying. I've been watching you, Penny. You're different. You notice things. Some of us aren't ever going to be part of the crowd." He wiped the lamb grease off his hands with a towelette. "And that's a good thing."

"It's just . . . I've been working toward this for three years. If I'm no good at it, what am I going to do?"

"You've been here, what, three weeks? Besides, you're twenty-one. A daily identity crisis pretty much goes with the territory. But you can always come to me for advice." He winked. "Think of me as your personal Buddha."

"But with better hair."

He laughed — a deep, reassuring chuckle. "So. The inevitable question. Why Turkey?"

"You first."

"I bid on Paris and Rome, but State sent me here. Some crap about serving my country." He grinned. "What's your excuse?"

She started to reel off the usual answer. "Turkey's such a fascinating crossroad of cultures. My grandparents came here on a cruise before I was born — it was my favorite photo album. So it makes me feel close to them. Plus, anthro majors have to take a non-Indo-European language, so . . ." She added more quietly, "U of M is a language flagship for Turkish. If you keep your grades up, summer intensives are free. Food, board, everything." She looks down at the cars crawling far below. "It meant I never had to go home."

"Cheers to that," said Zach. They clinked green glass bottles of apple pop. "Why do you think I love my job so much?"

27
Fairy Tales

O-52 Highway, Near Yarbaşi, Turkey
03:24 Local Time

Penny wakes disoriented.

A weak blue light is shining in her face.

"Cracker or chocolate?" repeats the bus attendant.

Penny squints at him. Every muscle in her legs has cramped up. Outside the window, there are no houses. The moon illuminates gray fields and low, jagged hills.

"What time is it?" she croaks.

"Almost three thirty," replies the woman in the window seat. Her accent is crisp, university educated — ladylike *hanımefendi* Turkish. But her round cheeks, Penny notices, are pink with sunburn. She must be at least forty, but her high color makes her look a decade younger. "I recommend the crackers."

Penny stifles a yawn. Her hands are freezing from the air-conditioning.

"Tea or Nescafé?"

Penny rubs her heavy eyes. "Do you have water?"

She turns to see how Connor will handle this. His eyes remain resolutely shut, even when the bus attendant shakes his shoulder. With an irritable mutter, the old man moves on. Connor catches Penny's eye and winks.

"Turkish isn't your mother tongue, is it?" says the sunburned woman at Penny's side.

Penny feels heat pool in her cheeks. Attention is the last thing she wants. "People don't usually notice."

"Ah" — the woman smiles — "but I am an archaeologist. I notice details." Her quick eyes fix on Penny's rustically tied head scarf. "You are visiting family in Mardin, maybe?"

Penny decides she won't lie if she doesn't have to. "I'm a student." She chooses her words carefully. "I've always wanted to see Mardin."

"You arrive at a troubled time. But, çok şükür, there is still much beauty to be found in Tur Abdin." She uses the ancient name for Mardin Province and the surrounding lands. "The last time I came, I gave a talk at a little primary school near Midyat. I saw three little girls playing hopscotch in the school yard. One was counting in Turkish, one in Kurdish, and one in Aramaic. You know, the language of the prophet Isa."

"The language of Jesus?" Penny stares. "I thought Aramaic was a dead language."

"The monks at Mor Samuel speak it, too. Or they did." The archaeologist sighs. "When my students in Istanbul think of Mardin now, they think of conflict. But for centuries, Jews, Christians, Muslims, and Yazidis farmed together in these hills, ate together, bought each other's pots, and mended each other's carpets."

"Istanbul used to be like that, too, didn't it? My professor said that in the reign of Sultan Mehmet the Conqueror, only half the people in Constantinople were even Muslim. She said the Conqueror built bath-houses and markets, not just mosques, so all his subjects could benefit, no matter how they prayed."

"We shouldn't make our past a fairy tale," says the archaeologist. "This land has seen no shortage of hard times. What country hasn't? But never in my lifetime has it been as hard as this. I fear that loving Turkey is leaving your heart on the railroad tracks. Sooner or later, it will get crushed."

Penny crunches the empty water cup. The sadness threatens to suck her down. Redirect. "Are you coming to Mardin for research?"

The archaeologist's mouth is full of cracker; she nods.

"Isn't it dangerous?"

"You're here, too, aren't you? Besides, I must keep coming, for as long as I can. My colleague was researching the Ottoman public architecture of Damascus. Bazaars, schools, fountains. She used to fly down every couple of months for field research and bring her kids in the summer." The archaeologist shakes her head. "Now . . ."

"But that won't happen here." Penny feels her stomach turn and tells herself it's just car sickness. "Turkey won't be another Syria. It can't. Palamut's no angel, but he'll defend his borders."

The archaeologist raises her eyebrows. "Look what he let them do to the American Embassy."

Penny hugs her arms to her chest. "It's not always possible to stop an attack."

"In the most secure building in the safest neighborhood in Ankara?" The archaeologist looks skeptical. "*Canım,* please. You don't think those murderers had help from the inside?" She drops her voice. "Did you hear about the leak?"

Penny leans closer. "What?"

The archaeologist pulls out her phone. "It's not in any of the Turkish press yet.

They're all too scared." She loads the VPN. "Do you read English?"

Penny nods.

The archaeologist holds out her phone. "There's a whisper going around Twitter that a journalist has credible evidence of Melek Palamut selling weapons to the Hashashin. Evidence from a U.S. government source."

"*Melek* selling weapons to the Hashashin?"

"Can you believe it?" The archaeologist shakes her head. "I don't like her father or her politics. But Melek *Hanım* always seemed the sanest of the bunch."

It takes Penny a long time to fall back asleep.

28
THE ABODE OF WAR

Ankara, Turkey
04:23 Local Time

"You cannot do this to me!" hisses Melek.

"It wasn't an official statement." Christina's voice comes through the phone calm and clear. "Just a little unauthorized leak."

"It is a forgery." For the first time in many years, Melek is fighting back tears. "I would never help those terrorists. They murdered hundreds of my people. Women. Children! They are a stain on the very word Islam!"

"Consider it a gentle warning."

Melek draws herself up, soldier straight. "In my country women bear the family honor. Do you think my father will stand by while you slander me?"

"In your country poor women who are raped get murdered by their own fathers and brothers to keep the family honor pure."

"In *your* country police shoot schoolchildren for the color of their skin!"

"In my country leaders can't afford to be associated with terrorists," says Christina calmly. "Your father will make an example of you. He'll have no choice. Not unless he wants to be implicated in your criminal, terrorist activity."

"The only criminal thing I've ever done is talk to you."

"The leak doesn't have to be substantiated. You can still make everything all right. I'm a reasonable woman, Melek. I'm just asking you to meet me halfway."

Şanliurfa Province, Turkey
04:45 Local Time

By the time the bus attendant returns with a plastic pouch of rubbery yellow cake, day has just begun to break. Light enough to distinguish a white thread from a dark. Shaggy brown goats nibble the lichen off ruined stone walls. Villages are no more than silhouettes, the softness of dawn smudging their TV aerials and cell towers into misleading timelessness.

The archaeologist is fast asleep, so Penny stares out the streaked window. The violet clouds sizzle off, replaced by glaring heat. Penny can feel it through the glass. A scorcher.

Soon, Penny can make out sharp, tawny

cliffs in the distance, and the odd dusty concrete house.

At eight thirty, the bus wheezes to a halt at Mardin's new bus station. A long portico of bright red concrete arches contrasts weirdly with the bland white buses and parched concrete.

For a moment, nauseating dread skewers Penny to her seat like a pin through a beetle.

This is it.

Last night in Ankara, her choice felt obvious, even heroic. Here, now, in this unfamiliar landscape, the danger feels horribly real. This city out the window — flat roofs and golden stone, sky-needling minarets — looks nothing like modern concrete Ankara.

Only twenty miles away, at Mor Samuel, the Hashashin are holding Zach captive. She won't let herself believe he might be dead.

Her courage blazes back to life. If Zach's alive, he needs her.

Penny steps down from the bus, into the shimmering heat. It's like climbing inside a kiln. She's grateful for the thin shelter of her head scarf.

"Take care." The archaeologist shakes Penny's hand and exclaims at the sight of the blue evil eye bracelet on her wrist. "A *nazar boncuğu*! You know, the Hittites used to use a pair of bull's horns on the wall."

Penny smiles. "I guess a blue bead's easier to wear than a pair of bull's horns."

"Some places it's the color red, or a touching wood or iron, or a silver hand at your throat. We humans love our apotropaic devices."

"We could all use a little luck."

"That is a corruption of the folklore," says the archaeologist firmly. "The *nazar boncuğu* does not bring luck. It turns away the power of evil."

Penny shivers in the heat. *"Inşallah,"* she mumbles. God willing.

"Do you need to share a taxi?" asks the archaeologist. "It's not like Ankara here. Stupid men can get the wrong idea."

Penny points to Connor, who is climbing down from the bus. "I'm with my cousin."

"Good." The archaeologist looks relieved. "I'm having tea with the director of the museum at four. Not many foreign students come here anymore. If you're at the museum then, come knock on her office door. Ask for Lale." She retrieves a tiny, modern Swiss suitcase and vanishes in a taxi.

Connor hurries to Penny's side. He seems surprisingly cheery; evidently, he's one of nature's early birds. She smiles, squinting in the intense light. "Enjoy your first Turkish bus ride?"

"What's up with the mandatory midnight snack?"

"Are you saying you don't enjoy a lovely Nescafé at three a.m.?"

"I'm not sure I've ever had a *lovely* Nescafé." His smile fades. "Now. Our plan of attack." They head toward the ribbon of shade cast by a minibus parked nearby. "They're meeting us at the Recep teahouse, right near the Zinciriye, uh, *medrese.*" He uses the word for a religious school.

"We have about twenty minutes."

"Just in case." Connor presses five hundred-lira notes into her hand.

"What's this for?"

"If anything goes wrong, you run. Promise me?"

Penny starts to tuck the money in her pocket.

"Not there," Connor corrects. "Pickpockets."

Penny tucks the money into her bra strap. "Come on. Let's get a taxi."

The flat-roofed golden stone houses of Mardin rise up the slopes to a castle-crowned citadel where Turkish military helicopters perch like sleeping dragonflies. Penny and Connor's smoke-saturated taxi speeds uphill, trailing a plume of yellow dust. A white donkey staggers up the highway beside them, laden with an ugly nylon carpet and a dozen frozen chicken carcasses, wrapped in plastic. Penny cranes around to see. Who knew that there were still places on earth that looked like this?

She notices that Connor hasn't buckled his seat belt. He perches on his seat as if he were in a helicopter about to make a jump, hand hovering over the door handle. Penny doesn't have to ask why.

Most buildings she's seen in Ankara are cereal boxes of steel and grotty concrete. Mardin's default is ornately carved sandstone structures, no more than a couple of stories high. Even the light is golden. The whole place looks like a film set of exaggerated medieval exoticism, except for the very ordinary pastry shops, hardware stores, and schizophrenically colorful bridal-couture emporia that fill the ground floors. The people running errands and sipping tea don't look that different from Penny's less prosperous neighbors in Ankara, except that more of the women are wearing white head scarves and more of the men are stooped over backgammon boards.

This muted normality isn't the way she'd imagined a town twenty miles from a war zone. How can people go about their lives with a Hashashin stronghold just over the border? And what about the hundreds of thousands of refugees billeted in this province? They've been dying of heatstroke this summer, just as they died of exposure last winter, unable to work, unable to study, forbidden to leave.

As the taxi climbs the cobbles toward the historic center, where tour groups used to come when tour groups came here, Penny notices heaps of spices and baskets of Antep pistachios outside the buildings. The scene is eerily pretty. A spotless neon HALK BANK sign glows beneath a golden sandstone balustrade on the façade of what looks like a Renaissance palace. Outside, kids in knockoff boy-band T-shirts are wheedling their dad for Max Duo chocolate ice pops.

The taxi pulls up in front of an imposing medieval building with two fluted domes of golden stone. Beneath the intricately carved geometric muqarnas of the arched doorway, a toothless old man with a large key around his neck is thumbing a string of *tespih* beads.

"*İşte Zinciriye Medresesi,*" says the driver.

"There. Recep teahouse." Connor nods at a few plastic tables outside a cinder-block house beside the *medrese*. The teahouse seems to have an exclusively male clientele. Two bearded men in military-looking fa-

292

tigues and sunglasses are lounging at the table nearest the road. Their impassivity makes them conspicuous; they're so self-conscious it's almost ostentatious. They're the only men who aren't smoking, sipping, talking, or smiling. "That's got to be them."

Penny's voice comes out as a rasp. "No Zach."

"No surprise. They want to see what we've got to bargain with."

Penny looks at the fluted dome of the *medrese.* Years of skill and training and labor and devotion went into making that beautiful shelter for learning and faith. And across the road are actual terrorists, just sitting in a teahouse.

Suddenly, all the normalcy feels like a flimsy plastic shell around a live grenade.

"You're scared," says Connor.

Penny makes a face. "Of course I am."

"You don't have to do this."

"This is *my* plan." Penny hopes she sounds tough. "Besides, they've seen both of us. If I don't come now, it'll look suspicious." She reaches for the door handle.

"Hang on." Connor pulls the tie out of his pocket. "Got to look the part."

She glances up at him. "I guess you've been on lots of dangerous assignments?"

"Loads." He tries to knot the tie around

his neck. Penny can see his hands are trembling.

"Here." She reaches up to help him. "My grandpa taught me how."

"Essential skill." He's clearly suppressing a smile. But his hands are steady now.

"Where I come from, not so many guys wear ties." Penny hands the fare up to the front seat. "You should have seen the way the people in the Crazy Wisdom Tea Room stared at the Special Investigator guy when he turned up in a suit to interview me for my clearance."

Connor makes a face. "*Everything* about that sentence is wrong."

"*Dikkat edin,*" the driver warns as they climb out. "Be careful. You find some bad people at that teahouse."

The light hammers at Penny's eyes. The heat as they cross toward the teahouse is lung crushing. It must be every bit of 110 degrees.

"No sudden moves," says Connor quietly. "There's a sniper on the roof of the *medrese.*"

Penny's neck throbs. So much for neutral ground. "What do we do?"

"Keep walking."

Penny doesn't trust herself to speak.

The men in sunglasses don't get up as

they approach the plastic table.

"Good morning," says Connor, touching a hand to his chest. "Is one of you Al-Sadiq?"

One of the men in sunglasses, the florid-faced one with the reddish-blond neck beard, gestures at Penny. "You did not mention a woman." His accent sounds German.

"You didn't mention a sniper," says Connor.

Both of the men in sunglasses stand up. Each has a knife and gun strapped to his belt.

The stocky, black-bearded older one says, "Explain yourself." Penny can't place his accent. Not Turkish or Arab, for sure. Some kind of Central Asian — Uzbek, maybe? "You said you had serious information to sell." He takes stock of them. "You don't look serious to me."

"Let's all sit down," says Penny.

The two men act as if they didn't hear her.

"Why is *she* here?" demands the German. His pale, fleshy lower lip pouts out.

"We're only authorized to speak with Al-Sadiq," says Connor.

"Authorized?" The German's already sunburned cheeks go even redder.

"Jamal," says Blackbeard in a low, warning voice. He frowns at Connor. "I am Al-Sadiq."

"Your execution of Davut Mehmetoğlu did not go unnoticed," says Connor.

"I told you. They are spies from Dar al-Kufr!" Jamal's whisper is ragged with eager rage. He uses an old extremist slur for the West, "the land of the infidel." In his German accent, it sounds like a kind of liverwurst.

"We are negotiators," says Penny.

Al-Sadiq looks to Connor. "Is this true?"

Connor nods. "Like I wrote on ExciDox, our employers were impressed by the Embassy bombing."

Al-Sadiq nods.

"Which is why," Connor continues, "we're prepared to extend you an offer. Bombs can only do so much harm. We have information far more damaging to both America and Palamut's government in Turkey than any bomb. Enough to push America out of the peace process. Information we're prepared to share. If we can find the right people. And the right terms."

"That's why we're here," says Al-Sadiq.

"Then you'll negotiate?" Penny can tell Connor is trying not to sound excited.

"It depends what you have," says Al-Sadiq drily. "And what exactly you are asking in exchange."

"We're not asking much. Just Zachary Robson. Don't bother denying it," Connor adds, as Al-Sadiq starts to speak. "We know he's here."

"No deal!" Jamal evidently relishes his own growl. The beard makes it hard to tell, but Penny's beginning to doubt that he's even out of his teens. "We do not bargain with infidels!"

"My brother," Al-Sadiq tells him sharply, "be humble."

Jamal bows his head and mutters a penitent apology. *"Astaghfirullah."*

Al-Sadiq turns back to Connor. His voice is flat, almost deadpan. "A deal?"

Connor nods.

"Whom do you represent?"

"I'm not able to disclose."

Al-Sadiq points at Connor's PB pistol and asks something in what sounds like Russian.

Connor pats the gun, smiling slightly. "Interesting theory."

"That's not an answer," says Al-Sadiq.

Connor shrugs. "You're a smart guy. If we are what you think we are, would we confirm it?"

Al-Sadiq's eyes are alert. "Why are you speaking English?"

"You want to speak Chinese?"

"Why Zach Robson?"

"I'm not able to disclose."

"Then I'm not able to negotiate."

"Shame." Connor turns to Penny and says something in Russian. She makes out the word *taksi*. She nods solemnly.

"If Zach Robson is so valuable," says Al-Sadiq, "why should we give him up?"

Connor gives the sigh of the long-suffering middleman. "Robson has specific information of great value to my employer, but worthless to anyone else."

"Convenient," scoffs Al-Sadiq. "And you think we will take all this on faith? Your employers won't identify themselves. They sent us a pair of children. Why should we even speak to you?"

"We wanted to give you room to maneuver," says Penny. "If our employers came, the eyes of the world would be on you. But to us, you can speak plainly."

Al-Sadiq still won't look at her. He takes a step toward Connor. "How do we know Daesh did not send you? Now that the Hashashin grow strong, those *nawasib* pigs get jealous."

"Do we look like the kind of people Daesh would send?" says Connor.

"No," says Al-Sadiq. "You look like the

kind of people the Americans would send."

Penny crosses her arms. "If the Americans sent us, you'd already be dead."

Al-Sadiq stares at Connor. "I don't like games."

"Neither do we," says Connor. "Which is why we came alone. You can check the entire province. No tanks. No backup. No eyes watching us. We're here to play clean."

"We shall see." Al-Sadiq gives an order in accented Arabic. Jamal pulls out his cell and steps away from the table.

"May we sit down while we wait?" asks Connor.

Al-Sadiq frowns. "The woman, she sits apart."

With ill grace, Penny drags a plastic chair a couple of feet away from the table. It scrapes loudly across the ground.

When they're all seated, Al-Sadiq says, "I will need proof that you have something worth negotiating for."

"I could tell you about Operation Liberty Echo."

Al-Sadiq's only visible reaction is to sit a little straighter.

Connor presses his advantage. "Maybe we could discuss the little assassination last month in Sharjah. Or I could tell you that as of Monday's satellite images, you have three dozen trucks at the Tel Ismail camp. Or —"

"So you have been monitoring the Americans monitoring us," says Al-Sadiq coldly. "If that is all you have, we are done here."

"Let's stop wasting time," says Connor. "Take a good look at my colleague's face."

Al-Sadiq recoils. "We do not . . ."

"Just look."

Al-Sadiq waits a full thirty seconds. At last, he pushes his sunglasses down his nose. He glances sidelong at Penny, as if the sight of a female might burn his retinas.

Irritated, she pulls her head scarf down around her neck.

He stares. "That girl. From the picture. With the flag?" Al-Sadiq turns back to Connor. "They said that she was dead."

Penny crosses her arms. "I guess they lied."

Jamal hurries back to them, his belly jiggling as he runs.

"Yes?" asks Al-Sadiq.

"What the *kuffār* say is true, my brother. There is no one following them."

Jamal's got to be new, thinks Penny. He keeps shoehorning in unnecessary Arabic, trying too hard.

"Well?" says Connor.

"What exactly are you offering?" says Al-Sadiq.

"You guys like making movies, don't you?" Connor turns to Penny. "I hear she photographs great."

"And I talk, too," says Penny. "Anything that you want me to say."

"Is that all?" says Al-Sadiq.

"We will discuss terms with your commander," says Penny. "When you bring us Zach Robson."

Al-Sadiq scowls at Connor. "You should remind the woman that you are not in a position to make demands."

"We must verify that Zach Robson is still alive and in appropriate condition," says Penny. "Otherwise, we have nothing to discuss."

Connor shrugs. "She's right, Mr. Al-Sadiq."

"We will discuss this somewhere more private." Al-Sadiq rises to his feet and begins to walk away. Connor and Penny jump up as well.

"What about the bill?" says Penny. "For your Fanta?"

"Affedersiniz!" The owner of the teahouse, hastening toward them, clearly has similar ideas. "That's four lira."

Al-Sadiq's face registers pure contempt.

He just keeps walking toward the white Toyota Land Cruiser parked a hundred feet down the road.

An old man nursing a purple sumac şerbet says, in Turkish, "Come on, Anas. What's the point?"

"No," says the teahouse owner. "These assholes only do what they can get away with. You've got to draw a line." He raises his voice. "Come on. This isn't Syria. The bill's four lira."

Al-Sadiq doesn't break stride. "Jamal."

The young man beams and pulls out his gun.

The owner ducks just in time. The window behind him shatters.

"No!" cries Penny. "Stop!"

"Leave him," Connor urges Jamal. "We have more important things to do."

Jamal's arm slackens.

Penny exhales. Thank God.

Bang.

The old man's head hits the table in a spreading pool of blood and sugary purple sumac şerbet. The man called Anas runs shouting to his side.

On the roof of the *medrese,* the sniper lowers his gun.

"Come," orders Al-Sadiq.

Connor tugs Penny's arm.

She whispers, "But he . . ."

"Say a prayer for the old man," says Connor. "There's nothing else we can do."

"Anyone calls the police, and you will die!" shouts Jamal in Turkish.

"Leave them alone!" Penny's hands clench into fists.

"Think," whispers Connor. "You can't help Zach if you get shot!"

Numbly, Penny falls in beside him. They follow Al-Sadiq down the yellow-dust road.

A couple of bearded men sporting machine guns step out of the white Land Cruiser.

"Oh, no," whispers Connor.

Penny gives him a sharp look. "What?"

His voice is urgent. "Just don't resist, okay?"

"What?"

Someone pulls an empty onion sack over her head.

Mor Samuel Monastery, Al-Hasakah
   Governorate, Syria
09:07 Local Time

The long, narrow refectory of Mor Samuel monastery is as quiet as it is dark. The Hashashin aren't much for breakfast chitchat — and most of the garrison ate four hours ago, at five, after morning prayers. Flies buzz in the sticky shadow of a jar of *pekmez,* sweet grape molasses.

Now, only two men are seated at a corner of the monks' old marble refectory table.

Outside the door, out of earshot, stand four high school dropouts with AK-47s.

"Explain," says the bearded man.

"I've told you everything."

"What are they doing here?"

"How should I know?" Zachary Robson pushes a hand through his hair, a nervous gesture. They drill those easy tells out of you pretty fast at the Farm. He's slipping.

"The brothers wanted to send you to hell with Mehmetoğlu. Perhaps I made a mistake in stopping them."

"I told you I'm worth more alive. Do you think those two would be here if I weren't?"

"We shall see what the girl can tell us," says Faisal.

"No." Zach's deep voice is urgent, almost desperate. "Let me question her."

"Look at my hands." Faisal can't be more than thirty-five, but he has the hands of an old man: pale, twisted, scarred. "Phosphoric acid. I learned a lot from you people at Abu Ghraib. I don't need your help with an interrogation."

"Let me question her." Zach's low voice is coaxing. "She trusts me."

The bearded man's face is stony.

Flies buzz in the silence.

"Look." Zach leans forward across the stone table. "She's an intern. She doesn't know what she knows. You wouldn't even know what to ask her."

"What is that saying?" Faisal's mouth twists. "You kill more flies with honey than with vinegar."

"Catch. It's 'catch more flies.' "

"I'm out of patience, Mr. Robson." Faisal stands up. "She talks, or you die."

Zach's hand slams down.

The flattened fly is splayed against the stone.

Mardin, Turkey
09:20 Local Time

Invisible hands pull Penny's wrists behind her back and shove her into the backseat of the Toyota. She can feel the heat of bodies on either side of her — smell the clovey cologne, too. The motion of the car throws her back in the seat.

Where are they going?

"Mr. Al-Sadiq!" Connor's muffled voice, on her left, is surprisingly controlled, but she can hear his anger. "Is this really necessary?"

Al-Sadiq's voice from the front of the

vehicle: "You come with us, you come on our terms."

"We're here to negotiate," splutters Penny, as self-righteously as she can manage through a faceful of cloth.

There's the dull thwack of a fist into a stomach, and a groan from Connor. Penny hunches forward, head throbbing again. The rough fiber grates against the cuts on her face. The money Connor entrusted to her is prickly under the left shoulder strap of her bra. Car sickness is boiling up. She thinks of the old man facedown in blood and purple sumac şerbet. Is there someone who loves him waiting for him to come home from that teahouse?

Concentrate on Zach, she tells herself. Al-Sadiq speaks in terse Arabic, apparently into his phone. No one else makes a sound.

Terror strips Penny of her sense of time. She can feel the Toyota rattling downhill, driving level, and then climbing upward again. Has it been five minutes? Half an hour? More?

A sudden splatter of gunshots. The crunch of punctured glass.

"Türkischen Soldaten!" cries Jamal.

This must be the Turkish border blockade.

Frantic hands shove Penny's shoulders down.

Someone next to her in the Toyota starts firing back, the breathless chink-and-sputter of a machine gun, intolerably loud.

Penny's unprotected eardrums feel like they're going to pop. She struggles, every muscle braced. "What's happening?"

The Toyota accelerates over bumpy ground, racing away from the sound of bullets. Another round of blasts beside her. She can hear the men breathing heavily.

The Toyota slopes down and over what feels like a bumpy dirt road. No light visible through the cloth. Cooler. A tunnel?

"Okay," says Al-Sadiq's voice. "Fast!"

Back up into daylight. A hand grabs Penny by the scruff of the neck and hauls her back up onto the seat.

Without warning, the Toyota rockets uphill. Penny hears shouts, and the squeak of hinges. Then, just as suddenly, the Toyota comes to an abrupt stop. With no seat belt to hold her back, Penny slams blindly into the back of the driver's seat. Hands pull her back, then outside into the unfiltered heat. They release her wrists, and she yanks off the sack. At first she still can't see; it's like staring into a white spotlight. Her cuts burn; that antibiotic ointment wore off a long time ago. The blue head scarf slips down around her neck like a heavy winter shawl; hot wind ruffles her jagged bangs. She squints around at the wide and ancient-looking courtyard, packed with a barracks' worth of men in various stages of battle dress. Around her rise sun-soaked walls of saffron-colored stone. The bullet-freckled Toyota is parked beside that unmistakable hexagonal tower.

They are inside Mor Samuel monastery.

Syria.

"Penny!" Connor is right next to her, thank goodness. Sweat streaks his face; his skin is blotchy with the first signs of heatstroke. His hands are knotted behind his back, with what looks like Liza's guitar-string garrote.

She grabs his arm. "They hit you?"

"Not that hard. But they took my gun, my wallet — everything. They frisk you, too?"

"Yeah. But they missed the money."

He cracks a grin.

"Who was shooting at us?" she asks.

"I'm guessing a Turkish government patrol." He glances up. "What the —"

Penny follows his gaze to a dark gray long-tailed aircraft nesting at the base of the hexagonal tower. "The plane?"

"Helicopter. Looks like some kind of modified Apache, but without the doors." His forehead wrinkles. "How'd the Hashashin afford a fifteen-million-dollar bird like that?"

Three tanks hulk near the courtyard wall. There's been a bonfire here; scorch marks still blacken the paving stones. Charred fragments of gilded, lapis-painted vellum flutter in the dust like candy wrappers. How many centuries did these manuscripts survive until the Hashashin rolled up here in their SUVs? The men doing target practice are using what looks like a mannequin in black monks' robes. But mannequins don't bleed.

Jamal starts to haul Connor in one direction, while two unfamiliar men grab Penny's arms.

"What do you think you're doing?" Connor objects, trying to sound commanding while in a choke hold.

Penny twists and kicks. "We're here to negotiate!"

"You said you came alone." Al-Sadiq's manner is markedly less civil. "So why were we attacked?"

"I don't know," says Connor. "Maybe the Turkish armed forces don't like you invading their territory and shooting people in broad daylight?"

Penny twists around, trying to look Al-Sadiq in the face. "We demand to speak with your commander immediately."

Al-Sadiq gives an order in Arabic. Four men grab Connor. Two more pull the onion sack back down over Penny's head. She kicks and bites and writhes. It has no effect whatsoever.

"Get off!" she can hear Connor shouting, from farther away. "Penny?"

"I'm here! Connor? Connor!"

Hands shove Penny forward, into an echoing place, where the air is colder and smells musty, like the used-book store near U of M where she works weekends during the semester.

She struggles. "Hey, watch your hands, you son of a —"

A creak of hinges, a shove on her shoulders, and she falls down a flight of stone stairs.

She rolls onto the floor, bruised and gasping on the cold, dusty stone.

She yanks the onion sack off again, in time to see the heavy door slam shut at the top of the staircase.

"Come back here!" she roars.

The lock clicks.

"Connor!" she screams. *"Connor!"*

No answer.

Penny pushes herself up onto her knees.

In the dim fluorescent glow, hundreds of

skulls stare back at her from their stone arches. The bones of ten thousand Syriac martyrs are crammed like scrolls into the shelves.

The monastery crypt.

Against the far wall, barely visible in the gloom, a dark-haired figure in jeans and a polo shirt sprawls on the floor as if he's too weak to get up.

"My God," Zach rasps. "Penny?"

29
WHAT YOU WISH FOR

"I don't believe it." Zach Robson shoves himself upright.

Penny kneels beside him, throat so tight she can hardly speak.

Zach reaches out. "They said you were dead —"

"They wish."

He pulls her into a tight hug and doesn't let go. "What in God's name are you doing here?"

"I wasn't about to let them kill you."

"Little miss tough guy." He leans back, hands on her shoulders. "You gonna translate all the Hashashin to death?"

"Something like that."

Zach's eyes crinkle in a real laugh. Except for a day's dark stubble and a few half-clotted gashes on his arms, he looks almost sleek, compared to her sore, travel-stained, felt-haired grunginess. He is remarkably un-flustered. But then, Penny tells herself, he's a professional.

She frowns. "They didn't tie you up?"

"You neither." His smile dies out. "The walls are four feet thick."

"Oh." Penny feels sick.

"Who's Connor? The one you were shouting for?"

"He's another officer from —" She hesitates. After all, he never actually told her. "From where you really work."

"Ah." Zach freezes. "They told you."

"You could've trusted me, Zach."

"It was too dangerous." He brushes the bangs from her face. His voice is softer, as if they were back in Ankara, back on the sun-warmed stone of the citadel. "I had to protect you."

"Zach." Penny meets his eyes. "What the hell is going on?"

"I can't talk." He casts a wary glance up at the door. "Not here. They're always listening."

"But, Zach . . ."

"It's just you and Connor?" he whispers. "They didn't send anyone else?"

"We . . ." She can explain later. Priorities. "It's just us."

Zach lowers his voice. "How the hell did you find me?"

"I saw the photo of what they did to Da-

313

vut Mehmetoğlu. We took a guess you'd be here, too."

Zach shakes his head. "They made me watch the beheadings," he says hoarsely. "Just stand and watch. I've never felt so goddamned useless in my life."

"Beheadings." Penny stands up so fast she gets dizzy. "Oh my God. Connor —"

He grabs her wrists. "Penny, calm down —"

"Zach, what if they . . . if they —"

"They're not going to kill him. You just got here. He hasn't even been interrogated yet —"

As if on cue, the door drags open.

Two heavy silhouettes against the light.

The guards throw a man's lanky body down the stairs.

30
QUESTIONS

"Connor!" Penny runs to him.

Connor curls on the stone floor. "I'm fine," he croaks.

"Yeah, just peachy." Penny kneels beside him, unknots the thin wire cord around his wrists, and helps him sit up. His left eye is already swelling. Bright blood stains his mouth and chin like a face-paint pirate beard. His shirt is smeared with dirt, and his necktie has been torn off.

"You okay?" he wheezes.

"Better than you." She takes off her blue-jean jacket and wipes blood off his face. "What happened?"

"Jamal and about twelve of his buddies started kicking me around, screaming questions. But then Al-Sadiq came and hollered at them, and" — Connor gestures, grimacing — "voilà." He eyes the skull-crowded arches. "Where's Count Dracula?"

"The name's Zach Robson." Zach

crouches down next to Penny. "And you're Connor . . . ?"

"Beauregard." Connor shakes his hand. "The way Penny talks about you, I was expecting Sean Connery."

"You should see me in white tie."

Connor doesn't laugh. "We've got a few questions."

"I've got a few myself."

"Careful." Penny lays a hand on Connor's arm. "Everything's bugged."

"Al-Sadiq speaks English plenty well." Connor rolls the thin wire cord around his hand like wool. "Why not just interrogate both of us right away?"

Zach looks up the stairs. "I'm sure they'll come back soon."

Penny swallows. "What happens when they do?"

Silence.

"We've got to get out of here," she whispers.

Zach shakes his head. "How?"

"Connor," says Penny. "Didn't you say your dad taught you to fly helicopters?"

"Hold your horses. Just because I know my way around a helo doesn't mean I can fly an *Apache*!"

Penny looks up the dark stairs to the light leaking under the door. "If we could just get back to the courtyard, we'd have a chance."

"We don't even know if that bird's fueled," says Connor. "If we even got that far. You saw how many Hashashin were in that courtyard."

"So we wait here to be beheaded?" she demands.

Connor squares his shoulders. "If you can get me in that cockpit, I'll give it my best shot."

"That's mighty heroic, cowboy," says Zach. "But the door is locked. The guards up there have semiautomatics. What have we got?"

Penny stands up. "Nothing to lose."

31
TURNED

Langley, Virginia
02:30 Local Time
The offices at the Original Headquarters Building on CIA's campus are as muggy as the inside of a rice cooker. Christina's office is white-green under the fluorescent lights. She sent most of her team home around midnight, but some of them refused to leave. Taylor, at her desk outside Christina's office, has munched her way through a tub of yogurt raisins and soaked most of a pack of Kleenex, watching the phone.

"Ma'am!" Taylor's ponytail swings around the edge of the door. "There's been a shooting in Mardin. Hashashin."

Christina tenses. "Mor Samuel?"

Taylor is breathless. "No, in the town center, but —"

"Are we talking dozens? Hundreds?"

"Just one guy —"

"AmCit?"

"Turkish, but —"

"*Turkish?*" Christina fixes her with an exasperated glare. "Taylor, you can log the little stuff without wasting my —"

"The witnesses described two foreigners at the scene with the Hashashin. Civilians, a young man and a woman, speaking English. The media doesn't seem to have picked up on it yet — it wasn't in the public police reports. No ID on the woman — we're guessing she's a local. But the description of the guy sounds exactly like Connor."

Christina sits very straight and very still. Her voice is quiet. "Incredible."

"So maybe he's got a lead to Zach Robson!"

"If it's him." Christina fixes Taylor with a laser stare. "Keep this strictly compartmented. We don't want to raise false hope. Any leads on the woman?"

"Not yet, ma'am," says Taylor brightly, "but I put in a request to Turkish intelligence."

"You *what*? On what authority?"

"Connor needs all the help we can send! I can call Incirlik. We can get planes, tanks, coordinate with Ankara —"

"Out of the question." Christina glances at Elastigirl. "We have no secure comms with him. The Hashashin could pick up on

319

anything we send. If it *is* Connor, we'd be signing his death warrant." She pauses. "There's something else. I wanted to substantiate first — I don't believe in tarnishing a good officer's name. But you deserve to know."

Taylor looks scared. "Ma'am?"

Christina sighs. "I have new intel from State indicating that shortly before his disappearance, Connor was behaving — suspiciously."

"Suspiciously?"

"To be perfectly candid, they think he may have turned."

"Connor?" Taylor blanches.

"And now, if he's gone rogue and run off to contact Zach Robson, there can be little doubt . . ."

"Ma'am, there must be some mistake. Connor would never —"

Christina gives Taylor a hard look. "It's never easy to realize how little we know the people closest to us."

32
NOTHING TO LOSE

Mor Samuel Monastery
10:18 Local Time

From beneath the earth, below the door of the monastery crypt, comes a man's howl of rage. A shattering crunch, as thousands of dry bones splinter against stone.

The two guards stationed outside the locked door of the crypt exchange glances.

Another man starts shouting, an ugly, furious bellow. Flesh punches into flesh. A woman screams.

One of the guards unlocks the crypt door and pulls it open. His companion stands poised behind him, gun at the ready.

In the beam of dusty daylight, the dark-haired prisoner stands over the bloodied blond one, fist raised. Broken skeletons are splayed around the floor, flotsam of their fight.

"Stop!" roars the guard in accented English. "Commander Faisal wants them alive!"

Heedless, the dark-haired man grips a femur and raises it over the fair one's head.

The guard, a heavyset Belgian, plunges halfway down the stairs.

The second guard steps into the doorway, Walther P99 raised.

From where she crouches near the door, Penny rears up out of the shadows. She wraps her hands around his knees and shoves him down the stairs.

With a shout, the first guard turns around. But Connor tackles him.

The second guard struggles to his feet with a strangled shout. He grasps for the trigger of his gun.

Penny leaps from the top of the staircase. She topples the guard to the ground, knocking the wind out of both of them and ripping open the knees of her leggings. Zach wrests the guard's gun away and smashes the grip across the man's face.

Connor is still grappling with the first guard. They slam into a rack of skulls, and bones crunch down around them. The guard lands a punch in Connor's gut. Connor staggers back, as if he's about to fall. The guard closes the gap, fist raised. Connor surges forward, grabs the guard by the shirt, and hurls him into the stone wall. The guard slumps like a scarecrow.

Penny is flushed, dizzy with the airless heat. Connor and Zach stand panting for a moment.

Zach checks the tiny round witness holes bored into the Walther 99's magazine. "Eight rounds left."

Connor examines the other guard's gun. "Same."

Zach grins. "A whole lot better than nothing."

"Sixteen bullets?" Penny shakes her head. "There are hundreds of Hashashin. The only way we're getting out of here alive is brains. Not guns."

Zach locks the magazine back into place. "Why not both?"

They climb the stairs, up into the light of a high, circular room. Zach turns the lock in the crypt door behind them.

The fifteen-hundred-year-old walls rise around them, smooth concentric circles of ancient golden stone. Hot white sun pours down from a single oculus, staring open to the sky in the center of the ancient dome.

Penny breathes in the library scent she'd smelled before. This must have been a church once, but now the only furnishings are rows of bookshelves, dozens of them, dark with that dim gloss ebony gets after a few centuries of careful tending. They're empty of everything but streaks of dust, where the contents have been pulled from the shelves.

A library without books.

Connor walks silently to the door and peers out through the keyhole.

"Can you see the helicopter?" whispers Penny.

"It's a different courtyard. A little one with an olive tree."

"The main courtyard is on the other side of the library," says Zach.

Connor leans away from the door. "There are at least a dozen guys out there. We'll never make it."

"If you distract them, Penny and I might make it to the next building."

"Thanks, but no thanks." Connor scowls. "Even if it worked, there would still be shots. The whole camp would come running. And even if you made it, who's going to fly the helo?"

Penny grabs one of the bookshelves. It must be every ounce of a hundred pounds. She heaves it a few inches toward the center of the room. Wood squeals across the stone floor.

Zach crosses his arms. "I've heard of rearranging deck chairs on the *Titanic,* but . . ."

Penny points upward. "We can reach the oculus if we stack them like a pyramid."

"A pyramid?" echoes Connor.

"We can climb across the roof." Penny leans against the side of the bookshelf, using her weight to shift it another few inches. It gives a resentful creak. She shoves harder. "It won't make so much noise if we all lift it." She tips the shelf gently over, staggering in an attempt to muffle the crack as it hits the stone floor. She wipes her forehead. Her hand comes away red. Blood is pumping again from the cut on her scalp.

Connor grabs the other end of the bookshelf. "Let's shove that one over here. Then we can lift another one on top."

"CIA Movers," Zach drawls. " 'We cover your assets.' "

Penny grits her teeth and grinds the second bookshelf toward the center of the room. "You want to help?"

A few minutes later, twenty feet up and kneeling on a pyramid of shelves, Penny grips the rim of the oculus and pulls herself up into the searing sunlight. She squints. "I can see the main courtyard."

Zach, one bookshelf down, glances back at the door. "We've got to hurry. They'll be back any minute."

"Come on, then." Penny grabs Zach's hand and helps him up beside her. It feels good to have him close.

Zach peers out at the helicopter and ducks back down. "That's just a two-seater!"

Connor hoists himself up on Penny's left. "The pilot station's in the back." He sounds clipped and startlingly assured. "You two go for the gunner's seat, in front. Robson, you ever have any missile training?"

"We had an Xbox in my prep-school common room," deadpans Zach. "If I played any more *Apache Death Ultra,* the Air Force would've owed me a medal."

"Lucky us," says Connor drily.

"The wall looks rough enough to climb down," says Penny. "We can hide behind the tank —"

Connor nods. "We wait for all three of us to reach the ground. Then we run. And then we pray."

"I'll go first." Penny grabs the rim of the oculus.

"Like hell you will!" says Zach.

"No," seconds Connor. "You have no training!"

"Exactly. I'm the expendable one!" She jabs Connor in the chest. "*You're* the one who can fly the helicopter. And you" — she puts a hand on Zach's arm — "*you're* the one with the information. So if anyone is going to get shot, it's going to be me!"

Zach grabs her wrist. "You are *not* expendable."

"Then I better not get shot."

Before either of them can say anything more, she heaves herself upward and pulls both her scabby knees up onto the hot stone.

She inches down the golden slope of the dome. In the main courtyard below, the helicopter sits only about fifty feet away, just at the base of the hexagonal tower. On the left, half a dozen teenagers are still doing target practice. At least they're facing the other wall, except for German Jamal, who is drilling them. A few more Hashashin, older guys, are hanging out around the Toyota beside the helicopter, joshing as the one in the black T-shirt rinses it off with a hose and a bucket of suds.

Penny loops her feet onto the outside wall and begins to climb down.

Ouch ouch ouch.

Her muscles haven't forgiven her for yesterday. Penny sets her teeth and hooks her toes into the cracks between the crumbly blocks of stone. She can only hold her fingers in one spot for a few seconds before they start to burn.

Laughter across the courtyard.

Penny freezes halfway down the wall, legs cramping, stone grit like cracker crumbs under her fingernails.

One stray glance and she's dead.

The guy in the black T-shirt spritzes water at his buddies. They laugh like kids around a sprinkler.

Penny inches another foot down the wall. Muscles she didn't know she had are twanging in her back.

The guy in the black T-shirt turns the hose on a white cat dozing in the sun. A yowl, more laughter. Assholes.

Penny lets go.

She hits the ground with a small billow of yellow dust.

Out of sight.

She crouches in the dusty shade beneath a parked tank, shaking slightly, every muscle throbbing, too-tight leggings cutting into her knees. Sweat stings like poison ivy in her cuts.

Gasoline reeks in the dry heat, even across the courtyard.

Connor drops down beside her, panting slightly and pasty with stone dust.

Penny squints up at the empty wall. "Where's Zach?"

"Your guy is smarter than he looks."

"Help!" Zach's voice bellows from inside the library, with the theatrical resonance of an operatic tenor. *"Help! GUARDS!"*

The Hashashin doing target practice don't turn. Of course not — they're wearing ear-guards. But the ones by the Toyota run inside.

Penny looks back up at the wall just in time to see Zach land.

Connor hisses, "Go!"

And she runs.

For the first three seconds, it's way too easy.

The sun blazes like a spotlight. Connor runs steadily to her left. Zach barrels forward on her right, pulling slightly ahead. Faster, faster, and they're halfway across the dusty stone.

Jamal's astonished voice cries, *"Zach?"*

"Go!" howls Connor, and shoves Penny forward.

Zach hoists himself into the front seat of the helicopter. "Penny, run!"

The firing squad turns in disarray. Jamal is screaming orders; he's grabbed a rifle. Four Hashashin are running toward them.

They'll never make it to the helicopter.

Penny grabs the bucket of suds and swings it wide.

Soapy water splashes the Hashashin in the eyes.

Jamal howls, firing blindly.

Connor screams, *"Run!"*

Penny's got one foot up on the helicopter.

A drum roll of cracking gunshots.

Penny cries, "Connor!"

Dust explodes like fireworks around her feet. Connor's sure hands shove her up to safety. She turns to help him follow.

His face is ashen. Blood streaks down his right hand, his gun knocked out of reach.

Penny grabs his left arm and helps haul him up. They collapse together into the narrow pilot's seat.

"Get down behind the windshield!" cries Zach from the gunner's seat. "It's bulletproof!"

A hailstorm of bullets against glass. Penny fights the instinct to duck.

Connor is panting as if he just finished a marathon. The cotton of his right sleeve is soaking red to the elbow. He grimaces, lip curling up over his gums.

"Oh my God." Penny presses her scarf to his arm, trying to stanch the blood.

Zach howls, "Take us up!"

Jamal and the four soaked, running Hashashin are fifty feet away. They veer toward the right. Without even a door to shut, there will be no protection against their bullets.

Connor grits his teeth. "It's gonna take a minute to get off the ground!" The lines across his forehead are deep with pain.

"Buy time!" Penny screams to Zach.

"Machine gun doesn't work without the engine!"

"So use your pistol!" Cradling his right hand, Connor stretches out his left and flicks a couple of switches.

Nothing happens.

"It's stuck in the fucking seat belt!" Zach tries to wrestles the Walther out. "Jesus fucking —"

"Zach, hurry!" screams Penny.

"We've got the fuel!" Frantic, left hand shaking, Connor tries again. *Rattle-snap.* "Why isn't it working?"

The Hashashin are twenty feet away.

The windshield is starting to fracture.

Bulletproof glass is only reinforced with polycarbonate. Shoot it enough, and it's just funny-looking shards.

Jamal howls as the Hashashin fan toward the open sides of the helicopter.

And in that moment, Penny realizes.

They're going to die.

33
DUST AND AIR

Gun raised, Jamal meets Penny's eyes. He aims and screams —

Nothing that she can hear.

The rising, high-pitched chain-saw buzz of two engines makes Penny's teeth vibrate in her jaw.

A sputtering round of explosions from the helicopter's machine gun.

Zach gives a whoop of triumph.

All five Hashashin are flat on the ground. Jamal was closest. Penny can see his limp flesh and wispy beard smoking by a puddle of red-laced gray. There's nothing left of his face. She feels like she's going to throw up.

Connor is struggling with the controls.

"Your hand!" she cries. "You can't drive!"

"I got the foot pedals and the cyclic!" Connor loops his right shoulder through one of the safety straps and grabs the joystick that rises from the floor. "But you're gonna have to steer the collective grip!"

Penny hooks her left arm through the other safety strap and clicks the seat belt around both of them. Squashed up against Connor, she can feel his chest shudder as he hyperventilates. Her eyes race across the control panel. Two large, flickering screens. What looks like a tiny, old-fashioned computer. Dials. Meters. Levers. Switches. Flashing lights. Buttons, dozens of them, enough to give a DJ a heart attack.

"The *what*?"

"The collective! That one!" Even with his mouth two inches away, she can hardly make out Connor's words over the screaming engines.

Penny wraps her sweaty hand around the large, button-studded, heat-sticky joystick-looking lever on her left. Through the windshield, she can see about two dozen armed Hashashin pounding toward them from the arched doorways around the courtyard. "What does it do?"

"Cyclic steers us backwards, forwards, sideways. Collective takes us up!" He jerks the rotors into life. They warm up sleepily, like an old ceiling fan. *Whup-whup-whup.* Connor digs a neatly folded Kleenex out of his pocket. "Grab the headset — hold it up so we can both hear! Stuff this in your other ear!"

The rotor blades are huge — they must be at least twenty feet apiece. Each quickening rotation slashes shadows across the cockpit like an accelerating strobe light.

Even through the tissue and the headset, Penny hears a rattle of machine-gun fire from the front, as Zach blasts the approaching Hashashin. The survivors stagger backward in the dusty blast of air as the rotors spin into high speed.

"Now?" Penny shouts.

Connor's left hand skims over the controls. "When I say go, pull up!"

"They're getting in the tank!" Zach's voice crackles back through the headset.

"Hold fire!" screams Connor. "We have to take off!" He grabs the cyclic. "Penny, *go!*"

Penny yanks up the collective grip.

The cockpit takes a sharp, nauseating stutter. It feels like being in a Ferris wheel pod in a high wind.

Then the helicopter lurches up into the free air. Wind rushes through the cockpit, getting colder as the ground falls away. They soar higher, up above the hexagonal tower, higher and higher, until Mor Samuel monastery is no more than a golden sandcastle beneath them.

Penny hears herself scream, "We did it!"

Connor's grin reaches almost to his ears.

"Woo hoo!" crackles through the headphones. Zach sounds as jubilant as Penny's ever heard him.

Penny spots a flash like a firework in the tiny courtyard. Half a dozen bright dots soar above the hexagonal tower, zinging up toward them. "What's that?"

"Pull up!" bellows Connor. He jerks the cyclic sideways. Penny yanks up on the collective grip.

Over the howling whir of the engines, the explosions sound like no more than a series of faint Rice Krispies pops.

Then, one bright blur explodes two feet from the left side of the helicopter. The blast of hot air scalds Penny's leg as Connor swerves the helicopter to the left. She drags up on the collective, and the helicopter rattles up another couple hundred feet.

"Hover!" Zach's voice shreds through the headphones.

"What?" yells Penny.

"Are you *nuts*?" Connor pitches the helicopter into a leftward lunge to duck another volley of bright fire. "We gotta get out of here!"

"Hover!" growls Zach. Penny can hear a series of electronic beeps through the headphones. "I'm gonna Hellfire those bastards!"

A blast barely misses the propellers.

"Target the tank!" yells Connor.

Penny hears a clank of metal below the left-hand side of the cockpit as Zach initializes the launch.

The helicopter lurches backward as the Hellfire missile blasts down toward the tank.

She sees tiny figures fan out around the courtyard, racing for shelter.

Not fast enough.

Even from a thousand feet up, Penny feels the blast resound in her skull.

A circle of fire and black smoke blooms where the tank used to be.

Zach whoops. "Score one for the good guys!"

"Celebrate later," shouts Connor. "Let's get out of here!"

Suddenly, Penny feels the Apache swerve backward again as a second Hellfire roars down.

A second later the library dome implodes.

Connor looks confused; sweat runs down his neck. "What the hell are you doing?"

"That's for our Embassy!" screams Zach.

"That's enough," yells Connor. "We might need the rockets later!"

"It's kill or be killed!" Zach fires one of the smaller rockets. Then another, then another, then another, pummeling the old monks' quarters. Acrid gray and black smoke streaks upward.

"Zach, no," Penny yells, coughing as the fumes reach her. "The monks. There could be hostages inside!"

Zach stops. She can hear him breathing raggedly. But it's too late. One of the rockets must have hit the munitions storeroom. The huge white blast rocks the helicopter. With a terrible scraping boom, the golden hexagonal tower collapses in a rock fall of shattered stone.

Connor slams forward on the cyclic. The seat belt digs into Penny's stomach as the helicopter roars out over the dry yellow plain. Wind eddies around her. This seat was only meant for one person — what if the buckle isn't strong enough to hold? The speedometer spins up over 180 miles per hour.

"Get a grip," Connor shouts to Zach. "You think the Turkish air force didn't notice your little show? The Syrians? The Russians? They'll blow us out of the sky!"

"Just radio air-traffic control!" Zach's voice crackles.

Connor rolls his eyes. "And say what?"

"Say we're Americans."

"Hi, we're a couple of CIA illegals and a girl everybody knows is dead. We just stole a helicopter and blew up a monastery. Everyone in DC's gonna say they never heard of us. But don't shoot us down, guys, okay?" Connor turns to Penny. "We're gonna dive."

Penny's teeth are rattling in her jaw. "Die?"

"Dive!"

They plummet toward an olive grove.

"Pull up, pull up! Jesus!" Connor is panting. "Try for a hundred feet! Stay below the peak of the hill!"

For a few minutes, they roller-coaster up and down, over dry fields and dry riverbeds. None of them has the breath to speak.

"We're back in Turkish airspace," yells Connor. "At least now there's only *one* air force that can shoot us down."

Over the roar of the engine, Penny can just make out Zach's "Now what?"

"I turned off the transponder," Connor shouts. "Our best chance is to keep off the radar. Fly as low as possible over deserted areas and pray to God some farmer doesn't spot us."

"How much fuel do we have?" Penny asks. Her throat is getting hoarse with all the shouting.

"In theory, we can go almost three hours. But if anybody's radar picks us up —"

"Then what?"

Connor shakes his head. "The Turks take down Russian bombers." The wind flattens his hair against his scalp. "If they clock us, we're dead."

"We have to tell the whole world we're alive," says Penny. "But first we've got to get somewhere safe — somewhere public."

"The NATO Summit in Istanbul starts tonight!" shouts Zach.

"We've got about five hundred and fifty miles in us," Connor yells back. He turns to Penny. "I say we head straight for Istanbul!"

Penny quickly calculates. "That's eight hundred miles."

"So we get as close as we can and nab some ground transport." Connor suddenly notices the Apache's trajectory. "Penny, watch it! We're getting over the line of sight!"

Penny slowly lowers the collective grip. The helicopter rattles down toward the parched earth. Connor holds his wounded hand above his head; a slower trickle of blood runs down his wrist.

Penny reaches out. "Your hand —"

Connor looks almost green. "Can't do anything until we land."

Even racing at 180 miles an hour, the rushing air feels oven hot. The relentless glare of the sun and the strobing shadows of the rotors are giving Penny a fierce headache. It's harder than it looks to hold the helicopter at a steady height. The machine is fighting her. Ten feet up they zag, then lurch ten feet down again.

"Don't trim our toenails!"

"I'm not doing it on purpose!"

"Relax your grip!" Connor shouts.

"What are you talking about?" Penny yells back. "I've never *been* so relaxed!"

Connor cracks a smile.

They're low enough that Penny can make out individual goats and the odd scrubby tree. The sun has a killing Midas touch: dry golden plants, dry golden fields, dry golden dust in the curling wind, dry golden stones of ruined huts that could have been abandoned fifty years ago or five hundred or five.

The miles blur. Hills bubble and recede into the dust. Farms and villages appear in the distance, and Connor veers around them. Penny tries to concentrate on nothing but the vibrating collective grip, and keeping the helicopter from bucking. The scream of the motors and roar of the rotors drown out all thought.

The smell of the air changes — something fresh and alive.

"What's that river?" Connor shouts.

Penny checks the monitor. "Fırat Nehri." Her heart does a strange lurch. Last time she heard that name was in Archaeology class in Ann Arbor, with fourteen inches of snow on the windowsill. "The Euphrates!"

Sharp cliffs plunge into bright water that glints and tumbles below the helicopter. The river stretches out into pale greens on the sloping opposite bank. Goats graze among the rocks. Penny feels a pang of longing as it vanishes.

Soon they're in the mountains. Penny lets the helicopter fly as low between the jagged rocks as she dares. Connor maneuvers them through the valleys, swaying to dodge the occasional grove of pines. Glancing at Connor, Penny notices that his milky skin is blistered red with sunburn, even up the part in his hair. She can feel her nose and cheeks starting to sting.

But it's not just sun. It's dust.

Churned up by the propellers, it fills the cracks in the windshield. Grit blasts their eyes, burning, blinding.

"Take us up!" Connor coughs. "We'll brownout!"

"We can't take the hill," chokes Zach. "Radar will pick us up if we go that high!"

"It's that or crash!"

They climb up to nine hundred feet, over the hill.

Clear lines of sight radiate in every direction. They're horribly exposed.

As soon as they're over the peak, Penny yanks them down. They can't have been visible on the radar for more than forty-five seconds. "You think they spotted us?"

Connor makes a face. "We'll find out."

They fly on. Once in a while, Zach's voice crackles through the earphones, prompting them ever farther north and west, into a pale volcanic landscape hollowed by the wind into lunar curves. They loop southwest around the foothills of Mount Erciyes. The mountain shrinks behind them as they speed over farms and dry valleys.

"No sign of any company." Connor looks at the monitor. "We should be safe for now."

Zach's faint, distorted voice scratches in Penny's ear: "We're coming up on Cappadocia!"

She shouts back, "Almost halfway." She feels Connor gasp. "What?" She follows his gaze to the radar screen. Fear twists in her stomach. "What are those dots?"

Connor grimaces. "Say hello to the Turkish air force."

"Just tell them who we are!" screams Zach through the earphones. "They can't murder

American diplomats in cold blood."

Connor wrestles with the transponder. "It won't turn back on."

Penny's hands shake. "They're gaining."

"This is an unmarked attack helicopter," Zach yells. "If we don't contact them, they'll blow us up!"

Connor's voice is surreally calm. "Penny, you see the parachute pack clipped to the ceiling? I want you to take it down and put it on. Robson, you ever jumped before?"

"In the Bahamas. Once!"

"Then you know what to do."

"Jump at a hundred and fifty feet?" Zach's voice comes through. "We'll die!"

Connor pulls the mouthpiece close. "Just do it."

Penny reaches up with her right hand and undoes the clasp. The harness is heavier than she expected. "There's only one!"

"Put your arms through the straps."

"No!" Penny yells. "What about you?"

"Most parachutes can take two people."

"Most?"

"Hurry!"

Penny shuffles the straps over her shoulders and slides her legs through the harness.

"Loosen the chest strap as much as you can."

On the screen, six dots draw closer.

"What now?" Penny yells.

Connor twists, so his back is to her. "Help me get my arms through the straps."

She hugs her arms around him, trying to fasten the harness around his chest. "I can't — quite —"

"Too tight." He takes a deep breath. "Unbuckle it and help me get my arms out."

"No!"

"The buckle's gonna snap," he yells. "We'll both die!"

"They're five minutes away," screams Zach. "What the hell are you doing?"

"Connor," Penny shouts, suddenly remembering. "Liza's cord! Is it still in your pocket?" She pulls out the thin steel cord and wraps it around the weak buckle, over and over, tight as she can.

"Penny, when I say go, you take us up as fast as you can." Connor shouts into the mouthpiece. "Robson. Are you set?"

Zach croaks, "You're crazy!"

"Are you ready?"

"Yes!"

The dots are drawing nearer.

"Penny, go!"

She yanks up on the collective grip. The air slams down at them as the helicopter soars up one, two thousand feet. Her ears pop as the dusty valley spreads beneath them. The dots on the radar race closer.

"On count of three, Robson!" screams Connor. "One, two, *now*!"

Zach leaps from the plane, his dark hair whipping wildly.

Penny gulps.

"Hold the grips." Connor undoes the seat buckle. "I'm gonna put the helo in hold. Face my back and lock your hands around my chest. You won't hear me without the earphones. Just jump with me when I squeeze your hand. Feet up when we get near the ground! And, Penny?" he catches her eye. "I'm sorry about that aspirin."

"Don't die," she shouts.

"I won't if you won't!"

Penny pulls off the earphones. The noise is physically painful. She hangs on to Connor. Together, like contestants in a three-legged race, they maneuver toward the open space where the helicopter door should be.

A red flash from the radar monitor.

Penny cranes her head. The text on screen reads: *MISSILE ALERT.*

Below, two thousand feet of air. Beneath that, only rock.

Connor squeezes her hand.

And they jump.

34
FREE FALL

The roaring air pillows around them as they fall.

Penny's fists lock around the buckle and the thin steel cord that binds it, eyes squeezed shut.

They plummet toward the rock.

If the buckle breaks —

If the cord snaps —

— then she'd rather die with her eyes open.

Penny forces herself to squint over Connor's shoulder, into the wind. Far below, she can make out Zach's white parachute zigzagging toward the wide, sandy-colored valley floor. Cold air tears at her loose clothes and snaps back her braid. It's so loud, she can't even hear the helicopter anymore. She cranes up, into the huge bright vastness of the sky, to see the Apache hurtling toward the wrinkly, sand-colored hills.

Connor reaches back and activates the parachute.

The shock as the chute opens knocks the wind out of Penny's lungs.

She feels the harness cut into her waist, and clings harder to Connor, feeling the ache in her arms.

The buckle cracks.

Connor's hands grip around hers.

She feels the steel cord strain.

But it holds.

Now they're flying, swooping almost gently toward the ground. She can make out tiny specks of color in the distant sky — hot-air balloons?

The empty helicopter continues on its arc, straight into the rocky flank of the hill. Penny can't hear the huge, flaming explosion. But she can feel the force of it in the sudden swerve of the parachute.

As the smoke rises from the wreck of the Apache, Connor and Penny float down past the ridges on either side of the valley. He's mouthing something over and over, like a mantra, but she can't hear anything.

The cliff faces are riddled with hundreds of caves.

On the ground, Zach's tiny figure stands up, struggling free of his parachute.

Sixty feet from the ground.

Penny's hands, locked around Connor, shake with adrenaline. She can't even scream.

Forty feet.

Twenty.

Connor folds his knees up, preparing to land. Penny barely remembers to pull up her feet before she slams tailbone-first into the dusty ground. Three bumps, and they skid to a halt. The parachute settles behind them.

Buzzed on relief and joy, Penny lets out a whoop.

"It worked!" Connor is laughing as if he can't stop. "It *worked*!"

Penny yanks the broken harness buckle out of the tangled cord. Her hands are still shaking as she helps Connor out of the harness.

Zach runs toward them, his deflated parachute balled under his arm. His knee is bleeding.

"We did it!" Penny calls.

Zach is shouting, but his voice is faint in her ringing ears. She can't quite make out his words. He's pointing upward.

A tiny missile zings overhead and explodes the wreck of the Apache into a second, larger inferno.

Penny licks her dry lips. "That seems redundant."

Zach pants into earshot. "Drones!"

About a mile off and rapidly approaching are what look like six curved, windowless gray planes, two larger than the others.

"Reapers," shouts Connor. "Run!"

Arms still stuck in the harness, Penny scoops up the billowy-soft parachute and races toward the shelter of the caves.

The three of them pile into one of the smaller openings in the rock. It's surprisingly cool inside, the pale cave walls as smooth as unglazed pottery. The cave isn't drippy or dank, but dusty dry, with the rich mineral scent of stone the wind has ground down for millennia.

"They'll have heat sensors," Zach pants. "Get all the way to the back!"

Penny shucks off her parachute harness and feels blindly for the back wall of the cave — which isn't there. She gropes into the blackness. "How far back does this cave go?"

Connor whistles. The sound echoes far away into the dark.

"There's a breeze coming up," Zach says, astonished. "It must be ventilated."

"I read that in Byzantine times, people built underground cities in Cappadocia to shelter from invaders," says Penny. "If this is part of an underground city, the tunnel might lead back to the surface."

"What if it's caved in?" Connor protests. "Or what if it's just a natural rock formation?"

Penny feels her way forward. "There are stairs carved into the stone."

"I think I saw this movie," says Zach. "We find the Ark of the Covenant, and the blonde turns out to be a Nazi."

Connor grins. "Wasn't the heroine secretly descended from Leonardo da Vinci?"

Penny crosses her arms. "Either of you comedians got a better idea?"

Outside, six drones growl low over the valley.

Zach digs a lighter out of his pocket. The tiny flame throws all of their faces into shadow.

"We can't go back out there," says Connor.

"Maybe *you* could." Zach's voice is quiet, and startlingly fierce.

Connor tenses. "What's that supposed to mean?"

"The second I saw you, I suspected you were here to take me on a little black-site vacation. But I wasn't sure until I saw those Reapers. Birds like that don't fly without a nod from Langley."

"Zach, listen to me," says Penny, "*I* convinced Connor to come help save you —"

"You think you did." There's a danger in Zach's calm. "Because, hey, *he's* not an intelligence officer specifically trained to manipulate vulnerable people."

"As if you're not?" snaps Connor.

"I get why Christina wants me out of the way," says Zach. "But I couldn't figure out why she'd send Penny with you." He shakes his head. "And then it hit me. Bait."

"Let's get something clear," says Connor. "I came to Mor Samuel for one reason. To get the information you got from Mehmetoğlu. The proof about what Melek Palamut and her father were up to with the Hashashin. The proof Christina will do anything to hide."

"You think it's *Palamut*?" Zach stares at them both in the darkness. And then he starts to laugh. Not an angry laugh, but deep and infectious.

"Want to share the joke with the rest of the class?" says Connor.

Zach catches his breath. "I've got to hand it to her. That woman knows her shit. You're just her type, too. Captain America. Not so experienced that you're expensive to replace, but, oh, so loyal. I bet she told you I was a traitor. I bet she even tried to smear

351

Penny." His smile fades. "But I bet she forgot to tell you it was a suicide mission."

Penny looks at Connor. "Just how psycho *is* this boss of yours?"

"Oh, Christina is perfectly sane," says Zach. "She's just scared."

"Is she a traitor?"

"Christina?" Zach sounds amused. "The woman bleeds stars and stripes."

"Then why is she trying to kill us? A car bomb, an assassin, Reaper drones? What the hell is all this *for*?"

"Sometimes the old clichés are the truest." Zach flicks the lighter and moves toward the mouth of the tunnel. "I know too much."

The tunnel slopes down into the cold of the earth. Penny can stand almost straight, but both of the guys have to crouch over. Stairs blur into a narrow slope, barely wide enough for the three of them side by side.

"You've got to understand," says Zach. "It wouldn't take much to bring Turkey from bad to catastrophic." In the faint flicker of the lighter, it's hard enough to see two feet ahead in the tunnel, let alone to read his face. "Either Palamut drives the country off a cliff, or someone shoots the bastard and they have a civil war."

Penny's eyes are growing accustomed to

the darkness. The bluish dot of Zach's lighter casts strange shadows on the curving walls.

Zach continues, "The border with Iraq and Syria is a potential war zone seven hundred miles long. The Kurds are sick of Palamut taking their taxes, then bombing the shit out of their villages. Palamut's sick of Kurdish separatists murdering his policemen. Then there's a metric fuckload of Syrian refugees and a crap economy."

Connor sounds dry. "You pack that much fertilizer in a barn, it's going to explode."

"Bingo," says Zach. "And where does that leave the U.S. of A.? It's time to be realistic. Trying to get rid of batshit Islamist fundamentalists by drone-striking their villages is like cleaning your sheets by washing them in dog shit. Stability costs years and billions and hearts and minds. It's never going to happen. So you make the best of reality. If we're going to have batshit Islamist fundamentalists, then we need batshit Islamist fundamentalists we can rely on. This operation was designed to get us in on the ground floor."

Penny is getting dizzy. "By financing terrorism? That's crazy!"

"Worked in Saudi, didn't it?" Zach helps Penny over a waist-high rockfall.

"Apples and oranges." Connor sounds terse. "If this is our strategy, why haven't I heard about it?"

"For the same reason I hadn't," Zach says bitterly. "I bust my ass in this country for three years, trying to get some decent HUMINT on the Hashashin. And then, back around Easter, I step into a little *ki-raathane.* And there's Martin MacGowan, my station chief, playing backgammon with one of the Hashashin's top dogs, the Old Man of the Mountain."

"So?" Connor edges around a hole in the rock floor. "Sounds like a great source."

"Yeah. Except I'd been tasked a Power-Point for the quarterly review. Puff stuff for Langley — we're the post-est with the most-est, give us more money, blah blah. That night was the Ankara Station St. Patrick's Day party, at MacGowan's house. I get MacGowan alone, ask if I can use the Old Man of the Mountain recruitment in my PowerPoint. MacGowan gets *furious.* Tells me to take it out and never mention it again. The next day, Langley tells me my job's on the line."

"So *that's* why," says Penny.

"Oh, Jesus." The flame reflects in Zach's mortified eyes. "They told you — ?"

"I told her what Christina told me," says

Connor. "About you and MacGowan's wife."

"I knew it wasn't true," says Penny.

"It is and isn't." Zach ducks under a bulge in the ceiling. "When I first got to post, I was still grieving Jess. I did some stuff I'm not proud of." His voice is quiet. "For what it's worth, Kate MacGowan told me they were about to get a divorce. A lot of people at post knew. But I had no idea MacGowan ever found out. It was all over years ago."

"So you told CIA it was over," says Connor. "And no one believed you."

"No." Zach flicks the lighter. "But I wasn't about to let them screw me over like that."

"What did you do?" asks Penny.

"I pulled every string I had. No go. I swallowed my pride and begged MacGowan for more time. The Agency said I could stay through the summer. They started making noises about revoking my clearance. My whole career was on the line. Not that it's so great. But it's all I've got. And my kid's counting on me."

"Oh, Zach."

He squeezes Penny's hand. "And then I got my miracle. A message slid under my door one night — just pencil and paper, from Eylo, a Kurdish peace group based in Diyarbakır. They claimed they had proof that the U.S. government was giving American weapons to the Hashashin."

Zach drops to his knees; the ceiling is barely three feet high.

"Oh, please." Connor crawls after him, wounded arm clutched against his stomach. "That is the definition of garbage intelligence. Have you *seen* the protocols for supplying weapons to Syrian nonstate groups? The Hashashin wouldn't qualify in a million years."

Penny crawls last, almost blind in the darkness, groping along the tufa stone. She tries not to notice her muscles seizing up.

"Let me tell you a story." Zach's voice echoes slightly in the tunnel. "Once upon a time in Syria there lived a band of Shia freedom fighters. They were kind of like Robin Hoods with AK-47s — hated Assad, no known ties to any terrorist groups, pretty open-minded about other sects. And most important, they were determined to destroy ISIS. Now, these Robin Hoods were a pretty tiny group, but they were unbelievably effective. Disciplined. Their branding was solid, too. The Hashashin? It sounds awesome and medieval, as if they're going to start scaling harem walls with daggers in their teeth. The group's founders actually met getting their master's degrees in computer science — smart guys. Their online presence was slick as hell — whole thing felt like an AO video game. Rebels you could really root for. CIA started paying attention. My boss, Christina, thought the Hashashin could take out ISIS for us. She thought all they needed was better equipment."

Penny makes a face. "Arming Islamist guerrillas who named themselves after an assassin cult?"

"The former President shared your skepticism," says Zach. "But Christina, she was convinced that she knew best. She secretly approached someone high up at the State Department. Somebody ambitious. Asked for his help delivering the weapons. If things worked out, he'd get all the glory. If not, they'd both deny everything."

"Why State?" says Connor. "Why not DOD?"

"State was on pretty good terms with the Kurds," says Zach. "Christina's special someone asked a Kurdish group named Eylo to smuggle a few truckloads of boxes, supposedly full of medical equipment, out of Turkey and across Rojava, supposedly for antiregime hospitals. The Hashashin retrieved the boxes, and blammo — overnight they've gone from the Iron Age to the most teched-out anti-ISIS militia in Syria. The problem was, that drew lots of new recruits. The group absorbed thousands of foreign fighters — brutalized Afghans and Iraqis with dangerous ideas. Robin Hood and his Merry Men stopped being so tolerant. In less than six months, they were gunning down U.S.-allied forces and making public vows to 'destroy America.' And staging all those fucking beheadings."

"I'm still not buying it." Connor shoves himself back onto his feet as the tunnel rises. "If that were true, why haven't the Hashashin gone public with it?"

" 'We took handouts from the CIA'? Doesn't play so well with that sexy-rebel brand identity of theirs."

"Zach," says Penny, dusting pebbles off her palms, "if a bunch of terrorists were running around with state-of-the-art American weapons, wouldn't someone somewhere have noticed something?"

"Someone did. You remember last month, the Hashashin bombed that maternity ward in Aleppo? I've seen credible reports they used American bombs."

Connor is unmoved. "*Stolen* American bombs."

"What if they weren't stolen?"

"You don't have a shred of proof," says

Connor.

"But Eylo said they did. Straight from the Kurdish guys who drove the trucks. Cold, hard, incontrovertible proof of Christina's involvement, and how she used the State Department to deliver weapons to the Hashashin."

"So these Kurdish terrorists — sorry, peace activists — are supposedly running around with secret information that gives them enormous leverage over the CIA?" demands Connor. "And you're telling me that hasn't leaked?"

"Their HQ in Diyarbakır got hit by a shell." Zach ducks to dodge a bulge in the tunnel roof. "Mehmetoğlu managed to save just one copy of the proof. And until the party, he'd been in hiding."

"Why didn't Eylo go to the press?" demands Penny. She stumbles on a crack in the rock.

"Eylo's noses aren't the cleanest. The evidence could be blown off as a malicious hoax. So they needed someone above reproach to break the story to the world. Someone people would listen to. An American government whistle-blower."

"Oh, sure," Connor snaps, " 'cause CIA officers are known for our snappy press releases. Haven't these guys ever heard of a

359

journalist?"

"That's what I thought," says Zach. This part of the tunnel is as wide as a school hallway; they can walk side by side again. "But you've got to remember, these guys grew up in Turkey. Journalists in this country are liable to end up tortured in a jail cell. They insisted it had to be me."

"What did you do?" asks Penny.

"I told Eylo if they wanted to play ball, I'd need hard proof ASAP. They agreed. The problem was, how? Now I'm being tailed every time I go outside — sometimes one guy, sometimes two. Could be the Agency. Could be the Turkish government. Could even be the Hashashin. Whoever it is, there's no way in hell I can arrange a meeting. My comms are all Agency systems, and if they catch me using a burner phone, I'll be guilty until proven innocent, even if they can't trace what I sent."

Penny's pulse races. "So how did you get the information?"

"Well . . ." Zach holds the lighter closer to his face. She can see he's smiling. "I'm under suspicion anyway, so I put on a show for the Agency to watch. That's where you come in, Penny. Davut Mehmetoğlu was one of Eylo's leaders. Used to be a pretty progressive politician — until Palamut screwed up his life and got him on the terror watchlist. He's gotten pretty friendly with the PKK since then — the kind of guy who would trigger an instant alert back at Langley. He wanted to meet me somewhere under U.S. protection. So I had you put him on the guest list. I knew MacGowan and Christina would let him come, just to watch what I'd do. Mehmetoğlu loved the idea of meeting at the party. He thought it would be hysterical — the Turks see him at the Embassy party and freak out that the Americans have suddenly swung wildly pro-Kurd."

"Wait," says Penny. "You had me put a guy you *knew* had PKK ties on an Embassy guest list?"

"Denize düşen yılana sarılır."

Connor sounds exasperated. "What?"

"No Turkish, huh?" Zach grins. "I see Christina sent you well prepared."

"It's a Turkish proverb." Penny takes a deep breath. "He who falls into the sea will clutch even a snake."

Connor isn't amused. "Who's the snake in this scenario?"

Zach ignores him. "The plan is, me and Mehmetoğlu, we just hang out and chat, then he goes home, and Langley's pissed and disappointed."

Connor sounds impatient. "What about the information?"

"Keep your shirt on, soldier. I knew all eyes would be on me and Mehmetoğlu. So I had Eylo slip someone low profile onto the guest list, too. Peace activist. Not Kurdish herself. Daughter of some big banking family — someone above reproach. She's on the up-and-up — a true pacifist. She had no idea what it was all about — just that she was supposed to give my courier the proof."

"How did the peace-activist lady get the proof?" says Connor. "I thought Mehmetoğlu had it."

"Mehmetoğlu couldn't meet her publicly — it would destroy her reputation. They overlapped going through security at the Embassy. He slipped it to her then. Everything went perfectly. The lady gave my courier the proof. But before I could retrieve it . . ." Zach shrugs. "Boom."

"Zach!" Penny cries. "You mean you didn't get the proof?"

"*I* didn't." There's something funny about the way he says it.

"Mehmetoğlu's text message." Connor comes to a dead halt. "Good luck to the girl with the flag."

Penny stops dead.

Zach squeezes her hand. "I knew I could trust you, Penny."

He's obviously expecting her to melt. But his presumption knocks the breath out of her. "Why didn't you tell me? Jesus Christ, Zach!"

"Did anyone question you, after the attack?"

"Well —"

"And were you honestly able to answer that you didn't know anything about what I'd been doing?"

"I guess, but —"

"What were you *thinking*?" says Connor. "Using an unwitting civilian as a courier? She could have been killed!"

"This is between me and Penny." Zach's voice is soft. "I knew I could trust her."

"But, Zach, this doesn't make any sense." Penny can hardly speak. "Nobody like that talked to me at the party! And even if they did, how on earth did you think I would remember some stranger when I didn't even know to be on the lookout for one?"

"Don't worry. I didn't expect you to remember. The information's on a microchip."

"What is this, 1985?" snaps Connor.

"This isn't the Gulf we're talking about," retorts Zach. "Eylo is a grassroots Kurdish peace group. We're lucky it's not on micro-*film*. Or fucking cuneiform."

Penny is glad it's too dark for Zach to see her face. Her voice comes out hardly more than a whisper. "When, exactly, were you planning to tell me about all this?"

"Well" — Zach's voice is gentler than usual — "I *was* planning to ask you out for a drink, after the party. A real date." He puts his arm around her waist. "Kind of overdue, don't you think?"

"I'd say," says Connor drily. "Since you'd been reporting her to us as a close and continuing intimate partner for two weeks. Care to explain that?"

Zach's voice is urgent: "Penny, the courier was told to ID herself to you with the code word *luck* —"

"*Excellent* choice," mutters Connor. "No risk of misidentification with something as rare as that."

Zach ignores him. "It would have been a woman, a Turkish woman."

"Zach, I got a concussion. I can't really remember —"

"Try, Penny. Think!"

Penny gropes forward in the blackness. The hard, uneven floor of the tunnel slopes slowly downward. She tries to keep her teeth from chattering.

The party.

A Turkish woman.

Smoke and pain and Matt and Ayla and Melek Palamut and the screaming toddler and the blaring saxophone . . .

Her memories slide steeper than the floor, piling into chaos.

No. No. Before all that.

"Try remembering the party from the start, step by step," suggests Zach. "Every person you talked to."

Penny screws up her face. "I was with Ayla Parlak. Everybody kept making fun of me for the flag, but they were all people from the Embassy —" She turns to Zach. "Did you really let me win bingo on purpose?"

"Brilliant, right? How could your contact miss the girl with the enormous flag?"

"Like a target on my back." Penny's mouth feels like cotton. She wishes he would take his hand off her.

"Keep thinking," Zach urges.

Penny takes a deep breath. Thinking of Ayla makes her stomach hurt as if she'd swallowed broken glass. "Ayla and I went to get ice cream. And —" She gasps. "The girl in the ice cream truck."

Zach can hardly contain himself. "The girl in the ice cream truck?"

"She wished me good luck. But, Zach, she

didn't give me anything, except the ice cream. Not even napkins!"

"Are you sure?" Zach's voice is hoarse with intensity. "Think, Penny! It would've been something small. An unusual coin, a pin, a flash drive —"

"I'd remember if a girl in an ice cream truck handed me a flash drive, Zach!"

"There *must* have been somebody else."

"Ayla wished me good luck."

"Who?"

"My friend. You know, the Public Diplomacy intern. From New Jersey?"

"Not her," snaps Zach. He grabs her arm so tight his nails dig into her skin. "*Think, Penny!*"

"Zach, you're hurting me!"

His grip tightens. "You *must* remember."

"Wait." Connor stops dead. "Do you hear that?"

From farther down the tunnel floats the sound of muffled laughter.

35
DERINKUYU

"And now we come to the final stop on our tour," a booming, Turkish-accented male voice declares, with the unmistakable synthetic charm of Tour Guide English. "I'll give you a clue: it was a lot more popular than the chapel!"

"Is it where they made the wine?"

Chuckles.

"Mr. George has a single-track mind!"

More chuckles.

"This is the ancient — excuse me — *tuvalet* of the underground city of Derinkuyu. You know, the little boys' room? Eighth century AD!"

An Australian voice: "But, Sully, how did they get decent plumbing six stories underground?"

"*Excellent* question, Mrs. Cochrane! The ancient Christians of Derinkuyu, they were very clever — almost as clever as Sully!"

Appreciative giggles.

"So they tapped into the *natural springs*! Like the ones at the hotel spa last night. And we all know how much Mr. George here enjoyed those! Especially with all these beautiful ladies, eh?"

This must be an easy crowd. Their laughter carries down the tunnel.

Penny can make out faint light against nubbly stone, fifty feet down the tunnel. She rips her arm away from Zach and breaks into a run. She's not even sure which she's trying to escape — the smothering dark, or the sudden, sickening certainty that the information on that microchip meant more to Zach than her safety. More than her life.

She runs harder toward the growing yellow light.

She remembers Zach's warmth beside her on the Ankara citadel in the sunset. The sense of safety he created. The way he carefully exposed just enough of his weaknesses so she could rush to his defense. How she felt at once that she could trust him.

His own words gouge into her: *An intelligence officer specifically trained to manipulate vulnerable people.*

Was that all it ever was?

Did he ever give a damn about her? Or did he just need a courier he could control, somebody too dumb and too desperate to be cared for to start asking inconvenient questions?

She rounds a corner in the tunnel, stumbling over a row of plastic orange warning cones into the startled stares of twenty tourists.

"Come out of there!" exclaims a man in alarmed Turkish. Penny follows the voice to a large, amiable-looking middle-aged man in a Red Sox T-shirt and an official guide badge that reads SÜLEYMAN AKARSU. The guide, Sully. "That part of the underground city is *yasak*! Hurry! It's very dangerous!"

"We — got lost," blurts Penny in English, at the same time that Zach says, "There was a landslide."

"You're American?" says Sully in English.

"We were hiking —" begins Zach.

A seventysomething woman in baggy khakis exclaims in a Bronx accent, "That young man's hurt!"

"I fell," says Connor quickly, cradling his bloody right hand. "I'm okay, ma'am."

"I've been a registered nurse for forty years, and take my word for it, young man, you are *not* okay. And *you*!" Her bifocal gaze locks on Zach. "That knee! Sully, is there a first-aid kit on the bus?"

"Of course, Mrs. Reid." Sully turns to the group. "We'll proceed back to the exit." He turns a concerned face to Penny, Connor, and Zach. "Did you come with a group?"

Penny's mind races. "We're . . ."

"Couchsurfing," Zach supplies without hesitation. "Junior and me" — Zach nods to Connor — "we always talked about going to Turkey. So when my girl here graduated, and Junior was on leave, we were, like, only one life to live, right? We figured we'd hike —"

Sully looks incredulous. "Didn't you take a map?"

"I thought my phone would work, but the signal out here isn't happening."

Mrs. Reid turns back to Connor. "Make sure you elevate that hand until I can get a better look. And keep constant pressure on it!"

"Yes, ma'am."

"I'll telephone an ambulance as soon as we reach the surface," says Sully.

"That's really not necessary, sir," says Connor. "I'm sure Mrs. Reid is all the help I'll need."

The yellow electric lights strung along the hollows in the low ceiling illuminate a medieval city in troglodyte miniature, carved room by room out of the crumbly tufa rock.

Filled with the sweet smell of perfume and

sunscreen, the subterranean air doesn't feel so cold. Everything has been carved from the living rock: benches and beds growing like mushrooms from the walls and floors. Penny tries to keep her head down. What if someone recognizes her?

One large, pretty lady, the one Sully called Mrs. Cochrane, pats Penny on the arm. "You must have taken an awful spill, darl."

Penny forces herself to smile. "I was lucky."

They climb a long stone staircase, so narrow Penny grazes her elbows against the rough walls.

Mrs. Cochrane sounds winded. "The tour company offered to evacuate us, after the tragedy in Ankara. Almost half our group left, but I wouldn't have missed this for the world."

"Are we really six stories down?"

"That's what Sully says. It's a good thing you found us, darl. These tunnels are supposed to go on for miles. You see those?" Mrs. Cochrane points to what look like enormous granite millstones, rolled to the side of the passageway. "Gates. Sully says when the invaders came, the Byzantine Christians would hide down here for months."

"Months?" Penny is suddenly painfully

aware of hundreds of thousands of tons of stone on every side.

"Kept 'em safe."

The last passage dumps them out into a bright parking lot. Mrs. Reid sits Zach and Connor on a bench in the shade of a lone tree. She flutters purposefully between them, applying iodine, ice packs, and bandages. The sky is cloudless, droneless blue. Mrs. Cochrane inspects lurid painted bowls and strands of flowery *oya* lace at the souvenir stall. Meanwhile, a trio of redheaded sisters take selfies with a camel, presumably imported from Saudi for the benefit of tourists.

"This is nasty," exclaims Mrs. Reid. "It goes right through your hand!"

"I fell on this huge old nail," says Connor through gritted teeth. The lines across his forehead are deep, his sunburned neck shiny with sweat. How has he tolerated the pain for so long?

"Do you know how lucky you are not to have crushed a bone?"

"That's Junior for you — Mr. Indestructible." Zach looks tanned and relaxed, his usually deep voice a dude-bro drawl. Somehow he's found time to ruffle his hair and undo the top buttons of his shirt, as if he's about to seek enlightenment and kombucha on some mountaintop.

Penny hovers at a distance. She can still feel the bruises on her arm where Zach's fingers gripped.

"Hey there." Zach saunters over to her and drops his voice. "No lurking. It looks weird."

"What if somebody recognizes me? All it takes is one. If Melek or Christina find out I'm alive before we can get to Istanbul . . ."

"Penny Kessler's dead, remember? You're Emma Bleecker from Ann Arbor."

"My face was on the cover of *every newspaper*, Zach! What are the odds that nobody recognizes me?"

"The bangs help a lot. People see what they expect to see." Zach rubs her shoulder. "You got this." He's cranking the charm up high. "Look, Pen. About what happened in the tunnel —"

Sully strides up beside them. "The bus heads out in a few minutes. You sure you don't want me to call a taxi? Or an ambulance?"

Penny pulls herself together. "Where is your group headed?"

"We won't be passing back through Nevşehir, I'm afraid. We stop at a caravanserai, and then straight on to Istanbul."

Penny holds out two of the hundred-lira

notes Connor had given her when they first reached Mardin. "Do you have three extra seats?"

36
ALLIES

Huber Mansion, Kalender, Istanbul
13:39 Local Time
"Why *not*?" demands Melek.

Far up the European shore of the Bosphorus near the Black Sea, the colossal wooden Huber Köşkü, was built for a pair of nineteenth-century German arms dealers. Like most men in dirty businesses, they liked their home lives pristine and orderly. Newly restored and cooled by breezes off the water, their former mansion is Melek's favorite of the presidential residences in Istanbul. She used to come here for peace. This time, she's here for privacy.

"Melek *Hanım,* with all due respect, such measures are not necessary." The air force general on the phone is flying a perilous course between reassurance and condescension. Life would be a whole lot simpler if the children of the powerful didn't have access to their daddies' contacts lists. But given President Palamut's paranoia about "traitors," the general can't afford anything less than complete obsequiousness. "The Hashashin terrorists could not possibly survive such a crash. The Americans even fired extra strikes, to make sure."

"Isn't it possible that the terrorists had parachutes?"

"They were flying far too low. Besides, Apaches are not typically equipped with —"

"Is it possible?"

The general waffles. "*Technically,* yes, Melek *Hanım.* But the heat sensor readings were negative. Not even a goat."

"They were in Cappadocia, weren't they? Do the sensors work through rock?"

"With all due respect —"

"If these terrorists flew due west, avoiding all major targets, it's reasonable to suppose their goal may have been the NATO Summit. If there's the slightest chance my father's life may still be in danger, surely, General Yağhane —"

The general is no fool; he can see where this is going. "We'll have troops in the area check the crash site."

"It's been an hour!" snaps Melek. "If they survived, they've surely escaped by now."

In the silence after she's hung up, Melek considers her options.

Christina has betrayed her.

But even a forged coin can be flipped.

Çırağan Palace Kempinski, Istanbul
14:04 Local Time

In the broad gardens of the Çırağan Palace Kempinski, U.S. Secretary of State Robert Winthrop steps out of the shadow of the rustling palm trees and up to the podium. To his left, in somber black, stand Moe Sokolof, Brenda Pelecchia, and Frank Lerman. To his right, Palamut, smirking at the vast crowd, and the puppyishly beaming Bolu.

"First of all," Winthrop booms, "I'd like to thank President Palamut and Prime Minister Bolu for such a warm welcome to this beautiful city of Istanbul."

The audience, decked out in more discreet jewelry, bulletproof shapewear, and security earpieces than even Istanbul's fanciest hotel usually sees, gives a resounding cheer. The noise carries beyond the white filigreed iron of the garden's seafront walls, and eastward out over the impossibly blue waters of the Bosphorus. Impossibly blue and improbably empty. Security has cleared all water traffic for a five-hundred-meter perimeter, effectively choking one of the world's busiest sea-traffic corridors. Taking advantage of the unusual stillness, slick black cormorants dive deep into the current in search of fish. Beyond the hundred-and-forty-year-old, twenty-foot stone barricade of the Kempinski garden's landward wall, a relic of its days as pleasure palace-prison to the last sultans, the busy coastal road is silent. Of the thousands of protesters who stood chanting there two hours ago, only fallen banners and tear-gas residue on the asphalt remain. Behind the intricate white façade of the Çırağan — one of the better-surviving remnants from a nineteenth-century imperial Versailles-or-bust building spree — black-suited members of Palamut's Presidential Guard keep watch at each window.

"Next, I'd like to thank the ladies and gentlemen of the press for joining us." As he's so often called upon to do, Winthrop strikes a carefully vetted chord between charm and gravitas. The breeze off the Bosphorus doesn't muss his thick dark hair.

"I was in a helicopter with the Secretary outside Kabul once," Moe whispers in Brenda's ear. "Even then, his hair didn't move."

Winthrop leans forward. "This press conference was intended as a kind of appetizer for tonight's big event." Polite laughter. "But in light of a communication we've just received, President Palamut and I will be making a special joint announcement." A murmur swells through the garden. "Today, the Republic of Turkey and the United States come together in a moment of terrible tragedy. We all pray that the NATO Summit that will commence this evening marks the beginning of a unified global effort towards peace." He stills the hair-trigger applause with his hand. "But sometimes, the vehicle of peace is force. The world must know that we stand strong against the armies of terrorism and chaos. We stand against those who would corrupt freedom. Against those whose only currency is fear and hate, whose only language is violence. Our enemies must know our strength, and that, when circumstances demand it, the United States will never fear to act!"

On cue, President Palamut steps forward. His stills the fevered clapping with a motion of his hand. "My people." His voice echoes up through the swaying palm fronds, echoed by a breathless English translation. "Our enemies have conspired against this day. Those so-called enlightened intellectuals — those traitorous Kurdish terrorists — they try to bring darkness, to make us weak. But we are stronger every day! We will destroy our enemies!" He waves away the cheers.

Brenda steels her face to blankness.

"I bring you news of a great victory," declares Palamut. "Yesterday, the Hashashin dared to occupy Mor Samuel. Today, the invaders are dead. They destroyed Mor Samuel, but we will rebuild it to twice the size. And now the Turkish flag will fly proudly above it!" Palamut clasps Winthrop's hand with both of his. The Secretary of State makes a visible effort not to look uncomfortable. Brenda can almost see him figuring the political calculus on how friendly to appear. "At eleven twenty-five this morning, the might of the Turkish air force joined with our American allies to destroy a Hashashin attack helicopter. A helicopter that took off from Mor Samuel armed with missiles intended to destroy the NATO conference." Palamut adds, with relish, "There were no survivors."

When the speeches are over, journalists jostle for the first question.

"Mr. Secretary." Nick Abensour, the BBC's bright-eyed Turkey correspondent, cuts through the clutter. "Mr. Secretary, we know Davut Mehmetoğlu was being held at Mor Samuel. What about the missing Foreign Service officer, Zachary Robson? Was he present at Mor Samuel, too?"

Winthrop speaks with quiet reproach. "We haven't been able to fully sweep the area and assess the situation yet. Until then, any statement about Mr. Robson would be pure speculation. And I'm sure we'd all condemn any cheap sensationalism in a moment of international tragedy."

Nick Abensour isn't so easily dismissed. "Any comment on the leak regarding President Palamut's daughter, Melek — that she's allegedly connected with the Hashashin?"

Winthrop frowns. "That has been thoroughly debunked." He points at the woman from CNN Türk.

But Abensour isn't finished. "Sir, you're saying a U.S. government employee leaked a forged document in an attempt to incriminate Melek Palamut?"

Winthrop smiles tightly. "Why don't we let one of your colleagues ask a question, too."

When the press have been shepherded away, Brenda finds Carolyn Sokolof staring out over the water, an unsipped glass of pale green melon juice in her fist.

Carolyn's back shudders in her tasteful black linen sheath. "So we blew up some of those bastards. Does that fix anything?"

"It doesn't hurt." Brenda shrugs.

"I don't know."

"Poor Zach," mutters Brenda. "Jack, I guess I should say. Apparently the whole Mehmetoğlu thing was a false lead, just some source he was chasing."

Carolyn takes a long sip.

Brenda rubs her old friend's arm. "You must be exhausted. Moe said you came straight from the Consulate."

"Yeah." Carolyn shakes her head. "I don't know how you're still standing."

"Because they can't. And I still can." Brenda blinks away the faces. "And maybe I'm still dumb enough to think that somehow we can make a real, decent peace, so I can go home and look my children in the eye."

Polite party noises in six languages eddy around them, pierced by the cries of jubilant seabirds. Waiters maneuver among the guests with trays of canapés. Apparently someone along the chain of command thought freestanding plastic soupspoons of garlicky cucumber-yogurt soup would make good power-broker party food.

Brenda and Carolyn politely decline.

"I can't get the kids' voices out of my head, Bren." Carolyn's voice breaks. "What do you say to a five-year-old who wants to know why her mommy and daddy can't come tuck her in?"

Brenda's phone rings. "Christ, I'm sorry. Let me just check . . ."

The caller ID reads: Dr. Ali Denizci.

Denizci? Memory kicks in. The hospital.

"I'd better take this." Brenda picks up. "Dr. Denizci, hello. Is everything —"

"I am profoundly sorry to interrupt, Ms. Pelecchia, but this is an emergency. I was the doctor responsible for Penny Kessler."

"I remember." Brenda's throat is tight. "Thank you for what you did for her."

"You seemed to care about her." There's something unsettling in his intensity.

"She's — she was an intern in my office. It's terrible."

"The newspapers reported that she died of a catastrophic cerebral hemorrhage triggered by the explosion. I could not believe it when I heard."

Brenda swallows hard. "That poor girl."

"You misunderstand." Dr. Denizci's voice is a whisper. "What the press reported was simply not credible. Not with that kind of cerebral trauma. I thought perhaps it had been a delayed adverse reaction to the methylphenidate. I felt responsible. I should never have prescribed it when it was not clinically necessary."

"It wasn't your fault." Brenda is struggling to keep her composure. "Frank Lerman should never have pressured you. I should have stopped him. Sometimes . . . these things . . ."

"If it was the methylphenidate, there should have been elevated heart rate, shock symptoms — the profile is very distinctive. I went to check her file. She was my patient. I owed her that."

Brenda feels ill. "And?"

"It was a fake."

"What do you mean?" whispers Brenda.

"I signed off on her chart myself. She had a moderate head injury — the survival rates are almost one hundred percent. But the paperwork in the file claimed she'd arrived from the Embassy with a traumatic brain injury — she wouldn't have been able to walk or talk, probably not even lift her head. And Ms. Pelecchia, *the document had my signature on it.*"

Brenda covers her mouth. "You have the file?"

He pauses. She can hear him take a deep breath. Then: "Yes."

"You did the right thing." Brenda tries to keep the urgency out of her voice; he already sounds terrified enough. "I'll send someone to pick you up. Are you still at the hospital?"

His voice is raw. "I left immediately."

"Where are you now?"

He hesitates. "If they find me —"

"Dr. Denizci, I am the acting Ambassador. You have the United States of America behind you. We'll keep you safe."

The doctor exhales shakily.

Brenda presses. "Where are you now?"

"Istanbul," he whispers. "I got in my car and drove straight here."

Brenda glances up. Frank is hovering at Secretary Winthrop's elbow, deep in negotiations with a server — *"I said Diet Pepsi. With ice. Ice! Where's the fucking translator?"*

Brenda drops her voice. "Meet me at the U.S. Consulate in İstinye in half an hour. Tell security you have a meeting with the Chargé d'Affaires." She hangs up and strides toward Secretary Winthrop.

Frank Lerman interposes himself. "Where are you going?"

"I need to speak to Secretary Winthrop."

"He's in conference with the Prime Minister," hisses Frank.

"It's an emergency." Brenda sidesteps him. "Mr. Secretary?"

"Brenda Pelecchia." Robert Winthrop gives his brilliant, dimpled smile. "Our acting Ambassador. You know Prime Minister Bolu, don't you?"

Brenda nods. "It's always an honor, Prime Minister."

Prime Minister Bolu nods cheerfully. His glass of *ayran* is nearly empty. "You will all take a picture with me?"

"Of course." Winthrop nods to a photographer and clasps Bolu's hand. Brenda and Frank smile tightly in the background.

"Mr. Secretary." Brenda blinks away the flash. "May we speak privately for a moment?"

"Ms. Pelecchia," says Frank, through his teeth. "I really don't think the Secretary —"

"Now, Frank." Winthrop shakes his head indulgently and claps Bolu on the back. "Prime Minister Bolu, I'll be right back with you. Maybe Frank can tell you about the Turkish-American sports championship idea we've been kicking around?" Winthrop steers Brenda a few feet away, where they are shielded by Diplomatic Security. "Brenda, you've got my full attention. What's wrong?"

"There's a situation at the Consulate General, sir. You know about Penny Kessler?"

"The flag girl." He shakes his head. "Horrific."

"The doctor who treated her at the hospital in Ankara just called me. He claims her records have been falsified. There's strong reason to suspect foul play in connection with her death."

Winthrop's face freezes. "This is the last damn thing we need right now. Can you put him on ice? At least until after the Summit."

"He's meeting me in İstinye in half an hour, sir. He claims he has hard proof. The sooner we secure it, the better."

"Good God." Winthrop drops his voice. "As soon as you debrief him, report directly to me. We don't want rumors flying around."

"Yes, sir."

Winthrop smiles, grave and reassuring. "Godspeed."

"Sir?" Frank hustles alongside. "Is everything all right?"

"It will be." Winthrop's smile has withered. "I need to make a call. Secure line. *Now.*"

Langley, Virginia
07:45 Local Time
The cars of graveyard shifters in the lot are streaked with condensation and pigeon droppings. Unfortunately, the Agency Starbucks is locked until eight a.m. Christina grips the phone between her ear and pad-

ded shoulder and slides a caramel ristretto pod into the backup machine. "Don't worry, Mr. Secretary."

"Don't *worry*?" Robert Winthrop's ragged whisper comes through the phone. "If he's telling the truth —"

"I've already issued the orders. You just go back to your party. It's better if you don't know the details."

She hangs up and shakes her head.

A ping from Sametime. Who on earth is writing to her at this hour?

Dan Bishop-TT: Chris, you in the office?
Christina Ekdahl: No. I'm on the beach in Palm Springs.
Christina Ekdahl: What are you doing at work? Barb dump your sorry tail?
Dan Bishop-TT: We've got some weird stuff coming over from NSA.
Christina Ekdahl: How weird?
Dan Bishop-TT: NSA read you into WALDO?
Christina Ekdahl: Why?
Dan Bishop-TT: Take it that's a no?
Christina Ekdahl: Really gunning for that TDY in Ouagadougou, Dan . . .
Dan Bishop-TT: Hey, don't shoot the messenger.
Dan Bishop-TT: WALDO's a pilot facial-

recognition program for all POI, focusing on SOCMINT in real time. They're letting NCTC kick the tires before they roll it out to the rest of the IC.

Christina Ekdahl: And your point is?

Dan Bishop-TT: Penny Kessler's name was still on my list of POI. And she just popped up in a social-media post tagged Derinkuyu, Turkey.

Christina Ekdahl: That's not possible.

Dan Bishop-TT: I pulled the photo. It's her. Sending now.

Dan Bishop-TT: She's in the background, on the left, next to the tall blond guy.

Christina Ekdahl: Not definitive. Lots of girls look like Penny Kessler.

Dan Bishop-TT: Lots of girls who happen to be 10 miles from the Apache shoot-down site?

37
AMERICAN FORTRESS

U.S. Consulate General, İstinye, Istanbul
15:36 Local Time

Like a Silicon Valley hoodie-zillionaire, a Secretary of State hardly scraping his forties is going to find himself having to project benevolent authority to intelligent, world-weathered men and women decades older. Usually, Winthrop does it with skill and grace, and an impressively low cringe factor. Brenda's always considered him thoughtful and fairly compassionate — especially for someone so privileged. The future-President rumors never even made her wince. America could do far worse.

She's starting to reconsider.

"Brenda," Winthrop says with the gentle confidence of a man who has been found charming all his life. "I'm so glad you came to me with this. The important thing is that we all communicate."

They're back up the Bosphorus, in the

concrete fortress of the U.S. Consulate General. The safe room is upscale bland — it could be any high-end lawyer's office. Just without windows. Even so, Brenda can hear the sirens outside.

"Forgive me, sir." Brenda's throat is tight. "But I think it's more important that a major source tries to alert us to the possible murder of one of our own interns, and he gets killed fifty feet from the Consulate!"

"It was an accident," says Frank. "The driver didn't see him —"

"The file was gone, Mr. Lerman! Do you think the wind just blew it away?"

"If there even was a file," says Frank. "The hospital says nothing was taken!"

"Brenda," Secretary Winthrop repeats, and she's certain he had to double-check her name with Frank. "You've been through hell. You've lost good friends and colleagues. You're hurting. You're angry. You're in shock. We all are. In the aftermath of a trauma like this, it's natural to look for answers. And we *are* looking, Brenda. The murderers who attacked our men and women will be brought to justice."

"But, sir —"

"Ms. Pelecchia, are you questioning the authority of the Secretary of State?"

"Down, Frank." Winthrop has the grace

to look embarrassed. "Brenda, I know it's hard. But we must never let grief make us lose hold of our rationality or reach for the false comfort of conspiracy theories. We don't know what Dr. Denizci's motives may have been, or even if he really had the files he claimed. The poor man just spent most of the past twenty-four hours trying to save bomb victims. You know better than I do that what came out of our Embassy was worse than anyone's worst nightmares. For all we know, this doctor had a breakdown. Maybe even a psychotic break."

"Mr. Secretary," says Moe Sokolof. "I'm not questioning your judgment. But if there's even the slightest chance that there was an irregularity —"

"And what if we find something?" says Winthrop. "I'm not denying it's a possibility. What do you want me to do, Moe? What would *you* do? Ask President Palamut? Penny Kessler was at his palace. Ask Prime Minister Bolu? That's a nice start to our new relationship — he's the one who appeared on camera inviting her. Whatever the hospital told us, we've already gone on record to the whole world endorsing it. Brenda said it. I said it. The President of the United States said it."

"Then we'll have to face the consequences," says Brenda.

"Consequences?" says Winthrop. "If we backpedal now, no matter what we do, no matter what we find, even if we find nothing, the United States will appear to be implicated in Penny Kessler's death. And in the process, we'll destroy whatever is left of our relationship with Turkey. You know this is true."

No one denies it.

Winthrop adds, "It's our responsibility to think of the future, Brenda. After you're officially confirmed as Ambassador —"

"Mr. Secretary," says Brenda, "I joined the Foreign Service straight out of graduate school. This is more than my career. This is who I am. I thought it meant more to me than anything but my children." She takes a slow, deliberate breath. "And I would sooner walk away right now than sit one day in office knowing I had any part in covering up the murder of a young woman whose only crime was wanting to serve her country!"

Frank is scarlet up to the dome of his shiny head. *"Ms. Pelecchia!"*

"Frank!" Winthrop silences him. His deep brown eyes fix on Brenda's. She can see his emotion, and she can tell it's real. "Brenda, please believe me. I feel as you do. But we both swore an oath to well and faithfully discharge our duties. Going down this kind of conspiracy-theory rabbit hole won't make anything better. And it won't bring Penny Kessler back. I cannot in good conscience take actions that may draw our country into another long, avoidable war. And don't kid yourself. If this NATO deal goes down the toilet, our relationship with Turkey is unlikely to recover. And without us, we all know where they'll turn. It's too late to save Penny. All we can do is try to stop this from ever happening again."

"Mr. Secretary, I accept that you're doing what you feel is right." Brenda means it. "And I must ask you to accept my resignation."

Moe grabs her arm. "Bren —"

Winthrop shakes his head. "You know I can't do that. Not now. We've got the Borusan reception in an hour. The NATO conference launches tonight. I need you, and I need Moe. I'm just the big guy from out of town. Your officers need leaders they believe in. They need *you.* You have a duty to them. To your country."

Brenda closes her eyes. "Most of my officers are dead, Mr. Secretary."

"Then do it for them." There's a rare fire in Winthrop's eyes. "Do it for Penny Kessler. Help make peace. If you want to quit after the Summit, I won't stop you. But you can't desert us now."

38
CARAVANSERAI

*Sultan Han Caravanserai, Central Natolia
15:40 Local Time*

In the dusty brightness of midafternoon, the tour bus rolls in air-conditioned comfort down the highway.

"And now," Sully's voice booms down from the bus speakers, "we approach the caravanserai!"

Seated beside Mrs. Cochrane, Penny shrinks back into the plush red seat. The caravanserai means a stop. A stop means she'll have to get out. And getting out means she'll have to face Zach.

Before they got on the bus, he urged her again to remember. But she can't. All she can see is pain and smoke, and dark bruises forming where Zach grabbed her arm.

Zach sits three rows back, across the aisle from Connor, smiling at her when she turns. Like she's a pot he doesn't want to boil over. Like she's a girl he's sweet on.

Like she's a bomb that might go off.

Always watching.

Zach's a hero, she reminds herself. A whistle-blower against the might of the CIA. Risking everything when he has a little girl at home to support. That takes courage. Honor. Conviction. He's been through hell. Maybe special rules apply. Maybe she's being selfish. How much does her safety really matter when things like this are at stake? He didn't know a bomb would go off. But she never agreed to be his courier. He didn't even ask.

She thinks of Connor, pushing her up to the shelter of the helicopter. An act of friendship that cost a bullet through his hand.

She doesn't know what to believe.

The bus bellies up beside its brethren in the caravanserai parking lot.

Sully tries to shepherd his flock past the souvenir hawkers at the gate, and into the caravanserai. But the siren song of the tchotchkes soon lures Mrs. Cochrane from the path of historical enlightenment.

"Look at those necklaces!" Mrs. Cochrane gravitates toward a rickety stall. "Don't you just love the evil eye jewelry?" She fingers a silver chain studded with glass eyes the color of cobalt. "I got evil eye rings for all my granddaughters at Ephesus, but these are so lovely, I might just have to get them, too, if I can bargain him down. You can't have too much good luck!"

Good luck.

Tens of thousands of staring blue glass eyes lie spread out on the little wooden tables, from tiny identical earring studs to dinner-plate-size slabs of heavy glass. Glass eyes tied like wishes to a little potted tree. Rows of sparkling glass eyes strung into bracelets and amulets and necklaces, studding gimcrack clay bowls and plastic wall ornaments.

Watching her. Watching over her.

Good luck to the girl with the flag.

And in that instant, Penny knows.

Triumph warms her like sunshine. Proof, real proof, and she had it all along. She's got to tell Connor and Zach. Where are they?

Connor is nodding agreeably as Sully makes cracks about camels. Zach loiters at the back of the tour group, schmoozing with Mr. George. Mr. George hands him a cigarette, and Zach pulls the lighter out of his pocket.

Then another memory slides into place with the leaden sureness of a key in a lock.

Zach's lighter.

The Hashashin would never have let a prisoner keep a lighter.

And if Zach wasn't their prisoner —

Penny hears the words of her companion on the journey to Mardin, the archaeologist. *You don't think those murderers had help from the inside?*

She remembers Zach's barrage of questions in the crypt. How fresh he looked. How unafraid.

She hears Jamal's puzzled cry across the dusty courtyard at Mor Samuel. Not *Robson,* not *Hey, you,* not some insult, but *Zach.*

She feels Zach's rage, when he gripped her arm in the darkness of Derinkuyu.

She sees the hexagonal tower of Mor Samuel falling.

Zach wasn't protecting her and Connor.

He was getting rid of all the witnesses.

And he'll never let her and Connor escape until he has what he wants.

Mrs. Cochrane has her paperback of *Stevie Tim's Turkey* splayed open to the vocabulary section. "*Ha-*yurr," she declares to the souvenir seller, shaking her head. "Chock pah-hah-luhh!"

"Not *pahalı!*" he protests. "Fifty lira for necklace is very *ucuz!*"

Penny reaches for a tray of simple bracelets, each a single blue evil eye on a colorful string — red or yellow or turquoise or hot pink — and fastened with a cheap-looking brass clasp. "How much are these?" she asks in English.

The seller beams at her. "For *you,* lady? Fifty lira for ten!"

"I just need one —"

"But your sisters! Your friends! Your mother! Your grandmother! Your cousins! Your neighbors! Your —"

"Fine!" Penny glances over her shoulder. Zach hasn't spotted her. "Just hurry." Back in the hot sun, she's sweating in the filthy green tunic. Her gaze falls on a stack of gleaming white T-shirts emblazoned with a cartoon of Nasreddin Hodja riding his donkey backward, and the immortal legend: ANCIENT KERVANSERAI CAMEL PALACE, TURKEY. "And one of those."

Sully leads Zach, Connor, and the rest of the tour group through the gate, into the caravanserai.

The seller slowly wraps each bracelet in a little cellophane pouch. He looks her up and down. "Where you are from?"

"Michigan. America. Please don't bother to wrap them —"

"Amerika! I love Amerika! My cousin, he —"

"How much?" says Penny urgently, snatching up the T-shirt.

"Two hundred lira" comes the serene reply.

Penny fixes him with a death glare. *"Bu tişört ipekten değil ki, lan!"*

He lurches back, startled into Turkish. "Forty lira, *efendim.* But —"

Penny slaps down two powder-blue hundred-lira notes, each adorned with the head of a whirling dervish. "That's twice what I owe," she says in Turkish. "Give my friend here the bargain of her life."

"Absolutely, *efendim!*" He hands her the bracelets in a plastic bag.

"You're incredible, darl," Mrs. Cochrane exclaims to Penny. "Did you use Berlitz, or Rosetta Stone?"

"Pimsleur. They're great!" Penny hurries into the caravanserai. It's an oasis of startling loveliness. A fountain splashes in the center of the courtyard. Flowering vines climb the exterior staircases. In a corner, Sully is gesturing at a carving.

"Hey." Zach strides toward her. "Shopping?"

"I needed a clean shirt." Penny glances at Sully.

She's got to time this perfectly. Zach has already killed. If he realizes what she's done before she gets away . . .

"Penny." Zach slides a hand around her waist. "On the bus. Did you remember any . . ."

"I have to use the ladies' room." She pulls away. "I'll be right back. Okay?"

He tries to mask his impatience with a syrupy grin. "Hurry back."

Penny almost retches.

She waits until the tourists are all seated for the dervish ceremony, then slips into the darkness of the caravanserai. Beneath the arches, dervishes in long white robes and tombstone caps stand still in the vibrations of the flutes.

Penny sits down at the back. As the dervishes begin to spin, she undoes the evil eye bracelet from her left wrist. She slips it into the plastic bag with the others. In its place, she fastens the almost-identical replacement: a little blue glass eye on a thin red cord.

The dervishes spin faster in the darkness, with the sureness of long practice.

Penny takes a deep breath. No mistakes.

"*There* you are!" exclaims Connor, when they emerge into the blazing parking lot. "I was getting worried —"

"I bought CDs for everyone's Christmas stocking." Mrs. Cochrane is starry-eyed. "It was the most moving —"

"Sunscreen check!" trumpets Mrs. Reid. She fixes Zach with a disapproving glance. "You're awfully burnt. Take some."

"Thanks, Mrs. Reid." He sidles up beside Penny. "Come on. I'll help you with yours."

It's her chance.

"Wait here." Penny presses the plastic bag full of bracelets on Connor. "Would you hold this for me? Please?"

He meets her eyes, questioning.

Desperately, she wills him to trust her and not argue.

"Okay." His voice is neutral. "I'll be right here if you need me."

Zach takes Penny by the hand. "Come on, babe. We don't want a repeat of what happened last year in Nantucket." He winks at Mrs. Reid, who is standing only a few feet away. "Two hours on the beach, and this one" — he nods at Penny — "was redder than a lobster."

As they walk away, Penny hears Mrs. Reid say, "Aren't they an adorable couple?"

When they're just out of earshot, Zach flips open the bottle and squeezes a pool of white lotion into his palm.

Penny's mouth is drier than the blowing dust. "Zach . . ."

"Hold still. I'll be your mirror." He leans in close and smears the cold sunscreen across her forehead, down her nose, and across each cheek like war paint. He squeezes out more sunscreen and puts his hand up to her neck. She gives an involuntary start. "Hey, it's all right. I got you." He rubs in the lotion, up to her jaw. He must be able to feel her pulse racing. But surely he's far too conceited to correctly interpret that.

There's a gentleness in his eyes. "You're safe now."

For a split second, doubt cuts in.

But she can still feel the sting where his nails dug into her arm.

"I'm sorry I got so emotional before," he whispers.

"That's okay." Her voice is hoarse.

He rubs the cold sunscreen into the back of her neck. "I'm glad I finally got you alone."

Penny doesn't trust herself to speak.

Then he does what she knew he would. "Penny, let's go back to the party. You can remember. I know you can. What happened after you got ice cream?"

Penny looks straight into his oh-so-honest brown eyes. "Well, Ayla and I went to sit under a tree."

"Uh-huh?" Zach smooths the lotion under her eyes and up to her temples.

Penny's voice gets stronger. "A woman came up to me and asked me if I was the girl who won the bingo. And then . . ." Penny gasps. "Oh, Zach."

"What?"

She holds up her left hand. "She gave me this."

"Good luck." A slow smile spreads across Zach's face. "Of *course*!" Thank God, he takes his hands off her face. He cradles her wrist and unclips the bracelet. Eagerness and sunscreen-greasy fingers make him clumsy. He gets the clasp open. "It must be in the bead. Oh, Penny. I knew I could count on you." Zach clasps both her hands, and she forces herself to look him in the face. "You know you can never tell anyone about this. Never. Not even Connor. If you tell, it could be a death sentence for you both. Do you understand?"

How can he possibly think she's dumb enough to fall for this crap? But, she reminds herself, she fell for it before. She widens her eyes. "What are you going to do?"

"I have to leave. I need to get this somewhere safe."

"But what should I tell Connor? And Sully will want to know why you disappeared."

"Tell Connor that Eylo contacted me.

405

They never managed to give you the proof at all. Now I've gone underground to get it. Tell Sully I loved the dervishes so much, I decided to hitch back to Konya and see Rumi's tomb. Can you remember that, Penny?"

Sully's voice carries across the parking lot. "Back on the bus, everybody! Time to go!"

Zach squares his jaw, every inch the handsome, self-sacrificing hero. "I'll never forget you, Penny."

With supreme self-control Penny bites back a retort. "I know."

He leans in to kiss her, but she holds up her hand. Her voice shakes a little. She hopes he can't tell it's with rage. "I can't let you do that."

He grins and dabs a white spot of lotion off her nose. "You're sweet." He hands her the bottle of sunscreen. "Bye, Penny."

She watches him stroll down to a motorcycle in the parking lot, fiddle with the ignition, and roar out of the parking lot.

Connor races up beside her, plastic bag on his wrist. "Where's he going?"

Penny swallows. "Not far enough."

39
GOLDEN BOY

Baltalimani, Istanbul
17:06 Local Time

Steel giant Borusan Holding's Bosphorus headquarters occupy a nine-floor turreted mansion, lodged on the European shore of the Bosphorus between the rambling stone castle Mehmet the Conqueror built in the mid-fifteenth century, and the swooping intercontinental suspension bridge named after him in the 1980s.

On the top floor is a boardroom. Swivel chairs surround a meeting table of flickering solid steel. The chairs are empty. Security staff prefer to stand, and in weather this fine, the VIPs are out on the terrace, fawning over President Palamut, sipping mint-cucumber lemonades and admiring the view.

Moe extracts Brenda from a tense and unpromising exchange with the Turkish Minister of Foreign Affairs.

Moe sounds haggard. "It's Winthrop. He got a message on his personal phone. Now he says he's got a headache and he has to leave."

"In the middle of the reception? Is he having a stroke?"

"He wants to go back to the Consulate."

Brenda takes a deep breath. "Palamut's not gonna be happy."

"Nope."

"You going with him?"

"Winthrop wants us to stay and gloss things over."

"President Palamut doesn't want *us*. He wants Mr. Golden Boy to make him feel special."

"You don't have to tell me, Bren."

"Moe . . ." Brenda keeps her bland party expression glued in place, but her blood pressure is spiking. "If there's another attack —"

"We'd know, Bren. I'm sure. It was his private line. It's probably just a family thing."

"Sir?" Across the terrace, Frank hurries alongside Secretary Winthrop. "Where are you going?"

"You stay here, Frank." Winthrop forces a smile. "I got this."

■ ■ ■ ■

Christina repositions her neck cushion and leans back in her ergonomic chair. "Mr. Secretary, there's no use panicking."

"How could this happen?"

"Leaks are a fact of life."

"I'm already fielding questions about Penny Kessler." His breath quickens. "I think, worst-case scenario, maybe Palamut has his hands dirty. And *now* —"

"It's clear from your cousin's message that he is deranged. Miss Kessler died in a hospital in Ankara. As for Connor Beauregard, we had credible evidence that he was a double agent instrumental in the July 4th attack. Sometimes you have to make the hard calls and act fast on the intel that you have."

"When you said local partners, I didn't think you meant the fucking *Hashashin*!"

"If you're that naïve Robert, I got an iceberg in Texas to sell you. Great price. And remember: location, location, location."

"Christina, so help me —"

"You closed your eyes because you wanted

409

to, Mr. Secretary. In any event, it's all resolved now."

"You promised me what we were doing would never endanger American lives. You promised me it was secure!"

"Situations evolve."

"You gave money to the *Hashashin*! How the fuck did you not see this coming?"

"Let's keep it clean, Mr. Secretary." Christina tears open a second packet of Splenda. "None of this is my fault. I'd have thought Melek would have stronger security. Everybody gets a mole once in a while, but seriously — Kurdish *peace activists*? And, I may add, you gave us no indication that your cousin was quite so volatile."

"I'm sorry, do you people not run clearances? Isn't this what the INSIDER THREAT program is supposed to catch? I haven't even seen Jack for — God, eight years? We don't even do Christmas cards. He's my fuckup little cousin! He was always a fuckup. When he was fifteen, he got so high he burned down our grandfather's summer house."

"Please spare me the family reminiscences."

"Why the hell was he even in on this at all?"

"Obviously that situation wasn't anticipated."

"Why *wasn't* it anticipated?"

"Mr. Secretary, hindsight is always 20/20."

Winthrop says through his perfect teeth, "Jack claims he has hard proof of our involvement in arming the Hashashin."

Winthrop's lack of control irritates Christina. "I got the message, too, Robert."

"Is it possible?" Winthrop's voice is a ragged whisper.

"What do you want me to say, Robert? You want me to lie to you?"

"My career." Winthrop's breathing is uneven. "I was supposed to run. What am I going to tell my wife?"

"Stop being emotional. Focus on what's important."

"If this gets out . . ."

"Robert. You've got to keep a 10,000-foot view. What we're doing is in the national interest. We all condemn the embassy bombing. But at least it will enrich government spending on security — rev people up. After this NATO Summit, you'll be the Secretary of State who brought peace to Syria and made America look strong again in the aftermath of a devastating attack. And when you run, it'll be my honor to accept your appointment as Director."

"On your advice. We gave. U.S. taxpayer-funded weapons. To a pack of terrorists. Who used the money. To blow up our Embassy. At the *Fourth of July* party!"

"In light of the recent leak, Robert, I question the wisdom of being quite so explicit, even on a secure line."

"You *promised* we could control them!"

"Well, thanks to Jack's little Mor Samuel stunt, our partners are all dead. So at least it's a clean break. Now the only unstable element remaining is Jack."

"Well, aren't you the little optimist."

"There's no need for that kind of tone, Robert."

"What are we going to *do*?"

"You need to focus on the NATO Summit. It's our best chance to salvage the peace process. Just do your job, and let me do mine."

"And what about Jack?"

"I'm taking care of it."

"What does that mean?"

"Robert. You're asking questions you don't want answers to."

"The Summit starts tonight!" Winthrop's voice is the bitterest she's ever heard it. "If I'm going to negotiate, at least I need to know who's pulling my strings."

"It should be over by then."

He takes a deep breath. "What if it's not?"

"Then we work around it."

"Did you hear what he *wants*?" Winthrop's whisper barely scratches through the connection. "A consulting contract for *every* Agency and DOS project that goes through Turkey? We're talking tens of millions of taxpayer dollars. And it's not even the money. He'll have us by the short hairs for the rest of our lives! Christina, in three years, if I run —"

"*When* you run. Like I said, I'll take care of it. With Palamut's collaboration, we've rolled up Eylo overnight. So as soon as we get Jack's copy, we're safe."

"*If* we get it."

"He's on his own, Robert. Every trick he knows, we taught him. It shouldn't be too hard."

40
SURROUNDED

"We're making great time," Sully chirps from the tour-bus speakers. "We're entering the outskirts of Istanbul now. In about half an hour we arrive at in the neighborhood of Kadıköy, on the Asian side. We'll stop for a traditional Anatolian feast at Çiya and then take the ferry across to our hotel in the old city!"

"Chia?" One of the trio of thirtysomething redheaded sisters looks up from her phone. "Like, superfoods?"

"Hey." Connor glances over at Penny in the seat beside him in the third row of the bus. Her knees are pulled up to her chest. Her eyes never leave the shifting cityscape. She's been quiet a long time, fingers tight around a paper sickbag. "You doing a little better?"

Penny takes a shuddering breath.

414

"Quit beating yourself up." Connor holds up the plastic bag of evil eye bracelets. "Thanks to this — thanks to you — we have enough to tell the world. If we can get you to the NATO Summit, we can fix this."

"What happens when Zach realizes the bracelet I gave him was a fake?"

"Let's focus on the things we can control."

"You need to steal another phone," says Penny. "If we get word out we're still alive . . ."

"One email, one post, one *anything,* and Christina will know exactly where we are."

"She can't cover up everything. Not if enough people know!"

"If she's desperate enough to be using Reapers, we'd still be dead. And so would everyone else on this bus."

Penny holds her head in her hands. "What are we going to do?"

"We'll be in Kadıköy at seven. The NATO Summit keynote starts at eight forty-five. I say we go directly there. Istanbul's got, what, fifteen million people? The odds are in our favor, as long as we keep our profile low."

"Even if we make it to the Summit, how on earth are we going to make it inside? Palamut's Presidential Guard is going to be there. The Turkish military. American Diplomatic Security —"

"The Kempinski's a hotel, not a government facility. There's got to be a back way in. Have you been there before?"

"I've never even been to Istanbul, except to change planes on the way to Ankara. Ayla and I were supposed to stay here this whole weekend for the Summit. We'd planned out everything. Hagia Sophia, the cisterns from that James Bond movie, the Blue Mosque. Ayla said her mom used to take her to this wonderful little teahouse behind Topkapı Palace, where the old sultans' rose garden used to be. . . ."

"Come here." Connor pulls her into a hug.

"I only knew her for six weeks." Tears are streaking down Penny's face into his shirt. "How can I miss her so much?"

"Nobody is ever made less by caring."

"It's my fault." Penny squeezes her eyes shut. "If I hadn't trusted Zach —"

"If I hadn't trusted Christina, Faruk would probably still be alive."

"But that wasn't your fault!"

"And this isn't yours."

"Zach *must* have known about the Embassy attack," she whispers. "He must have helped the Hashashin plan it. . . ."

"He'll go to jail," says Connor with conviction. "Christina, too."

"What about the scandal? Don't your employers prefer to sweep the bad stuff under the rug?"

"Once the truth's out, it's out." Connor's pale eyes are bright. "When you walk into the main lobby where I work, there's a quote from the New Testament carved into the wall: 'And ye shall know the truth, and the truth shall make you free.' We make plenty of stupid mistakes. But I believe in our country. I believe in our ideals. And we've got to be better than that."

They are quiet together for a while. Against all logic, Penny feels a deep, sheltering peace.

"Connor?"

"Yeah?"

"What were you saying, when we jumped out of the helicopter?"

He laughs. "Pierrepont Sands, Pierrepont Sands, Pierrepont Sands. It's a beach in the middle of nowhere, South Carolina. Alex and I drive down there sometimes. His parents have a little shack in the woods, a mile from the beach — really a shack, just a generator for the lights. There are pelicans and loggerhead turtles, and the best sunsets you ever saw. It's where I go in my head when things get really bad."

She smiles. "To the turtles."

The microphone clicks back to life. Sully's ballooning enthusiasm fills the bus. "We are now approaching Kadıköy! We learned what *köy* means — does anyone remember?"

" 'Village'!" comes the prompt reply.

"Penny." Connor's face is tense. "Do you see those two black SUVs?"

Penny's heart plummets.

"One has been following us for a couple minutes. I wasn't sure before, but another one just pulled up behind us."

"That's *right,* Mrs. Reid! And Kadıköy means the 'village of the judge'!"

Penny whispers, "Those are Turkish government plates."

Connor straightens his collar. "Looks like we've got a bigger problem than Mr. Robson."

Penny struggles to keep calm. "How could Melek possibly know where we are?"

"Gotta be Zach. Who else could it be?"

"Known to the ancients as Chalcedon, Kadıköy was founded before Byzantium itself, over on the European side. The first human settlement here was over three thousand years ago!"

"Back when I was growing up," crows Mr. George.

"The shoppers in our group — you know who you are — will love it," continues Sully.

418

"Kadıköy has one of Istanbul's best street markets!"

Penny digs into the plastic bag. "If it's Zach, he'll expect me to have the evil eye." She leans down and clips a decoy bracelet around her right ankle.

"An anklet?" says Connor drily. "Isn't that a little tacky?"

She sits up and meets his eyes. "You've got to take the real one." She pulls it out of the bag. It's easy to identify — the only one with a stained, fraying cord.

"And how do we keep Robson from noticing my new bling?"

Carefully, Penny unwraps the bandages at the base of his wounded hand. She fastens the real evil eye around his wrist and rewraps the bandages.

The soundtrack of normalcy fills the bus: excited chatter, hushed predinner squabbles, the rustling of food wrappers and empty water bottles, Sully's patter.

At Fenerbahçe Stadium the tour bus turns off the Istanbul ring road.

"Look at those big black cars," exclaims Mrs. Cochrane.

Mrs. Reid has an explanation at the ready. "It must be something to do with the NATO conference. I read that Robert Winthrop is giving the keynote. He spoke at our library benefit, when he was first elected to Congress. Such a *charming* young man, really presidential . . ."

The SUVs flank the bus fore and aft.

Closing in on them.

Penny leans back into the plush of the bus seat. Panic slides in, swift and gentle as a needle.

Sully frowns. He stoops to whisper to the driver.

"We're putting everyone in danger." Penny turns to Connor. "It's me they want. If I get out first and distract them, you can run. Just get to the NATO Summit, and tell them —"

Connor shakes his head. "We're in this together."

As the tour bus inches under the squat overpass and down Söğütlü Çeşme Avenue, Penny tunnels through thickening panic. *Söğütlü çeşme.* The fountain with willows. Boxy stores and residential blocks of stained concrete rise several stories high on either side; fast-food chains and offices. Hard to imagine swaying willow branches and icy water bubbling up through the rock.

Flanked by the black SUVs, the tour bus pulls out into the wide square that abuts the Bosphorus. The blue water is hardly visible past the huge spread of asphalt, which is jammed with old minibuses and city buses bound for every corner of this rambling megalopolis. Beyond the parking lot, a low ferry terminal is just visible.

The bus wheezes to a halt. The black SUVs swerve around it.

"What on earth —" exclaims Mrs. Cochrane.

"Keep calm, ladies and gentlemen!" urges Sully. "Do not be alarmed — they are police. There is no reason to panic."

"We'll never make it," says Penny.

Connor frantically scans the scene. "If we can just get as far as the crowd, blend in —"

"How?"

Four Kevlar-vested members of Palamut's Presidential Guard step up to the bus, brandishing machine guns.

Penny jumps to her feet. "Listen, everyone," she shouts. "I'm Penny Kessler. The" — she winces — "girl with the flag. From the U.S. Embassy." She grabs Connor's arm. "My friend works for the American government. The Turkish police want to kill us. You've got to help us. Please."

Mrs. Cochrane holds out her hand. "It's all right, dear. You're — upset —"

"I'm not crazy! Don't any of you recognize me?" Penny turns to Sully in desperation.

"*Doğru söylüyorum!* I'm telling the truth!"

"*Hay Allah.*" Sully stares at her.

Palamut's Presidential Guards scream to open the bus.

"Just let us off," says Connor. "They won't hurt any of you!"

Sully turns to the driver. "Open the door!"

The door wheezes open.

Penny grips Connor's left hand in hers as they step down onto the asphalt.

A woman's shriek pierces the parking lot, followed by gunshots.

The Presidential Guards turn around.

A motorcycle barrels straight toward the tour bus, scattering the screaming crowd. The rider is wearing a black helmet, visor down, and a bulky black vest.

"*TERÖRIST VAR! TERÖRIST!*"

41
LUCKY

A widening black circle of empty asphalt spreads around the motorcycle. The crowd pulls back in a stumbling, frightened tide. One peddler selling *köfte* meatballs off a little charcoal grill jumps up so fast he knocks the coals onto the dry grass of the median, which catches fire.

The four Presidential Guards advance cautiously.

"Why don't they shoot him?" cries Mrs. Cochrane.

"He's wearing a suicide vest!" Mrs. Reid screams. "If they shoot him, he might blow up the whole square!"

"That bastard." Connor pulls his hand free, grabs the large plastic watercooler from the front of the bus, and runs directly toward the motorcycle.

Two more shots.

"Connor! No!" Penny tears after him. *"Connor!"*

Not fast enough.

"Everybody back!" Connor's almost there.

The rider fires at him.

Misses.

Connor hurls the watercooler under the motorcycle's front wheel. The motorcycle screams a wild half circle, straight into the smoldering dry grass of the median, throwing the rider across the asphalt.

No explosion.

The Presidential Guards head in.

But the rider has one more shot in his gun.

Just as the Presidential Guards approach the motorcycle on the burning median, he fires. Straight at the motorcycle's fuel tank. For an instant, there's nothing but the trickle of gasoline.

Then the motorcycle explodes, knocking the guards to the ground. Connor tackles the rider, pinning him to the asphalt. He pulls off the rider's helmet.

The rider grabs Connor's wounded hand and twists. As Connor doubles up, the rider sits up and smashes him in the jaw. The rider's eyes fix on Penny.

Zach.

She turns and bolts. Zach races after her, and the guards follow Zach.

Penny pounds past abandoned minibuses and screaming stragglers. She doesn't dare look behind.

She drops to the ground and rolls under a parked minibus. Gasoline fumes make her choke. Zach shucks off the vest and dives in after her. Penny drags herself out the other side. The asphalt claws into her palms as she springs up. She races out along the waterside promenade, up to the old white ferry terminal.

The ferrymen are unlooping the snake-thick rope that ties the lumbering commuter ferry to the dock.

The vest didn't blow up when Zach hit the asphalt.

Sometimes a black vest in summertime is only a black vest.

Penny's legs burn as she runs. Fresh blood is running down her asphalt-ripped palms.

She has to get Zach as far as possible away from Connor. From the real evil eye.

She summons every last fragment of strength and races into the ferry terminal. The bomb panic has spread. People are struggling for the exits. Penny hoists herself over the metal turnstile and scrambles toward the dock.

"Penny!" Zach's deep voice cuts through the screaming. "Penny, stop!"

Angry shouts chase her through the high, white-plastered hall of the ferry terminal's old waiting room.

Stop!

Where are you going?

She races out the high doors and along the salt-worn concrete of the dock, against the brisk damp breeze off the water.

The ferrymen are pulling away the two parallel gangways. Penny's feet skid on the wet, ribbed-steel plank as she scrambles onto the ship. Surprised faces turn to her as she lands hard on the deck.

"Are you all right?"

She pushes herself up. "I'm fine —"

"Late for dinner?" joshes a father, with a tiny pigtailed girl on his shoulders.

Penny freezes.

Under his windbreaker, the young father's shirt has a half-visible police logo embroidered on it. Undercover? On his way home from work?

"Fast!" The toddler claps her hands at Penny. Like most Turkish babies, she has an evil eye pinned to her sleeve.

With a mechanical roar and a stream of tiny pale blue bubbles, the ferry pulls away from the dock.

Penny turns around, breathing hard. Where's Zach? She races to the lower-level railing. No sign of him on the dock. The cool breeze slaps back her hair as the ferry grinds past the long stone breakwater into open water, toward Eminönü. Seagulls dive like *simit*-seeking missiles in the wake. The people around her are laughing, chatting, on their way home for dinner on an easy summer evening. Even at seven, the light is still lustrous. Not brash gold like the sun that hammers down on Mardin, but soft as water, almost pearly.

Penny runs along the narrow outer deck that rings the ferry. The sharpening breeze has chased the other passenger indoors.

Didn't Zach follow her? Where is he? She holds on to the railing, gasping for breath. The silhouette of old Istanbul spreads in front of her: trees, domes, minarets.

A hand loops around her waist and pulls her close. She can feel the prickle of something sharp and metallic at the base of her spine.

Zach says, in a low voice, "Sightseeing?"

42
CROSSING

Penny squirms. "Let me go."

"Isn't it pretty?" He points at the grandest of all the domes, squared in by four stocky minarets. "Hagia Sophia. Almost fifteen hundred years old."

"Same as Mor Samuel *was.*" She braces against his grip, but he holds tight. "Let me go."

"You can't possibly think that's going to work."

She grits her teeth. "I'm not afraid of you."

The knife's point scrapes her back. "You know," he says, "it makes a big difference where on the spine an injury occurs. If I cut where the knife is now, you might walk again eventually. On crutches. Whereas if I push through the vertebrae here" — he draws the knife up her spine, between her shoulder blades — "you'll never get out of a wheelchair. Hooked up to a ventilator for life."

Penny draws a deep breath.

The knife presses into the skin between her shoulder blades, just enough to sting. "Screaming would be a very bad idea."

She exhales and cranes her head around. Maybe it would hurt less if he suddenly looked evil, but he doesn't.

It's just Zach.

The ferry rounds Sarayburnu, where the European shore buckles outward in a peninsula. It chugs toward the Golden Horn, where it will dock at Eminönü, across a broad square from the Spice Bazaar.

If she can just stall long enough to reach Eminönü . . . "And if I give you the evil eye, what? You'll just let me walk away?"

"Why not? You won't get far with Melek and Christina after you. And even if you do, you have no proof of anything. If you show up babbling about plots and terrorists and evil eyes and secret CIA conspiracies . . . well, everyone knows you had a head injury, you poor little thing. Plus, State told the press you were dead. Winthrop can have fun explaining *that* away."

Penny stomps on Zach's foot.

Zach tightens his hold. "I know you hate me right now. But it's Christina you should be angry with. I never tried to hurt you. I made sure you didn't go near the Embassy bomb. And it's thanks to me you aren't playing hide-the-electrodes with Palamut's Presidential Guard right now."

"You're sweet," she snaps.

"I'm really not the bad guy here, Penny."

"Dressing up as a suicide bomber? Threatening to cripple me?"

"*Bad* is Christina arming the Hashashin. *Bad* is my perfect cousin screwing everybody over twelve ways to Sunday. But they love him. Me? I fuck up once, and they try to take my whole career away. Everything. And when I ask my cousin for help? He gives me a fucking campaign speech about integrity. No." Zach shakes his head. "My only crime is not being high enough up the totem pole. Yet."

"Wow." She shakes her head.

"Aw. Did I shock the innocent little intern?"

"You know," says Penny through her teeth, "when the Hashashin blow themselves up, at least those bastards believe it's for a cause. But murdering hundreds of people because you're mediocre at your job? That's just pathetic."

"That wasn't supposed to happen." Zach's grip tightens. "It was supposed to be a controlled explosion. Just enough to compromise him. To give me maximum leverage."

"Compromise who?"

"Believe me, I had no idea the Hashashin were planning a bomb that size."

"But you *did* know they were planning one." Her hands are shaking. "You said you kept me away from it."

"Yes."

"Which means you must have known *exactly* where and when it was going to be. Which means you let everyone else die. Ayla. The Ambassador. Martin MacGowan. Practically every single person in POL Section. Almost three hundred people. You murdered them. You murdered them all."

"The Embassy bomb was remotely detonated. Somewhere, some Hashashin terrorist was watching a live stream of the party. And then, boom, he pressed a button. Is that supposed to be my fault?"

"You dropped your drink."

"What?"

Penny squeezes her eyes shut. "You're not a clumsy guy. After Mehmetoğlu got that text that said the microchip had been delivered — as soon as you made sure I wasn't going anywhere — you dropped your drink. And then the bomb went off." Bile stings her throat. "You were giving the order

431

to press the button."

Zach says nothing.

"It seems pretty stupid to make sure I had the microchip and then just let me go." Penny swallows. "Why didn't you just take the microchip at the party? Or at least have the Hashashin kidnap me, too?"

"I wasn't supposed to be knocked out." The point of the knife presses into the base of her neck. She can feel the angry tremor in Zach's hand. "I was going to carry you heroically to safety and retrieve the chip. But those assholes got greedy. That fucking bomb was ten times bigger than we agreed. I woke up in the van halfway to Mardin. The Hashashin didn't know about the chip. We agreed they could take Mehmetoğlu — a kind of freebie. But Kurds are just target practice. They wanted me, too."

"Ten times bigger than you *agreed*?" Penny's voice is raw. "Did you negotiate about how many people you were willing to kill? You knew there would be children there. And you let those bastards put the bomb *in the ice cream truck.*" She cranes around to see his face. "What about Mia? Did you think about what it would mean for her, having a father who's a traitor and murderer? What about all the children at the Embassy party? Did you think about

432

them? About their parents?"

"Mia." Zach chuckles. "What the fuck would I want with a kid? Mia is a bunch of photos I copied off some mommy blogger on Instagram."

"You fucking sociopath."

He shrugs. "You wouldn't sleep with me. You're too boring to blackmail and too uptight to bribe. I had to find another way to synthesize a bond." He grins. "You said we had to trust each other, remember?"

Penny can barely get the words out. "I told you about my childhood. You knew I'd do anything to keep a little kid from getting hurt."

"Penny?" He leans his chin on the hollow of her shoulder. His breath is warm against her cheek, his voice amused. "*I know you're stalling.* You're talented, don't get me wrong. But it's another fifteen minutes before we get to Eminönü. You know you can't go crying for help; if Palamut's police get hold of you, you're dead. So come on. Just give me the evil eye, and I won't hurt you. I'll even buy you an apple soda from the bar."

"It's on my right ankle. See for yourself."

"How unobservant of me."

She watches him. "Aren't you going to take it?"

"So you can kick me in the face?" He

chuckles. "Oh, don't look so disappointed. No, you're going to unbuckle it for me." He traces the knife point up her neck. "Now."

"Baba!" A tiny pigtailed figure races toward the railing. "Look, *Baba*! Seagulls!"

"Careful, *Nur'cuğum*!" The father scoops the giggling child away from danger and cuddles her close.

The toddler waves at Penny. "Fast!"

The father turns.

Words rise in Penny's throat.

Zach pulls her closer. She feels a sharp sting and a small drip of warm blood down the back of her neck.

The young father smiles. "Now I know why you were in such a hurry!" He carries the toddler back inside.

Zach waits until they're alone again. The besotted smile slides off his face. "Crouch down slowly and take off the evil eye."

With exaggerated molasses slowness, Penny stoops. She fumbles with the bracelet clasp, stalling for time, praying for some kind of last-second inspiration.

And then it comes.

"What about Connor?" She rises, bracelet in her fist. "Maybe you're right. Nobody would believe me alone. But Connor's a CIA officer. A military vet. He isn't like you, Zach. He's brave and he's honest and he'll *fight* for what he knows is true." Her voice strengthens in triumph as she looks up at Zach. "All he has to do is get to the NATO Summit. And you're too late to stop him now."

"He was out cold, Penny. I saw those guards shove him into the back of a car. I don't think anybody will ever be seeing Connor again."

"How do I know that's not another lie?" Penny fights through the nausea.

"You don't. But it's true."

The horrible thing is, she believes him.

She blusters. What else can she do? "So what if Melek's got him? I escaped from her with no training and no weapons. I'm sure Connor can waltz out in half the time."

"You escaped *because* you had no training and no weapons. They were careless. They won't be that sloppy again." Zach leans down to look her in the eye. "Melek has a certain way of doing business. I know where she's taking Connor. He won't get out."

"You can't know that."

"Look. Even if, by some freakish chance, Captain Wonderful escapes, nobody is going to believe a word he says. He has no proof." Zach holds out his hand. "Give me the evil eye."

The ferry draws near the mouth of the Golden Horn. Smaller ferries jostle around them in a bobbing traffic jam.

"I can't," Penny whispers.

"No is really not an option."

Penny opens her fist. "It's just another decoy."

He rolls his eyes. "Sure it is."

"You studied me, didn't you? You worked me all summer. Does that sound like something I'd do?"

"You lied at the caravanserai."

"See for yourself, Mr. Honesty!"

He reaches out warily and takes the bracelet. Keeping the knife at her neck, he holds the evil eye up to the sun. The light shines clear through, blue and pure. Nothing but glass.

His voice is surprisingly calm. "Where is the real one?"

"Connor has it."

Zach exhales hard.

Penny snatches back the bracelet and fixes it around her left wrist.

The ferry bellies up the Golden Horn toward the Galata Bridge. A little white ferry — one of the small shore-hoppers, almost empty — roars perilously close beside them, obviously determined to beat its big sibling to the landing. Oblivious, the big commuter ferry cuts it off, veering toward Eminönü on the left bank, where the New Mosque's dozens of dove-gray domes rise beside the crowded plaza of the Spice Bazaar. Behind the ferry landing, silent squad cars line the road. Waiting.

Penny turns to Zach. "You said you know where Melek's taking Connor. Is that true?"

"Why?"

"I can't save Connor alone." Penny swallows hard. "Help me, and you can have the evil eye. The real one."

Zach's expression is sardonic, but he lowers the knife. "What time yesterday do you think I was born?"

"Connor would die before he gave it to you. You need me."

"And you'd just hand it over?"

"I don't want my friend to die. And I'm prepared to guess that you're prepared to guess that you can probably force me to give it to you."

"Touché."

Onshore, armed police file onto the ferry landing.

Penny backs away. "Did you *have* to impersonate a suicide bomber?"

Zach sheathes the knife. "Follow me."

Penny races after him to the back of the

boat. Zach hoists himself up onto the railing.

"Are you *crazy*?"

He lunges out over the water.

No splash.

Penny scrambles across the slippery deck, toward the railing of the ferry.

Eight feet down, across two feet of choppy water, on the empty rear deck of the little white ferry, Zach straightens up and beckons her.

Penny pulls herself up on the metal railing. Her bloody palms leave prints on the peeling white paint.

The big ferry grinds against the rocky bed as it maneuvers toward the dock.

"Hurry!" hisses Zach.

Penny jumps. She barely clears the iron side of the little ferry and lands painfully on her knees.

Did anyone see her? Penny cranes around to see the window of the big ferry. Nobody was watching; all faces are turned to the police on the dock.

Except for one. The tiny pigtailed girl is watching gravely over her father's shoulder, fingers in her mouth. She pulls her hand out for a rather slimy wave.

Penny waves back.

The larger ferry docks. No sooner do the

ferrymen slide the ramp into place than dozens of dark-uniformed policemen charge on board. The little ferry slips into a smaller berth, closer to the Galata Bridge, its lip protruding over the concrete. Without waiting for the dockhands to slide the disembarking stairs into place, Penny and Zach hop onto solid ground.

Zach's arm slips back around her waist. Penny flinches.

"Smile," he whispers. "And walk nice and slow." He pulls a smartphone out of his pocket and holds it up to his face as they cross the road to the tram stop, pretending to photograph the Spice Bazaar. "Have you got coins?"

Penny digs a few lira out of her pocket to buy plastic *jetons* for the tram. On the docks, police are swarming all over the large ferry.

"Which way?" asks Penny. "Bağcılar or Kabataş?"

"Kabataş. Stay on till the last stop."

The tram is painfully crowded — a gauntlet of sharp elbows, overcooked tourists in Hawaiian shirts, and swinging shopping bags. The clock over the door reads 19:36.

Penny reaches up to a slippery yellow plastic grip and holds tight, so the blood from her palms won't run.

With a cartoonish strum of electronic harmonies, the tram glides out of the stop, up onto the Galata Bridge, and across to Karaköy, at the foot of the faded hill that rises to the Galata Tower. How can there already be another stop? They've hardly gone a quarter of a mile!

More passengers crush aboard. Finally, the doors close again. A soft female voice issues from the speakers: "Next stop: Tophane."

Penny stoops under a businessman's sleeve to meet Zach's eyes. He looks straight through her and leans casually against the pole, the quintessence of a bored commuter. The tram pulls beneath the old Ottoman cannon foundry and out past the naval offices and insurance-company buildings that line this semi-deindustrialized patch of the European shore.

She could scream. People would help her. She might even escape. Make it to the Consulate. Tell them, convince them —

And in some lonely room, Connor would die, long before help could reach him.

"Fındıklı," coos the recording as the tram whirrs alongside a waterfront park. "Next stop: Kabataş."

At Kabataş, passengers uncramp themselves and hustle onto the platform. Penny and Zach cross to the right side of the road. Penny takes a deep breath of cool air off the water. The light is getting redder now. Zach hails a cab and both of them climb into the back.

"Tarabya'ya," orders Zach. His Turkish is slicker than Penny's, more colloquial, but his accent remains as gummily American as a slice of Kraft cheese.

The cabbie warns him that the coastal road is closed through Ortaköy.

"Cut up Barbaros and over to Maslak, then down to the coast from there. Can you turn the radio off, buddy?"

"Tarabya?" asks Penny.

"Old presidential residence down near there," Zach replies in English. "Melek's been having it fixed up. She's the only one who uses it these days."

"And you think . . ."

"Nice and quiet for interrogations. And if she wants to get rid of a body, there's plenty of room."

European Shore, Istanbul
19:34 Local Time
Connor wakes with an aching jaw as the SUV speeds down an unfamiliar, leafy boulevard. On the left, gated mansions. On the right, glittering blue water. Blaring

441

sirens echo in his sore skull. Through frosted windows, he can see cars swerving out of their way.

The driver is on his cell phone, expostulating in Turkish. Sounds defensive, but careful, like he's breaking bad news to a superior.

Penny would understand exactly what he's saying.

Penny.

"Where is she?" Connor straightens up in his seat, to find his hands and feet are bound. "Do any of you speak English? Where are you taking me?"

The young Presidential Guard buckled beside him just stares straight ahead.

"Where are we going?"

No answer. But that doesn't mean that they can't understand.

"Where's Penny Kessler? What did you do to her?"

The SUV turns left, swerving uphill on a shaded side road, to the service entrance in a high wall. Connor recognizes the insignia on the gate.

The SUV pulls up at a small brick outbuilding. The guards shove Connor inside and muscle him down a brightly lit flight of stairs.

At the bottom is what looks like a suburban finished basement.

Still no sign of Penny.

In the corner, one of the Guards bends over what looks like a stove, holding a tiny metal pot.

With agonizing clarity, Connor's remembers his anti-interrogation training down on the Farm. Acid. Hot lead poured on bare skin. Even plain boiling water can do terrible things to human flesh. He wishes he still had those white pills. A quick fistful and no power on earth could make him speak.

A thirtyish, dark-eyed woman in a tasteful violet turban and matching silk tunic is poised at a glass table in the center of the basement, her hands steepled in front of her.

There is a sweet scent of roses.

And . . . coffee?

U.S. Consul General's Residence, Istanbul
19:39 Local Time

"Excuse me, sir, ma'am." One of Moe Sokolof's bodyguards hurries into the living room of the CG's residence. "The driver asked me please to inform you that if the car doesn't leave soon, it won't be possible to get to the Kempinski on schedule."

Carolyn Sokolof nods. "Thank you, Ah-met. I'll let my husband know."

Brenda is bent over her BlackBerry, nursing a glass of ginger ale. She's changed into another, more formal black pantsuit, black ribbon pinned beside the flag pin on her lapel. "I just heard from Frank Lerman. Winthrop's already on his way to the keynote. Security precaution. That bomb scare in Kadıköy is making security extra jumpy."

"How thoughtful of Mr. Lerman to let us know *after* we waited twenty minutes." Carolyn slides her feet back into her heels and looks up as her husband comes hurrying in. "Moe, where've you been?"

Moe holds up his phone, looking dazed. "There was a call to the consular emergency line about half an hour ago. Just made it up the ladder to me. Mary Reid, one of the tourists affected by the Kadıköy bomb scare, reported that a girl who joined her tour bus in Cappadocia identified herself as Penny Kessler, and then disappeared, pursued by the motorcycle bomber."

"What?"

"That's insane," says Carolyn. "Why are they even forwarding that kind of craziness to you?"

"They managed to get a photo from one of the other tourists on the bus." Moe grimaces. "It does look kind of like the girl

444

in the flag photo. You knew her, Bren. What do you think?"

"It can't be." But Brenda takes the phone.

Ginger ale and glass shards splatter on the carpet.

Büyükdere Avenue, Istanbul
19:41 Local Time

The taxi bumps away from the skyscrapers of the Maslak financial district, down the slope to the glitzy coastal hamlet of Tarabya and the outcropping at Kalender.

Penny fixes her eyes on the horizon, fighting the car sickness. Zach has bummed a cigarette off the driver, and clovey smoke fills the cab.

They pull up on the coastal road, beside the high walls of the Huber Mansion.

"Burada mı?" asks the cabbie incredulously. He nods at the empty road. "There's nothing here, *abi.*"

Zach gestures toward the wide sweep of the Bosphorus. The slow sunset settles in broken pinks and scarlets across the face of the water. *"Romantik."*

Penny and Zach step out into the fresh breeze as the cab speeds away.

Penny looks up at the mansion's forbidding wall. "What now? Do we just go introduce ourselves to the guards at the gate?"

"Pretty much." Zach shrugs. "Getting in isn't the tricky part."

43
CLUTCHING AT SNAKES

Huber Mansion, Kalender, Istanbul
19:43 Local Time

"Mr. Beauregard. Thank you for coming." The Turkish woman doesn't rise. "How much sugar do you take?"

Connor stares. "Ms. Palamut?"

"Please, sit. Sugar. In your coffee." Melek gives him a mild hostess smile. "Don't tell me you haven't tried Turkish coffee?"

Connor perches on the edge of one of the wooden chairs. His voice comes out hoarse. "I only arrived in Turkey yesterday, ma'am."

"Melek *Hanım*?" One of the guards hurries down the stairs.

Melek looks exasperated.

Before she can speak, the guard bursts out in a flurry of low Turkish. Emotions flicker across Melek Palamut's mobile features: astonishment, triumph, caution. Then, with regal gentleness, she gives a brisk order. She turns back to Connor. *"Anladınız mı?"*

"I'm sorry, ma'am?"

"Of course not." Her smile is tight, voice dry. "Christina never wanted you to understand." She looks up at the stairs behind him. "How much sugar, Mr. Beauregard?"

Ortaköy, Istanbul
19:45 Local Time
The Consul General's black SUV and identical follow car race up the coastal road toward the Kempinski.

Secretary Winthrop's voice comes through the speaker of Brenda's BlackBerry, conciliatory and assured. "That's simply not possible."

"Mr. Secretary, I saw the photo myself. She's sunburnt, and her hair's different, but it's Penny. I'm sure it is. And that means that an hour ago, she was alive, and in Istanbul."

"You're sure a dead girl is alive? Brenda, you've got to understand how this sounds."

"Sir, the photo —"

"Frank Lerman's taken some people to go check it out." Winthrop's voice sharpens. "And I have to ask you to stop chasing ghosts and do your job. The NATO Summit is wheels up in half an hour. We simply can't afford this kind of distraction. I certainly can't."

Brenda exhales. "Yes, sir."

"Am I on speaker? Can Moe hear me?"

Moe Sokolof leans forward. "Yes, Mr. Secretary."

"When you arrive, I want you both to come directly to my suite. I'm hearing from DC that we may be looking at some last-minute adjustments."

Huber Mansion, Kalender, Istanbul
19:48 Local Time

The small door in the high seafront wall of the Huber Mansion complex swings open. Four Presidential Guards escort Penny and Zach as they cross the grassy compound into the dark leafy shade, toward a low brick outbuilding.

"We're here to see Melek *Hanım,*" says Zach in Turkish. "Not tour the parking lot."

One of the guards gestures down the stairs. "She is waiting."

Penny glances at Zach. "What if it's a trap?"

"Kind of late to worry about that."

"Penny?" shouts a familiar voice from below. "Is that you?"

Penny plunges down the stairs two at a time.

Connor, wrists unbound, is sitting at a table with Melek Palamut. Two tiny cups of

Turkish coffee steam in the fluorescent glow. His face crumples. "They got you."

She rushes up to him. "Are you okay?"

"You're just in time, Penny." Melek stands up. "And this is Mr. Robson, no?"

Connor recoils. "What's *he* doing here?"

Melek gives a gracious nod. "Mr. Robson, I believe we met at the German Ambassador's Labor Day reception."

Zach slips seamlessly into diplomat mode. "I'm honored that you remember, Melek *Hanım.*"

"Türk kahvesi?"

Zach smiles. *"Çok şekerli olsun."*

"You have a sweet tooth," observes Melek. "And you, Penny? You look exhausted."

Penny stands straighter. "No, thank you."

One of the guards locks the door. There are six of them, all heavily armed.

"Now," says Melek, resuming her chair, "please sit. I'd like to discuss the future."

Penny tries to mask terror with sarcasm. "Are you going to read our future in the coffee grounds?"

Melek actually laughs. It makes her look more human, and about a decade younger. "I don't have time to waste on theatrics, Penny. Sit."

Penny and Zach obey.

Melek folds her hands. "Are you familiar

450

with a woman at the CIA who calls herself Christina?"

"Why?" asks Connor.

Melek levels a hard stare at him and Penny. "Because earlier today, she asked me to kill you both."

Penny and Connor exchange a glance.

"My faith teaches that if you take a single life outside the strictures of the law, it's as if you've killed all mankind. And to save a single human life is to save all humanity." Melek tilts her head. "We must all learn to temper our ideals with practicality. Belief is no magic pill against hard choices. But I've never taken a life. I'd prefer not to start today."

Penny crosses her arms. "That sounds awfully sanctimonious coming from the woman who threatened to torture me yesterday."

"*Threatened,* Penny. But I never touched you."

"Only because you didn't get the chance!"

"You don't know that."

"I've got a question, ma'am," says Connor, his hand in the air.

Melek's mouth twitches. "You really don't have to raise your hand."

Connor lowers it, ears red. "What are *you* doing taking orders from CIA?"

451

"I'm trying not to." Melek takes a deep breath. "Christina is attempting to blackmail me. I would prefer she didn't succeed."

One of the guards sets down a coffee by Zach, and a water in front of Penny.

"I see, ma'am," says Connor. "And you figure if she wants us dead, we must have something on her."

"Just so." Melek takes a sip.

"And you think we'll tell *you*?" says Penny.

"I suspect it is a question of giving, not telling. I know Christina tried and failed to kill two of her own citizens. Yet neither of you, Penny and Mr. Beauregard, are of particular importance — your word alone would carry very little weight. So whatever it is she wants hidden, you must have some kind of proof. And that proof is what I need. Along with her title, and her full name."

"You know, I've read the dossier on you, Melek *Hanım,*" says Zach. "They're right. You *are* the intelligent one."

Melek looks neither flattered nor annoyed; her voice is neutral. "I've read your dossier, too, Mr. Robson. Christina told me you were a terrorist sympathizer, working with the Hashashin. Yet it very much appears that prior to the Embassy bombing, you were also cooperating with the Kurds. Clearly, you're not a man of God. So far as I can

452

tell, you act neither from madness, nor principle, nor duress. So you're acting for gain — or possibly revenge. Given Christina's interest in you, I take it your efforts have met with some success."

Zach smiles.

"But," says Melek, "your willingness to come here tells me that you haven't yet got what you wanted."

"So you won't let us go unless we tell you what Christina did?" says Penny.

"The proof you hold can buy you life or it can buy you death. Frankly, I think my offer's the better of the two."

"What if we do give it to you?" Zach doesn't touch his coffee. "How do we know you won't just kill us anyway?"

"I swear on my father's life."

"That isn't good enough," says Zach.

Connor meets Melek's eyes. "You know what happened in Kadıköy, ma'am. And so do all the hundreds of other people in that parking lot. Even Christina can't hide the truth much longer. There are too many loose ends. The world is going to know that we survived. It's one thing to be a murderer. It's another for everyone to *know* you are. Especially if you don't want to implicate your father." Connor takes a deep breath. "You can't afford to kill us."

Melek sets down her coffee. "Your line of reasoning is not without its flaws, Mr. Beauregard. You assume that my guards shooting foreign spies who attempted to break into a presidential residence in the wake of a devastating terrorist attack would reflect badly on *me*. I encourage you to rethink that assumption."

"It would still be very messy for you, and for your father," says Penny.

"A week of rain will wash away your little mess. Your country does not want another stupid war."

Penny tries another tack. "You know we can't go to the media with this — who would believe us?"

"Who indeed?"

"So why murder us?" Penny switches into Turkish. "Is that really what you want right now? Don't we all need less killing? Don't we all want peace?"

"You presumptuous child," Melek replies in the same language, quiet and calm. "You think you know everything about my situation, don't you?"

"I . . ."

"You think because you can read our newspapers and watch our television, because you come and stay in my country for a few weeks, you *understand*? You really

454

think you're ready to play this game?"

"I'm not playing games." Penny looks Melek square in the eye. "I told you. I'm not a spy. I'm not even a diplomat. And I'm not a child. I may not understand your country, but I care about this place and these people. Killing us won't make anything better. It just makes you as bad as Christina. I sure wouldn't want to be like her. And I *definitely* wouldn't want to do her dirty work for her. Do you?"

Melek is very still.

Penny switches back into English. "You can get us inside the Kempinski, can't you?"

"A police launch is at the Tarabya pier," says Melek. "*If* you give me what I need."

Penny looks to Connor. "What do you think?"

Three deep lines crease Connor's forehead. "I can't."

"Connor, Christina tried to murder both of us!"

"It isn't that." Connor takes a deep breath. "Penny, if I tell — you've got to understand. I took an oath. If I betray Christina to a foreign power . . ."

"So she pays a price for what she did!"

"It isn't for her." Connor swallows.

"Jesus Christ." Zach shakes his head. "Death's staring you straight in the face,

455

and you still don't dare break the rules, do you? The good little soldier. What is it with you assholes? They wave a flag in front of you, and you're so damn hypnotized you forget to act in your own best interest."

"I know the difference between what's right and what's convenient. And that has nothing to do with Christina's rules." Connor turns to Penny. "When I gave you those pills, my conscience told me it was wrong. But I followed orders and did it anyway. When I tried to take you to that safe house, I knew in my gut that it was wrong. But I followed orders and did it. Our choices add up to who we are. And I chose wrong." He squares his shoulders. "Not anymore. If we give up everything good about who we are, what are we even fighting for? *Fuck* Christina. She deserves to pay for what she did. But I won't sell her out to a hostile foreign power. Because if you think Zach could cause trouble by blackmailing the CIA, *imagine* what Ms. Palamut could do." His eyes are bright in the gloom. "If you want to tell her what you know, I won't blame you —"

Penny's throat feels like it's closing. "Connor . . ."

"Really. I won't. You're a civilian. You never asked for this — you shouldn't have to sacrifice yourself." He scrunches up his face. "But I won't do it. I can't."

Penny says nothing.

Melek watches them both.

"Her full name is Christina Ekdahl," says Zach. "She bought bombs with U.S. tax dollars and used the State Department as cover to ship them to the Hashashin." Zach takes a swig of his coffee. "Then the Hashashin used one of those bombs to blow up the U.S. Embassy. I'll give you specs and numbers, if you want."

Melek smiles. "That's more like it, Mr. Robson."

"Actually, since I'm leaving government service, there's really no need to use my cover name. After all, I'm confident we'll be working very closely over the next few years."

"Indeed?" Melek raises an eyebrow.

Zach grins, triumphant and cocksure. "My new consulting firm is about to be awarded quite a number of intelligence and security contracts. As soon as the NATO wonks finish brokering that Syria deal."

"In that case, it is a pleasure to meet you, Mr. . . . ?"

"Cabot. Jack Winthrop Cabot."

"Winthrop?" says Melek.

"Cousins." Zach shrugs. "He got the rich

dad. I got the brains."

Penny feels as if she's going to be sick.

"I'm sure we'll have a great deal to discuss, Mr. Cabot." Melek turns to Penny and Connor. "But I believe I promised Penny a ride to the Kempinski."

Zach leans back in his chair. "I think that would create unnecessary complications."

Melek's expression doesn't change. "How so?"

"This doesn't have to be embarrassing for any of us. Dye Mr. Beauregard's hair, and you've got your Kadıköy motorcycle bomber. CIA's already repudiated him as a traitor. He was even captured on the scene."

"Not the bad guy, huh?" Penny feels her cheeks go hot. "I wish I'd pushed you out of the helicopter!"

Melek conceals her look of surprise, but not quite fast enough.

Zach continues, "And everyone already knows Penny's dead. Send the body back to Ankara. How is anyone ever going to prove it wasn't always there?"

"You bastard." Connor tries to get up, but two Presidential Guards hold him down.

Melek has eyes only for Zach. "And may I ask how you know the hair color of the Kadıköy bomber, Mr. Cabot?"

"I was on the scene."

"You certainly were."

Goose bumps rise on Penny's arms.

Melek leans forward. "My people identified you from the CCTV in the Kadıköy ferry terminal." Her gaze slides over to Penny. "You, too. That's three lira you owe the Istanbul Municipality."

Zach leans forward, voice suddenly rough. "Have you told . . . anyone?"

"Not yet." Melek raises her eyebrows. "But it seems courteous to give Secretary Winthrop fair warning before we release the information to the press."

Zach takes this news much better than Penny would have expected. "He's my cousin. He wants to be President. I'm sure he would prefer to keep this quiet."

"Unfortunately for both of you, Mr. Cabot, your cousin has no authority to do so. America can hardly continue holding the Embassy bombing over our heads if not only a senior CIA official but also the Secretary of State's own cousin are directly implicated."

Zach has mustered his wits, and his deepest, most charming voice. "I don't think you realize what a valuable friend I can be, Melek. My consulting firm will be handling huge volumes of classified information. I'm sure we can come to an understanding."

Melek stands up. "What is it you people say? 'We don't negotiate with terrorists.' "

Zach grins. "You and I both know that's not true."

"The thing about traitors, Mr. Cabot, is that they can't be trusted. You betrayed your own people. Why wouldn't you betray me?"

"I don't know anything these two don't know. The difference is, I have a working relationship with you to protect."

"Work with *you*?" Melek looks disgusted. "I know about your dealings with the Kurdish rebels, Mr. Cabot."

"Exactly," Zach says quickly. "I have an open line of communication —"

Melek crosses her arms. "I'm finished clutching at snakes."

"What if I told you there's hard proof of everything Christina did," says Zach. "Not only what she did with the Hashashin?"

Penny holds her breath. She doesn't dare even look at Connor.

"If you had that," says Melek, "you wouldn't be here."

Zach points at Connor. "He's got it. Search him. It's on a microchip, inside an evil eye bead."

"Really." Melek's expression is profoundly skeptical.

"I deliver," declares Zach.

Melek nods slightly. Two guards pull Connor into a standing position and pat him down. They're well-trained and thorough, pulling out his pockets and unlacing his shoes.

Penny watches, motionless. What can she do?

Connor stands like a scarecrow, face blank. No one speaks. Zach's heavy, eager breathing fills the silence.

The guards pat down Connor's back, his shoulders, his arms. They're almost at the bandage on his wrist.

"Stop!" Penny bursts into tears. "Stop, please! I can't stand it."

Everyone stares at her.

"I lied, okay? I lied!" Penny meets Zach's eyes, lip trembling. "I knew you wouldn't help me find Connor — unless you thought he had it. When I realized what it was, I got scared. I threw the real one away. At the caravanserai."

"If that's true," says Melek, "then why are you here?"

Penny says simply, "Connor."

"Oh, please," says Zach. "Don't believe a word she says. Why would she throw away something so valuable?"

Penny turns tearfully to Melek. "I was terrified! You kidnapped me. Christina tried to

461

blow us up." She gulps. "I thought maybe if I got rid of it, I'd be safe. I thought maybe it would all be over."

Melek looks unconvinced. She turns to her guards. *"Var mı?"*

"Yok," declares one of the guards, stepping away from Connor.

"Well, Mr. Cabot?" says Melek.

"Search the girl!" splutters Zach. "She's lying. They must have swapped it!"

Melek's lips purse. "Mr. Cabot . . ."

"Go ahead and search me," says Penny, straightening her shoulders. "I've got nothing to hide."

The guards' hands are brisk and professional, as if she were made of dynamite. They don't meet her eyes.

One of them holds up her left wrist, with the evil eye bead on it.

"Ha!" Zach strides over, unclips the bracelet, and hands it to Melek.

The President's daughter holds the evil eye up to the light. "There's nothing. Only glass."

"İki yüz lira." One of the guards searching Penny holds up a few warm, folded bills. "That's it."

They step away from Penny.

Melek raises a single eyebrow. "Well, Mr. Cabot?"

Zach turns on Penny. His expression hits her like a lead pipe. Hate and rage, untainted by charm or artifice or hope. "You. Lying. Bitch."

Two of Melek's guards grab him and haul him, kicking and yelling, into an adjoining room.

"Who'd you give it to?" Zach screams. "Where is it?"

Penny catches sight of what looks like a surgical table. The door slams shut behind them.

"Stop!" Penny jumps up. "What are you going to do to him?"

"That is not your concern." Melek nods to her guards, who grab Penny and Connor by both arms and haul them toward the stairs.

"He needs to stand trial, ma'am." Connor's voice is raw.

"That won't be necessary," says Melek.

From the adjoining room comes a single, muffled shot.

"Take it." Melek tosses the evil eye bracelet back to Penny. "I don't believe in luck."

44
THE ÇIRAĞAN
PALACE KEMPINSKI

Çirağan Palace Kempinski, Istanbul
20:10 Local Time

By 8:10 p.m., so many black-armbanded
diplomats and staffers are crammed into
Secretary Winthrop's suite at the Çirağan
Palace Kempinski that it resembles a funeral
reception populated entirely by jittery
workaholics. Outside, Diplomatic Security
special agents prowl the marble balconies
and crowd the corridor. Everyone is on high
alert. Moe is consulting with five members
of his staff, each stressing about a different
last-minute disaster. Brenda is in a huddle
with what remains of the political team. At
the center of it all, the charismatic Secretary
of State leans back in a satiny armchair, flip-
ping through talking points. A young female
staffer who flew over with Winthrop from
Foggy Bottom hurries to the Secretary's
side, proffering a phone. "Sir, it's Mr. Lerman for you."

"Jimena, right?" Winthrop flashes a benign-but-commanding twinkle.

"Yes, sir." She blushes, delighted.

Winthrop knows all his staffers' names. It's a pain, but, hey — ten minutes every morning with that flash-card app, and your staffers tell *Politico* you're the nicest boss they ever had. "Not the best moment, Jimena."

"Sir, I'm so sorry, but Mr. Lerman says it's extremely urgent."

Winthrop sighs, takes the phone, and veers into the bedroom, closing the door behind him. "Frank. Make it fast."

"So, so sorry to interrupt you, Mr. Secretary." Frank Lerman sounds miserable. "I had to be sure to catch you before the keynote. They've got a tentative ID on the failed motorcycle bomber in Kadıköy. And I don't know how much longer I can get the Turks to keep it quiet."

"Why would we keep that quiet? Can we get a nice cooperation angle? America helps Turkey catch the bad guys?"

"Mr. Secretary . . ." Frank's voice is hollow. "Don't shoot the messenger, okay?"

Sixty seconds later, Winthrop hangs up. He's barely had time to exhale when he feels a buzz from his jacket pocket — his private cell. Christina. Thank God. She'll know what to do. He pulls out the phone. Caller ID blocked. He can count on his right hand how many people have this number. He presses talk and tries to sound tough. "Hello?"

A woman's voice fills his ear. Not Christina. Not his wife. Not his mistress. Sweet, cultured, slightly foreign sounding. "Secretary Winthrop. I'm so glad I caught you."

"Who is this? How did you get this number?"

The answer makes him sit heavily on the edge of the bed. But his voice remains confident. "What an unexpected pleasure, Ms. Palamut. What can I do for you?"

A pause.

Color drains from Winthrop's face. "What?" He swallows. "I'll have to ask you to verify that."

A text message beep.

The body in the photo is unmistakable. Right in the forehead.

Winthrop can hardly keep the giddy relief out of his voice. "At least it was quick." His manner becomes almost jolly, as if they'd just signed a satisfactorily lopsided treaty. "Well, that's *most* considerate. Thank you. I would appreciate that very much. And I'm sure my government will show their appreciation."

Winthrop holds the phone tight to his ear, listening. When he speaks again, his voice is grim. "You realize that goes directly against our policy."

Another pause.

"I see." Winthrop sticks out his chin. "Well, under the circumstances that seems extremely . . . reasonable." He closes his eyes in resignation — then opens them with a start. "*What?* Right now?"

Winthrop steps up to the high window. Commotion on the Bosphorus. A Turkish police launch splashes through the empty red waters around the Kempinski, scattering indignant cormorants into the twilight.

Winthrop shoves the phone in his pocket and steps back into the anteroom, a huge, convincing grin across his face. "Down to the dock, everyone! We've got some very special guests!"

"Mr. Secretary?" Brenda hurries across to him.

"Congratulations!" Winthrop claps her on the back. At 6'3", he towers over her. "I had to keep the operation quiet until I was sure. But I want you to be the first to know."

Brenda looks up at him. "Sir?"

Winthrop beams. "Penny Kessler's coming home."

■ ■ ■ ■

Çirağan Palace Kempinski, Istanbul
20:31 Local Time

Penny leans into the cool spray as the police launch draws up to the wrought-iron water gate of the Kempinski. Not sad. Not scared. Not even angry anymore. Connor sits silently beside her. All the way down the Bosphorus, they haven't dared speak — not with Melek's guards on either side.

"Connor." Penny nervously twists the evil eye bracelet on her wrist. "Is that . . . ?"

Framed in the water gate, wide fatherly smiles glued to their faces, stand Secretary Winthrop and President Palamut.

The launch bumps against the dock. Policemen usher Penny and Connor ashore. As the cameras flash, Red Crescent workers drape silver blankets around their shoulders.

The Secretary of State clasps Penny's hand. Dark wavy hair, intent brown eyes, that smile. Winthrop's a good twelve years older than Zach, but in person, the resemblance is striking. "Welcome back, Penny," he says in a heartfelt stage whisper, and turns to Connor. "You've done well, young man."

Penny grabs Connor's arm. "He's —" She

468

hesitates.

"Our Turkish Agricultural Policy and Food Security desk officer." Winthrop shakes his hand. "I know all about you."

Connor is visibly startled. "Yes, sir."

"This brave young man was kidnapped by the Hashashin while trying to protect Miss Kessler," says Secretary Winthrop loudly, clasping Connor's shoulder. "Welcome back, son. The Department of State is very proud of you."

Penny and Connor exchange a look.

President Palamut strides down the dock, trailing Prime Minister Bolu and a gaggle of aides.

"Things are extremely delicate," whispers Winthrop. "Please don't say anything."

Cameras press in close around Penny as President Palamut steps up beside her.

Huber Mansion, Kalender, Istanbul
20:42 Local Time
In the dry and muffled stillness of the basement corridor, Melek's ballet flats pad noiselessly along the hard blue carpet.

Winthrop had melted like woolly *pişmaniye* cotton candy under a faucet. Victory. But it felt as triumphant as squashing a slug in her fist, and just as dirty.

Her father will come out stronger, Melek

469

tells herself. What else matters? So what if she didn't get the microchip? The information her new prisoner can give more than makes up for the loss.

She quickens her pace.

Chipped and dynamited out of the limestone bed of the Bosphorus in the dying days of the nineteenth century, the old basements of the Huber Mansion used to resemble abandoned mine shafts — all rotting wood and dripping stone, soggy forgotten files, and the odd Prussian rifle bleeding rust. But last year's renovation pumped the old stone with concrete and hammered smooth drywall down the decaying halls. It's the only kind of renovation her father believes in: the kind that obliterates. It's clean down here now. Comfortable. They even put a TV in the cell. She can hear it — the canned distortion of her father's voice.

There's a one-way mirror set in the cell door.

Melek's breath doesn't fog it; it's too warm down here for that.

Inside, Zach Robson lounges on what looks like a hospital bed. The guards have wiped the fake blood off his forehead, but carelessly, leaving an absurd pink smear across his tan as if he'd had his face painted at a children's party. His hands and ankles are zip-tied, but he's otherwise unconfined. Two guards sit watch, guns resting on their knees. But their eyes are on the TV.

President Palamut's face fills the large flatscreen. Beside him, clutching the Red Crescent blanket around her shoulders, Penny looks pale and dazed. She glances occasionally up at Secretary Winthrop, as if for reassurance.

Even without a microphone, President Palamut's voice resonates. "When we recaptured Mor Samuel from the terrorists, we discovered that a fraud had been perpetrated at the hospital by Kurdish doctors plotting against our national security. These villains will be punished!"

Secretary Winthrop visibly tries not to wince. Prime Minister Bolu is attempting to get into the frame, but no matter how he maneuvers, somehow Palamut's security seems to be in the way.

"Look at this young woman!" Palamut grabs Penny's hand and holds it up like a trophy, ignoring the way she flinches. The iconic image of Flag Girl flashes in the upper corner of the screen.

Palamut turns theatrically to Penny. "What is your name?"

Penny's voice comes out hoarse, but startlingly strong. "Penny Kessler."

A huge cheer from off camera.

"You see!" roars Palamut. "Penny Kessler did not die, as the Kurdish terrorists tried to deceive us into believing! She was kidnapped by the Hashashin and taken to Mor Samuel monastery as a hostage."

It's Winthrop's turn. "When the terrorists destroyed Mor Samuel monastery, a U.S. Foreign Service officer, Zachary Robson, was tragically killed. America will grieve the loss of this brave, promising young man. Zachary died as he lived: in service to his country. I understand the loss all too well." Winthrop bows his head. "Now that his parents have been informed, I can tell the world that my own first cousin John Winthrop Cabot was also murdered in the July 4th attack on our Embassy. My family's sacrifice has only increased my resolve to continue fighting to keep the United States of America strong and proud."

In the comfortable sanctuary of the basement, Zach Robson laughs until he can hardly breathe.

Melek pulls open the cell door, sending the guards lurching to their feet. "Enough." She scowls at the guards. *"Televizyonu kapatın."*

They obediently switch it off.

"Melek *Hanım.*" Zach grins up at her.

"Make yourself at home."

Her silent stare holds nothing but contempt.

"This doesn't have to be an interrogation. I cooperated. Your guards can tell you. I *want* to help."

She turns to the guards. "Wait outside."

They look worried. "Melek *Hanım* . . ."

"Merak etmeyin," she assures them.

Unconvinced, the senior guard extends his gun, grip first.

"Tamam." She takes it.

The door whispers shut.

Zach leans toward her. "We should be allies."

Melek is silent for a moment, twisting her long fingers together. "This morning, before I flew to Istanbul, I went to the children's hospital in Ankara. Some of your little victims have no hands. Some lost their eyes. Some of them had their legs ripped off. One little boy — he's in a coma. But you killed both his parents, so his grandmother sits with him alone." Tears gather in her eyes. "And those are the children who *survived.*"

Zach stands up. "Thanks to those children's sacrifice, your country will be stronger."

"Sit down."

"I heard the speeches. From now on, my

cousin will be your father's biggest advocate in Washington. Don't pretend you aren't happy about that."

Melek levels the gun at his chest. "Sit *down.*"

He doesn't move. "You should be thanking me. If it weren't for what I did at the Embassy, I wouldn't be here now." As his confidence grows, his voice takes on its old charm. "And *you* wouldn't have the best source on the CIA you're ever going to get."

"You're a terrorist."

"I'm a pragmatist," says Zach. "And so are you. Or you wouldn't be here."

"I'm interrogating a criminal."

"Is that why you had the guards step outside?"

Melek says nothing.

"You don't have to put on the righteous princess act for me. I know who you are, Melek. You're not sentimental. You do whatever it takes to get what you want. Same as me."

"I don't murder innocents."

"Just think of them as martyrs."

Melek presses the gun to his forehead. She cocks it. Her expression has not changed; she's far too disciplined. But her breath, more honest, is ragged with rage.

Zach's eyes meet hers. "If you were going

to kill me, you already would have."

For a moment, Melek simply looks at him. When she speaks, her voice is soft. "I'm not going to kill you, Mr. Cabot." She lowers the gun. "You're already dead."

"If this is heaven, I'm a few virgins short."

"I hear that you set great store by your charm." Melek walks toward the door. "I thought you'd talk more easily if you thought you were winning." She looks back at him. "I've changed my mind." She opens the door. *Gelin buraya.*

The guards stand at attention.

"You want my information." For the first time, Zach sounds agitated. "You can't just leave me here."

"No. I won't leave you here. We have real prisons for people like you, Mr. Cabot. And real interrogators." Melek nods to the guards, who grab Zach firmly by the arms.

"You're bluffing." Zach's laugh verges on the hysterical.

"Good-bye, Mr. Cabot." Melek crosses her arms. "You will not see me again."

His face is white. "You think you'll get anything out of me this way?"

"You'll talk," says Melek. "I know a coward when I see one."

■ ■ ■ ■

Çirağan Palace Kempinski, Istanbul
20:44 Local Time
In service to his country.

Penny opens her mouth — and closes it. She can't contradict the Secretary of State on camera. He knew who Connor was. He must know about Zach. He must have a reason. He *must.*

Winthrop continues, "Thanks to the courage of President Palamut's Presidential Guard and the swift action of U.S. forces, Penny Kessler was rescued." Winthrop reaches across Penny to shake President Palamut's hand. "The United States couldn't ask for a better partner in the global fight against terror than President Palamut. We look forward to continuing our fruitful partnership with him for many years to come."

Behind the cameras, Prime Minister Bolu looks like somebody put bleach in his glass of *ayran.*

"Now that the world knows that Penny Kessler is safe, I will lead my very dear friend Robert into the NATO keynote," says President Palamut. He smiles down at Penny. "You are speechless, my dear. I

476

understand." He presses his hand to his chest. "But I feel your gratitude in my heart."

The cameras follow Winthrop and Palamut like a tide as they maneuver back into the floodlit Kempinski gardens.

"Penny." Brenda Pelecchia folds her into a fierce hug. Tears are running down her face. "Thank God. Oh, thank God."

As the last light fades, the call to prayer echoes across the water.

45
WHAT SETS YOU FREE

Since Brenda refuses to let Penny out of her sight, Red Crescent workers turn the gold-brocaded sitting room of Secretary Winthrop's decoy suite into a makeshift hospital. The IV drip stings, but Penny can feel her cramped muscles relax as painkillers and saline wash through her. A Red Crescent worker dabs stinging iodine on the wound on Penny's head.

Penny grits her teeth. "Brenda, we have to talk to you privately."

"Secretary Winthrop asked to debrief you both himself." Brenda picks up an embossed leather portfolio from the rococo desk. "I'm under orders to get you guys anything you want for dinner. How do you feel about" — she squints at the room-service menu — "Ottoman-style rosewater yogurt soup?"

"It's extremely urgent, ma'am," says Connor, from a plush armchair with a sterile plastic sheet draped over the arm.

"Keep that ice on your jaw," orders the nurse. Connor holds the white ice pack up to where Zach punched him. The nurse unwraps the bandage on Connor's hand.

"An evil eye bracelet?" says Brenda.

The nurse sees Connor's half-clotted bullet wound and sucks in her breath. "What this man needs is a surgeon, not a good luck charm!"

"I can call an ambulance," says Brenda.

Connor squares his shoulders. "I'm staying with Penny. At least until Secretary Winthrop comes."

"Only if you want to lose the use of that hand," warns the nurse.

Connor blanches.

Brenda says firmly, "I'm calling the ambulance."

"Go!" Penny touches his shoulder.

"You sure?" His forehead creases. He looks like he's been dragged through hell backward: filthy shirt and no tie, hair wild, face pummeled and lobster red, slightly upturned nose bleeding again. Penny remembers when she first saw him in the Ulus State Hospital.

"You look smiley." Connor raises an eyebrow. "Concussion catching up with you?"

"Just tired." She grins. "I could use some

aspirin."

He smiles. "My aspirin-giving days are over."

She blinks hard. "Connor, I just want you to know . . ."

"No need for big good-byes," says Brenda. "You're both getting medevaced back home on the same plane."

"Medevaced?" Penny hasn't forgotten how Christina blew up Faruk's car. She tries not to panic. "You mean alone, on a government plane?"

"Don't get too excited. It's just a seat on a commercial flight." Brenda makes a face. "They wouldn't shell out for an air ambulance."

Connor stands up, wincing. "Alex and I have a comfortable futon in Virginia. Promise you'll come stay with us. As long as you need."

Penny hugs him. "I promise."

"Haydi." The nurse urges Connor toward the door.

"Okay." He squeezes Penny's hand. "Good luck."

In her palm, where Connor pressed it, is the real evil eye bracelet. She closes her fist tight and shoves it deep in her pocket.

The door closes behind Connor. Outside, on the dark waters of the Bosphorus, a container ship blasts its horn.

"Haydi, canım." The nurse sits Penny back down in the silk-upholstered armchair.

Brenda exhales. "Penny."

"Yes?"

"I'm just so sorry." Brenda's voice is thick. "I should never have let Prime Minister Bolu take you —"

"It wasn't your fault." Penny stares at the floor as the nurse wraps gauze around her head wound.

Brenda shakes her head. "I should have fought harder."

Penny closes her eyes; her head is throbbing again. "Maybe next time."

"Christ, I hope there's never a next time." Brenda sits down next to her. "Penny, will you do me a favor?"

"Me?"

"Don't let this put you off a career in the Foreign Service. We could use young people like you."

"Honestly" — Penny looks at her — "you didn't seem to think I was very good at my job."

"The last thing you needed was another pat on the head. You shouldn't rely so much on other people's approval. You have to know your own center of gravity."

"I'm working on it."

"Good." Brenda flips on the gigantic flatscreen TV. CNN Türk is replaying footage of Secretary Winthrop and President Palamut's handshake. "The Secretary is skipping the reception. He'll be up as soon as the keynote's over. Not long now."

Winthrop is as good as Brenda's word. He strides into the sitting room of his suite looking tired but triumphant, hair rigidly perfect as ever. Aides escort the medical staff out of the room.

"Let's move it, folks!" Frank Lerman claps his hands like a middle-school football coach. "The Secretary hasn't got all night! Clear the room!"

Disgruntled Red Crescent workers file out as Diplomatic Security special agents check for listening devices.

"You, too, all of you!" Frank hustles a young staffer out the high wooden doors. "This is top-level only. Me, the Secretary, and the Chargé d'Affaires. That's *it.* DS agents, you wait in the hall." Frank slams the door and shakes his head at the sheer burden of always having to tell lesser mortals what to do.

"You, too, Frank," says Winthrop.

Frank's face falls. "But, sir —"

"Frank." Winthrop raises an eyebrow.

"Yes, Mr. Secretary." Frank's little eyes

dart at Brenda. "But I'd like to remind you, sir, that I have higher clearance than the *acting* Ambassador."

"I'm going to ask Brenda to step outside for a moment, too." Winthrop sits down next to Penny on the couch.

Brenda's hand rests on Penny's shoulder. "Mr. Secretary, if you wouldn't mind . . ."

Winthrop grins. "I'm not going to lose her, Brenda."

Frank stalks out. Brenda closes the door carefully.

It's just the two of them.

"Thank you for your cooperation," Winthrop says.

"Of course, sir."

"There's no 'of course' about it," says Winthrop warmly. "I've never heard anything like it. Punching out Palamut's Chief of Staff? Sneaking out of the palace down a construction tube?" He shakes his head. "That's sure not what we put in the internship brochure."

Penny's breath catches in her throat.

She never told him about the palace. She hasn't told anyone but Connor. So how does Winthrop know exactly how she escaped from Melek? There's no time to think about that now.

She stammers, "I guess you rise to the occasion."

"Well, you certainly rose. I'll see to it that you and Connor Beauregard both receive official commendations for bravery." Winthrop smiles at Penny. "That will look pretty good on job applications, huh? Now" — he leans forward — "I hear you have something to tell me."

"Mr. Secretary . . ." Penny swallows hard. "Why did you tell them Zach — Jack — died at Mor Samuel? Melek Palamut —"

Winthrop nods wearily. "I'm aware of what she did."

"You are, sir?"

"I know it's hard to understand." Winthrop sighs.

"She murdered him! That's not justice!"

"No." Winthrop walks to the high windows and looks out across the Bosphorus. The shoulders of his well-cut suit slump. "But sometimes we must make sacrifices for a greater truth. Given the nature of my cousin's work with the CIA, if his morally repugnant conduct came to light, it would undermine everything we're trying to achieve." Winthrop turns back to her, eyes sad. "It's a painful lesson. I'm sorry you have to learn it so young."

"You know what Zach did, sir?"

"Yes, Penny. I do."

"Then you know about Christina Ekdahl."

Winthrop is suddenly very still. "What do you know about Christina Ekdahl?"

Penny takes a deep breath. "She's been deliberately collaborating with the Hashashin. When Zach found out, she tried to have him transferred and threatened to pull his clearance."

Winthrop stares.

"She thought I might know, so she sent Connor Beauregard to pick me up. And then she blew up our car. Our driver was killed. She sent an assassin after us. And *then* we think she tipped off the Turkish air force to take out our helicopter — and apparently she told the State Department that Connor was a traitor —"

Winthrop holds up his elegant hands. "These are *extremely* serious allegations. Christina Ekdahl is one of our most trusted senior intelligence officials."

Penny's heart pounds. "I have proof."

Winthrop speaks with exaggerated calm, as if he were talking a madwoman off the edge of a cliff. "Proof?"

"Zach was trying to get an evil eye bead with a microchip inside it. It's the only copy. A microchip full of proof that Christina Ekdahl used the State Department to secretly smuggle American weapons to the Hashashin. Including the Embassy bomb."

"And you have it? You have the microchip?"

There is a raw desperation in Winthrop's face.

Suddenly Penny remembers Zach's voice on the ferry: *It was supposed to be a controlled explosion. Just enough to compromise him.*

She looks up at Secretary Winthrop, her mouth dry as dust.

Zach said a senior State Department official had cooperated with Christina to smuggle weapons to the Hashashin.

But Zach lied about so much. And Robert Winthrop is the Secretary of State.

"It's okay, Penny." Winthrop's smile is as fixed as his hair. His chuckle is ingratiating, scared. "You're safe now."

In that instant, Penny is certain beyond doubt.

In the end, you have to trust yourself.

Hand trembling, Penny unfastens the bracelet from her wrist.

Winthrop's fingers close around the evil eye. "No one else knows?"

She shakes her head.

Winthrop looks down at her with obvious emotion. "You don't know what a service you've done for your country."

Penny swallows. "I hope I did the right thing."

"You did, Penny." His relief is visible. "If this had fallen into the wrong hands . . ." He shakes his head.

"What now?"

"Now, you should put this trying time behind you, take a very well-deserved vacation, and *heal.*" Winthrop stands up and shakes her hand. "You know I can't announce this publicly. But you've shown extraordinary courage and patriotism today. You make me very proud."

"That means a lot, sir."

"You've done great." Winthrop grows jolly as he guides her toward the door to the hallway. "You're almost free."

"Almost?"

"Frank wants you for one more interview."

"Mr. Lerman is very . . . persistent, isn't he, sir?"

Secretary Winthrop throws back his immobile coif and laughs. "A diplomatic answer if ever I heard one. Tell Frank I'll be right out." Winthrop shakes her hand once more, his voice deepening for the benefit of the listeners in the corridor. "Well done, Penny. God bless you. And God bless America."

Winthrop closes the door behind her and walks across the suite, into the bathroom.

He smiles. For an ugly moment, he looks just like Zach.

He opens the toilet lid and drops the evil eye into the water.

One flush, and it's all gone.

Brenda and Frank steer Penny down the second-floor hallway of the Çırağan Palace Kempinski, away from Secretary Winthrop's suite. Penny feels jittery, as if she'd jammed her fingers in a socket. Her eyes won't focus. She hardly feels their hands on her back as they guide her down the high white corridor. Their squabbling sounds like an unknown language, until one furious exclamation breaks through.

"An *interview*?" On Penny's right, Brenda sounds livid. "No. No. I absolutely forbid it."

"Come on." To the left, Frank Lerman looks irritable, his pink pate shining with sweat. "It's a puff piece! You know, 'What's next for Flag Girl?' Blah blah American resilience blah blah blah. I had to get the fucker off my back. This is his reward for shutting up about that fucking Melek Palamut fake document leak." Frank glares at Penny. "Which you are *not* going to say anything about, right?"

"She's not going to say anything about anything," says Brenda, "because she's going to go lie down in a quiet room and rest!"

"What fucker?" Penny asks Frank.

"Nick Abensour from the BBC." Frank rolls his eyes. "Their 'Turkey whisperer.' Gobble, gobble. I had him checked out. Wasted ten years with Amnesty International, and he thinks he's the fucking King of Democracy —"

"I'll talk to him for a few minutes," says Penny. "But only if we can talk alone."

"Penny . . ." Brenda frowns.

"Don't worry." Penny's fingers close around the evil eye in her pocket. Between two disks of glass, the tiny black microchip rests intact. "I'll be fine."

EPILOGUE

D100 Highway, Bakirköy, Istanbul
22:55 Local Time

Brenda insisted on accompanying Penny to the airport in her official car, the big black SUV with its heavy bombproof doors. It's almost eleven, but Brenda is still on her BlackBerry, fielding call after call — a hailstorm of crisis fallout.

"No more hospital photo ops," snaps Brenda. "You tell Frank Lerman I don't care *what* he says about the goddamn optics —"

Penny shifts on the waxy leather, staring at the high-rise hotels that cluster around the highway to Atatürk International. She remembers Nick Abensour's astonished face two hours before, when she handed him the evil eye.

"Say you found it," she whispered. "Just lying on the ground, outside the Embassy."

"I'll get this where it needs to go." Nick

490

slipped the evil eye into his pocket. "Thank you for trusting me."

The black SUV speeds toward Atatürk airport. The highway is almost empty at this hour. Penny watches the signs flick past. Turkish signs. Words she memorized, flash card after flash card, long ago in Michigan.

Brenda is already on another call. "I want to approve the schedule *myself.* Okay? Good." She hangs up. "Jesus."

Penny forces a smile. "You really didn't have to come out here with me."

"Of course I did. Anyway, what am I going to do? Sleep?" Brenda fumbles in her purse and pulls out a plain white envelope. "Here. Don't open it."

"What is it?"

"Money," says Brenda. "Not that much. Just enough to help get you through the next few weeks."

"Thank you," Penny stammers, "but —"

"I won't take it back." Brenda purses her lips. "I read the obituary they put together for you. You worked forty hours a week *during the semester* to afford this internship. I'm damned if I'll let you get into debt for surviving the attack."

"It was my dream." Penny feels a lump in her throat. "I was proud to work hard for it." She tries to smile. "I even loved filling out the SF-86 for my security clearance."

"You're kidding."

"No." Penny's voice is hoarse. "It meant that I was part of it. Being at the Embassy meant the world to me." She holds out the envelope. "You don't need to do this."

Brenda crosses her arms. "You think it's guilt, don't you?"

Penny suddenly feels sorry for Brenda. "No, I —"

"Well, what if it *is*?" There are tears in Brenda's eyes. "I can't fix this fucking mess. Are you going to take away my chance to make some tiny part of this all right?"

Penny shakes her head.

"Okay?"

"Okay." Penny folds the envelope in half. "Thank you."

"Dış hatlar," Brenda directs the driver. He steers toward the low white concrete of the International Terminal. Connor is waiting for them outside, his freshly bandaged hand in a sling.

Penny beams when she sees him. She'd give anything to tell him about Nick Abensour. But she knows she can't. Connor's a CIA officer. Anyone with a clearance that high is legally bound to report leaks. He'll just have to find out for himself.

■ ■ ■ ■

*Turkish Airlines Flight TK 7 to Washington
  Dulles*
23:32 Local Time
Connor squeezes into the window seat, his
bony knees pressed against the seat in front
of him. Penny takes the middle. She has no
luggage — just her boarding pass, Brenda's
envelope, and an emergency passport,
tucked into the string backpack Carolyn
Sokolof found for Penny at the Consulate.
Relic of some long-forgotten election night
party, it's printed with an American flag and
the jaunty slogan BE SMART! DO YOUR PART!
VOTE!

"Uçaktayım. Evet." A pudgy, shaggy-haired
Turkish executive plops down beside her in
the aisle seat, speaking loudly into his
enormous shiny phone. *"Öptüm. Haydi bye-
bye."* He holds out his smartphone, scroll-
ing through the news, flicking past a photo
of police outside the latticed marble of the
Çırağan Palace Kempinski. "Not again," he
groans in English. *"Fuck."*

Penny feels suddenly sick. "Was there
another attack?"

"No, no." The shaggy-haired executive
shakes his head. "You know about the peace

493

summit? There were protesters. Peaceful. Then the police came. Arrested them all. Kids. Journalists. Everybody." He scrolls down. On the bright rectangle of the screen burns a photo of a handsome dark-haired man in his early forties: nose bleeding into his close-cropped beard, both arms pinned back by helmeted Turkish riot police.

Nick Abensour.

Oh, God, what will they do to him?

"Some of the signs were in Kurdish. Palamut's threatening terrorism charges — pretending the protesters are PKK." The executive makes a face. "Those poor bastards."

Penny feels like her throat is closing. "Yeah."

"Sir." A flight attendant stands over them. "You need to put that phone in flight mode."

Penny grips the armrests. She gave Nick Abensour the only proof she had. There's nothing left. Was Melek behind the arrests? Winthrop? Christina?

She realizes with a jolt that the plane is already arcing up into the air.

Istanbul falls away beneath them. And then it's gone. She can never go back. Not while Palamut's in power, and that bastard will rule until he dies.

"You look gray," Connor says, laying a hand on her arm. "You've got to try and rest."

Six hours later, Penny stares through the condensation on the oval window, out at the blank darkness, miles above the sea.

Beside her in seat 39A, Connor sleeps heavily, still on major painkillers. His bandaged hand is braced in the sling against his chest, rising and falling with his slow breaths. The young Turkish executive snores like a congested rhino. One of the *Mission: Impossible* movies plays silently on his little seatback screen — tiny harmless explosions, blood that's really nothing but red pixels.

Wrapped in her blanket in the desiccated half-light, Penny feels hot and strangled. As long as she held on to hope, as long as she believed some justice would come out of this, she could bear it.

But now?

She fought. She survived. She did the right thing. And none of it made a goddamn bit of difference.

So much for truth.

The clouds are pale pink now. She can see trees and houses far below. America. She's home.

495

■ ■ ■ ■

"Alex is meeting us near baggage claim fourteen," says Connor, as they head out of passport control and into the international-arrivals area.

Penny nods numbly.

"Penny." Connor grabs her shoulder, pointing at the TV suspended from the ceiling. "Look."

The TV is set to CNN. A green-and-black graphic swoops across the screen: *The Abensour Files.*

"Breaking news in the scandal now rocking the administration," says the pancaked anchorwoman, eyes wide. "Last night, BBC journalist Nick Abensour was deported from Turkey. Less than an hour ago, he broke what many are already calling one of the most explosive stories of the decade. A thumb drive Abensour miraculously recovered near the wreckage of the U.S. Embassy in Ankara allegedly implicates senior U.S. government officials, including Secretary of State Robert Winthrop, in the illegal supply of weapons to the Hashashin terrorist group, possibly including the actual bomb

496

used in the devastating attack in Ankara on the Fourth of July. We take you live to David Zhang in Istanbul."

"Thank you, Meg." Zhang is clutching a microphone in front of the Kempinski. "This is shocking. Secretary Winthrop has been recalled from his scene of triumph at the NATO Summit in Istanbul. Leaders on both sides of the aisle have already issued statements demanding Winthrop's immediate dismissal. So far, no word from the White House. The State Department has refused to comment, but it's pretty obvious: if the Abensour Files are authenticated, losing his job will be the least of Secretary Winthrop's problems. In fact —"

"Sorry, David," interrupts the anchorwoman, "we're getting exclusive breaking news from Howard Hennessey, outside CIA headquarters in Langley, Virginia. Howard?"

The screen splits in three.

"Meg, I can't believe what we're seeing here." Hennessey can barely contain his excitement. "This is unprecedented. Christina Ekdahl, a *very* senior CIA official implicated in the scandal, has just been escorted from CIA headquarters by *multiple* police cars. According to sources, she may be facing not just civil but *criminal* charges —"

Connor turns to Penny. "You didn't . . ."

She smiles. "Of course not."

He pulls her into a hug. "I take my eyes off you for five minutes . . ."

"I have no idea what you're talking about."

He shakes his head, laughing. *"Miraculously* recovered."

"He must just have good luck." Penny slings the American flag backpack over her shoulder. "I'm starving. Let's go."

ACKNOWLEDGMENTS

Many thanks to Piers, who has stuck by me since the reign of Richard III. Thank you to Rick for dedication and a leap of faith. I never imagined eastern Bulgaria would be the place where dreams come true. Thanks to Jo, Nita, Sally, Emily, and everyone else who has helped *Liar's Candle* become a book. DITD was there from the start. JKCF helped give me the freedom to try. Many thanks and much love to the London Wing. Elizabeth Hunt Davis Mazzocco was a wonderful mentor, a dear friend, and a "kindred spirit." She never saw this book, but she helped make it possible. Thank you to the FSOs who serve with integrity and humanity, often in hardship. To my professors, classmates, friends, and neighbors in Turkey: your courage and kindness remain an inspiration. My mother raised me to be a writer and showed me how to be brave. She stood by me every step of the way. This book is for her.

ABOUT THE AUTHOR

August Thomas began her first novel, *Liar's Candle,* at age twenty-three. Fluent in Turkish, she has traveled and studied in Turkey as the recipient of a Fulbright Scholarship, and holds Master's degrees from Bogaziçi, Istanbul's top public university, as well as the University of Edinburgh. She also has two degrees from the University of Massachusetts. A travel writer as well as a novelist, she lives in Massachusetts.